Ali Harper writes feminist crime fiction. *The Runaway* is her second novel. An option for TV and film rights has also been signed with Yorkshire-based Duck Soup Films. Ali lives in Leeds, where she teaches creative writing, has just completed a PhD, and plays netball badly.

 @AliHarperWrites
aliharperwrites.wordpress.com

Also by Ali Harper

The Disappeared

The Runaway

Ali Harper

OneMoreChapter

One More Chapter
an imprint of HarperCollins*Publishers*
The News Building
1 London Bridge Street
London SE1 9GF

www.harpercollins.co.uk

This paperback edition 2019

First published in Great Britain in ebook format by
HarperCollins*Publishers* 2019

A catalogue record for this book
is available from the British Library

ISBN: 978-0-00-835431-2

Set in Birka by Palimpsest Book Production Ltd,
Falkirk Stirlingshire

Printed and bound in Great Britain by
CPI Group (UK) Ltd, Croydon CR0 4YY

This one is for my netball team.
We've never lost a game – we just occasionally
run out of time.

Chapter 1

I was bent double when she pushed open the office door, my sides aching so much I thought I was going to wet myself. A moment before, Aunt Edie had been up the set of stepladders, brushing away the cobwebs in the cornices with a bright blue and purple plastic feather duster. Jo had made some joke about how it was fortunate we didn't have any men in the office as the sight of Aunt Edie's pop socks would drive them wild, and Aunt Edie had swiped at her with the feather duster. The steps had toppled, Aunt Edie grabbed hold of the filing cabinet and the pot plant on top of it got knocked over, landing on Jo's Afro. Jo was spitting out polystyrene balls and dry compost when the bell chimed and this young woman, with dreads and a silver cannabis leaf nose stud, marched into our office.

Aunt Edie was the first to recover. 'Welcome to No Stone Unturned,' she said, clambering down from the filing cabinet. 'The,' – she rhymed the word with bee – 'the most successful private investigation bureau in the north of England.' She pushed past me, stuffing the feather duster behind Jo's chair as she bustled across the room. 'Edith Caudwell, Office Manager.'

Aunt Edie had been installed as receptionist only the week before, having swapped her terraced house in Accrington for a housing association flat down the road from our offices in Royal Park. 'Are you missing someone, pet?'

'My boyfriend,' the woman said, her eyes settling on Aunt Edie. 'I don't know where he is and I need to find him. Like now.'

She held the left sleeve of her rainbow-coloured top in her right hand, twisting the material. I glanced across at Jo and noticed a polystyrene ball clinging to her eyebrow. I was about to point it out when our visitor's face crumpled and her shoulders sagged, like someone had let the wind out of her.

'Oh, now. Don't you go getting yourself worked up,' said Aunt Edie, putting her arm around the woman's shoulders. They were almost the same height, which is no height at all. 'Come on, take a seat and tell us all about it. Did you read about these two,' – she turned and pushed Jo's DMs off the desk – 'in the papers? If anyone can find your missing fella, they can.'

I pulled a face at Aunt Edie. Our first case had gone well, but if this woman hired us to find her missing boyfriend, it would make her only our second client. My lungs buzzed at the thought, although it was early days and she didn't look like she could afford shoes, let alone private investigators. However, if I've learned one thing from living in this part of Leeds, it's not to judge a book by its cover. Trustafarians, Jo calls them. Kids that get off on looking poverty-stricken while their parents run Barclays.

'We'll go through to the back room,' I said, having finally

got control of my vocal cords. 'Tea would be great, Aun— er, Edie. Would you mind?'

Aunt Edie pouted. I knew she itched to get the details, but she was the receptionist, something Jo and I had gone to great lengths to explain when we agreed to let her work here. Tea-making went with the territory.

'I'm Lee and this is Jo,' I said to the woman. 'What's your name?'

She held her hand over her eyes, like we might not notice her crying. 'Nikki.'

She didn't volunteer a surname and I didn't push it. Jo grabbed a new client file and I led the way to our interview room. It's tiny, the proportions not helped by the dark laminate panelling that lines the walls. We've got a card table with a green felt top, three wooden chairs and a punch bag strapped to the ceiling in the far corner. 'Take a seat, Nikki,' I said. 'And take a minute. We've plenty of time.'

She sank into a chair and held her head in her hands.

'Fag?' asked Jo, tugging a pack of Marlboro Lights from the front pocket of her dungarees and taking her own seat at the table.

'Please.' A hand snaked out, with silver rings on every finger, even her thumbs. 'Oh, shit, no. I can't. I've given up.' Her head bowed. 'Why the fuck anyone ...?'

Her voice trailed off, or maybe I just didn't hear the end of her sentence. I swallowed and took the last seat, the one across from Nikki. I dragged it a little to one side, set it at an angle. Jo opened the file, glanced at me and cleared her throat.

'So, probably best to start by taking some details. Nikki what?'

'Cooper-Clarke,' she said. She put her hands on the table and sat up a little. 'With an e.'

'With an e.' Jo raised an eyebrow as she wrote on the form. 'And your boyfriend's missing?'

Nikki nodded, and I heard the sound of tinkling bells. It took me a moment to trace the source – Nikki wore silver rings in her dreads. I scooped my hair back off my face and tied it up with a spare band I had round my wrist.

'Let's start with the easy ones,' said Jo. 'What's his name?'

Nikki wiped her eyes on the hem of her top. Questions are good. We're trained from childhood to want to provide answers. 'Matt,' she said. 'Matt Williams.'

'That's great,' I said, in what I hoped was an encouraging voice. Jo frowned at me. I interlaced my fingers, let my hands rest on the table. It felt weird, like I was praying. I unlaced them and folded my arms across my chest.

Jo kept a stream of easy to answer questions coming – occupation, phone number, height, weight, next of kin, date of birth, star sign – until Nikki's shoulders had fallen an inch or so and she'd lifted her gaze to meet Jo's. 'Pisces,' she said and tried to smile. 'Creative genius.'

'Frustrated alcoholics,' said Jo as she glanced at me and shifted in her chair.

'I'm Virgo,' I said.

'When,' said Jo, ignoring me and speaking to Nikki, 'did you last see him?'

'Saturday.'

4

Jo checked the calendar we had tacked to the wall. 'The eighth?'

Nikki shrugged.

'What happened?' I asked. 'When you last saw him?'

'Nothing,' said Nikki, turning to me. Her eyes were almost violet and I wondered whether she wore coloured contact lenses. 'Nothing,' she said again, as if that was the most frustrating thing. 'It was just ordinary. Friday night, we went to The Hyde, played some pool. He stayed at mine. I got up Saturday, went to the Union. That's the last time I saw him.'

'You're a student.' Jo raised an eyebrow at me.

'English Lit.,' she said. 'Saw the article about you in *The Gryphon*.'

'And Matt's a student too?'

'MSc.' The bells tinkled again. 'Actually, can I have that fag?' she asked Jo.

'How was he when you left?' I asked.

'Asleep.'

'And no one's seen him since?' asked Jo, as she pushed the pack of Marlboros across the table.

Nikki rested her hand on it but didn't pick it up. 'His mates have,' she said.

'Go on,' said Jo, and I didn't know whether she meant to tell Nikki to take a fag or to carry on speaking.

'We were supposed to be going to a party on Saturday night – but I didn't go coz I felt like shit. Ha.' She forced out what I think was supposed to be a laugh but sounded more like a shriek. I watched her fingers tremble over the cigarettes. 'I spoke to him on the phone that afternoon, asked if he

5

fancied coming to mine instead, but he wanted to go. So he went. No one's seen him since.'

'He disappeared at the party?'

'Tuff said he left him there.'

'Tuff?'

'His best mate.'

'Where was this party?'

'Lincolnshire.'

'Lincolnshire?' Geography's never been my strong point but that struck me as a long way to go for a night out.

Nikki's hand left the cigarette packet and picked at the tassels on the edge of her sleeves. 'Sunday afternoon, I went round to Matt's. Tuff was there. I asked where Matty was and Tuff was like really cagey.'

'Matty went to the party with Tuff?' Jo asked as she continued to scribble the information down.

'Whose party was it?' I asked.

'A free party,' she said.

'You mean, like a rave?' Jo asked.

'Wasn't that the nineties?' I said.

Jo pulled a face at me. 'Whereabouts in Lincolnshire?'

'Don't know.' She picked up the cigarettes and extracted one from the packet. 'A field somewhere.'

I glanced at Jo and she stuck out her bottom lip. I've known her long enough to know what that look means. Jo's one of the most open-minded people I've ever met, except when it comes to men. Truth is, since she caught Andy, her ex, in bed with another woman, she's got about as much faith in men as she has in the Tory government. Not that I can talk. But I know my failure with the opposite sex is down to me, not them.

Jo put her pen down and pulled her fingers through her hair. A drop more compost fell out. 'How long you been seeing him?' she asked.

'A year. Nearly.'

'Have you thought,' – Jo paused and passed Nikki a lighter – 'have you thought maybe he's dumped you?'

Nikki lit her cigarette, her eyes half-closed against the smoke. She didn't speak.

Jo tried again. 'How would you describe your relationship?'

The questions were getting too complex for Nikki. I saw a fresh batch of tears threaten. 'He hasn't dumped me,' she said.

'Wonder where Edie is with that tea?' I made a half-hearted attempt to get up from the table, but Jo glared at me.

'Why hasn't he rung anyone?' Nikki screwed up her nose and exhaled the smoke from her lungs. 'His phone goes straight to voicemail.'

'Does he have a job?' asked Jo.

'No, but he's missed his final tutorial. He's so close to finishing, why disappear the week his dissertation is due to be handed in?'

'Maybe that's why he's disappeared.' Jo glanced at me again and this time the look was serious. 'Maybe the pressure was getting to him. Does he suffer from depression, low mood, anxiety?'

Nikki's violet eyes flashed. 'He hasn't killed himself, if that's what you're thinking.'

Jo pressed her fingertips down on the edge of the table, making her knuckles crack. 'Exclusive?' asked Jo. 'Or open?'

'Exclusive,' said Nikki, without a moment's hesitation. She pushed the lighter back across the table to Jo. 'He's lovely. Ask anyone. He's—'

'You can't think of a single reason why he might have needed to get away?'

'No. I mean, at least, no, I don't think so.'

I felt sorry for her, as I watched her trawl her memory banks, because I've been there. I know what it's like to try and find a clue, something you may have missed, a sentence that with hindsight had a different meaning, an action that foreshadowed subsequent events.

'I don't think so,' she said again. 'I wanted him to stay in with me. He needed a night out.'

'Have you been to the police?'

'No.' She turned to me and I sensed she was glad of the distraction. 'I didn't want to get anyone into trouble. That's why I came to you.'

'Trouble?'

'Drugs,' Jo said, folding her arms across her chest.

Of course. It was only Wednesday. If this guy had gone to a rave on Saturday night it was possible he hadn't come down yet. We'd probably find him in a field, telling a tree how much he loved everyone.

Nikki rubbed her face with her left hand before speaking. 'He's not really a drugs person.'

I leaned closer to her, inhaled some of her second-hand smoke. Its warmth crept down my throat. 'What does that mean?'

'Well, he does. Sometimes. But, I don't know ...' She leant back in the chair. 'I'm worried about him.'

'Maybe the party isn't over,' said Jo.

'It's been four days,' said Nikki, her voice rising.

'You tried his family?'

'I don't know where they live.'

'You've been together a year and you don't know where his family live?'

'I know it's Somerset.'

'He never took you to meet them?' I was surprised at that. Not that I'd ever been to visit a boyfriend's parents, but I'd never had a year-long relationship either. As I've probably already said, I'm not the relationship type. And one of the reasons I've never had a year-long relationship is because I don't ever want to meet someone's parents. Or, more to the point, have someone want to meet mine.

'They don't get on,' Nikki said but I got the feeling she wasn't happy with the situation.

Jo stretched out her fingers. 'Best thing you can do is relax,' she said. 'Men are like dogs—'

Nikki wrinkled her nose. 'I need to find him now.'

'Dogs,' said Jo, crossing her arms behind her head. 'Simple needs. The trick is not to—'

'You don't understand,' said Nikki, grinding out her half-smoked cigarette into the ashtray. 'I've not got time to—'

'What's the rush?'

As the question came out of my mouth I realized I already knew the answer. 'You're pregnant,' I said.

She nodded and another wave of tears welled, smudging her eyeliner before spilling down her cheeks.

'And Matt knows,' said Jo. I knew from the tone of her voice what she was thinking.

'No.' Nikki shook her head and a tear flew from her cheek and landed on Jo's new client interview form. I watched it absorb into the paper. 'He doesn't know. I didn't even know. I only did the test the day before yesterday. It sounds stupid, but I never thought. I didn't feel right Friday, thought I'd eaten something bad. Felt sick all weekend. Then Monday, I was watching *Jeremy Kyle*, and this girl with the most awful mother ... well, anyway, it just hit me. I went to the chemist, got a test and two minutes later there's these two blue fucking lines.'

'How pregnant?' Jo asked.

'Who can remember the first day of their last period? I mean, Jesus.' She paused and I felt the rage radiating from her.

I was lost, but fascinated. Like when you pass a car wreck on the motorway. I didn't want to look but I couldn't help myself.

'How pregnant?' said Jo again.

'His birthday.' She let the words hang in the air.

'So,' said Jo, re-reading the form, as I tried to remember whether Pisces was February or March. 'What's that, two months?'

I glanced at Jo. I know very little about pregnancy but I know there's a cut-off point, when it all becomes a definite rather than a possibility. From the look of Nikki's wide eyes, that point wasn't too far away.

As if to reiterate my thoughts she said in a quiet voice, 'I've not got long.'

The unspoken words hung between us all. I didn't envy her. I dodge decisions whenever possible. This one was inescapable. Not deciding was a decision all in itself.

She seemed to sense my sympathy because she grabbed my arm and her eyes bored into mine. 'I can't do this, not without him. My mum's going to flip her wig. And my dad ...' She didn't finish the sentence, crumpled like a wet cardboard box. I wanted to say something comforting but I couldn't think of the words.

Aunt Edie chose that moment to crash through the door. I stood up, bashing my knee against the table leg. I took the tray from Aunt Edie and set it on the table in front of us. Aunt Edie passed a box of tissues to Nikki as I hovered by the door, my back to the wall. The room felt smaller than normal.

I try not to think about the past. Nothing good comes from raking over coals or making plans for an unpredictable future. There is only the here and the now. But I couldn't stop the images flooding my brain. Another young woman I once knew, who didn't mean to get pregnant.

Fiona.

My half-sister.

A sister I didn't know I had until four or so years ago, when I first set out to find my dad, a man who'd disappeared the day I was born, a man I'd never met. A man I now wish I'd never met, pray I'll never meet again. The man that haunts my nightmares. It's his face I see when I jolt awake in the pitch-dark, panicked and drenched in cold, wet sweat.

I wasn't there for my seventeen-year-old sister when she discovered she was pregnant. I wasn't there when she had to break the news to our father. I wasn't there to protect her. I'll pay the price for that as long as I live.

I watched Aunt Edie cluck around, handing out mugs of builder-strength tea, and knew that it didn't matter whether Nikki Cooper-Clarke could pay for our services. It didn't matter that Jo was convinced Matt had done a runner because somehow he'd sensed his girlfriend was up the duff. I knew there and then that I'd go and find him and I'd force him to face up to the consequences of his actions. Decision implies rational consideration of the facts. Choice is a leap of faith. In that moment, I chose.

We'd got our second case.

Chapter 2

I mumbled something about having to make a phone call and left the room. When the three of them came out, a few minutes later, I was behind the desk, pretending to type up case files. As Nikki left, her cheeks mascara-streaked, I asked her to bring in a photograph of Matt – the most recent she could find. She nodded and I promised her we'd give it everything we had. For an awful moment, I thought she was going to hug me, but the desk blocked the space between us. 'We bill by the hour,' I said.

'I've paid the deposit.' She gestured towards Jo, who, I noticed for the first time, held a wad of £20 notes in her left hand.

*

'Poor lamb,' Aunt Edie declared from the kitchenette, once Nikki had gone. 'Still, least it's not like it was in my day. She'd be shipped off faster than you could say, "Up the duff without a paddle." Never knew who was going to disappear next. It was like those murder-mystery parties where they pick you off, one at a time.'

'Let's start with his mate,' I said to Jo. 'Clearly Nikki thinks he knows something.'

I googled the address Nikki had given us for Matt, The Turnways – up near the cricket ground. 'No time like the present.' I grabbed my jacket from the peg by the door. 'Come on.'

Jo drove the company van as I gave directions. We found a nice little residential street in the heart of Headingley. At least, it was probably a nice little residential street once upon a time, before students had overrun the area and landlords disregarded their obligation to keep properties in a good state of repair. The houses were identical, substantial semi-detacheds, arranged in a gently curving semi-circle. Jo parked up and we knocked on the door, waited a few minutes, knocked some more. No answer. I patted my jacket pockets for a pen.

'A note?'

Jo wrinkled her nose. 'Let's keep the element of surprise. Least till we know what we're dealing with.'

'What then?' I glanced up, spotted an open window on the first floor. An open sash window. No window easier to get through, even without my ironing-board physique.

Jo caught me scoping it out and shook her head. 'Give him a chance. We'll come back.' She left the garden and strode towards the van. 'Let's try the uni.'

*

We detoured via the office to drop off the van – getting into the University of Leeds' car park is harder than getting into Glastonbury. 'Nikki gave us the name of his tutor, didn't she? I'll get the form.'

'I've had a Martin Blink on the blower,' said Aunt Edie as soon as I stepped through the door. I keep telling her she watches too many cop shows.

Martin Blink. I grinned. If it wasn't for Martin Blink, Jo might be on remand in Armley nick, waiting for some pen-pusher to decide whether self-defence is now an offence. 'What's he want?'

'Says he's got a case for you,' Aunt Edie said in a tone that suggested she had trouble believing him. 'A suicide.'

'We're a missing persons' bureau.' I hung my jacket back on its peg. The day was warmer than I'd realized. 'What we going to do with a suicide?'

'Wouldn't give any details,' Aunt Edie continued. 'Like I might not have the wherewithal to take a proper message.' She tutted and balled up the piece of paper in the palm of her hand. 'Insisted on coming to see you.' She took aim at the wastepaper bin next to my desk. 'I told him we can't have people dropping in willy-nilly. I told him, you're both busy women.'

The ball of paper flew through the air and landed dead centre in the bin.

'Not that busy, Aunt Edie.'

'He said you'd make time for him.' She raised eyebrows at his temerity. 'I said, "Oh, will they now? And who might you be?" Bloody cheek.'

'He's the journalist I told you—'

'Retired journalist. Talks like he's part of the team. Well, I told him, I don't care who you are, you have to have an appointment.'

I narrowed my eyes. 'And did you make him one?'

Jo pushed open the door. 'Come on,' she said, tapping at an imaginary watch on her wrist.

'Martin Blink wants to see us,' I said.

'Ace. Let's go.'

'He needs reminding that this is a female detective agency, isn't it?' Aunt Edie looked to Jo for support.

I've given up trying to explain the difference between a detective agency and a missing persons' bureau to Aunt Edie. At times I think she's deliberately trying to misunderstand.

'That's right, Edie,' said Jo. 'No persons with dangly bits will ever work in this office.' She made a diagonal cross over her left breast as she spoke. 'You know what it's like. Let one in and they'll all want to start waving them around.'

I frowned at Jo. I put my hands on my hips and tried to adopt a managerial tone. 'Did you make him an appointment?'

'In the diary.' Aunt Edie sniffed.

'When?'

'Half past four.'

'Today?' I glanced at the clock.

'I squeezed him in.' She switched on her computer screen and took a seat at the desk. 'Not that he was grateful.'

*

It's only a ten-minute walk from our offices to the uni, through Hyde Park, the decompression chamber between city centre and student-ghetto. Jo found the Earth and Environment building on a map of the campus while I checked the form. Nikki had given us the name of Matt's tutor – Professor Kenrick, or Kennick.

We found the name – Kendrick – on a tutorial list; office was on the eleventh floor. It was already two o'clock in the afternoon and it appeared that the university had done its main business of the day and was winding down to home time. We passed several empty seminar rooms as we marched along the corridors, reading the names on the doors. We climbed another flight of stairs and encountered an identical set of corridors before we found the room we were looking for. I glanced through the window. A woman with short hair, hunched over a desk.

Jo knocked and pushed open the door. 'Professor Kendrick?'

The professor glanced up from her desk, and the familiar feeling of being a schoolgirl in the firing line washed through me. I braced myself for her displeasure at being disturbed. She looked us both up and down.

'You've found me.' She placed her pen down on the pile of paper in front of her and pushed her glasses up into her short, spiky hair. 'And provided a welcome distraction. What can I do you for?'

'We're looking for Matt Williams.'

The professor inclined her head. She was younger than I first thought. Perhaps not even forty. 'Popular chap.'

'We're private investigators,' said Jo. 'We need to talk to him.'

The academic stood up and I realized how tall she was. Impossible to miss, she must have been over six foot. In the small room she took on almost comedy proportions.

'I do beg your pardon. I thought you were students.' She brushed down her rumpled suit trousers with one hand as she held the other out to shake Jo's. 'Private investigators. Fascinating.'

'Thanks,' said Jo.

'How long have you been in this line of business?'

'Long enough,' said Jo.

'Do come in, and close the door. If I move this pile of papers,' she grabbed a stack from a chair in the corner of her shoebox-sized room, 'you'll even be able to have a seat.'

Jo didn't move and as I was stood behind her, I didn't either. The professor didn't appear to notice as she continued to rearrange the boxes and piles of paper. 'So, Matthew. Matty, I believe the girls call him. Obviously, I'm too old to be swayed by his charms, but not so old I can't appreciate why he causes such a stir.' She turned to smile at us both.

'Do you know where we might find him?' asked Jo.

'Afraid not. Haven't seen him, not recently.'

'It's rather urgent,' said Jo.

She finally cleared both chairs and crossed to the doorframe. Jo moved aside to let her pass, which put Jo deeply inside the room. I followed, inching past the professor, straining to avoid body contact. After glancing out into the corridor, Professor Kendrick closed the door and returned to perch on the edge of her desk. She folded her hands across her knees. 'Take a seat.'

Jo sank into one so I took the other. This gave Professor Kendrick an even bigger advantage and she loomed over us. Her white shirt tucked in at the waist, emphasizing her slender frame. 'Now, what's this about?'

'Matt's missing,' I said. 'No one's seen him since a party on Saturday night.'

'Then I suggest you talk to admin and see whether they'd be willing to contact his parents. You can leave—'

'We've spoken to his mother,' Jo lied.

Professor Kendrick raised her voice and continued speaking as if Jo hadn't interrupted, 'Your number with me, and if I see him, I would certainly be happy to pass it on. Although I suspect he may be in hiding.'

'In hiding? Who from?'

She pulled her glasses down to the brim of her nose. 'From whom?' She peered at me over the top of the frames. 'Well, from me I suppose. It's the deadline for his dissertation. We were supposed to be having a final run over it on Monday afternoon and he didn't show. Not like him, I must say. I intend to email him.'

I didn't like the feeling of claustrophobia that had settled over me as soon as Professor Kendrick had closed the door. I like always to know my escape route, and as we were on the eleventh floor, she'd just sealed the only real option.

'Any concerns about his work up until this point?' asked Jo.

'No, he's a committed student. One of my best. More or

less on target, as on target as any of us ever are. But he's not the first student to go AWOL in the month running up to submission. What did his mother say?'

'She hasn't heard from him,' Jo said, and even I wouldn't have known she was making this up. 'That's why we're here.'

The professor stuck out her bottom lip. 'She's hired a firm of private investigators to find him? As far as I'm aware she hasn't contacted the university. I'm his supervisor, I'd expect that message to come to me.'

I pretended my interest had been caught by the poster about climate change pinned to the wall.

'You said he was popular,' said Jo. 'What did you mean by that?'

Professor Kendrick's grey hair fell forward to partially obscure her glasses. She flicked it away with the back of her hand. 'You're not the only ones looking for him.'

'Other people are looking for him?' I asked.

'Other women.'

'How many other women?'

She smiled. 'I am perhaps exaggerating for dramatic effect. Forgive me, a knee-jerk reaction to reading the musings of my undergrads.' She nodded at the pile of papers that towered on her desk.

Jo raised a single eyebrow. 'How many?'

'Undergrads?'

'Women looking for Matt.'

'Two, that I'm aware of.'

'Of whom you are aware?' I couldn't resist.

'Who?' asked Jo, shooting me a look that left me in no doubt I should shut up. I went back to the poster.

'I'm not sure it's any of my business.'

I'd had enough of the professor, and I worried the oxygen supply was depleting. I'd never survive working in this rabbit hutch. Books lined the walls, giving it an underground bunker-like feel, despite its high-rise situation. 'People are worried,' I said.

'What did they look like? The two women looking for him?' asked Jo.

'One had hair like rattlesnakes.'

'Dreads?' said Jo. She turned to me. 'Nikki.'

'Nikki?' asked the professor.

'His girlfriend.'

Professor Kendrick nodded. 'I've seen her hanging about before.'

'What about the other one?'

'Well, I'm not one to gossip, and there might not be anything in this.'

'We're professional private investigators,' said Jo. She showed our police-issued identity card. 'It's not gossip, it's helping with our enquiries. Anything you tell us will be treated in the strictest confidence.'

The professor's brow creased as she took in the badge. 'The police are involved?'

'They've been informed,' Jo lied again.

'And?'

'They share your view – nothing too ominous in a student disappearing the week before his dissertation is due.'

Professor Kendrick put Jo's ID down on her desk. 'There was an incident. A strange incident. Not strange, that's too strong. Was it yesterday? What's today?'

'Wednesday.'

'Yes, must have been. I wasn't in Monday, not in the morning. Yesterday morning, Sally from the office came to see me to say she'd caught a young woman taking mail from the pigeon-holes. The student pigeonholes. She'd asked said young woman what she was doing, and, she said, the woman had seemed,' Kendrick paused, searching for the right word, 'flustered.'

'Did she stop her taking the mail?'

'Of course. Not that any of it would be of any interest. Hell, it's not of interest to me and I wrote most of it. The system is mainly used for hard-copy submissions and leaflets about forthcoming symposiums, information we can't email. To be honest, hardly anyone uses them anymore. I can't think why on earth—'

'It was Matt's pigeonhole?'

'She may have thought she'd find a timetable, perhaps.'

'Where's Sally now?'

'Probably her office.'

Jo got up, filling the air space between me and the professor. I wondered again whether there was enough oxygen in the room to support three people. If anyone was going to keel over, like the sacrificial canary in the coal mines, it was going to be me.

'Can we talk to her?' Jo asked.

'Follow me.'

*

Sally was housed in a much bigger office, but she shared it with at least three others.

'Could we have a word, please,' said Professor Kendrick, indicating to the middle-aged woman to step outside the room.

'These two young women are private investigators,' the professor said to Sally once we were all standing together in the corridor. 'They want to know more about the woman you saw interfering with the pigeonholes yesterday.'

Sally's cheeks reddened but I didn't read anything in to it. The smallest hint of official enquiry can cause some people to colour up.

'I didn't recognize her so I asked her what she was doing.'

'Professor Kendrick says you thought she was flustered.'

'She struck me that way.'

'What did she take?'

'Nothing. I didn't let her. I asked her what she was doing and she said she was on the wrong floor. She left very quickly.'

'Can we see the pigeonholes?'

Sally glanced at the professor.

The professor shrugged. 'Well, they are open mailboxes. We've never considered locking them – which goes to show how uncontentious the contents are.'

'They're this way,' Sally said, and we trooped round the corner to where the lifts were.

Outside a room that bore a plaque stating 'Earth and Earth Sciences Department', was a grid of shelves – four wide and about a dozen high – each one about the size of a shoebox. Each box had a name tag. Matt Williams was easy to find – the last one on the right-hand side.

'Are you sure it was Matt's pigeonhole she was interested in?'

'Yes,' said Sally. 'It was the bottom one.'

'Can I?' I crouched so I was level with Matt's mail.

'It goes without saying I'm not condoning such behaviour,' Professor Kendrick said.

I scooped up a handful of paper. The professor was right. Flyers about upcoming conferences, speakers from foreign countries coming to lecture, discount offers on everything from books to nightclubs. I frowned at Jo and handed the pile to her.

'Are you sure she was taking mail?' I turned back to Sally. 'Perhaps she was leaving him a note?'

Sally pulled a face as she considered what I'd just said. 'I didn't think of that. But if she was, why didn't she just say? Instead of running off?'

Jo sifted through the papers. And sure enough, there amongst the bumf I caught a glimpse of A4 lined paper, torn from a book and folded in half. I snatched it and opened it up.

Professor Kendrick peered over my shoulder as I read:

Matt. I'll be in Old Bar, Thursday two o'clock. Be there. I mean it.

The note wasn't signed but there was a letter at the end of it. The letter 'S'. No kiss, not underlined, just an S and a full stop, all in purple biro.

'When did you see this woman?' Jo asked Sally.

'Yesterday, just before lunch.'

I turned to the professor. 'What's he like, Matt?'

'Bright. Well-bred. Popular.' She pushed her glasses back up her nose. 'I ought to inform administration.'

I wasn't keen to get any kind of authority involved, not until we knew what we were dealing with. 'He might just have had a row with his girlfriend.'

'And you said his parents are aware?'

'If there's another woman on the scene,' said Jo, waving the piece of paper in the air, 'he might be in hiding from his girlfriend. Case she breaks his legs.'

'The eternal curse of good-looking men.' Professor Kendrick shrugged her shoulders. 'I imagine.'

'Of course, the girl you saw might not have left this note. It's not dated.' I turned back to Sally. 'What did she look like?'

Professor Kendrick took off her glasses, polished them with a cloth handkerchief.

'I don't know,' said Sally. 'She was young. I assumed she was a student.'

'Glasses? Braces? Blonde, redhead?' asked Jo. 'Clothes?'

Professor Kendrick returned her glasses to her face and checked her watch. 'I expect she wore clothes, didn't she, Sally?'

Sally's cheeks grew pink and she threw a grateful glance at the professor. 'I didn't take much notice, I was late for my meeting. She had dark hair, I think. About this long.' She pointed to her shoulders.

'Young, female and dark, long hair? Anything else?'

'I'm sorry. I'm not very good at this kind of thing.'

'Anything at all.'

'Eyeliner,' said Sally with a note of triumph in her voice. 'I remember thinking she wore too much eyeliner.'

Great. That should narrow it down to well over eighty per cent of the student population, even if you included the boys.

'Well,' said Jo. 'Here's our card. If you remember anything, give us a ring, let us know. There's a ... an office manager if we're not available. You can leave a message with her.'

Chapter 3

We trudged back up the hill towards the office. We hadn't found out a right lot, and it was hard not to feel a bit deflated. We decided we'd wait till teatime to go round to Matt's house on The Turnways again, see if anyone turned up. Before that we were meeting Martin Blink.

Martin arrived at the offices on the stroke of half past four. He limped through the front door, and Jo jumped up from her desk and hugged the life out of him. They'd spent a lot of time together, after our last case, when Jo was in hospital recovering from her surgery on her shoulder, and I was trying to handle the chaos of the aftermath of what had happened. I think now he sees her as his protégée.

I hung back, tried to position myself so that Aunt Edie wouldn't see Jo's eyes tight shut in the embrace. 'Good to see you,' I said. 'How you doing?'

He didn't answer me, staring instead at Jo, running his eyes up and down her frame like he was looking for weak spots.

I tried to see Jo through Martin's eyes. I know I take her for granted. She's the stronger one, I mean, mentally – the least neurotic person I ever met. To Jo everything is black or white. There's the wrong way and the right way. Good versus evil. If there's ever anything on her mind, she'll go out, get hammered and forget about it. She doesn't have brain worms – the things that wriggle around in your headspace, won't let you go.

I had noticed that since the last investigation she was smoking and drinking a bit more than she used to, and I was keeping an eye on it. But who wouldn't be, in her position, after what had happened? She'd been shot and the physical scars were still healing. The mental scars might take even longer. She'd get there though. I'd make damned sure of that.

Jo seemed to pass Martin's inspection, because he took a step back, nodded and said, 'Doing all right, kid.'

And I felt my shoulders give a little.

'I'm hanging in there,' said Jo.

She pushed a chair towards Martin and as soon as he sat down he didn't look old. His face tells a lot of stories – frown lines buried deep in his forehead, but laughter lines like spiders' webs criss-crossing from the corner of his eyes and disappearing into his hairline. When he's not trying to walk you'd think he was in his fifties.

'Doing just fine,' said Aunt Edie.

'Any ghosts?' said Martin, setting a battered leather briefcase on the desk.

Jo glanced at me and a wash of something that felt like acid burned my veins. I know she hates talking about the fact she killed a man. Even a man as bad as the one she killed. I tell her she did the world a favour, but I know she doesn't believe me. Not yet.

'I'm coping,' said Jo.

'It's ace to see you, Martin.' As I said the words I felt my breathing deepen, so that air made it past my chest and into the rest of my body. 'What brings you here?'

'Private matters.' He tapped one finger against the side of his nose and then glanced across at Aunt Edie. 'If your receptionist here could make us a cup of tea, I've a thirst like the Sahara. You got a room we could talk in?'

I think I actually ducked. When I did dare risk a glance in Aunt Edie's direction, she was holding on to the back of her office chair, her knuckles white under the fluorescent lights.

'I'm the office manager, not the receptionist,' she said in the tightest of voices.

'Sorry, love.' Martin held up his hands. 'Didn't mean to cause offence.'

Aunt Edie bridled but managed to bite her tongue. She pushed her chair under the desk. 'I'll happily put the kettle on,' she said. 'And I was going to leave a bit early tonight, so no need to go through to the back. You can have the place to yourselves. Talk about your privates to your heart's content.' She stared unblinking at Martin as she spoke.

I felt my cheeks burn.

Once Aunt Edie had switched the kettle on and her computer off, she buttoned up her coat and let herself out.

Martin loosened his tie.

'Got off on the wrong foot there.'

'Don't worry. Her bark's worse than her bite,' I lied. 'So, come on, spill.'

'I want to hire you girls.'

'Hire us?'

'Women,' said Jo.

'I want to hire you women?' asked Martin. 'Really?'

Jo nodded and put her feet up on the desk.

'OK,' said Martin, shrugging his shoulders. 'I want to hire you women.'

If I've got a weak spot, it's lonely old men. You see them, shuffling round Morrisons, mismatched clothes, in need of a haircut. I can't bear to think of them fumbling with the tin opener and being unable to reach out to people. Jo gives me hell for my sexism and it's true – I don't worry about women in the same way. I guess I think women have an advantage.

I knew Martin was divorced, that he lived on his own, but I didn't like to think of him living with the ghosts of the disappeared.

'You're missing someone?' I wondered who it might be. He'd never mentioned much about his private life.

'Been thinking, since you solved that last case. You found the answer to something that happened seventeen years ago. You went back and found something we all missed.'

'Couldn't have done it without you,' I said. 'And the—'

'Enough, already. Don't need to be damned with your faint praise, thanks all the same. Never doubted my investigative skills.' He fiddled with the clasp on his briefcase and pulled out a newspaper. 'But sometimes you got to wait till the window opens.'

'Go on,' said Jo, taking the paper from him.

'Page thirteen.' He pulled at his tie and loosened the knot. 'Another one I never got to the bottom of. And this one nags me, buzzes round my head like an angry wasp. You know, when the 3 a.m. gets you?' He looked to Jo and I found myself feeling resentful. I'm more than familiar with the early hours, thank you very much.

Jo read while Martin continued, 'One that won't let me lie. And I thought well, if you could have a go at it, maybe the time is right.'

'The body?' said Jo.

'Let me see.' I peered over Jo's shoulder, saw a small article, only a few lines with the headline: 'Police discover woman's body in garden of luxury flats.'

'It's worth a crack, that's what I'm saying.'

We heard the kettle whistle in the kitchenette out back. Martin Blink looked up at the clock. 'Sun's almost over the yard arm. You gi— women got a local?'

Martin doesn't know about my issues with alcohol. Not that I've had a drink since the last case. And I try not to beat myself up too much about that one. Surely anyone in that situation, faced with the immediate prospect of their own death, would succumb to one last shot? Especially when it was one of the finest whiskies money could buy. So fine that when I close my eyes, I can still taste it.

But before that one slip, in extreme circumstances, it had been nearly a full twelve months since I'd given up drinking.

I know now that that's the difference between the addict and the social drinker. To the addict, it doesn't matter how long it's been since the last one, because they're focused on the next. The social drinker can enjoy a drink, the one they have in their hands – as a self-contained event, an occasion all in itself. Which is a nice idea, but a single drink doesn't exist for the addict. The addict is thinking about the future, about what will happen when the one in their hands runs out. To the addict one drink is only ever the start.

Addicts are people who have never experienced enough. Enough of what, I don't know. Therapists would tell you they haven't had enough love. I don't know about that. I just know there's never enough alcohol to get me out of my mind.

'Well?' asked Martin.

I nearly said no, but I caught the look on Jo's face. And, I reminded myself, it's good for me to be challenged. An opportunity to reassert my faith, my resolve. Least, that's what the textbooks tell me.

I switched the phones over to the night-service and unhooked my jacket from its peg. 'There's The Brudenell,' I said as Jo's eyes lit up. 'Just round the corner.'

Chapter 4

The Brudenell is a social club but it's not like your average working men's club. For a start, nearly everyone in it is a student and probably not one of them has ever done a full day's work in their lives – at least, not the kind of work that working men's club implies. Recently, The Brudenell has been building a solid reputation as a kind of secret gig venue, with unadvertised performances by some big-name bands.

We were seated in the bar less than ten minutes after leaving the office, Martin and Jo both with pints – Landlord for Martin, lager and lime for Jo. I nursed a blackcurrant and soda. I can't drink cola because the caffeine makes my heart race, and I'm never sure what else to order. 'Let's hear it then.'

He glanced around but it was still early, even by student standards. The closest drinkers were seated three tables away. 'Trouble was no one was pushing for it to be solved. A body – young girl – young woman, a prostitute—'

'Sex worker,' said Jo.

Martin nodded and took a swig of his pint. The head of his beer left a foam moustache along his top lip. It suited him, matched the white of his hair. 'Sex worker. Like it. Anyway, that was as far as they got. A body. A sex worker, they decided. No one ever came forward to claim her.'

'Murdered?'

Martin popped a Fisherman's Friend in his mouth and crunched. 'She was dead. That's about the only fact. Police decided it was suicide although they never found a note. Pathologist said somewhere between twenty-two and twenty-five. Autopsy showed she'd carried a child. Slip of a thing. Bruises that looked like she'd had some kind of fight, but they were old – not related to her death.'

'Suicide?' I know I've got an issue with suicide. To me, it's selfish and passive-aggressive – a way of handing on your problems to someone else. It's the easy way out. Jo gives me hell for my views but I can't seem to change them. It's like they're ingrained in me. I took a sip of my blackcurrant and tried not to gag. 'How she do it?'

He slapped me on the knuckles. 'Not proved.'

'Well, how'd she die?'

'Poisoned.'

'Poisoned? What, like an overdose?'

'Strychnine – know how that works?'

I shook my head.

'Starts with twitching. Facial muscles go first.' Martin clenched and unclenched his fingers, balling his hand into a fist, then flinging his fingers back. He still wore his wedding ring and it squeezed the flesh of his third finger. 'Spasms spread throughout the body, progressing to convulsions as the nervous system runs out of control.'

'Weird way to kill yourself,' said Jo.

'Eventually the muscles that control breathing become paralyzed and the victim suffocates,' Martin continued. 'Stays conscious and aware the whole time up to death – in fact the nerves of the brain are stimulated, gives heightened perception.'

'Christ,' said Jo.

He took another mouthful of beer. 'Hard to think of a worse way to go.'

'Where'd she get strychnine from?' I asked. 'Is it legal?'

'It was. Used by mole-catchers – but you had to be a licensed pest controller to get hold of it. Police never found where she got it from, least not that they told me.'

'You don't think it was suicide?'

'She was found in the communal garden of a block of flats, overlooking Roundhay Park.'

I'd never been to Roundhay Park, but I'd heard of it. It was out to the north of the city, only about four miles away; but we've got Hyde Park right on our doorstep, so why travel?

'She killed herself outside?' asked Jo and I knew by the tone of her voice that she didn't believe it. I could see where she was coming from – when you think of suicide, especially women, you think of pills in the bath, head in the oven. But then there were the jumpers, I thought. Beachy Head and that bridge near Hull. They were outdoors.

'Perhaps she didn't want a relative to find her,' I said. 'I mean, if it was suicide, and she'd killed herself in her own flat, chances are it would have been someone she knew who discovered her. Perhaps that's why she went to the garden – she wanted a stranger to find her.' Which, I thought, although

I didn't say aloud, made her more thoughtful than your average suicide. I don't know how the tube drivers ever recover from what they must see when someone decides they can't go on.

'She didn't live in the flats,' said Martin.

'Oh.' I considered this for a moment. It didn't make sense. 'Why would you kill yourself in someone else's garden?'

'Where *did* she live?' asked Jo.

Martin shrugged. 'That's the trouble. We don't know. No one knows who she is. No ID on her; all they found was a train ticket from Nottingham. Like she'd travelled all the way from Nottingham to kill herself in the garden of this particular block of flats.'

'She must have known someone in the flats,' I said.

'She'd tied herself to a statue. Right in the middle of the grass.'

'If they didn't know who she was, how did they know she was a sex worker?' asked Jo.

Martin shrugged again. 'Don't know. And I've got to tell you here, after ...' He paused, looked at Jo again. 'After last time. I want to put my cards right out there on the table, so you know what you're getting into. I didn't like the way the investigation was handled, if you catch my drift.'

'Come on, Martin,' I said. I banged my drink down on the table harder than I expected and caused the table to wobble and Jo's pint to slop. I lowered my voice. 'You can't put your cards on the table and then ask us to catch your drift. What do you mean?'

Jo mopped at the spillage with a beer mat.

'The policeman in charge. I had my doubts. That's all.

Nothing concrete, just a feeling that perhaps he wasn't as committed as he could have been.'

'Wasn't committed or was bent? Massive difference.'

'Lee,' Jo said. She put a hand on my arm. 'We've got to come to each case blank, you know that. Empty.'

I reminded myself to breathe. Martin looked at me and then at Jo, like he was watching a tennis match.

'I don't know why he decided she was a sex worker. That's all. Maybe she was known to the police, or him; maybe he was working from the fact that no one ever claimed her, the bus driver's impression ... I don't know. It might not be important. Anyway, to me it felt like she was trying to tell someone something. She was naked. Did I say that?'

'She committed suicide naked?'

'Bollocks,' said Jo.

'The report said she was naked as the day she was born except for a necklace,' said Martin.

'If she was naked, where was her train ticket?'

'All her clothes were folded neatly next to the body. The train ticket was found in bushes less than three metres away.'

'Might not be hers then?' Jo said.

'It had her fingerprints on it. And they found a bus driver who thought he remembered her getting the bus from the station.'

'Did they check the CCTV?'

Martin nodded. 'Nothing.'

'Not a lot to go on,' I said.

'I looked into the residents. Posh flats, owned by the well-to-do. Rob Hamilton was one of the residents.'

Even I've heard of Rob Hamilton and I don't watch TV.

'If in doubt, deal,' said Jo.

I frowned at her.

'That's his catchphrase,' she said.

'And Jimmy McFly lived there too – the celebrity chef. Before he got done for drunk driving.'

'Didn't he go out with Gabby Fairweather?' asked Jo. She pointed a finger at me. 'She left him when he went to prison. Before she met that singer from that boy band.'

I was totally lost.

'The Wranglers. God, what was his name? Chris somebody.'

For a radical feminist socialist, Jo is surprisingly well-informed on celebrity culture.

I turned to Martin. 'Anyone with any links to the body?' I said, my voice a little pointed.

'I've got the full list here.' Martin bent to pick his briefcase from the floor, opened it and took out a reporter's spiral bound notebook.

I read the neatly written label on the front. Jane Doe; 29 August and the year. I did the maths. Almost seven years ago.

'There were a couple of people of interest. One resident who'd been prosecuted for tax evasion.' He flicked through the pages of the notebook. 'There.' He pointed to a name that had been highlighted. 'And Blake Jeffries – the whisper was he'd made his money on the club scene ... and not just through door entry charges, if you know what I mean.'

Jo grabbed for the notebook before I could get there and settled herself to read its contents.

'You mean drugs?' I said.

'According to a source. I looked into it but nothing provable.'

'We're a missing persons' bureau,' I said. I folded my arms. 'She's like the opposite of missing. She's found. I mean, all right, she's dead, but she's not—'

Martin opened his mouth to say something but Jo got there before him. 'Somewhere she's missing,' she said. 'That's the thing. These women, they've been isolated—'

'What women?' I asked.

'Cut off from society, precisely so no one cares when they're abused, raped, killed ... whatever.'

'What women?' I said again.

'Sex workers,' said Jo.

I knew her patience was stretching and truth was I was trying to stretch it on purpose. Don't ask me why. I get like this sometimes. You'd think I'd learn, but no.

'Somewhere,' Jo said, 'they're missing.'

'Somewhere there has to be a family or a past lover,' Martin explained, and I noticed the similarity in the two pairs of steely blue eyes staring at me. 'Or a friend. Someone who's missing her. She had a child. That child must be somewhere, wondering where their mother is. She died anonymous. Seven years later, no one even knows her name.'

Jo continued to flick through the pages of Martin's notebook. There didn't seem to be many, perhaps half a dozen, the rest of the pages virgin white. I knew from the way she closed the front cover I wasn't going to get much say in this one. Resistance was futile. 'And that's all you got?' I asked. 'A list of people who lived in the flats and a train ticket?'

'They're a subclass of people,' said Jo. 'Cynics might think these women are bred for abuse and murder. Most sex workers grew up in care.'

'We don't actually know she was a sex worker.'

'Abusers, murderers know they stand a good chance of getting away with the shit they get away with—'

'She wasn't murdered. And we don't know she was abused.' Jo obviously wasn't going to let any of the facts stand in her way.

'Because no one cares,' she said, her eyes boring into mine. Her voice was so loud the people at the other table had stopped speaking.

'I do care,' I said. 'I just think we need to be clear—'

'They're the world's missing, the world's lost.'

'OK.' I held my hands up.

'They're so missing, so off radar, no one even knows they're missing. They're more than missing, they're fucking invisible.'

'That's the thing,' said Martin, nodding with approval at Jo. 'There was no one stamping feet, demanding answers. The case got pushed aside. She had no one. That's why it won't let me go.'

'If the kind of men who prey on these women knew there were people like us out there, people who care and want to find out what happened, maybe, just maybe, it might make them think twice before they do the fucked-up shit that they do.'

'OK,' I said. The expression on Jo's face made me feel like crying. 'I guess it wouldn't hurt, having a look at it.'

I turned to Martin because I couldn't bear to look at Jo

anymore. 'You don't have to pay us though, we owe you one.'

'We owe you more than that,' said Jo.

He drained his pint and waved at the barman, indicating another round, the same again. I wanted to point out it wasn't waitress service, but the barman smiled and reached up for a pint glass from the rack above his head. Martin turned back to us.

'I do have to pay you. And I'll tell you why. If I don't, I have to be nice to you because you're doing me a favour. There's no pressure on you to succeed.' He grinned at me and the twinkle returned to his eye.

'You want to be able to boss us around, is that what you're saying?' said Jo.

'Precisely.' Martin patted Jo on the hand. 'And besides, that battleaxe you've hired as your receptionist, sorry, office manager ... she'd kick all our backsides if you said you'd taken on a freebie. I need to be able to stand my ground with her.'

Jo shook her head. 'You'll learn. Complete surrender is the only way with Aunt Edie.'

'Yes, well, I'm too old. And you know what they say about old dogs and new tricks. I don't surrender to anyone. Never have, never will.'

Jo laughed and it struck me that I hadn't seen her laugh for ages. Not like that, head back, square white teeth on show.

Chapter 5

We stayed in The Brudenell till closing time. Martin had booked himself a couple of nights in a B&B on Cardigan Road in order to watch the cricket. As Jo tried to wheedle another round out of the barman I noticed the skin on my forearms was scratched red and tugged my sleeves down. Once the barman had convinced Jo there wasn't going to be any after hours, we poured Martin into a taxi from the rank opposite and I linked arms with Jo as we waved him off, Jo swaying as I held onto her. When the taxi turned the corner, I half-pulled, half-pushed her up the hill towards our flat on Hyde Park Road.

She stumbled over the kerb on Royal Park Mount and fell on her arse. I tried to pull her up, but Jo found it too hilarious for words and I gave up and sat next to her at the roadside. We shared a fag, which got so damp from the tears streaming down her face I had to light another. I put my arm around her shoulders and her body warmth seeped into me. Must have looked like a right pair. Just as I thought she'd fallen asleep and I'd have to roll her up the hill, she clambered to her feet.

'Chris Goodall.'

'Who?'

'The bloke from The Wranglers.'

'Right.' I had no idea what she was talking about, and I'm not sure she did either.

'The one who went out with Gabby Fairweather. After she finished with Jimmy McFly.'

I nodded.

'Doesn't matter. It's not important.' She took a moment to steady herself and then set off at such a pace that I had to jog to keep up with her.

When we got to the flat, I let us in as quietly as possible so as not to disturb our downstairs neighbour, who happens to be the only full-time worker within about a two-mile radius. She hates us and our unsociable hours. I went into the kitchen to put the kettle on while Jo crashed into the front room. When I joined her with a freshly brewed pot of tea – milk in a jug, just how she likes it – she was out cold on the settee with her Doc Martens still on. I put the tray down, untied her laces, tugged the boots off her feet and fetched the duvet from her bed. I floated it over her body. She looks different asleep, less fierce, her face softer, unlined.

She didn't stir so I took the crumpled Rizlas, the tobacco tin and the tea tray upstairs. My bedroom is in the attic, a bolthole from the hustle of the streets. My bed nestles in the space beneath the dormer, and the garret window looks out over the treetops of Hyde Park. Here I can convince myself that I'm not in the city, that there's clean air and a world of space. I lay half-propped on my pillows, trying to memorize

the star constellations. I made a spliff, but my heart wasn't in
it and I stubbed it out before I was halfway done. A line from
an old Billy Bragg song looped in my head. It's never the same
after the first time, but it doesn't stop you coming back for
more.

The next thing I knew the alarm clock glowed out 4:03 a.m.
I lay in bed feeling unsettled and trying to remember my
dream, but it floated just outside my grasp, leaving me worried
but without knowing why. I'd fallen asleep without closing
the curtain and when I saw the first trace of dawn across the
park, I pulled on a pair of denim cut-offs and my T-shirt and
went downstairs.

Jo was still comatose on the settee, so I opened the front
room curtains, knowing that before long the sun would be
beaming down through the tall sash windows. Jo grunted and
turned away.

I laced my trainers on the bottom stair, shoved a jacket and
notebook in my backpack, then jogged, slowly, my usual two
laps round the park. I intended to stop there, then walk round
the corner to the office and pick up the van, but the sun was
breaking through the red clouds, and I got into my stride and
decided to run down into Woodhouse and then up The Ridge
to Headingley. Leeds 6 doesn't really stir much before lunchtime and I live for these glimpses, the moments when I'm the
only one awake.

By the time I got to Headingley sweat dripped from my forehead, but the voices had gone. It was almost eight, so I sat

on the brick wall of a flowerbed until Sainsbury's opened, bought a bottle of water and made my way through the empty streets to The Turnways.

As I got close to number 24 I saw the curtains were still open and the house looked just the same as it had the previous day. The thought crossed my mind that perhaps it wasn't just Matt that had done a disappearing act. I walked up the path, hammered on the door and jumped when it opened straight-away.

'Yes?' said a young woman in a round-necked striped jumper. She had mid-calf-length boots on and I had the impression she was about to go out. I felt underdressed next to her, in my T-shirt and knee-length shorts. I wished I'd put my jacket on before knocking on the door.

'Sorry to bother you,' I said. 'Is Matt in?'

She frowned. 'Who are you?'

I wasn't used to doing this without Jo and it reminded me how much I rely on her, especially to break the ice. 'I'm Lee, Lee Winters. I'm a private detective.' It sounded stupid to my ears, but I persevered. 'Investigator. I run a missing persons' bureau. We're ... I mean, I'm looking for Matt.'

'Oh,' she said. Her forehead creased and she paused for a moment. 'You mean someone hired you? Someone hired you to find Matt?'

'Is he in?' I straightened my spine, adjusted the weight on my feet so I grew a couple of centimetres.

'No. No, he's not here. Haven't seen him since last week. I don't know where he is.'

'Can I come in?'

She checked the time on her watch. 'I've got lectures.'

Not at eight fifteen in the morning, she didn't. I might not have spent that long in higher education, but long enough to learn the basics. I took a step forward. She held her ground and so we stood too close to each other, so close I could smell the mint of her toothpaste.

'It won't take long,' I said.

She hesitated. I knew she didn't want to talk to me but I guessed she was too polite to say. 'I said we should have reported it,' she said, 'but Tuff thinks he's holed up somewhere. He's about to submit his dissertation.'

'Tuff?'

'No. I meant Matt's about to submit his dissertation.'

I was having difficulty keeping up with the conversation. 'Who's Tuff?'

'My flatmate. Matt's best friend.'

I went for it, taking another bite out of the distance between us, and this time she stepped back which allowed me to move inside, into the hallway. I swung the backpack off my shoulders. 'I'm going to need to take notes.' I opened the drawstring and pulled out my notebook. 'You got somewhere we could sit?'

'I guess. Front room.' She pointed to the first door on the right.

'I'm Lee,' I said again. 'What did you say your name was?'

'Someone's hired you to find Matt?' She emphasized the word hired, and I read it to mean paid.

'Yeah.' I followed her into the front room, which was neat and tidy by student standards. The coffee table had a pile of textbooks on it, a picture of a microscope on the front of the top one. I took a seat in the armchair and turned to a clean page in my notebook. 'What's your name?'

'Who?'

'What?'

'Who hired you to find him?'

I cleared my throat. 'I can't tell you. It's against—'

'Nikki,' she said. She shook her head and stared right at me. 'I'm guessing the police told her to fuck off?'

'I'm not at liberty—'

'She's nuts.'

I gestured at the chair opposite me, trying to indicate she should take a seat. She didn't comply, choosing instead to stay standing by the door. 'She's nuts?' I wrote the word nuts in my notebook, looked up at her again. 'Like you mean she has a mental health issue?'

She stood with her back to the wall. 'She's nuts about Matt.'

'Maybe she's worried? I mean, you said yourself you don't know where he is.'

She picked at her fingernail. 'Matt has that effect on women.'

I saw where this one was going. I offered up my usual silent prayer of thanks that I'd put all that behind me. I'm not quite a virgin, but it's been so long I might as well be. It's better that way. Me and men, me and relationships, it's just not my strong point. Play to your strengths, someone once told me. I tried to keep the knowing tone from my voice. 'How long you lived with him?'

I failed.

She swiped her dark fringe back with one hand so that she could see to stare at me. 'We share a house.'

'Why don't you take a seat?'

She pointed a finger at me. 'I've never, ever thought about him that way. Which is probably why this houseshare thing works.' She stepped forward and moved the pile of books out of my way so I could put my notebook on the coffee table. 'This is our second year. They're both all right, mostly.'

'Meaning?'

'Well, you know, I've had to break it to them that the cleaning fairy doesn't exist. And Matt spends more time in the bathroom than any woman I've ever met, but apart from that, it's OK.'

'How old is Matt?'

'Twenty-three.'

'And he's an MA student?'

'MSc.'

'And, sorry, I don't know your name?'

'Jan.'

I wrote that down. 'When did you last see him, Jan?'

'I'm sure Nikki's told you.'

I opted for flattery. 'It would be great to hear it from you. Just to make sure I've got my facts straight.' I grinned at her. Aunt Edie's always saying I've got a nice smile and I should use it more.

Jan took a breath, released it slowly. 'I was away for the weekend. Went back home to see my parents.'

'When?'

'Last Friday.'

'Where?'

'York, well, just outside. All I know is Matt and Tuff went to a party – on Saturday night. These outdoor parties – you know?'

I shook my head. 'I've heard of them but thought they'd got rid of them back in the nineties. They're illegal now, right?'

'I don't know much about it.' She finally lowered herself into the chair opposite me and rubbed at an imaginary spot on her jeans. 'Sounds like a bunch of hippies, taking drugs and dancing till sunrise, but Nikki's got them into it. Tuff came back on Sunday, about lunchtime, he said – I wasn't back. He said Matt stayed.'

'When did you get back?'

'Teatime. I was hoping to get some work done. Fat chance. Nikki came round, twice, looking for Matt.'

'Sunday evening?'

She nodded.

'What did,' I checked my notes, 'Tuff say had happened to Matt?'

'I didn't see Tuff till Monday.'

'He got back Sunday lunchtime, you said?'

'Yes, but he'd gone out again by the time I got here. And I was in bed by the time he came home. I didn't see him till Monday.'

'And?'

'And he said he came back Sunday lunchtime and Matt had decided to stay at the party.'

'Did he say anything else?'

'Not really. Nikki came round again, screaming that she's

going to call the police. Like I'm personally responsible for the fact that her boyfriend's not here.'

'Must be hard for her —'

'Matt's problem is he's too pretty. He's got too many options.'

'You mean – there's someone else?'

'I wouldn't blame him, that's all I'm saying.'

'You really don't like Nikki.' It wasn't a question, more a statement of fact. I probably sounded peeved. I hate women doing other women down, especially over a man.

'I don't not like her. I just wish ... Oh I don't know.' She stood up. 'Tuff's right. Matt's probably holed up, writing up his dissertation.'

'His tutor says he should have just about finished it.'

'I think that's probably being optimistic.'

'Have you rung his parents?'

'Tuff's known Matt the longest.'

'Where is Tuff?'

'He'll be at uni by now.'

I frowned and glanced at the clock on the wall above the fireplace. 'Bit early.'

'Yeah, well.' She smiled for the first time and I had the sense that she felt better for talking to me. 'They're both feeling the pressure. And the library opens at 8.' She paused a moment, drew a breath. 'It is weird.'

I thought she meant the library. 'Weird?'

'Tuff's, well, I don't know. Maybe it's just the stress.'

'Tuff's what? What were you going to say?'

She didn't answer me, was lost in her own thoughts. 'If Matt'd taken his laptop with him, I'd agree he's holed up somewhere, ignoring Nikki and trying to get his dissertation finished. But he went missing at a party.'

'Could he have come home on the Sunday? If Tuff was out and you were out? Maybe he picked up his stuff?'

'Maybe. I did have a look in his room, but it's impossible to tell. I'd have thought he'd have left a note though if he'd done that. Unless he didn't trust us not to tell Nikki. That's the only thing I can think of – he wants to disappear till he gets it in.'

'How long's he got?'

'It's due Monday.'

'And you don't think you should ring his parents?'

'He did disappear before you know.'

'Disappear?'

'Well, took off for a few days. Never said where he'd gone or anything.'

'Did you ever find out where he went?'

She shook her head. 'That was before Nikki.'

'What's their relationship like?'

Jan pulled a face. 'Nikki knows Matt's out of her league – that's what's driving her mental.'

'He must like her. They've been going out together for nearly a year,' I said.

'Yeah.' She shrugged her shoulders like she was genuinely bemused by the whole thing.

'Is there someone else?' I asked again.

She hesitated and I knew she was searching her conscience. I leaned closer to her. 'We're just trying to make sure he's OK,' I said. 'We're not looking to get him into trouble.'

'Last night, I got a few phone calls where the phone was silent every time I picked it up. I don't know whether it was Nikki, or just ...'

Jan's gaze had fixed on the window. She stood up and crossed the room and stared out into the street. I couldn't see what had caught her interest. She swore under her breath and it sounded like a gust of wind.

'What?' I asked.

'That's Matt's car.'

I got up and peered out of the bay window in the direction she pointed, followed her gaze to the burgundy Volkswagen Polo parked a few hundred yards further down the street. I hadn't noticed it on my way there, but I'd come from the other direction.

Jan turned and ran from the room. I followed her, through the front door back into the street. I wondered how I'd not noticed it earlier, but I'd been focused on the house, and a car with a smashed window isn't that much of an unusual occurrence in Leeds 6. As I got closer though, I realized it wasn't just a smashed window. In fact there wasn't a single pane of glass intact – front and rear windscreen, every window, shattered. Another couple of steps and I realized the headlights and taillights were destroyed as well. The shards crunched under my feet.

'Shit,' said Jan again.

'Vandals?' I said.

Jan looked up and down the street. 'Why just his car?'

She had a point. There were other, more attractive cars parked along the street. 'Which is Tuff's?' I asked.

'Tuff doesn't have a car.'

'Oh. How did he get back from the party?'

'Should I ring the police?'

'He must have come back in a car. The party was in Lincolnshire.'

Jan stood blinking at the Volkswagen like she was willing the glass back into the panes. I looped around it and tried to read the message it sent. Anger. Raw, unchannelled anger, you could smell it. Every single body panel was dented, same for the bonnet. It looked like it had been attacked with a baseball bat.

'Didn't you hear anything?'

'You don't think Nikki ...?' Jan's voice tailed off.

I frowned as I considered the idea, but it didn't add up. 'Don't think so. I mean she's worried, but she didn't strike me as angry. Least, not this angry.'

'What should I do?' Jan turned to me and I realized she'd got worried for the first time.

'Phone the police. Report it.'

'And tell them Matt's missing?'

I still find it difficult to think of the police as anything other than the enemy. Too much soft drug consumption. That's my soft drug consumption, not theirs. But I remembered the roasting we'd got from not involving them earlier in our last case. 'Don't think you've got a choice,' I said. I peered in through the driver's window. Or the space where the window once was. 'Radio's still there. Doesn't look like anything's been stolen.' The glove box was closed. I pulled my head back out. 'Is Tuff insured? To drive it?'

'I'm not dealing with this,' Jan said. She held up her hands in front of her like she was trying to stop traffic. She turned towards the house. I still had my notebook and pen in hand so I wrote down the registration number and followed Jan back across the road.

'I don't know anything about it,' she said, talking to herself. 'This is Tuff''s problem.'

I followed her into the house, back into the front room. She picked up a denim jacket from the back of the settee. 'I don't know anything. I haven't got time. I'm late. They're not the only ones with deadlines.'

'Why don't I tell Tuff, then he can sort it?' I said. 'You said he's at the library?'

'Not my drama,' she said, still shaking her head.

I stuffed my notebook into my bag. We were obviously leaving. 'What time will he be there till?'

'Don't know. He works Thursdays.' She grabbed a bag and a ring binder from the floor in the hall.

'Works where?'

'The bookshop.' She was out the front door, standing on the step waiting for me to leave so she could shut the front door. 'The one opposite the uni.'

I stepped out of the house and she slammed the door behind me, locked it and put the key in her pocket.

'What time does he start?'

But she didn't hear me. Or if she did she didn't acknowledge it. She was already out of the gate and headed down the street towards town. I watched her stride away until she turned left at the end and disappeared from sight.

Chapter 6

I caught the bus to Hyde Park Corner and threaded my way through the streets back to the office. Aunt Edie was at the computer, two-finger typing and swearing under her breath as I slung my bag onto my desk. I noticed Jo was wearing her hangover lipstick – dark purple, like crushed blueberries.

'Where've you been?' she asked.

'Matt's house.'

'Why didn't you answer your mobile?'

'Oh.' I pulled open my desk drawer and rummaged. 'It needs charging,' I said, holding my new iPhone aloft.

'You're supposed to charge it at night so that it's ready every morning,' Jo said, snatching it off me and plugging it into the wall socket. 'How many more times?'

'I went for a run – had a chat with Matt's housemate, Jan. She said he disappeared once before – didn't show for days.'

'Told you,' said Jo. 'He'll show up with numb nuts and a hangover, I'd bet money on it. Or he knows she's preggers and he's moved to the Outer Hebrides. You know what men are like.'

'But,' I said, crossing the room and pulling the file from the cabinet, 'his car's been done over, like, seriously done over.'

'Crap,' said Aunt Edie.

I frowned at Jo. 'What's she doing?'

'She's doing my head in, that's what she's doing.'

I glanced back at Aunt Edie. Her glasses had fallen to the tip of her nose and her lips were pursed but she didn't appear to have heard Jo's comment. I raised my eyebrows at Jo. We both know Aunt Edie doesn't take criticism well.

Jo shrugged her shoulders like she didn't care. 'She's typing up Martin's notes. Thought I might as well get her doing something, seeing as how we didn't know where you were.'

I put my notes from my interview with Jan into the file and thought about what we had. A possible date in Old Bar today at 2 p.m. And Tuff. We needed to speak to him – it looked like he was the last person to see Matt – and maybe he could shed some light on what had happened to Matt's car. The bookshop was opposite the university Union, which housed Old Bar. It made sense to combine the two appointments, not that Tuff knew we were coming. A glance at the clock above the filing cabinet told me it wasn't even ten. I dropped the file with my notes onto Aunt Edie's desk so she could type them up later. She peered at her computer screen and cursed again.

Call me sensitive, but I was picking up on an atmosphere. Luckily, I've been mates with Jo long enough to know what she needed. 'Why don't we take a drive to see the flats where the woman's body was found? Martin said they overlook Roundhay Park. There's got to be a café round there somewhere. I'll buy breakfast.'

*

Jo and I left the office together. I didn't even take my jacket. The van was parked just round the corner, and I clambered into the passenger seat and got that buzz I always get when I know we're leaving our normal. A trip. Probably I need to get out more.

We had to negotiate the mad ballet dance that is the Sheepscar Interchange, which involved a few car horns and Jo sticking the Vs up out of the window as the satnav lady fired directions at us. We eventually joined Roundhay Road, which takes you out to the north-east of the city.

Leeds 6 is a bubble: it insulates against the real world. Its only inhabitants are the young, the impressionable and the idealistic. The shops are all takeaways, off-licences, laundrettes and taxi firms, so there's never any pressing reason to go anywhere else. But as Jo drove us down a hill, into Roundhay Park, and we caught a glimpse of the enormous lake, I thought perhaps we should have made more of an effort and visited before.

'I googled Roundhay Park this morning, while you were out, running.' Jo made the last word sound like a euphemism.

I rose above it. 'And?'

'It was bought by the mayor of the city, for the people of Leeds, a couple of hundred years ago.'

'That was nice of him.'

'Before that it was privately owned. There's a stately home at the top.'

I peered out of the windows but all I could see was park-land.

Jo turned into the car park at the bottom of the hill and

reverse parked into a space. 'Roundhay Park had its own serial killer, once upon a time,' she said.

'The Park Killer? That was here?'

You couldn't live in Leeds and not have heard of the Park Killer. He was a serial killer who'd killed all of his female victims in parks, hence the moniker. He'd been caught by a late-night dog-walker, who'd discovered him cutting up his final victim in bushes and had made a citizen's arrest. According to folklore, the dog, a black Labrador, had pinned the killer down, holding him until the police arrived. Some people claimed the Park Killer had been inspired by the Yorkshire Ripper, who'd stalked Leeds' streets back in the seventies, but the truth was no one really knew what had motivated him to do what he had done, because the Park Killer committed suicide in prison, before his case had come to trial. I glanced around.

'He killed two women here,' Jo said. 'Think the others were in Meanwood.'

'Fucked up,' I said.

We climbed out of the van and surveyed our surroundings. 'The flats are up there,' said Jo, pointing to the crest of the park.

'Food first,' I said. I'm not stupid. Hanging out with Jo when her blood sugar is low is taking your life in your hands.

We made our way over to the Lakeside café – a wooden building jutting out over the lake – and I ordered us both a full English breakfast with an espresso for Jo. We sat on the balcony, the sun glistened off the water, swans and ducks glided past, and I filled Jo in on the details of my conversation with Jan while we waited for breakfast to arrive.

'Matt could have easily popped home Sunday,' Jo said when I told her everything I could remember. 'Picked up his stuff and bought a single ticket away from planet parenthood.'

'Seems weird that he'd know Nikki was pregnant before she even did. And Jan said she couldn't tell whether any of his stuff was missing.'

'He's probably out getting laid in between typing up his dissertation.'

'What about his car?'

'Or getting laid while some woman types up his dissertation. A woman on my course did that. Typed up her boyfriend's dissertation. He dumped her like a week later.'

I paused as the waitress arrived and handed us two plates brimming with sausage, eggs and beans. Jo poured vinegar onto her fried eggs – she likes them dripping with the stuff.

'There's the note in the pigeonhole as well,' I pointed out. 'Someone else is looking for him.'

'Could be weeks old, that note. And from anybody.' Jo spooned a forkful of baked beans on her slice of bread, folded it over and took a bite.

'We'll find out this afternoon,' I said. 'Even if Matt doesn't turn up, the person who wrote it might.'

'Might,' Jo stressed as she chewed on her baked bean sandwich.

'Not like we've got anything else to go on.'

We ate the rest of our breakfast in silence. I watched the colour return to Jo's skin as she ate. When her plate was empty she poured the last of her coffee down her throat and licked her fingers. 'Delish. I'll have that sausage if you're not going to eat it.'

*

After breakfast, we climbed the steep hill to the flats at the top. When I think flats I always picture council sky-rises, like the ones that mark the edge of the city in Little London, or new-build student halls of residence, which remind me of battery hen coops. These flats weren't like those. White stucco, with huge portrait-shaped windows, built on the crest of the hill overlooking the park and the lake. Location-wise, it didn't get much better. Apart from the wooden café, there wasn't a single building in sight from the top of the hill, just miles of green parkland.

Jo put her hands in the small of her back as we surveyed the vista. 'Not bad, eh?' Roundhay Park stretched before us, a natural flat-bottomed bowl, with what looked like a cricket pitch at its base. I was reminded of school and my geography teacher droning on and on about glaciation. We were high up, above the trees. From where we were it looked like you'd be able to trampoline in them. 'U2 played there,' said Jo, pointing down the slopes. 'And Madonna, Bruce Springsteen, Robbie Williams, Ed Sheeran – apparently the acoustics are well good.'

Martin's notes included a detailed description of where the woman's body was found. To get into the grounds we had to walk down a small road that ended just behind the flats. The gates were open and it was easy to slip inside. A car park with more than its fair share of convertibles and BMWs stood between us and the rear of the building. Surrounding the car park were well-established trees and shrubs. 'What are we going to say? If anyone asks?'

That's the thing about leaving the Leeds 6 bubble – you become aware of how different you are to 'normal' society. It's unusual to see anyone over twenty-five in Leeds 6 and the dress code is relaxed to say the least. I was still wearing my denim cut-offs and Jo was in her hangover outfit – baggy trousers she'd picked up in Thailand and a sweatshirt that had the neck and cuffs removed.

In the park and around the café, I'd seen old people walking dogs, kids running around, an Asian couple feeding the ducks, mothers with prams. The prams had made me think of Nikki. What a weird thing, to grow another life. I shook the thought from my head and concentrated on our surroundings.

'We're gardeners,' I said. 'Here to price up a job.'

Jo tugged Martin's notebook out of her bag. 'OK.'

I wasn't sure that anyone would fall for it because the gardens were immaculate. The hedges ruler straight, the soil finely tilled, the roses all neatly budding. We made our way down a small path, around the building to the front – the side of the flats that overlooked the park – Jo reading from Martin's notes. 'Middle of the garden, by the statue.'

'The statue?'

'Apparently.'

'Of?'

'There.' We rounded the corner and sure enough there was

a statue in the middle of the front gardens. A statue of a woman, naked and kneeling, holding what looked like a large pitcher, water flowing from it into the well next to her.

Jo read from Martin's notes. 'Vic. discovered by statue, right wrist attached to statue's right arm. Cable tie. Black.'

'Weirder and weirder.'

Jo paused from reading. She dropped her bag on the floor and looped a full circle around the stone woman, the gravel crunching under her feet as she walked. When she'd done the full three hundred and sixty degrees she turned to me. 'She's like the suffragettes, chaining themselves to railings. Solidarity?'

'Who is she?' I peered up close at the statue woman's face, freckled with lichen, her hair tied in a topknot, the ponytail swirling around her moss-green neck. 'Aquarius?'

'Don't know.' Jo crouched to the ground and pulled the camera out of her bag. 'Knew this baby would come in handy.'

'Martin's right,' I said. 'There's something wrong here.' I couldn't put into words why, but every part of my body refused to accept the narrative we'd been given. I glanced around the garden. It was completely cut off from the park by an eight-foot hedge, anyone in the park wouldn't be able to see into the gardens. There were three benches arranged at the east, west and south ends and bird feeders swung from a metal pole. The beds were planted with the kind of shrubs that don't take much looking after. Jo snapped pictures of the statue as I tried to put my sense of unease into words. 'You'd be scared someone would see you for one thing.'

Not someone from the park, but someone from the flats. I glanced up at the many windows of the numerous flats that overlooked us. The windows got bigger the higher up the building you went – so that on the top floor they were floor to ceiling. Huge windows. I counted the number of floors and did a rough estimate. At least sixty of them.

'Would have been dark,' said Jo. She put the camera on the stone at the base of the statue and picked up the notebook again. 'Vic. discovered by newspaper boy: 6.50 a.m.'

'Time of death?'

Jo flicked through the pages. 'Pathologist reckoned she'd been dead between three and four hours.'

'Let's give her a name. I don't like calling her Vic.'

'Vicky?'

Despite myself, I half-smiled. That's what I love about Jo. Even in the hard times, the darkest of dark times, she can make me smile. 'Why would the newspaper boy be round here? The entrance to the flats is at the rear.'

'No, there's another one there, look. Some residents must use that one.'

'We need a plan of the flats. I'll put Aunt Edie on it.'

I kept looking up at the windows, hit by the enormity of the task ahead. There must be at least thirty flats in the building, thirty owners to track down – possibly more because some of the flats would have been sold in the seven years since our woman's body had been discovered. Some of them were probably sublet. The theme tune to *Mission Impossible* started up in my mind. I tried to get a more precise count of the number of windows, and that was when I first noticed her.

On the third or fourth floor, the face of a woman, an older

woman, pressed against the glass, the palm of her hand also raised and touching the window. When she saw me spot her, she pulled back, so quick I wasn't sure whether I'd imagined her. Just a dark space where she once stood and perhaps the smudge of her fingerprints, although I was far too far away to see for sure. 'This place gives me the creeps,' I said to Jo.

'Nutter. This is the pinnacle of human achievement. You live here, you've made it. Bet these cost a bomb,' she said.

'Someone's watching us,' I said, scanning the building again. The hairs on the back of my neck prickled and I felt the shudder run all the way to my toes.

Jo lifted the camera and rapid-snapped photos of the building. Nothing moved but I couldn't shake the feeling. I stepped away from Jo and tried to imagine the scene. A naked woman, cable-tied to the statue. I sat on the ground next to the statue, held my wrist against hers.

Jo returned the camera to the bag. 'There's something missing. Something we're not seeing.'

'Besides her clothes?'

'Yeah, besides her clothes. Although, actually they were there; Martin said they were neatly folded, next to her body.'

I shook my head. 'Who'd get naked to commit suicide?'

'I know right.'

'So what's missing?'

Jo flicked through Martin's notebook. 'We've got a list of her possessions. Brown ankle boots, scuffed. Denim-effect dress, belt, bra, red knickers. Train ticket dated 28th of August – the day before her body was found. Stamped.'

'Didn't Martin mention a necklace?'

'Yes. She was wearing that. The only thing she was wearing.'

'Go on.'

'The train ticket was found in bushes near the body.' We both glanced around at the perfectly manicured shrubs. 'So where was her purse?'

'Good point. Maybe she didn't have one?'

'And the other thing – what did she carry the strychnine in? Had to be some kind of container.'

'Is it a powder or a liquid?'

'Her bag's what's missing,' said Jo, bending to scribble something in the notebook. 'It's obvious. Every woman has a handbag.'

I pulled a face at that. I've never owned a handbag in my life.

Jo straightened up. 'Women that wear dresses have handbags. Dresses don't have pockets.'

I thought about this. 'She'd have needed money for the train fare.'

'She would have had a handbag,' said Jo, again. ''S'obvious. Can't believe we didn't think of it sooner.'

'Maybe there was one and Martin's not noted it.' I glanced at Martin's pristine notebook and knew I was clutching at straws.

'We need to speak to the police – the person in charge of the original investigation,' said Jo. 'DI Roberts, according to the notes here.'

'Wasn't that the one that Martin said he wasn't sure about?'

'And what about the necklace? What kind of necklace was it? It's got to be important if she kept it on.'

'Wonder what they do with it? The evidence? Do they store it all somewhere?'

'It's an unsolved case,' said Jo. 'They can't throw everything away. There must be a warehouse somewhere with Vicky's possessions in it.' Jo's eyes lit up at the thought.

'You're right,' I said. 'We're going to need to speak to the police.' My heart sank at the thought. Neither Jo nor I are keen on involving the police in the business, even though we know it's going to be unavoidable at times. We've both grown up seeing them as the enemy – due to a couple of student demonstrations where they've seemed more concerned with social control than upholding the freedoms of the general public.

Jo sat on the bench by the bird feeders and wrote something in Martin's notebook. I took a walk around the small enclosed garden before taking a seat next to her and lighting a cigarette. 'Why here?' I said. 'She caught a train from Nottingham. Why come all this way to die? Martin's right, it's like she was trying to draw attention to something, but what? The flats? Someone who lived in one of the flats?'

'Possible.'

'The statue?'

'The park?'

'If it was the park, you'd think she'd have killed herself in the park.'

'What about the Park Killer?' I said. I'd been unable to get him out of my thoughts since we arrived.

'He'd been dead five years before Vicky got the train here.'

'Maybe she wanted someone to find her,' I said, looking

up again at all the windows in front of us. 'I mean, before she died. Maybe it was a cry for help.'

'Aspirin is crying for help,' said Jo. 'She's hard-core. She didn't want to be found, not alive at any rate.'

'How did she know the statue was there?'

'Maybe she didn't. Maybe the idea only struck her when she got here.'

'What about the cable tie? She had to have brought that with her. Is there anything on that in the notes?'

Jo flicked through the pages of the notebook. 'No. Only that they're standard issue, available in every DIY shop in the country. Black plastic.'

'She chose this spot. It's so, so,' – I struggled to find the right word – 'premeditated. There's no reason to ever come here unless you were coming here.' What little road there was stopped at the flats, the rest was trees and parkland. 'And naked. Why would you strip to commit suicide?'

'It was August,' said Jo, as if that made any sense at all.

I shook my head. 'It's another statement. Naked and tied.'

'The statue's naked.'

'Why go to all this trouble to make such a statement but then not leave a note?' I kicked at the grass. 'It's like she wanted to make a statement, but it's one no one can understand.'

'Maybe the message wasn't aimed at us. Maybe it was aimed at someone else.'

I thought about this for a moment.

'Maybe it wasn't suicide,' said Jo.

That was the thought that had been playing in my head

since the moment I'd seen the statue. Maybe she'd been forced to ingest the strychnine. Maybe she'd been tied to the statue once she was already dead. 'We need to know more,' I said. 'More about her, more about her background. Jesus. How are we going to do that if the police didn't even manage it at the time?'

Jo slung her backpack over her shoulders and linked arms with me. 'Martin doesn't think the police were trying very hard.'

'Well, we're going to try harder. Much fucking harder,' I said.

Jo grinned at me and I noticed she'd got lipstick on her teeth. 'Right.'

'First things first. We need to know who she was. Martin's right. Somewhere she's missing. We need to find out who's missing her.'

Chapter 7

When we got back to the office, I rang directory enquiries and got the number for the missing persons' helpline. I rang them straight away and gave them the few details we had for Vicky Doe: white, female, previously given birth, aged between twenty-two and twenty-five when she died seven years ago; possibly from either Leeds or Nottingham. Not much to go on really.

'I'll check our database,' the woman on the phone said.

'The police probably checked at the time,' I said.

'You never know. We get new reports all the time – sometimes for people who've been missing for years.'

'Why would someone not report them missing at the time?'

'Sometimes it takes a while for people to realize their loved ones are actually missing, not just out of touch.' She checked herself. 'But you shouldn't get your hopes up too high. Hundreds of women go missing and are never reported.'

It makes you think, doesn't it? Hundreds of women go missing and no one ever reports their disappearance? I glanced across at Jo and she raised her eyebrows as if to say I told you so. And of course she had. I'm not naive, I know there's a lot goes on in this world that most people would rather not know about, but it takes a lot to have *no one* care – to have no one in your life that cares enough to report you as missing? These women were ghosts, drifting in and out of people's lives, not having made enough of an impact to even be sought.

The woman on the phone said she'd get someone to call me back, but warned it might take a few hours.

'I'll put the kettle on,' said Aunt Edie, as she dropped an envelope into the out tray.

'We need you to get us a plan of the flats. Either from the management company, or the fire service or something,' I said to Aunt Edie.

'Don't forget – we've got to be at Old Bar at two o'clock,' Jo reminded me. 'Are we going to walk?'

I glanced at the clock. It was just past one.

'It'd be great if Matt just turns up,' said Jo. 'Easiest case ever.'

'Mmm. Although Nikki's still got the job of breaking the news to her parents.'

'Poor mite,' said Edie, coming back from the kitchen. 'She rang this morning to see if there was any news. I told her she'd have to be patient.'

'We can call in and see Tuff while we're there – he works in the bookshop just opposite the uni. Jan seemed to think he knew something but wasn't telling. And he needs to report the damage to Matt's car.'

The click of the kettle sounded and Aunt Edie made to get up, but I beat her to it.

'My turn.'

I picked up Aunt Edie's mug.

'Tenner still says he's with a woman somewhere,' said Jo.

'He might be finishing his essay. They work very hard, these students, and no one gives them credit,' said Aunt Edie, as I made my way through to the back.

Which would make him difficult to find. I poured the water from the kettle. He'd be leaving the house only to buy fags and Pro-Plus tablets. I thought back to our trip to Roundhay Park and how out of the ordinary it had felt. As a general rule, Leeds 6 residents don't travel. They might go home to see their parents once a term, but other than that they wore grooves in the pavement going from Leeds 6 to the edges of the city and back again. Chances were Matt was holed up in a house a stone's throw from where I was standing. Didn't make the job any easier though.

'Or trying to ditch a clingy girlfriend.' I used my back to push open the office door as my hands were full with the three mugs of tea. I turned to see a grimace on Jo's face and Nikki standing in the front office. She wore a pink and orange top that reminded me of ruby grapefruits.

'Clingy girlfriend?' The bangles on her arms jangled.

'Another case,' said Jo. 'Take a seat.'

'Who said that?'

'Nikki, hi,' I said, my knuckles burning against the mugs. I put them down on Aunt Edie's desk. 'What brings you here?'

She carried an envelope, which she waved at me while she spoke. 'Clingy?'

'Come on in, take a seat. I'm glad you're here.' The lie was obvious to the both of us. I sat at my desk and pulled out the notebook from the top drawer. I gestured for her to take a seat, but she ignored me. 'We've made extensive enquiries.'

'Have you found him?'

'We've spoken to his tutor, people at the uni, his housem—'

'Jan. Jan told you I was clingy. Bitch.'

I flicked through some pages, pretending to scan my notes. 'Jan told us it's not the first time Matt's done a runner.'

'Have you found him?'

'No.'

'No? Nothing?'

'We've got a few leads to follow up.'

'Like?'

'Listen,' said Jo. She guided Nikki into the seat in front of my desk. 'You have to let us do our job. We've not had twenty-four hours yet. As soon as we know anything, we'll tell you, I promise.'

'I brought the photos.' She handed me the envelope. I flipped it open and pulled out half a dozen snapshots of a man: standing on a beach in a pair of shorts in the first one, his torso bronzed and firm. *Nice*, I caught myself thinking. Nice ... if you like that kind of thing. Which I don't. I mean, I can appreciate art – doesn't mean I want to learn how to paint. I handed the pictures to Jo.

'Probably the next step is to contact his parents,' I said. 'Unless—'

'Mmm,' said Jo. 'Tasty, isn't he?'

Nikki glared at her for a moment before turning back to me. 'Unless?'

'Just saying,' said Jo as Aunt Edie crowded in for a look.

'Someone may have arranged to meet him.' I put a hand up to quell the excitement that that news generated. 'We don't know whether he'll show. He might not have got the note.'

'The note?'

'I can't tell you anymore at this time, Nikki. Jo's right – you have to let us get on with things.'

'Do you know anyone with the initial S?' Jo asked. 'Someone who might want to meet up with Matty?'

She shook her head. 'I'm going home this weekend,' she said. 'It's my dad's sixtieth.' She slung her shoulder bag on the desk, and in doing so knocked over my mug of tea. Aunt Edie threw herself across the desk and grabbed my laptop. Boiling hot liquid seeped across my desk and burned through the leg of my denim shorts.

'Sorry,' said Nikki, a wobble in her voice. 'It's like an alien has taken over my body. I can't stand it.'

Aunt Edie sat the laptop on the filing cabinet and went through to the kitchenette as Jo moved everything off my desk and onto Aunt Edie's. I did a quick risk assessment and led Nikki over to the coffee table and chairs in the corner of the room. 'Take a seat.'

'I just want to eat and throw up. That's my whole life. And I can't do this without Matt.'

'Look,' I said, almost pushing her into the chair, 'we'll go along to this meeting. Even if he doesn't show up the person might know something about where he is.'

'Where is this meeting?'

'Nikki, you have to leave this to us. Trust me.'

Aunt Edie came back into the office with an armful of tea towels. I glanced up at the clock on the wall. 'We've got to run. Here, drink Jo's tea. Edie will look after you, won't you?'

Jo unhooked her jacket from the peg by the door and we bustled out the door.

We got to Old Bar ten minutes before 2 p.m. We were looking for a young woman with long hair and too much eyeliner. Not the most accurate description to go on, but at least we now had a photo of Matt. I wouldn't have any trouble recognizing him if he showed up.

We got a drink and took a table. Jo pulled a packet of cards from her pocket and we played a game of Spite and Malice. I was grateful she'd brought the cards – I'm never very sure what to do with my hands when I can't wrap them around a cold pint of lager.

We'd only been there a few minutes when another woman entered the room and sat down. She didn't order a drink – just sat at a table and took out a file. Once she'd settled, Jo sidled up to her and said in that conspiratorial way that she has, 'You waiting for Matt?' The woman frowned and shook her head.

Jo returned to her seat and we played another three or four games (I won but I don't think Jo's heart was in it) until another lone woman entered the bar. She didn't look like our woman – because her hair was short, really short – but there was something about her demeanour that made me stare at her. She was furtive, wary almost. Like she was sticking to the shadows. I glanced at the clock. It was twenty past two.

She bought a pint and made her way to a table at the far side of the room. Jo and I carried on playing, but I couldn't help glancing over every minute or two. Her pint sat, untouched, on the table in front of her. Women drinking alone are still a rarity, even now. Jo saw me noticing her and raised an eyebrow. Worth a shot, I knew she was saying.

I packed away the cards as Jo crossed the room. I watched her place both her palms on the table and lean across to the woman. The music had increased in volume since we'd arrived and I knew Jo was having to raise her voice to make herself heard. I watched the woman's face turn from indifference, to engaged and then to something else I didn't quite recognize from my position at the other side of the room. Was it fear? She'd jolted when Jo had first approached her, like she'd been disturbed from her own private world, even though it was clear she was waiting for someone.

I slipped the boxes of cards into my pocket and made my way to join them.

'... not until you've told me who you are,' the woman was saying.

'Keep your voice down.'

'Fuck off.'

'Hang on.' I pulled one of our business cards from my back pocket. The trouble is, in the Students' Union, everyone assumes we're students. 'We're private investigators,' I said. She snatched the card from me and I noticed the tremor that seemed to run through her entire body. 'We're looking for Matt,' I said.

She turned to stare at me and her huge green eyes were

like pools, open wide, framed by the longest black lashes and thick eyeliner. She was stunningly beautiful in a Betty Blue kind of a way. 'Why?'

'We can't tell you that.'

'Do you know?' she said. The fear in her voice unmistakeable, she might as well have unwrapped it and placed it on the table in front of us.

'Do we know what?' asked Jo.

'We found your note,' I said. I felt the need to reassure her, although I didn't really know why. 'That's all we know – that you're looking for him too.'

She stared at me for a moment and I knew she was working out whether to trust me. 'I don't have his phone number. He didn't reply to my Facebook message. I didn't know what else to do.'

'He's not answering his phone,' I said. 'We've tried too.'

'He's not coming, is he?'

I shook my head. 'No one's seen him since the weekend.'

She nodded, like she wasn't surprised. 'I don't know what to do,' she said. Her voice quiet, matter of fact.

'Shall we go somewhere else – somewhere where we can talk?' I asked. Jo wasn't saying much, I noticed. 'What's your name?'

'Sara.'

'I'm Lee. This is Jo. Maybe we can help you. You're trying to find him. We're trying to find him. Maybe we can help each other.'

She stared at me like she had no idea what I was talking about.

'Find him, I mean,' I said. I coughed to clear the frog in my throat but it didn't seem to make any difference.

'You won't,' she said.

'Not saying much for our fine detective skills.' I tried a smile to show I was joking.

'He doesn't want to be found,' she said.

'Well, we've been there before.' I frowned at Jo. She hadn't said a word for the last minute.

Jo licked her lips and the saliva shone under the UV light. 'At least hear us out,' she said. 'Give us half a chance.'

Sara nodded. 'No point waiting here. What was I thinking? Fucking moron.' I didn't know whether she was referring to herself or Matt. She pulled the pint towards her and necked half of it.

'Shall we—?' Jo started, but I didn't get to hear the end of her sentence because a dash of orange filled my vision and I heard someone shout, 'Where is he?'

I felt the wet splash of cold lager down my right thigh. The other leg of my shorts was still damp from the cup of tea incident back at the office. Sara's forehead creased up.

'Get lost.'

'Don't you dare, you cow.'

I turned round, already knowing what I was going to see. Nikki, standing behind me, empty pint glass in her hand, her face red, spit flying from her lips. 'Might have known you'd be sniffing around. Can't keep your hands—'

'All right, Nikki.' Jo grabbed her arm. 'Let's not turn this into an episode of *Eastenders*, eh?' She turned Nikki around and pushed her in the direction of the exit.

'I want to know where he is,' Nikki shouted over her shoulder. She hurled the pint glass to the floor and shards of glass splintered across the wooden floorboards.

The barman stared at us. He wasn't much older than Nikki. I looked at Sara. She shrugged her shoulders.

'Shall we?' I said.

Sara drained the remainder of her pint and stood up. It felt like every single person in the bar had stopped speaking. Sara, to give her credit, held her head up and made her way through the bar towards the door.

A man with a nose stud put his hand on my arm. 'That was my pint,' he said, gesturing towards the remains of the glass Nikki had smashed.

'Sorry.' I tried to shake his hand off.

'You owe me a pint.'

'I didn't chuck it.'

'Your mate did.'

I lost sight of Sara as she disappeared through the door of the bar and into the corridor outside. I fished in my pocket and found a crumpled fiver and shoved it into his hands. 'Here.'

When I emerged through the door into the corridor outside, Sara was over by the far wall, bent down to tie her shoelace.

As I got closer, I realized she wasn't tying her shoelace. In fact her boots didn't have laces.

'I can't deal with this,' she said, and I saw that she was crying. Not crying like she was sad. Crying like she was in pain.

'What's the matter?' I said. I glanced around for Jo.

'Leave me alone,' she said. And I wanted to, I really did. Emotional scenes are not my strong point.

She jumped up, turned and ran and I hesitated, didn't know what to do. I'd probably be able to match her for speed but something held me back from chasing. I scanned the corridor again and saw Jo, the back of her, heading the other way, leading Nikki in the direction of the laundrette. I considered the options for a moment. The look on Sara's face scared me. I couldn't let her go. I yelled, 'Back in a minute,' to Jo and set off. I chased Sara through the Student Union building, up from the basement, out through the main door and down the steps into the courtyard.

I was still wearing my trainers so I had the advantage. There were lots of students milling about but Sara was tall so she stood out. She turned left and ran in the direction of Hyde Park, but when she got to the end of the courtyard, she paused, turned and stared at me. I was fifty yards behind. She shook her head at me, took a sharp left and disappeared. I felt chastened by her stare, but I carried on. A porter came out of one of the buildings pushing a trolley stacked with cardboard boxes, I had to pause a second so that we didn't collide. When he'd moved, I continued on round the corner, watched her climb up the steps to one of the buildings, a substantial terraced house. I put on speed, felt my heart start to pound and charged after her. I pushed my way through the front door.

'Where you running to?' asked a man sitting behind a reception desk.

'Did you see a woman come in here? With black hair?' I took a breath, tried to compose myself.

'You have to sign in,' he said. 'Who's your appointment with?'

'Did you see her?' I turned and surveyed my surroundings. There was a staircase up to the left and off the corridor on the right-hand side of the staircase there was another three or four doors. All of them closed.

He stood up, I think to show he was much bigger than me. He stared at me, like he was waiting for the answer to his question rather than having any intention of answering mine. 'You're not a student of this department,' he said.

'What is this department?'

'There's a sign on the door,' he said. 'You can read it on your way out.'

I thought about arguing with him, but knew it wasn't going to get me anywhere. It wasn't going to get me inside. I shrugged like I couldn't care less and turned to leave. As I closed the front door behind me I noticed the sign by the side of it: 'University of Leeds, School of Fine Art and Cultural Studies'. I'd be back.

*

I found Jo and Nikki sitting on the wall outside the Students' Union. Well, Jo sat and smoked while Nikki paced, chewing a thumbnail.

'What the fuck did you do that for?' I shouted at Nikki soon as I was close enough.

'It's not my fault.'

'You just chased off our only witness.'

Nikki snorted air through her nostrils. 'Might have known she'd be involved.'

'Who is she?'

'She's sex mad. Everyone knows.'

'What?'

'Nikki thinks Sara might have "stolen" Matt,' Jo explained, raising her eyebrows and shaking her head at the same time.

I took the cigarette from Jo's fingers and had a drag. 'Stolen him?'

'Yes,' said Jo. 'Kidnapped him, held him against his will in her sex dungeon. You know, like women do.'

I didn't think Jo was helping. 'We needed to speak to her,' I said to Nikki. 'She might have been able to help. Do you want us to find your boyfriend or what?'

'I'm sorry, I'm sorry. I can't take the sitting around.'

'So, Sara knows Matt?'

Nikki sat down on the wall next to Jo and folded her arms across her chest. 'They're both in Greenpeace. She thinks she's God's gift.'

I remembered the look on Sara's face. It didn't strike me as the look of someone who thought they were God's gift. What did she know? What did she want from Matt? I wiped the sweat from my forehead with the back of my hand. 'Who told you where we'd be?'

Nikki didn't answer. Jo and I glanced at each other.

'Aunt Edie,' we both said at the same time.

'It wasn't her fault,' Nikki said. 'I asked her for a glass of water, and while she was out of the room, I read the notes she was typing up.'

I made a mental note to have a word with our receptionist-stroke-office-manager when we got back to the office.

Chapter 8

We managed to dump Nikki in the Students' Union and, once I was convinced she wasn't following us, Jo and I made our way out of campus and across Woodhouse Lane to the university bookshop.

We pushed through the door and looked around. A tall gangly man stood behind the till; a couple of young customers browsed the shelves. I headed to the counter. 'Tuff?'

He frowned at me. 'Yeah?'

'Hi, we'd like to talk to you.' He looked confused, and I realized I used the word 'we' and Jo was not by my side. I glanced around and saw her over in the Sex and Gender Section, her head at a right angle to her body. I turned back to the man in front of me. 'I'd like to talk to you. Have you got a minute?'

He didn't look busy. 'Well, I'm at work. What's it about?'

'It's about your housemate, Matt Williams.'

I know I didn't imagine it. A look of complete panic passed through his eyes. He turned his attention to the pile of books he was stickering with price labels.

'You know where he is,' I said.

'No.'

'So he's missing?'

He didn't speak.

'Are you worried about him?'

'Who are you?'

I showed him my badge. He held it steady in my hand so he could read it. 'Private investigators? Really? Who—?'

'I know you left him at a party on Saturday night. You drove his car back on Sunday morning, but you left him there.'

'I've got to work.'

'You took his car and left him in Lincolnshire. How did you think he was going to get home?'

'He said he'd get a lift. There was a crew from Leeds.'

'Are you insured to drive his car?'

'What, so you're the police now?'

'No, the police are the next people you're going to be talking to, if we don't find Matt. That car that you drove back, illegally, from an illegal party where I'm fairly certain you were taking illegal substances, that car has been smashed to bits by someone who doesn't seem very happy, either with you or with Matt.'

He carried on stickering the books, and I knew I wasn't telling him anything he didn't already know.

'You saw his car?' I asked.

'Nothing to do with me.'

'Jan says it's your responsibility to report it.'

He picked up an armful of books and made his way from behind the counter to one of the shelves. I followed him.

'It's in your interests to help us find him.'

He stacked the books on the shelves in silence, seemingly engrossed in his task.

'Come on, Tuff. As far as we can work out, you were the last person to see him alive.'

'He's not dead.' There was scorn in his voice.

'How do you know?'

'Why would he be dead?'

'Well, he's missing. Someone's trashed his car. His girlfriend doesn't know where he is.'

'Yeah, well. She might be glad of that one day.'

'Meaning?'

He didn't answer my question. I pressed on. 'I thought you were best mates.'

'That makes two of us.'

'You're very cryptic.'

He put the last book on the shelf and turned to face me. 'He'll be back. And when he is, it's up to him to tell everyone what's going on.'

'You left him at a party at the weekend and he's not back by Thursday and you're not worried?'

'No.'

'He missed a tutorial.'

'Peak.'

'Did something happen at the party? Did you guys fall out?'

'No.'

'Did he meet a girl? Is that why he stayed?'

'Don't ask me. I left early.'

'Why?'

'I had to give someone a lift.'

'Who?'

'No one. Look, when Matt turns up, I'll ring you. He can explain.'

'You left him in the middle of the countryside, took his car, you don't know how or if he managed to get back to Leeds, but you're not going to help us find him because you're being loyal to him?'

'Something like that, yes.' He walked back to the counter. Jo was waiting with a couple of books in her hand.

'That makes no sense,' I said, as I trailed behind him.

He shrugged and I had the feeling it didn't make much sense to him either.

I took a stride forward so that I was standing between him and the counter. 'Who's Sara?'

A look of pure panic flashed through his face.

'How's it going?' asked Jo. 'Any joy?'

'There's something you're not telling us,' I said.

'Do you want to buy those?' he asked Jo, as he pushed past me and got behind the till.

'If we can't find him, Tuff, we'll have to go to the police,' I said. 'And they're going to be way less understanding than us about a lot of this stuff ...'

'That's £12.98,' he said.

We didn't bother going back to the office. I phoned Aunt Edie and told her she could go home early. Jo made us fish-finger sandwiches and we ate them with the TV on. Not that we were watching it; I just think neither of us were in the mood for talking.

Jo was in the bath when my phone rang. I took the call into the front room, switched the TV off.

'Is that Lee Winters?'

I recognized the voice but couldn't place it straightaway. 'Who's this?'

As I asked the question my stomach flipped, my veins opened and the stuff that I live for, the quick fix of something so pure, so delicious pumped into my system. It was the woman from the missing persons' hotline – what was her name? I'd written it down somewhere.

'It's Mae. From—'

'Oh my God, you know who she is?'

'Steady on.' She laughed. 'No. I'm not that good. I mean, I've a few possibles. They might be something. They might not.'

I swear at that moment a ghost stepped into the room. I felt a presence, or something. The hairs on my neck, my arms, my legs, they all rose, like cool air had hit my skin. 'Really?'

'They're only possibles,' Mae said. 'I've trawled through all the white women we've got listed that are around the right age with any known links to Leeds or Nottingham, whose disappearance fits the timescale you mentioned. Oh and that have had a child.'

'Let me grab a pen.'

I found a biro on the mantelpiece and an envelope on the hall table – our unopened gas bill. I sat cross-legged on the floor. It was seven years since Vicky Doe's body had been discovered. Mae gave me the name of three women who had disappeared seven or more years ago and remained missing to this day. I wrote each one down, printing their names down one side of the gas bill:

Marcia Stevens
Jenny Crawley
Danielle Goodwin

As I spelled out each name, I thought about their families, left behind to live with the uncertainty. For a moment I wondered whether I had the stomach for this job.

'Marcia might be too long ago – she's been missing for almost twelve years. Eighteen when she went missing, so she'd be thirty now.'

I divided my list into three columns and did some maths in my head. 'Twenty-three when the body was found. That fits.'

'Her file says she grew up in Chapeltown, which is a suburb of Leeds.'

Suburb didn't really cover Chapeltown. It was inner city, home to most of the Afro-Caribbean population of Leeds, huge brick-built Victorian houses, all faded former glory. 'Chapeltown's about a mile or so down the road from where the body was found,' I said.

'Well, she lived there until she was thirteen,' said Mae. 'Then her family moved to London.' I could tell she was reading from notes, as I scribbled mine down. 'Had a baby at sixteen – a baby girl, who was placed with a foster family, after concerns about Marcia's known associates. Marcia disappeared not long afterwards. Maybe she decided to go back to her roots. A lot of people do.'

'How did she disappear?'

'She lived alone, a flat in Peckham. Her family said they hadn't heard from her for a while, so the brother went round. Her belongings were still in the flat, but there was no note or any clue as to where she might have gone. No one's heard from her since.'

I got a picture in my head of the kind of predators that stalk herds of deer, looking for the weakest one to pick off. Lions and tigers lying in wait, watching for the most vulnerable. 'What about the other two?'

'Danielle Goodwin's from Nottingham. She's the best bet when it comes to time frame. She was seventeen when she disappeared seven years ago, in August.'

My pulse got a bit faster, made my veins throb. 'Our victim was found on the 29th of August.'

'Danielle disappeared the twenty-third. Still lived at home – her mother reported her missing, first to the police and then to us. According to our notes, the mother seemed to think her boyfriend was involved. Police interviewed him but never pressed charges.'

'The mother's boyfriend?'

'No, sorry, the mother suspected Danielle's boyfriend of being involved in her disappearance. Said he had a violent temper.'

I couldn't imagine what that must feel like – to suspect someone of killing your child, but to have no evidence. That must be the path to madness.

Mae continued, 'Think there'd been one or two incidents of abuse, but obviously the police couldn't find anything to prove he'd had anything to do with her disappearance.'

'And she had a child?'

'Yes. A little boy. Looked after by Danielle's mother now, or was when we last heard from the mother. Mum keeps in quite regular contact – wants to be able to tell her grandchild what happened.'

'Christ. That's awful. What's the Leeds connection?'

'Tenuous but Danielle'd got tickets for Leeds Fest and was really excited about going. She disappeared three days before she was supposed to be getting the train. Her mother said she wouldn't have missed it for the world.'

'Right.' I scribbled a note to look up the dates for Leeds Fest that year. 'Do you think the police might have contacted her mother? I mean when our Vicky Doe turned up – she seems like a good fit?'

'I don't know. There's nothing about that in the file.'

Martin had said he didn't think the police had given this much attention. He'd said no one was pushing to get the case solved. Things disappeared down cracks, I knew that much. 'You said she was seventeen?'

'Yes. So she'd be twenty-four now, if she was still alive.'

Seventeen made her a bit young for our body, but I wondered how accurate post-mortems could be, in the absence of an identity. 'Do you think her mother will speak to us?'

'I'll contact her and give her your details.'

'That would be great. Thanks.'

'And then there's Jenny. Jenny Crawley. She's been missing for nine years.'

'That's probably too long ago too. It's only seven since our body was found.'

'Yes but often one leads to the other.'

I switched ears with my phone, worried that my brain was overheating. 'I don't understand.'

'In many cases disappearance precedes death. It's often the death of the missing person that solves the disappearance. People disappear because they get involved with the wrong crowd. And that sets in motion a chain of events that eventually leads to the loss of life. Their death is often what brings them home to their families.'

'Do you think a lot of the missing are actually dead?'

'Jenny used to live in Leeds,' Mae continued, as if she hadn't heard me. Perhaps she didn't want to answer the question. 'She was reported missing by her social worker, four years ago.'

My envelope was filling up as I tried to scribble all the information down. 'Hang on, I thought you said she'd been missing nine years?'

'As far as we're aware, no one has seen Jenny since she was about nineteen, nine years ago. At the time, she told her social worker she was moving back to Poland. The social worker hasn't been able to find anyone who has had any contact with her since then.'

I fished another envelope out of the bin. I'd have to write everything up into proper notes as soon as I ended the call. 'What about her family?'

'Her mother's Polish – apparently the mother went back to Poland. Jenny stayed in England. No one has managed to contact the mother since Jenny went missing.'

I wrote 'Mum' and drew an arrow and wrote 'Poland'. 'Dad?'

'No mention.'

'Dad', question mark. 'Why'd she have a social worker?'

'Jenny had a son on the at-risk register. Social worker is on file as saying that maybe Jenny had got wind of the fact they were moving towards taking her child into care. She took off.'

'No other family?'

'Not that I know of. There's not much here.' I heard the rustle of paper down the phone.

'What about the police?'

'According to this, social services decided she'd most likely gone back to her mum in Poland. Apparently there were a couple of letters from Jenny suggesting that's what she was going to do. Case closed. Remember it's not illegal to disappear if there's nothing to suggest a crime has taken place. The social worker rings us once a year to see if there's any news. Apparently she told one of my colleagues she feels like there's a ghost out there trying to tell her something.'

I didn't want to think about ghosts. 'If it was Jenny she'd have had to have been missing for two years before her body turned up.'

'I know. And she'd have been twenty-one years old at the time of death.'

'She might be alive and well and living in Poland.'

'The social worker's not convinced. She said England was the only country Jenny had ever known.'

I thought about this for a moment. Thought about the feeling I get whenever I drive over the tops and into Lancashire. The feeling of coming home, even though I hate the place. 'What's the Nottingham connection?'

'The father of her baby was from Nottingham. It's where the social worker thinks she went.'

'Where is this social worker? Can I speak to her?'

'Leeds. I tried ringing her earlier, but no answer. She's retired now so it's her home phone. I left a message.'

'Leeds?'

'Yes. Jenny lived in Harehills.' She pronounced it with its aitches, which made it sound like somewhere to aspire to, which it isn't. Harehills isn't very far from Roundhay Park, but culturally it's a million miles apart. Small redbrick terraced houses, no gardens, cheap shops and takeaways. If our body belonged to Jenny Crawley she'd almost made it home. I felt a shiver run down my back.

'What happened to her child?'

'Don't know. The assumption was she took him with her, when she left.'

I checked back over my notes. Three missing women. All mothers. One child in care, one child being raised by its grandparents and one child disappeared alongside its mother. It didn't make for uplifting reading. 'Can you give me the numbers of next of kin?'

'No. But I'll ring them now and offer to give them yours. It will be up to them whether they get in touch.'

'Will you ring them before the weekend?' I checked the time. It was nearly seven o'clock on Thursday evening. Mae obviously wasn't the kind of worker that switched off at 5 p.m.

'Yes. I'll do it as soon as put the phone down. This is your office number, right?'

'Yes, and it gets forwarded to my mobile out of hours.' I checked my notes, to see if there was anything I hadn't asked. 'Who reported Marcia missing?'

'The brother. To be honest, I don't know whether you'll hear from him. We contact families on a fairly regular basis, just to see whether there's any updates. The last time I spoke to him, I got the distinct impression he felt there was no point raking it all up again.'

'But he must want to know what happened to his sister?'

She exhaled. 'People deal with disappearances in different ways. Some people move on. Some people can't. I've been to houses where there's a shrine to the person who's disappeared and I've been to others where there's not so much as a photo. They're the ones I feel most sorry for. The ones that have left no mark. It's like they're invisible.'

As I put the phone down I thought about what Mae had said. The same word Jo had used in The Brudenell. Invisible. These women had left no imprint on the world.

I turned on the gas fire and felt soothed by its soft hum. I couldn't wrap my head around the fact that you could die without anyone knowing your name. Which brought another question to my mind. Where was Vicky buried? And what about her child? Was he or she out there somewhere, lying awake at night, wondering what had happened to their mother? The pathologist reckoned Vicky Doe was early twenties when she died, seven years ago. The child couldn't be more than ten or so years old. Who was looking after them?

'What's up?' said Jo, coming back into the front room, wrapped in two towels, one around her body, the other around her head.

'I'm not cut out for this.' I picked myself up from the floor and climbed onto the settee.

'You so are.'

'That was Mae from the missing persons' thing. She's given me details of three women who might be Vicky. Three women who disappeared seven or more years ago. That's three families who've spent at least seven years wondering what the fuck happened to their sister, or daughter, or girlfriend, or mother. Imagine not knowing where your child is, not knowing whether they're dead or alive, having to raise your orphaned grandson without any help from anyone and all the while thinking that maybe someone killed your daughter.'

'Awful.' Jo sat on the settee and rubbed my back. 'Who are we talking about?'

'All of them. Mae said hundreds of women disappear each year who aren't even reported as missing. It's fucking tragic.'

'I know.'

'The world's fucked up.'

'I know. But that's why we started No Stone Unturned. To put some of it right.' Jo pulled me up so that I was sitting next to her. 'It's the best thing I've ever done, Lee. It's like, it's like I've got a mission. And it's all thanks to you.' She put an arm around my shoulders and drew me into her body and the warmth of her freshly bathed skin immediately hit, made me feel like I had an aura around me. 'The world needs us; these women need us. We're not going to find every single missing one, but we might get justice for Vicky; we might make some sense of her life. That's worth fighting for. You can't give up; we're not giving up, not ever.'

Chapter 9

She was waiting for us as we rounded the corner to the office on Friday morning. Sitting on the stone doorstep, outside our front door, which has only recently been replaced after the break-in during our last case. Her arms wrapped around her knees. I nudged Jo.

'Hi, Sara,' I said as we drew closer. 'You OK?'

I wasn't sure if she was crying. She looked like she hadn't slept, and I was fairly certain she was still wearing the same clothes she'd had on the day before.

'I need someone to talk to and I figure you guys are as good as anyone.'

'Thanks,' I said, not making too much of an effort to hide my sarcasm. Jo elbowed me in the ribs.

It was a beautiful spring morning, the sun had a real warmth to it. 'Let's go to the park,' said Jo. 'Better than sitting indoors on a day like this.'

So we walked up the hill together, retracing our steps for me and Jo. We found a bench in the middle of Hyde Park – it's only a small park, more of an expanse of green – but it's a breath of fresh air in an urban environment; in the middle of it you can almost believe you're not surrounded by traffic on all four sides. It was too early for it to be busy, but by ten o'clock a stream of students would flow through the middle of it, making their way to the two universities on the other side.

'So, go on,' said Jo, sitting herself on one side of Sara. I took my seat on her left. 'We're listening.'

'Nikki hired you to find Matt because he didn't come back from the party on Saturday night? Is that right?' asked Sara.

I glanced at Jo and I know we were both thinking the same thing. Aunt Edie was becoming a liability.

'Your card says you're a missing persons' bureau,' said Sara. 'Matt's missing. Nikki's on one. It's not rocket science.'

'No,' I said, 'I don't suppose it is.' I ticked myself off for jumping to conclusions and being too quick to blame Aunt Edie. If Nikki wanted to keep her business private, she needed to stop gatecrashing our investigation.

'Nikki's worried about him. She's his girlfriend. Or at least, she thinks she's his girlfriend,' said Jo, going cross-eyed.

Sara couldn't help herself, she smiled at Jo's expression and I was struck again by how attractive Sara was. There was something so compelling about her. The contrast of her bright red lipstick, blue eyes and black hair – Snow White with smudged eyeliner and a small gap between her front teeth. Snow White with flaws.

'You obviously know Nikki,' I said.

Jo offered Sara a cigarette, and then lit it for her. Then she put one to her own lips and lit that. I coughed to let her know I'd like a fag too.

'I don't really,' said Sara. 'I know she's doing English – I needed some text for my end of year show. We're not what you'd call friends.'

'You're an artist?' said Jo.

'Photographer.'

'How do you know Matt?'

She closed her eyes for a second, then opened them again. 'We're both in Greenpeace. I've known him a couple of years, since my first year.'

'And Nikki thinks you're competition?' I asked.

Sara scratched at the back of her hair. 'Got it cut off, two days ago. My neck feels weird.'

'I love it,' said Jo. 'Really suits you.'

'Thanks.'

'What would you call you and Nikki then?' I said. 'If not friends?'

'Nikki's terminally insecure.'

'You're not the first to say that,' said Jo, exhaling a plume of smoke as she extended an arm along the back of the bench.

'Well, Matt has disappeared after going to a party. And he hasn't rung her to tell her where he is,' I felt obliged to point out. 'Not the kind of behaviour that fosters trust.'

'She's in denial,' Sara said.

'Who isn't?' said Jo. 'When it comes to men?'

'I'm not,' said Sara, like she'd taken Jo's comment as a direct attack on her. 'Just don't know what the fuck to do.'

They stared right at each other and as they were sat next to each other on the bench I could feel the intensity of their gaze. 'To do about what?' I asked.

Silence for a moment. Jo and Sara continued to stare at each other. I felt like moving places, sitting between them, but I didn't have the nerve. A group of students walked along the path towards us. 'Shall we go and sit on the grass?' I said, when they'd passed. 'It's dry enough.'

We left the bench and walked a hundred or so yards away from the path into the middle of the grass. I took my jacket off and laid it on the ground. Jo did the same. We sat in a triangle and I felt a bit better.

'You don't know what the fuck to do about what?' I said again.

Sara turned to me. 'I was at the party on Saturday night.'

'Ah,' I said. I knew where this was heading. Least, I thought I did.

'I was twatted.' Sara paused and glanced at Jo, then back at me, sizing us up. We obviously passed the test because she continued, 'Some pills, a bit of speed.' Another pause. No one spoke. Maybe she was waiting for our reaction to the news of drug taking, but it's kind of obvious neither of us are the judging kind. 'I felt a bit queasy. I think I threw up. I don't know.' She tugged at handfuls of grass, uprooting small fist-fuls. 'All I remember is thinking I needed to lie down. The next thing I know, it's morning. The sun's up, there's blue sky and trees above me. And ...'

Her blue eyes brightened but in a way that made my guts clench.

'And?' said Jo.

The park was so quiet I heard birds singing and it struck me I'd never really noticed birds in the park before.

'And Matt's on top of me.'

'On top of you?' said Jo.

Sara nodded and didn't speak for a while. When the words came they came in a rush, a stampede. 'Can't remember the order. But there's pain in my legs. And his cock, hard, well hard-ish, out of his pants. I'm like, "What the fuck?" I can't see anyone else but I can hear Massive Attack. It's come-down time, you know.'

Another pause. Neither I nor Jo spoke.

'There's sunlight through the trees. I don't know what happened. And he gets up, and says, "Sorry, sorry, sorry", over and over, and he's nearly crying. He stuffs his cock back into his pants. We're in trees, in the woods, there's no one around. It's daylight, and he tries to hold me, like hug me. I push him off. Tell him to fuck off, but I can't wrap my fucking head 'round it. He says, "I know what I'm like, and it's not like that", or something, and he staggers off and I look down because it's cold on my skin. Cold where he was. Cold and wet, and my tights are ripped, my knickers are ripped and there's spunk mixed with blood running between my thighs and I don't know what to do. I don't know what the fuck to do.'

We sat in silence for a while, perhaps me and Jo were waiting for her to say something further, I don't know.

'God,' said Jo, after ages had passed. 'Fucking hell.'

Tears welled at Sara's blue eyes, and I wanted to run. To run and run. To find the better world, the one where this kind of shit doesn't happen.

'I can't remember,' she said. 'That's the worst thing. I don't know what happened before he got up. It's like I'd been beamed down there, or something. I don't know how it started. There's just this black fucking hole.'

'You've known him two years?'

'Near enough.' She pulled her sleeve over her hand and wiped under each eye. 'He's a really nice guy.'

'He fucking isn't,' said Jo.

'I thought he was,' she said. 'He's sound – you know. I've leafleted with him, seen him at a few actions. Last summer we both worked at the dairy together. We've hung out at parties. He's basically an all-round good guy and—'

'And a rapist,' said Jo.

Chapter 10

Jo moved closer towards Sara and put an arm around her shoulders. Their heads bent close together: Jo's bleached blonde Afro curls contrasting with Sara's black, shiny, short straight hair. I glanced around the park. There were students on the path walking towards the city, but no one close enough to hear what we were talking about.

'I don't know what happened before,' Sara blurted, raising her chin as tears streamed down her face, her eye make-up smudged. 'I can't remember anything.'

I've been there – when there's just a blackness where memories should be – and I know how disorientating it is. It's one of the reasons I'm glad I don't drink anymore.

'Did I get off with him?' she asked the question like she genuinely believed we might have an answer for her.

I shrugged my shoulders.

'I've never fancied him,' she said.

I remembered the photos Nikki had given me. The tanned torso.

'He's not my type,' Sara said.

Jo kept her arm across Sara's shoulders.

Sara chewed on her thumbnail. 'Did I flirt? Lead him on? Can't remember kissing him. I don't remember even talking to him. All I can remember is thinking I'm going to be sick.'

'Then it's rape,' said Jo, in a quiet, steady voice and I was grateful for her certainty. 'If you can't remember giving consent you either didn't or you weren't in a fit state to consent. Either way, that's rape. Consent has to be informed.'

'I've never fancied him,' Sara said again, and I wasn't sure she'd even heard Jo. 'I know everyone does, but I don't. He's too, too ...' she searched for the right word. 'Too waxy.'

I agreed. From the pictures I'd seen, he was too plastic, trying too hard. Not my type either. Not that I have a type.

'You're not to blame,' said Jo.

'That's not how others will see it.' Sara rubbed her eyes with the corner of her sleeve, leaving a thin line of mascara running from the corner of her eye up towards her hair, like her eyes had wings.

'What others?' Jo asked.

'Nikki for one.'

'Nikki.' Christ, just hearing the name of our client made my stomach flip. 'What about Nikki?'

Jo glared at me.

'Afterwards,' Sara said, like she hadn't heard my question, 'I didn't know what to do. I mean we're in some bit of a wood somewhere in Lincolnshire, I think. Like Lord of the Fucking Flies. I don't know if anyone saw, if anyone else ... I didn't know where Matt was, didn't know where he'd gone. I took my tights off and tried to clean myself up. When I got back to the main bit – the clearing – someone had made a fire, a kettle boiling, steam billowing. Loads of people sitting around, getting stoned, a few still dancing, but I couldn't find the guys I'd gone there with. Then I saw Tuff – he's a friend of Matt.'

'We've spoken to him,' I said.

'What did he say?' The hope in her eyes was painful.

'Not much,' I said. 'Doesn't know where Matt is.'

'I just wanted to get home. I begged him to take me, told him I was ill and in the end he said OK.'

'Did you see Matt?'

'No. Tuff said he was going to find him to tell him we were going, and I freaked out. Tuff obviously thought I was nuts, but in the end he agreed to take me. He must have known something was wrong. I had twigs in my hair, my legs were bruised. He didn't ask any questions. All the way back to Leeds.'

Jo and I were silent.

'He dropped me outside uni, and I went to my studio. Couldn't bear the thought of seeing anyone. Had to come down. Jesus.'

I've taken party drugs a couple of times, most students have, but I can't handle the unbearable emptiness that comes after the event. Those kind of drugs lift your mood, take you to previously unimagined levels of happiness – there's a reason why it's called Ecstasy. But, what goes up has to come down, and, afterwards, my mind gets taken to places I don't ever want to go back to. How she survived that on top of what had happened to her, I didn't want to think.

'That was the worst. All Monday and Tuesday, I wanted to die. I-I need to find Matt and find out what the fuck happened.'

'He's not going to tell you,' said Jo. 'He's not going to want to own up to what he did.'

'It's just a hole in my brain. I've got nothing.'

'You've got to go to the police,' I said.

Jo pulled a face at me that suggested she didn't agree with my assessment of the situation. She turned to Sara. 'Who did you go to the party with?'

'I wasn't even going to go. Got talked into it by a couple of guys.'

I didn't like the look that Jo was giving me. 'What? He raped her,' I said.

'Do you think Tuff might ...?' Sara asked.

'He knows nothing,' Jo said. 'Apparently.'

'He might now,' I said, 'if we report—'

Jo shook her head at me, like she was exasperated. 'She's taken drugs, can't remember anything. Defence'll have an absolute field day. She'll be raped again, for a second time, up on the witness stand – that's if she ever manages to persuade the police, and the CPS, to take the case.'

'Don't feel like you have to sugar-coat it.' I nodded towards Sara who was sitting in an almost foetal position, her knees clasped to her chest, upright, her face buried.

Jo still held her arm around Sara's shoulders. 'She knows. All women know.'

'This is why rapes go unreported,' I said.

'You want to sacrifice her into the criminal justice system so you can feel better?'

'What about truth and justice? He needs taking to court.'

'Don't act fucking stupid, Lee. Courts aren't about truth

and sodding justice. They're about law. She doesn't need some doddery old guy telling her she should have kept her legs together, all the while getting a half-stiffy while she goes through the details for the seventeenth time under hostile cross-examination from some prick from law school, who probably fantasizes about doing something similar to the women at the lap-dancing clubs he goes to. Women are asking for it by wearing short skirts. God knows what a judge's going to make of someone who would have to admit to taking so many drugs she blacked out. She doesn't stand a chance.'

Sara raised her head. Mascara ran in two slender rivers down her cheeks. 'My show's called *The Dominatrix*,' she said.

We both stared at her. 'What show?'

'My finals. My exhibition. My photographs.'

She was trying to laugh but it wasn't working. 'All staged, one of the guys on my course – modelled for me. I've spent the last few days coming down, trying to work out the gaps of what happened on Saturday night, surrounded by pictures of women with whips in their hands while Brad's handcuffed to a bedframe.'

I saw something flicker across Jo's face but it was gone too quick for me to read. 'She's into sex,' Jo said to me, like that was the final nail in the coffin.

She turned to Sara. 'You don't stand a chance,' Jo said, her voice low.

'I know.'

'Well, that stinks,' I said.

'Yeah,' said Jo, and I could see the anger in her eyes boiling up at me, as if it was my fault. 'Welcome to the real world.'

Chapter 11

We walked with Sara back to her studio, which was a room in the building I'd chased her into after we'd met her in Old Bar the day before. I'd never been in an artist's studio – it had obviously once been a much bigger room, but at some point had been partitioned to form several smaller studio spaces. It was on the second floor, and the light from the tall windows at the far end flooded the room. It didn't take long to realize she hadn't exaggerated about the photographs. Black-and-white stills lined every wall. The same beautiful, long-haired man in each, his long, tapered body, not an inch of spare flesh. In one, draped across a bed, his hands handcuffed above his head, a woman with hair shaved at the sides, butch but beautiful. I tried not to see but everywhere I turned there were photographs. A woman in a mask and thigh-high black boots. An androgynous figure, black shorts, dark nipples, holding a leather strap between both hands.

I try not to think about sex most of the time. It only leads to trouble, in my experience. But suddenly there it was, the sun glinting off the shiny photographic paper. Skin and sex. Inescapable, unavoidable.

Jo was less reserved, closely examining each frame while I squirmed in the corner and muttered about whether Sara needed us to get her anything. When she said she needed more fags, I ran to the Union, never more glad to leave a room. I bought her a ready-made sandwich, tea bags, milk and a packet of chocolate Hobnobs. I handed over the company bank card at the checkout.

When I got back Sara and Jo were sitting on a makeshift bed in the corner of the room – it wasn't much more than a camping mat, with a duvet and a couple of pillows. There was also a small kitchen unit – a couple of cupboards under a stretch of worktop that had been fixed to the wall at some point – just a sink and a kettle from what I could see. Jo had her arm around Sara's shoulders again and I marvelled at her ability to get past the physical boundaries. I hesitated in the doorway, unsure of whether to intrude, but Jo glanced up and gestured me over. I put the provisions next to the kettle and made us all a cup of tea. I was the only one that drank it.

Before Jo and I left the studio, Sara made us promise not to tell anyone what she'd said. I knew she was in shock – the shock of having said the words aloud for the first time. That's when the thing becomes real. Out there as a narrative, as a true fact, rather than inside and under your control. I heard the lock turn on the door behind us as we walked down the corridor.

*

Jo and I didn't speak until we were heading out to the north of the university campus, across Clarendon Road and back into the park.

I kicked at a Coke can and this wave of frustration overwhelmed me, threatened to knock me off my feet. 'We're being paid to find a rapist so we can tell him he's about to be a father. This isn't the kind of reuniting I had in mind.'

Jo shrugged. 'I guess people go missing for a reason. And one of those reasons is they can't face up to what absolute cunts they are.'

'I can't believe everyone thinks he's such a great guy. Nikki. Jan. Tuff is obviously protecting him, even though he must have figured out what happened. Professor whatsherface said he was well-bred, popular. Even Sara said he's lovely.'

'Rapists are ordinary men.' Jo lit a cigarette and scrunched her eyes up against the initial cloud of smoke.

'Oh come on, Jo. You can't believe that.'

'The Park Killer had a girlfriend.'

'A nutcase.'

'The Yorkshire Ripper gets love letters from women all over the world. It's a sign of how damaged we are as a gender. Women are so confused about sex. Hardly surprising when you think of the stories we get told.'

I changed the subject. 'We could just tell Nikki we can't find him.'

'Or develop a sideline?'

'A sideline?' I saw the glint in Jo's eyes as she exhaled a plume of smoke into the fresh air, and I knew what she meant,

113

even before she said the words. 'No Stone Unturned, No Mercy Given?'

We both grinned at the thought and the world tilted back a little.

Another thought hit me. 'Do we tell Nikki what Matt's done?'

'We can't. We promised Sara.'

'Nikki's our client,' I reminded Jo but I already knew that Nikki wasn't where Jo's loyalties lay. We had to think of the person paying our wages though. That was the point. 'Jan said he'd disappeared before – do you think that means he's raped before? If we could find someone else—'

'We need to go to one of those parties,' said Jo as we passed a group of students playing Ultimate Frisbee. 'They must have their regulars – the same crowd every week. Someone must have seen something. While you were at the shop, Sara said the party organizers are somehow connected to travellers' sites, so maybe someone there will know where Matt went. We'll get the details from Nikki.' Jo's eyes brightened. 'We can go down if there's one tomorrow.'

'What the fuck do we do if we find him?'

'There's only one thing we can do.'

'Which is?'

'Get him to confess.'

'Confess? Why's he going to do that?'

'Because it's good for the soul,' Jo said, grinding the stub of her cigarette into the path with her boot.

Back at the offices Aunt Edie looked flustered. 'Where've you been? Nikki's been looking for you. Dreadfully upset. She's supposed to get the train back to her parents this evening. She's desperate for news.'

She wasn't desperate for the news we had.

'And that bloody Blink man's sniffing around. Said to tell you he was coming in. In fact,' she glanced at the clock, 'he should be here in a minute. And then there's Sheila.'

'Sheila?'

'Cracked pot, if ever I saw one. Still in her slippers; there's no excuse for that.' She looked at me pointedly. 'You get dressed, every morning, no matter what.'

'I know,' I said. It wasn't like I hadn't heard that a million times before. 'What does Slippers Sheila want?'

'Says she's lost her cat. I told her we only did humans. That is right, isn't it?'

I couldn't help myself, I grinned. 'Well, cats sound more tempting than humans, this morning.' I wasn't sure what to tell Aunt Edie about Matt. 'What colour is it?'

Aunt Edie clutched a stack of papers to her chest. 'I didn't ask.'

'Well, if she comes back, get a description and tell her we'll keep an eye out.'

Jo took a seat at her desk and got straight on the phone to West Yorkshire Police. She'd been trying since the day before to get hold of the officer who'd led the initial investigation into Vicky Doe's suicide at the flats. I knew she was hoping to get some information about the necklace Vicky had been wearing. If she'd removed her clothes but kept the necklace, it had to mean something.

'Where's Nikki now?' I asked Aunt Edie, as I hung my jacket up.

'I told her to go and take a walk around the park, get some fresh air. She'll be back. Twenty minutes.'

My stomach flipped at the words. What the fuck were we going to tell Nikki? I glanced at Jo but she was busy trying to explain why she needed to speak to DI Roberts. She was speaking slowly and loudly to the person on the other end, like they were incapable of understanding.

I peered through the blinds. Suddenly having an office felt like being in a target range – anyone could walk in and take a shot at us. I felt encumbered, trapped, tied down. I felt like running.

I flicked the blinds back into position and forced myself to breathe, five times. In through the nose and out through the mouth. 'Aunt Edie, can you come in the back a minute, I need to tell you something.'

I worry about introducing Aunt Edie to the dark side. She's, well, I don't know exactly how old she is, but she remembers rationing. She's from a different era, a gentler time. She never had any children and I'm guessing Arthur was the only man she ever, well, you know. And even then. Well.

I didn't really know how to broach the concept of rape. And rape of a woman comatose because she'd taken illegal drugs. I shouldn't have let Aunt Edie come here, to the dark underbelly of the city. She might have been better off staying in her small town in Lancashire, with its tight community and focus on the soap operas.

Aunt Edie followed me into the back room with an armful of files clutched to her chest. I closed the door behind her.

'Well, come on, spit it out,' she said. 'I've a million things to see to.'

'Right. The thing is, Aunt Edie.' I held onto the back of the chair. 'The thing is, I'd be grateful if you could try and keep Nikki away from us today. We've found out some information about Matt, and I don't know how we're going to break it to her.'

'Another woman, has he?'

'Er, no. Well, not in a straightforward kind of a way, no.'

'What then?' She peered at me and I felt myself colouring up like a six-year-old caught for stealing ginger biscuits from the pantry. 'What's he done?'

'I mean, nothing's proven. He's not had a chance to give his side of the story.'

'Let me hear the other side,' she said, putting her papers down on the card table.

'When we got here this morning, there was a woman sitting on the doorstep.'

'And?'

'She was upset. I mean, like really upset. She seems to think, well she said, I mean—'

'He never did.'

'She was at the party—'

'He did. He bloody did. I knew it.' Aunt Edie punched her right hand into her left palm, like she was splatting a fly.

'What? What do you mean, you knew it?'

'I sodding knew it. If it's too bloody good to be true, then it is.'

'Come again?'

Aunt Edie lowered herself into the chair and rubbed at her shin. 'If there's one thing living this long has taught me, it's that there's no such thing as a man who's too good to be true.'

'Are you spending too much time with Jo?'

'We're all flawed, Lee.' Aunt Edie stressed the word flawed. 'My Arthur, flawed as they come: that's how I know he was decent.'

I wasn't sure I was following her logic. I took the seat next to her. 'Well, we mustn't get carried away. Like I said, nothing's proved.'

Aunt Edie cuffed me round the head. 'Don't be stupid, Lee. Women don't make up stories like that. You know she's telling the truth, I can see it on your face. Two rules for women.' She stuck up a bony finger. 'One, trust your gut. Two, stick together. Only way for this shit to get better is for women to stick together.'

I coughed. 'Not sure Nikki's going to see it that way.'

'Ignorance isn't bliss. It's ignorance. Educate to liberate.'

I made a mental note to have a word with Jo.

'Not telling her is only going to make it worse,' Aunt Edie continued. 'What Nikki Cooper-Clarke needs now is facts. F – A – C – T – S. Not fantasies. She's about to make the biggest decision of her life. No going back, not ever, not for a single second. Imagine how you'd feel if she took that decision based on a lie.'

'I'm not suggesting we lie, more—'

Aunt Edie wasn't having a bar of it. 'Not telling the truth is lying, however you dress it up, Lee. Think about how you felt about your mum not telling you …'

Aunt Edie must have caught a look on my face because she finished the sentence limply, 'about all that business.'

She paused, cleared her throat and regrouped. Found herself some firmer ground. 'Nikki needs to know.'

And it was firmer ground. I knew Aunt Edie was right, but it was a question of timing.

'And she needs to know before she gets on that train, Lee. Before she tells her parents something she might decide they have no business knowing. You can't play God and decide what to say and when to say it. She's paying our wages, you owe her the truth.'

'Bloody, fucking, authoritative, arrogant, sexist, up his own arse, misogynistic wanker,' said Jo, crashing through the door.

Aunt Edie didn't stop glaring at me. I turned to Jo. Her troubles seemed more attractive than my own. 'Problem?' I said.

'All bent. Every last bloody one of them.'

'Go on.'

'DI Roberts no longer works for West Yorkshire Police and no one seems to know where he's gone or whether he's even still alive. And apparently I can't access any evidence of past crimes, even ones that aren't being prosecuted or even bloody investigated, due to health and fucking safety concerns.'

'Aunt Edie thinks we have to tell Nikki about Matt before she goes to visit her parents.'

Jo shook her head and her Afro bobbed. 'We can't, we promised Sara.'

'It's in the client contract,' said Aunt Edie, hands on her hips. 'You've signed to say you'll hand over all relevant information.'

It's true. I put that clause in myself, because of what Aunt Edie had just described as 'all that business'.

'Paragraph 4, Subsection b,' Aunt Edie said, in case we were interested.

'So we tell her we've been told something but we can't tell her what.' Jo picked up the papers Aunt Edie had put on the table.

'She has a right to know, Jo.' Aunt Edie had her hands on her hips. 'She's paid you to find out what's happened to her boyfriend. You can't not tell her.'

'I can. And I'm not,' said Jo.

'You don't, I will,' said Aunt Edie, as she snatched her papers back from Jo's hands. They stood face-to-face and I wouldn't bet money on either of them backing down this side of Christmas. This was where being the company director came in. I didn't like it but I knew what I had to do.

I stood up and went to stand in the corner of the room, by the punch bag. Perhaps I thought I could use it to deflect any blows. I didn't want to take sides but there was a higher principle at stake. 'Aunt Edie's right, Jo. We have to tell Nikki.'

My mouth got dry. I hate arguing with Jo because she's so passionate and she says whatever she thinks and her argument swells over you like waves on a beach, each affront bigger than the last, until you're pounded into the sand, wishing you'd never even had the thought to put your swimming costume on. I breathed out and stretched out my toes in my boots. 'We can't let her tell her parents she's pregnant, not without telling her what we know.'

'I promised Sara I wouldn't tell, so I'm not,' said Jo. She stared at me, her blue eyes darkening.

'Fine,' I said, swallowing the lump in my throat. 'I will.'

*

I didn't have time to get too worked up about it, which is probably a good thing because I could have whipped myself into a frenzied maelstrom of anticipation, anxiety and adrenalin. But fortunately, or perhaps unfortunately, we heard the front door go. I prayed it was Martin, or the woman in her slippers that Edie had been on about. Or perhaps the photocopier service man, even though he could talk the hind leg off a donkey.

We all hurried through into the front office, bottlenecking as we squeezed through the door.

And there was Nikki.

Paler than I remembered, her dreads neatly tied back, wearing a black skirt and cream jumper that didn't look anything like the sort of thing she'd wear. A small rucksack sat at her feet, like a dog. We stood facing each other in the front office, the unexploded bomb on the desk in front of me, about to blow out the walls. 'I'm off,' she said. 'It's my dad's birthday. I just wanted to know if—'

'Come through, Nikki,' I said. 'I have some news.'

'I'll put the kettle on,' said Aunt Edie, hurrying off in the direction of the kitchenette. Jo took up a seat at the desk, not looking at anyone.

*

'What?' said Nikki as soon as we were in the back office.

'Take a seat.' I wanted her sitting, less mobile. Just in case. 'There's no easy way to tell you this.'

'You've found him?'

I moved quickly to extinguish any good feelings she may have been developing. 'No. But I think we may have discovered the reason he's disappeared.'

'What?' She looked hopeful and confused all at the same time and I knew in that moment that she had only ever thought that this was going to turn out all right. That we'd find her missing boyfriend, and that there'd be some simple explanation for it all, that they'd be reunited to continue along their path to happiness.

'I can't tell you much, because none of this is on record, and I don't know whether it ever will be. I also want to promise you that we haven't finished. We will keep going till we find him, if that's what you want, after I've told you what I'm about to tell you.'

Nikki slipped into a seat. 'Go on.'

Still no fear in her eyes. Curiosity, not fear. Puppy-dog eyes. Like she didn't believe the world was capable of bad.

I swallowed and wiped my palms on my cut-offs. 'We spoke to someone who was at the party on Saturday night. I can't tell you who at this stage. But I can tell you that they've accused Matt of a serious crime.'

'A crime?' She pulled a face, like she was waiting for the punchline. I didn't say anything. 'What crime?'

'Nikki, I'm really sorry.'

'You mean drugs?' She frowned at me as if surprised by my reaction. 'I told you—'

'He's been accused of rape, Nikki.'

The air stilled for a moment. Time splintered. The room felt too warm. She stared at me, waiting for the next sentence. I chewed on a lump of skin inside my lip.

'Bullshit,' she finally said. 'That's crazy. Bullshit. I don't believe it.'

'Nikki,' I said. I crouched on the floor in front of her, so that I was at eye level, held her gaze. 'I do. I spoke to the woman myself and I believe her.'

Nikki narrowed her eyes, willed me to change the words, but I kept myself as absolutely open and centred and present as I have ever been. I wanted her to read the truth out of me, in case I got the words wrong. 'Obviously, I wasn't there. You weren't there. We haven't heard from Matt. But I'm certain that this person was telling the truth. It's not been reported to the police; there's nothing for this person to gain. I believed every word she said.'

'She might have got the wrong person.'

'It was Matt.'

'It can't be.'

'Nikki, I didn't want to tell you now. I wanted to wait until we've got more to give you, but I know you're going to your mum and dad's.' At this a single tear appeared at the corner of her right eye. It hovered for a moment, made my own eyes sting, until it fell forward, over the rim of her eyelashes and made its way down the side of her nose. 'And I know you've got some fairly huge decisions to make—'

'Why would Matt rape someone? He could have his pick of women. Honestly, girls throw themselves at him. Once, we were playing pool in The Hyde and I went to the toilet and when I came back this girl had offered to meet him in the gents for a shag. Why would he rape someone?'

'Rape isn't about sex,' I said. 'It's about power, entitlement.'

'He's not even that into sex, most of the time.'

I didn't want to get too involved in the details of Matt and Nikki's sex life. Or indeed anyone's sex life. I cleared my throat. 'I promise, I'll do everything I can to find him, if you still want me to. But it's whether you want—'

'I want you to find him,' she said.

She put her elbows on the table. There was something I wasn't quite grasping, something in the room that was beyond my reach. 'Nikki, do you believe me?'

I had a feeling she did.

'No.'

'Has something happened to you?'

She didn't answer. Aunt Edie chose that moment to knock on the door and I was startled to realize I was cross at the interruption. I yanked open the door. Aunt Edie handed me the tray, gave me a nod and turned away. I put the tray down on the table.

'Nikki?'

'I want you to find him,' she repeated. 'I need to hear it from him.'

'What about ... I mean, your mum and dad?' I nodded my head in the direction of her belly. I didn't want to use words like baby or pregnancy.

'Uncle Stephen's flying in from Perth. I haven't seen him since I was like five.'

'Have you got someone on your side? A brother or sister?'

'An older brother. Ten years older. He's disabled. There's only me. The great white hope.'

I poured the tea and we sat in silence for a moment, while Nikki added three heaped teaspoons of sugar to her cup.

'Listen,' I said. 'I don't know anything about having kids. But I know a lot about growing up with a mother who wasn't ready. At the end of the day, this might have done you a favour.'

I realized I hadn't quite got the words right as Nikki half-choked on her drink.

'Nikki, how old are you?'

'Twenty, in July.'

'So, even if Matt was the most amazing guy in the world, even if he hadn't gone missing, even if he hadn't been accused of rape' – she closed her eyes at the mention of the word – 'you still have to decide based on you. The chances of you having a baby with someone at nineteen and them sticking by your side through thick and thin until the baby's grown up – that's fantasy land.'

'My mum got married when she was twenty-one.'

'So did mine. My dad left the day I was born.'

'Not everyone—'

'Plan for the worst.'

'If he did ...' She looked up at me. 'What about ...?' She cradled her hand to her belly, like she was trying to protect whatever was in there from hearing the words. Her words reduced to a whisper. 'What if it's a boy?'

Fresh tears fell down her cheeks.

I handed her a tissue.

'Did your parents know your brother was going to be disabled?'

She shook her head.

'That's the thing, isn't it?' I said. And the reason I knew with absolute certainty I was never going to have a child. 'You've got no control. The way I see it, unless you're ready for anything, you're not.'

'So now I have to go and tell my parents that I'm pregnant, the father's missing and he's possibly a rapist?' Her voice grew louder and shriller as the sentence progressed.

I thought about my half-sister, Fiona, who's buried in a graveyard in Skipton that I can't bear to visit. She was two years younger than Nikki when she got pregnant. Seventeen. What would I have said to her, if I'd had the chance, when she'd first found out about the baby growing inside her? I'd have told her she didn't have to tell her parents anything, if she didn't want to. Telling our dad she was pregnant was the reason she was no longer here. He'd lost the plot when he'd heard, gone out to France to force her into a decision she didn't want to make. They'd argued, and who knows what happened? He said she fell backwards, hit her head on the glass coffee table. The pathologist's report said she suffered a fatal trauma to the back of the head. The only person that could tell us the absolute truth was no longer here. I missed her more the longer it got without her, despite the fact I hadn't even known she existed for most of my life.

I stood up and stared at the top of Nikki's head. What

should I say to her? I had a chance to make amends for my failure with Fiona. The chance to put a little part of it right. Still the words weren't there. I practised possibilities in my head. *You don't have to tell your parents anything. You don't owe them explanations. If you do tell them, tell them in a public place, somewhere where they can't lose it, somewhere where they can't hit out. Truth is, my only experience of family is dysfunction.* I shook the thoughts from my head. I remembered Yuki's words. The here and the now. Only the present.

'Don't think about them, Nikki. Think about you. What do you want? Once you've got that bit right, the rest will follow, I promise. Whatever you decide, I'll back you all the way.'

The words sounded trite even to my own ears. She shrugged my arm off and got to her feet with all the enthusiasm of someone going to the dentist for root canal work. I didn't envy her, but Aunt Edie was right. At least now she was armed with the facts.

Chapter 12

I don't want to sound dramatic, but I came out of that room a new woman. I felt taller, reborn, which is possibly too strong a way of putting it, but something had changed inside me. I'd handled it. I'd faced emotional trauma and I'd stood my ground. The only fly in the ointment was that as I'd grown, Nikki had diminished, like I'd leeched some of the confidence from her and put it under my own skin. She didn't speak as she walked through the front office and out the door.

'So you told her,' said Jo, as we watched Nikki trudge past the window.

'I told her Matt had been accused of rape. I didn't say by who.' It was only then that it occurred to me that Nikki hadn't actually asked anything about Matt's accuser.

'It's hardly rocket science,' said Jo. 'She saw us talking to Sara.'

'I guess she might put two and two together on the train.' I waited a moment, squaring my shoulders, waiting for the inevitable onslaught, but it didn't come. 'Then again, she might not. She's a woman with a lot on her mind – she's got to work out what to tell her parents. What she's going to do about the baby.' It wasn't a baby yet, I reminded myself. Just a clump of cells. The potential of life, not an actual person.

'Glad I'm not in her shoes. Pregnant. Yuck.' Jo hunched her shoulders and shuddered her whole body. 'Another plus for political lesbianism.'

'You've cheered up,' I said. I took my seat at the desk. 'What's happened?'

'I spoke to Martin. He's got us a contact at the West Yorkshire Police's Property Store.' She grinned.

'No way.'

'Yes way. We're meeting the guy in thirty minutes. Get your coat. I've nearly finished.'

'How?'

'How what?' Jo returned to her typing.

'How did he set it up?'

'Contact from his journalist days, I guess. Martin was going to come with us, but she said it's better we go alone.'

'She?'

'Someone Martin trusts.' Jo clicked her mouse a couple of times and the computer fan stopped whirring.

'Why is it better we go alone?'

'Apparently the copper we're meeting is a ladies' man.' She popped a pen she'd been using back into the holder and stood up. 'Whatever the fuck that means.'

We drove into town and parked the van near the train station on a patch of wasteland, which some joker had decided was a car park, and had the balls to charge us a fiver for the privilege. It took ten minutes to walk down to the waterfront,

past the Dark Arches and under the railway tracks, me struggling to keep up with Jo as she marched us past the trendy
coffee shops that are springing up all around the place. I
linked arms with her in a bid to slow her down.

'Martin said the coppers who work in Property Stores are
the ones that have to be kept away from the public.'

'Say again?'

'Property Stores is where the bad apples get sent.'

My skin shivered. Jo squeezed my arm and let it go. 'The
guy we're meeting may have been implicated in the Dave
Hammer business.'

'The Dave Hammer business?'

'See, this is what happens if you don't read a newspaper.'
Jo shook her head in disgust at my perceived lack of aware-
ness about world events. She's got a point. I hate the news. It
brings me down, makes me feel small, helpless. I've found the
only way I can stay sane in this fucked-up world we live in
is to concentrate my energy on the things I can change. Just
that which is in front of me. The present. My present.

Jo's the opposite. She drowns herself in current affairs. Reads
The Guardian on her phone every single day, usually before
she gets out of bed. She surfs the internet, watches the news,
listens to the BBC World Service as she falls asleep. She's an
information junkie, always searching for her next fix. She
made me stay up all night for the last election, even though
the result was obvious.

'Dave Hammer is ... well, was the policeman responsible
for ensuring West Yorkshire Police's seized property got
disposed of.'

'And?'

'Well, he did dispose of it. Just not in the way they envisioned when they gave him the job.'

'How are they supposed to dispose of seized property?' I hadn't really thought about it before, but it struck me that the police must end up with a lot of stuff. Evidence from crime scenes, stolen goods, lost property. Nicked cars. 'Ebay?'

'Depends what it is – they keep cash. Auction off the good stuff – cars, unclaimed jewellery, anything that's been deemed to have been bought with ill-gotten gains. Drugs get incinerated – least that's the plan.'

'All that hash going up in smoke.' I pictured stoned council workers standing around a bonfire. 'What a job.'

'Or not as the case might be.'

I pulled a face at Jo. Sometimes she talks in riddles.

'Hammer got caught with a few spare kilos of cocaine stashed in his tumble drier,' she explained. 'Instead of incinerating it, he was selling their entire back catalogue.'

'Shit. Bet that didn't go down well.'

'He got thirty years. Doubt he'll ever get out. Which is why they're a bit cagey about their Property Stores.'

'And this guy we're about to meet worked with him?'

'We don't know that for certain. But he works there now.'

'Right. With all the other bad apples?'

'Depends on whether you think it's the apples or the barrel itself that needs work.' We skirted round a circular tower block of yuppie flats and arrived at a bridge. The steps at the side of the bridge led to the canal. 'Ready?' Jo asked.

'Weird place to meet,' I said.

Jo took a breath, pushed back her shoulders and made her way down the stone stairs. I followed her along the canal path heading out towards the west of the city. Four or five minutes later, I saw him, standing under another bridge, a few hundred yards in front of us. He nodded at us as we got closer, his hands shoved in his trouser pockets.

'Topper?' Jo said as we approached. 'Jo and Lee.' Jo pointed to me.

He turned to walk the same way we'd been heading and we fell into step beside him. 'Nice day for it,' he said.

He wore a blue shirt with the sleeves rolled up, but it wasn't that warm. He was one of those men that look like he carried his own heating system under his skin, muscles tugging at the shirt fabric. He had a tattoo on his forearm but his arm was so hairy I couldn't see what it was supposed to be.

'Thanks for meeting us,' said Jo.

'What can I do for you girls?'

He licked his lower lip and I fought the impulse to say, *Trust me, there's nothing in this whole world you could do for me*. But instead I smiled in what I hoped might be interpreted as a sign of my willingness to be open to suggestion. I felt Jo bristle next to me, and I knew I'd have to be the lead on this one, or things might get ugly. I went for bright and breezy. 'Apparently if we want to know anything about police property, you're the man to ask.'

'Possibly.'

'We're investigating a cold case. We want to take a look at the evidence.'

He didn't break stride. 'Don't look like coppers to me.'

'We're private investigators. We run a missing persons' bureau.'

'Stores are only open to coppers.'

'Amanda said you'd be willing to be flexible,' said Jo.

'Did she now?'

'The case is seven years old,' I said. 'No one's interested anymore.'

'There's no way I can get you into the Property Stores. Not now. Not since ... They've tightened up. CCTV everywhere.'

'Could you have a look at something for us? Perhaps describe it to us?'

He stopped to light a cigarette. 'What's in it for me?'

'Truth and justice?' said Jo. She lowered her voice and muttered under her breath, 'But you're probably not interested in that.'

I frowned at Jo and turned to Topper. 'Look we're trying to solve a crime that the police gave up on.'

Topper hesitated, like he was about to argue with us. 'You got a POO number?'

'Yes.' Jo pulled out Martin's notebook from her bag and read a series of random numbers and letters, beginning with the letters P-O-O. I didn't ask what they stood for.

'So what's the case?' he asked.

'Suicide,' I said. 'A young woman. We're just trying to find out who she was.'

'We wouldn't keep anything that long. Not for a suicide.'

'There must be something on file.'

'I'll have a look, see. But I wouldn't hold your breath. Chances are we'll have got shut.'

'That would be great,' I said. 'We'd really appreciate it.'

He stopped walking and turned to stare at Jo, or, more specifically, he turned to stare at Jo's breasts. I flinched under his gaze and he wasn't even staring at me. I watched Jo's fists clench.

'If I find anything, none of this happened, OK?'

'You have our word,' said Jo, and I remembered the promises we made at the end of our last case to keep the police informed about everything we did. We were making and breaking promises on what felt like an hourly basis and it didn't sit right with me. I kept my mouth closed and hoped I'd be able to wriggle out on a technicality later – Jo promised, I told. I promised, Jo told.

*

He left us by the side of the canal, ducking up a set of steps by the side of another bridge.

'Why don't you go home and get tea on? I'm starving,' said Jo.

'Oh, OK. What do you fancy?'

'Anything so long as it's not from a pig.' She half-laughed at her own joke, hit me on the upper arm and tossed me the van keys. 'You take the van; I fancy a walk.'

I frowned at her departing back. Jo never fancied a walk. Topper had obviously got under her skin more than I thought, but I guessed it was best to leave her to burn it off. Maybe she just needed a bit of time on her own. We all do sometimes. In fact, I often feel bad because I need it more than Jo. She's socially-brained – always up for the party. I told myself I shouldn't feel peeved when she finally asked for some space.

I'm not the world's greatest driver. Truth is, I don't like driving at all. Too much power at my fingertips. I worry about going mad, just for a second and deciding to nail it into a wall or a tree. You see those bouquets tied to trees or lampposts and I know that's what happened to them. A split-second tidal wave that hits you, and that's it. Game over.

I pushed the thoughts away and concentrated on the next moment. One turn at a time until I made it back home. I parked the van at the kerbside and went into the flats. A quick look through the cupboards and I decided on corned beef hash, cos it's quick and easy and Jo loves it. Something to do with growing up on the Mersey, I think.

I was peeling spuds and listening to Radio 6 when my mobile rang. I switched off my speakers and took the phone through to the front room.

A woman's voice asked to speak to me. 'I hope it's not too late,' she said. 'I've been out for most of the day. Just got back at teatime and got the message. And I know it's Friday and it's past five and everything but Mae said you worked weekends. I couldn't bear the thought of waiting till Monday morning. I thought with it still being before, well it's almost seven, but I had to get the tea done and then I didn't want bug-a-lugs hearing everything. I've got him settled now, watching Power Rangers – he's mad on it – and I thought if I just left you a message even, that would be something.'

I realized I was holding my breath. I released it. 'Who's speaking?' I said.

'Sorry. I should have said that bit first. Sorry.' I felt her pause, like she was resetting herself. 'I'm Louise, Louise Goodwin. I'm Danielle Goodwin's mother. She's been missing for—'

'Seven years,' I said. I sat down on the settee because my legs felt weak. 'I'm sorry.'

'Can't really remember any other way now.' She cleared her throat. 'Kyle keeps me going.'

'Did Mae tell you why we wanted to speak to you?'

'She left a message on the answer-machine. I forget to check it half the time. She said you were private investigators, and you were looking at an old case. From Leeds. She said you'd found a body.'

'Have the police ever spoken to you about this?'

'They've told me about six girls, over the last seven years. I've been to the morgue to see three of them.'

I felt her shudder at the memories.

'None in Leeds, though,' she continued. 'We live in Nottingham, see. Although, it's funny you say Leeds, because Danielle was supposed to be going to the music festival there: she'd got tickets, her and her friend, before she disappeared.'

'Yes, the Leeds Fest. Mae mentioned—'

'How did she die? Your girl?'

I took a deep breath to buy myself some time. I wasn't sure how much to say but then I heard Aunt Edie having a go about truth. 'Suicide, we think. Or at least that's what the police thought at the time.'

'Oh that is terrible. I don't understand how anyone can ... How did she ... you know, how did she do it?'

I didn't really want to talk to her about that. Couldn't tell this poor woman that if Vicky Doe was her daughter she'd chosen such a brutal way to die. 'She took an overdose,' I said, hoping she wouldn't ask me anymore questions. 'I'm very sorry but I'd really like to ask you some quest—'

'It's not Danielle.'

She sounded so utterly sure, I was wrong-footed for a moment. 'How do you know?'

'Danielle would never kill herself. She wasn't that kind of person. She had Kyle to think about. She had too much to live for.'

I noticed Mrs Goodwin was talking about her daughter in the past tense. 'What do you think happened to her?' I asked.

She made a noise that might have been a small sneeze, or it might have been her spitting, or clearing her throat or something. 'I'm sorry,' she said. 'It's just every time this happens, it brings it all back.'

'I know,' I said. And I do know. I know what it's like to live with the uncertainty, the false hope, the absence, the ghosts. I wanted to help. More than that, I needed to help. 'Mae said you had a bad feeling about Danielle's boyfriend. Could you tell me something about him?'

'Hmph.' She paused. 'Bad news. Simon James, called himself "Ink". Stupid name for a DJ. But Danielle was besotted. He turned her head, he did. I'm not saying they weren't happy enough at first, and after what happened with – well, it's not a secret.'

I paused, sensing she wanted to tell me, but that she was struggling to find the words.

'Did Mae tell you?' she asked. She didn't pause long enough for me to answer. 'Danielle got pregnant when she was only fifteen.'

'Wow, that is young.' Younger even than Fiona, who I still thought of as my baby half-sister.

'She made a mistake. A terrible mistake. A one-off thing; she'd been drinking, made me swear not to report it.'

'Report it?'

'It was statutory rape. But she never told me the man's name. He was married, she said. That's all I know. I did wonder if it was one of her teachers at school, but she got so upset when I asked, I had to let it go. Thought she'd tell me in her own time. One thing I do know is, whoever he is, he's had nothing to do with Kyle, not even since Danielle disappeared.'

'Poor Kyle.' The boy didn't know whether his mother was alive or dead. Didn't know who his father was. I tried to work out in my head how old he'd be. Danielle had been seventeen when she disappeared, so Kyle must have been young, a toddler really. Which made him eight or nine now. 'And you've looked after him ever since?'

'He thinks of me as his mum, bless him. It's just the two of us, now.'

'What about Danielle's dad?'

She sighed. 'I'm a widow. John died nearly ten years ago now.'

God. The poor woman.

'The stress of all this,' she continued. 'Unless you've been

through it, you can't imagine.' I heard the catch in her throat.
'I'm sorry.'

I felt bad for making her revisit old wounds. 'I'm sorry, too,'
I said. 'You've been through a terrible time.'

'Danielle struggled to adapt to being a mother. I can't blame
her for that – she was only a child herself. That first year was
terrible.' She took a deep breath. 'But then she met Simon
and things were looking up, least for a while. He's charming
on the outside, but there was always something about him,
something I couldn't quite put my finger on. He was jealous
of Kyle.'

'Jealous?'

'I know – who can be jealous of a toddler? But he was
– he resented the time Danielle spent with her own child.
He wanted her by his side while he was doing his DJing,
and of course those kind of hours don't fit with having a
little one. I did what I could to help out but I knew they'd
been having rows.'

'Danielle told you?'

'I noticed bruises on her arm and when I asked her about
them – something wasn't right. It's easy with hindsight, but
at the time you don't know what to believe. If your own
daughter is telling you everything is OK, you have to believe
that it is. And I had my hands full, what with work, and Kyle,
I didn't really take the time to talk to her about it.' She sniffed.
'I blame myself.'

'It's not your fault,' I said.

'Do you have children?' she asked.

'No.' No one had ever asked me that question before and

it surprised me that anyone would ever think for a moment that I might.

'You can't know until you do, what's it like. I had three miscarriages before Danielle, four after. And Sophie. She only lived a few short days, God rest her soul.'

I didn't know what to say. I switched my phone to my other ear.

'I'm sorry, love,' she said. 'You don't want to be listening to all this. And like I say, I've got Kyle now. He keeps me focused on the future. That's the best way.'

'You're very strong,' I said.

'What doesn't kill you ...' she said. 'That's what my mother always used to say.'

'Can I ask you some questions about Danielle?'

'Well, I don't mind. Most people don't like to mention her, not anymore, after all this time. But it's not Danielle.'

I knew she didn't want to believe her daughter was capable of killing herself – who would? But there were too many coincidences – the time frame; the fact she was on her way to Leeds Fest. And the father of her baby, a married man who didn't want anyone to know about her pregnancy. I wondered whether he could be one of the names on the list of residents at the flat. 'When did you last see Danielle? Can you tell me about how she disappeared?'

'The 23rd of August, seven years ago. She went to a club with Simon. He says she'd had a bit to drink and had a funny turn. At quarter past two in the morning, she told him she needed some air. He couldn't go with her because he was in the middle of his set. No one's seen her since. She disappeared into thin air.

'The police found two images of her on CCTV. On her own, walking through the town centre, heading back in the direction of the club. But whether she went back inside, no one knows. Simon says she didn't and there were no other witnesses. No other *reliable* witnesses at any rate.'

She stressed the word reliable, and I felt some sympathy for the police. Trying to build a picture of events from the collective memory of a couple of hundred clubbers couldn't be a whole heap of fun.

'Trouble was, at first the police assumed she'd run away. Thought she'd had enough of being a single parent, of responsibility – that she'd be back within a couple of days with her tail between her legs. Then, when she wasn't, they thought she might have fallen into the river or something. They got divers in and everything. So, by the time they started treating it as a possible crime, a lot of CCTV had been lost. The police have been good to me over the years, and I'm not complaining, but those first few weeks, well, I wouldn't wish those on anyone.'

'Did Simon have an alibi?'

'He said he was at the club, and a couple of his friends vouched for him, but who knows? He could have easily sneaked out. You could have killed elephants and none of that lot would have noticed, all smoking their funny tobacco and whatnot. He told the police he'd assumed she'd gone home, because she often got worried about Kyle. He finished at the club, went home to his flat. Apparently had a friend stay the night, but who knows.'

'When did you report Danielle missing?'

'The following morning. I got up about seven. I knew Danielle wasn't back because she always left her bag and coat on the floor when she came in. And often she'd make a snack in the kitchen and there'd be bread and the butter knife – you know stuff lying around everywhere, like teenagers do. I wasn't worried, because sometimes she'd go back to Simon's, so as not to wake us up. I waited until nine and I rang her but there was no answer, which wasn't unusual. I left it another hour and rang again. Straight to voicemail. So, I rang Simon's flat – the landline – and he answered the phone. I asked to speak to Danielle and that's when we realized she wasn't there and she wasn't here.'

'The police interviewed him?'

'Yes, but without a body, they didn't have any evidence. Not enough to charge him.'

'Where is Simon now?'

'Last I heard he'd left Nottingham. Good riddance, I say. I bumped into him a few times, after Danielle disappeared. Couldn't bear to see his smug grin.'

'Yes, that must have been awful.'

'It's funny that it's Leeds. That's the only thing that gets me thinking – she was so excited about going to Leeds Fest. But she'd never commit suicide. Not my Danielle. Did she leave a note – your girl?'

'No, I don't think so. At least if she did, we haven't found it.'

'Poor lamb. It's her family I feel sorry for – out there flinching every time the phone rings. They never found Danielle's mobile. I still ring it from time to time. Just in case.'

That reminded me about Vicky's possessions. 'Did Danielle wear a necklace, do you know?'

'Yes. She never took off – a locket, not an expensive one. One of those ones that's shaped like a love heart. Had a picture of Simon in it, of course.'

I put the phone down on Mrs Goodwin, after promising to get back in touch if we found out anymore information. I wondered whether Topper had managed to come up with anything. Surely the police kept DNA samples of every discovered body in case years later a relative turned up? Which made me wonder again where Vicky Doe was buried. Had anyone gone to a funeral for her? Or was her body put in the incinerator along with all the other discarded evidence of her life?

*

I must have fallen asleep pondering these questions, because the next thing I knew it was almost midnight and I'd dribbled down the side of my mouth. I flicked the gas fire off, shut the door to the kitchen where my pile of half-peeled potatoes sat on the kitchen table, and staggered up to bed, wondering why Jo hadn't woken me up. But as I got to the top of the stairs, the answer to that question became clear. Jo's bedroom door was ajar and her curtains were open. I switched on her light. Her room was empty. Jo wasn't back.

Chapter 13

It took about three seconds for me to go from semi-comatose to adrenalin-fuelled-hyper-awake. I stood in the doorway to Jo's room, staring at the empty double bed. Random phrases rushing through my brain. I'm not Jo's mother. She's entitled to stay out overnight. I mean she's a big girl and all that but it was weird that she hadn't rung. I stumbled back down the stairs. My phone was still in the front room, but the screen was blank. I didn't see the point of a mobile phone if it needed charging every five minutes. I plugged it in, waited until the screen came to life and checked voicemail. No messages.

Knowing Jo, she'd have bumped into someone she knew in town, ending up going for a pint, which would lead to several. I wouldn't have thought she'd have gone for an all-nighter though, not in the middle of a case. I flicked through my contacts, all three of them, until I came to her number and pressed call. It went straight to voicemail. I hung up without leaving a message. I went back upstairs and stared at her empty bed for a few more moments and then went into my own room, because I couldn't think of anything else to do. I knew sleep was no longer an option. A few hours of pacing the floorboards, at least metaphorically speaking, waiting for dawn, beckoned. I didn't know where to start looking. If she hadn't shown up by morning I'd have to decide what to do.

*

I was propped up in bed, smoking a cigarette, when I heard the front door go. Heard footsteps on the stairs, the first flight from the ground floor up to our flat. Then the second set, from the lounge up to our bedrooms. I sat up straighter, listening, ready to call out, but something stopped me. I paused, trying to think what that something was. Jo was creeping up the stairs; in fact, I'd swear she'd taken off her boots, which would have accounted for the pause between the two steps of stairs. She also didn't sound drunk. I checked myself and all those weird sentences that were playing round my head. *What time do you call this?; Look what the cat dragged in* ...

I didn't move. I refused to play the wounded, Billy No-mates flatmate. She was entitled to go out without me. I heard her bedroom door close and checked the time. Twelve minutes past four. I stubbed out my cigarette, closed my sash window and pulled the duvet over my head.

Having spent half the night awake, I didn't wake up until gone nine. I crept out of bed and listened outside Jo's bedroom door until I heard her gentle snores. I knew it would be lunchtime before she surfaced.

I went downstairs and into the kitchen. Saturday morning and again the weather looked dry. I put my trainers on and went for a run, thinking I'd just do a lap or two of the park. But once I started I couldn't stop and I ran and ran, down to Kirkstall and along the canal, until my lungs felt like they were bleeding and my legs refused to take me any further. I got my breath back sitting on a park bench watching the skateboarders.

When I got back to the flat, Jo was in the kitchen, eating a fried egg sandwich. Yolk dripped down her chin. It was just after twelve.

'What happened to you last night?' I asked in the most casual voice I could muster. 'I made you tea.'

Jo pulled a face at the pile of half-peeled potatoes that I'd forgotten to clear from the kitchen table. 'Sorry I missed it.'

'I was going to make your tea,' I said, as I kicked off my trainers. 'I gave up when you didn't come home.'

'Soz.' Jo picked the plate containing her half-eaten egg sandwich and a glass of water up from the worktop and moved towards the kitchen door. 'Make us a brew, will you? Kettle's boiled.'

Jo's mug was already on the worktop, next to the kettle. I pushed a teabag into it. 'So, where were you?'

She turned her back to me and opened the door with her elbow. 'Thought I'd call in on Sara on the way back, make sure she was OK.'

'Oh.' I let that information sink in and realized it hadn't come as a shock. 'Right. What, you were with her all night?'

'Good run?'

'What time did you get back?'

'Dunno. Lost track of time.' She stepped into the hall and I followed her through into the lounge.

'Right.' I realized I'd said that already. 'So, what did you do, I mean talk about? With Sara?'

'I got a contact for the free party network thing. There's one tonight.'

'A party?'

'I think we should go. Mind if I put the news on?'

'Where?'

'That's part of the adventure. They put the details up on this closed Facebook Group after six. Magical mystery trip.'

'Right.' I cursed myself and wished I could stop saying that word – I sounded worse than Aunt Edie when she'd got the hump. I tried to shake myself out of it.

'Up for it?'

'What else?' I asked.

'Eh?'

'What else did you talk about? You spent all night with her. Getting the details of a Facebook Group can't have taken that long.'

'Not all night.' Jo flicked the TV on.

'It was after four.'

'God. Really?' She sounded genuinely surprised.

I pulled a face at her.

'What's with all the questions? I just thought she might need a friend. Thought I'd show my solidarity with her.'

'Solidarity?'

'Sisterhood.'

'Sisterhood?'

'Why are you repeating everything I say?'

I stopped myself. Took a breath. 'I'm not. It just seems like a weird thing to do. And why didn't you ring?'

'I did. Your phone was switched off.'

'I didn't have a missed call.'

Jo picked up my phone where it was still charging. 'Yes, you do. Look.'

I stared at the screen. 'That wasn't there last night.'

'Thought you were in one of your "I need to be alone" heads. Thought I'd give you a bit of space.'

'Right.'

'She's been raped, Lee. She needs support.' Jo sat down on the settee and took another mouthful of her sandwich. She held up her hand in front of her mouth so I wouldn't see the contents when she spoke. 'What's rattled your cage?'

'Nothing.'

'Sure?'

'Positive.'

'OK. Great. What did you get up to?' Jo turned her attention to the TV. I listened to the presenter announce another set of cutbacks to essential social services. I picked up the remote and switched the TV off. Jo stared at me, like she didn't recognize me.

'I spoke to Louise Goodwin. She's Danielle's mother, one of the missing women Mae told me about.' I admit I might have been trying to make it sound like I'd been hard on the case while she'd been 'chatting' to Sara, but the subtext appeared to go unnoticed. 'I think Danielle might be Vicky.'

'Fucking hell. Why didn't you say?'

'You weren't here.'

'What makes you so sure?'

I considered withholding my information. I didn't feel like Jo had earned the right to it. But the truth was I couldn't contain it. I was desperate to discuss it. 'She disappeared six days before Vicky's body turned up.'

'Could be coincidence.'

'She was supposed to be going to Leeds Fest, which puts her in Leeds. She'd have got the train from Nottingham to Leeds. And she might have been depressed. Her mum said she'd really struggled after the birth. The father of her baby wanted nothing to do with her after she got pregnant. Then she meets a new man who turns out to be a wanker. That's enough reasons to want to kill yourself.'

'Sounds promising.'

'AND she wore a necklace. Never took it off, her mother said.'

'Why Roundhay Park? That's nowhere near Leeds Fest.'

'I've got a theory about that too. Want to bet the father of her child lived there? He was married, and maybe a teacher, her mum said. A man with a lot to lose.'

'How old was Danielle?'

'Seventeen when she disappeared. I know, it's a bit young.' Martin had said the post-mortem had put Vicky somewhere in her early twenties. 'Wonder how reliable those post-mortems are? How do they tell? I mean girls can make themselves look miles older than they are.'

'I'm sure they're not relying on her make-up.'

'I know but it's not like counting the rings in trees, is it? What's the scope for error?'

'So what do we do next? Should we tell the police?'

'Mrs Goodwin doesn't want to believe that it's Danielle. She says her daughter wouldn't have committed suicide.'

'What about the strychnine? Any idea where she might have got that from?'

I hadn't thought to ask about that, mainly because I hadn't wanted Louise Goodwin to know how her daughter chose to die. If it was her daughter. And if it was a choice. 'No.'

Jo switched the TV back on. 'We have to hope Topper comes through for us.'

'Great, we're pinning our hopes on someone I wouldn't trust to feed the cat. I think we go see this boyfriend of Danielle's. Simon. Mrs Goodwin thinks he killed her.'

'Did she say that?'

'It was obvious that's what she thinks. He's a DJ – can't be that hard to find, surely.'

'Let's have a look then. See if he's still going.'

Jo got on Google and found him within minutes, still DJing. 'Aren't blogs great,' said Jo. 'The answer to the universe is out there on a blog, somewhere.'

'Surely that means he can't have killed her,' I said. 'If you'd got away with murder you wouldn't be advertising yourself on Facebook?'

Jo shrugged. 'Seven years on, I guess you might start to feel confident you'd got away with it. He's playing a gig on Monday night. Perhaps we should go and pay him a visit?'

'Playing a gig where?' I leaned over Jo's shoulder to look at her phone screen.

'Bristol.'

'Bristol. That's miles away, isn't it?' Geography was never my strong point.

'It's at the bottom of Wales,' said Jo. 'Not that far.'

'Better see what kind of state we're in after tonight.' I thought about the party ahead of us and my stomach flipped, in anticipation or fear, I couldn't say. I hadn't been out for a long time, not since I gave up drinking. And I hadn't done two nights out in a row in years. Growing older has taught me I'm not that much of a going out kind of person. Strip away alcohol from your average night out and there's very little to recommend the experience. After my momentary lapse on the last case, I was scared of putting my sobriety to the test. I was scared of going to pubs and clubs because I knew what temptations lay there. I could smell the alcohol before I stepped through the door.

Of course, going to a free party was a different kind of test. It wouldn't be alcohol there, but recreational party drugs. I don't have the same problem with party drugs. I never got addicted to them because the come downs were always too much of an ask. And, I learned the hard way, you can't dodge them, you have to come down, eventually. I hadn't taken any drugs, apart from the odd spliff, for a long time, probably a year or more.

My phone rang. I glanced at Jo before I pressed answer.

'Who's that?' said a voice.

'Lee,' I said.

'Skinny one?'

'Topper,' I mouthed to Jo. 'Hi,' I said into the phone. 'How—?'

'Info.'

'What?'

'Same place.'

'You mean meet by the canal again?'

'In an hour.'

The phone clicked. 'Man of few words,' I said to Jo.

I finished telling Jo about my conversation with Louise Goodwin as we got ready to drive into town to meet Topper. 'I said we'd ring her as soon as we knew anything more.'

'There's still the other two as well, don't forget,' said Jo. 'Marcia and Jenny. We have to keep an open mind.'

'I know.' But even as I said the words, I was sure it was Danielle.

'What a pisser, not knowing whether your relatives are dead or alive.'

'Innit.' I tried to keep the sarcasm from my voice but I knew I'd failed. Jo knew I'd grown up without knowing anything about my dad, or any of my relatives on his side of the family. I didn't meet him until after my mum died.

'Soz. I didn't—'

'I told Mae to give them all my mobile number. All three families, I mean. Actually, one didn't have a family – just a social worker. That's Jenny. She lived in Harehills.'

'And have you actually got it with you?'

'What?'

'Your phone?'

I pulled it out of my back pocket and held it up like a policewoman might hold up her warrant card.

Jo grinned and punched me on the arm. 'First time for everything,' she said.

Topper was leaning against the same wall. A man of habit, I couldn't help but think, but I scotched the thought as quickly as I could. I didn't want to think about his habits.

'No joy,' he said, as we approached him. He stood up straighter, kept his hands in his pockets.

'You brought us all this way to tell us, "No joy"?' I said. 'You said you had information.'

'The property of the deceased has been disposed of. Cleaned out four years ago.' He shrugged. 'Can't keep everything. You should see the mountain of crap we have to deal with.'

'Where did it go?'

'Gets burned. Most of it. Anything valuable is flogged. Or it should be.'

'Should be?' Jo had noticed the same niggle of something in his voice that I had.

He paused, glanced around. 'When we get ready to dispose of evidence we let the original investigating officer know. They're sent an email, giving them two weeks' notice.'

'And?'

'And sometimes they write back saying, no don't – something's come up, but usually we don't hear anything and everything's destroyed.'

'Go on.'

'Well, I pulled the records of this one. We emailed the

investigation team, as per. Never heard anything back. So we disposed of all the evidence.'

'Great.' I couldn't really see where he was going with this. 'So there's nothing?'

'Well.' He grinned. 'I noticed that one of the original investigation team had come back.'

'What do you mean?'

'He'd signed into the Property Stores – everything is logged these days, Jesus, you want to see the paperwork – and he'd asked for a look at the box again.'

'Why had he done that?'

'Great minds. That's what I thought. So, I thought I'd do you girls a favour. I went to see him.'

'And?' It was like pulling teeth. I couldn't help but think Topper was loving the power he had over us.

'Now I don't want you going shouting about any of this. Policemen aren't what you think.' He nodded towards Jo. 'We're only human. We're just trying to keep the good guys alive and the bad guys off the street.'

'I know that,' I said as Jo raised her eyebrows. I nipped her on her arm.

'Anyway, this policeman, let's call him Fred, had only just started when your body turned up. He was first on the scene – just round the corner when it got called in. You never know which ones are going to speak to you – just sometimes something'll get under your skin and you can't say why. Well, this had happened to our Fred. So when we write in, a couple of years later, saying we're about to chuck all the stuff, he comes for a last look.'

'Right,' said Jo and I knew she was having trouble working with Topper's explanation of Fred's motivation, but I willed her to let it slide.

'He takes a look and sees all her possessions laid out and it takes him back to that day, to feeling helpless.'

'Cut to the chase, Topper,' said Jo. 'What did he do?'

'He took something.'

'He took something?' I repeated as the implications sank in.

'Which is, of course, strictly against the rules, especially the new rules. Mind, this was before the Hammer business.'

'What did he take?'

'Nothing valuable, nothing he could have profited from. There's no ulterior motive. But if anyone ever found out, he'd get into serious trouble and he's a good copper.'

'We won't tell a soul,' I said.

'He knew it was all about to be destroyed.'

'What did he take?' The suspense was killing me.

He pulled something from his pocket and dangled it from his fingers. A fine silver chain with a small pendant. I grabbed at the pendant so I could see it more clearly, laid it on the palm of my hand. It was half a silver heart, the right-hand side, with a jagged cut down the middle. It wasn't a locket though. It was a thin sliver of silver and it had been engraved. It said 'ters'. And then underneath 'ever'. I held it up so Jo could see it clearer.

'Where was it?' I asked. I turned it over in the vain hope it might look more like a locket from the back.

'In his desk drawer. He couldn't really explain it. Just said he had a feeling to keep it, that's all.'

'Can we have it?'

'Don't see why not. It's down as destroyed. And I told Fred it wasn't a good idea to hang onto it. You can never tell anyone where you got it though.'

'Promise.'

'There's one condition.' He dangled the pendant in front of my face.

'What's that?'

'If you find out who she is, Fred wants to know.'

I nodded. Topper dropped the chain into my hand and I clasped my fingers around the metal. I felt a fizz of something and I knew we were a step closer to Vicky. I felt her in me, around me. I know that sounds weird but it's how it was. Jo linked arms with me and we said goodbye to Topper. A decent bloke, I thought, in the end. Just goes to show you never can tell.

'What do you think it means?' I said as Jo and I walked back down the canal towards town. '"ters, ever".'

'I know what it means,' said Jo. 'I've seen them before – somewhere there's another chain with the other half heart. They usually say "best friends forever". Suzie Hall got me one when we were like nine.'

'Best friends?'

'Yes. And the heart is split down the middle and you each wear half. This one didn't say "Best Friends Forever", though, it said "Sisters, Forever". Somewhere there's a sister with a chain with a half a heart pendant and she's got the left-hand side which says "Sis" and "For". When you join them together you get "Sisters Forever".'

When I hear the word 'sister' it's like putting on tight shoes when you have blisters on your heel. 'Vicky has a sister.'

'And because Vicky had the ends of the words, I'm betting she was the younger sister. So make that an older sister.'

I clutched Jo's arm tighter. 'Mrs Goodwin told me she had a baby girl – Sophie, she said. She died, only lived a few days. But that would still make her Danielle's sister.'

'Did you ask Mrs Goodwin about the necklace?'

'Yes. She said it was a locket. With a photo of Danielle's boyfriend, the DJ, in it. But maybe she had two necklaces.'

Jo pulled a face and I knew she wasn't convinced, but it was possible. Maybe Danielle didn't want her mother to know that she was upset about her lost sister. People with depression clung to all kinds of morbid thoughts; I knew that from my mother. Maybe Danielle had kept her feelings about the dead baby hidden because she didn't want to upset her mother.

'We should check whether either of the other two had sisters,' said Jo.

'I'll ring Mae and see what she knows. And I'd better ring Mrs Goodwin too – see whether it's possible this belonged to Danielle. Maybe we should drive down to Nottingham and show it to her?'

'Let's try Mae first,' said Jo.

I still had the necklace in my hand, felt the metal warm in

my grasp. I knew we were getting closer to finding out who Vicky was. And when we knew who she was, we'd find out why she'd done what she'd done. I let go of Jo's arm and sprinted back towards the van.

Chapter 14

Mrs Goodwin didn't answer her phone so I left a message asking her to call me. Even though it was Saturday, Mae had given me her personal mobile number and she struck me as the kind of person who would want to be kept up to date – the kind of person who wasn't in her job for the wage. I told her I'd spoken to Danielle's mother the day before, and I told her about the necklace we'd just been given. I didn't tell her where we'd got it from and she didn't ask. 'Brilliant,' she said. 'That gives you a real chance.'

'Did any of the three of them have a sister, do you know?' I pressed to put the speakerphone on so that Jo could hear both sides of the conversation as we sat side by side in the van.

'Stupidly, I've left my notes at work,' said Mae. 'I know Marcia has a brother. She's the one that grew up in Chapeltown, has been missing for nearly twelve years. I'm fairly certain there's just him now Marcia's gone. And I'm not sure how much help you'll get there. I spoke to him yesterday. Their mother's in a home with early-onset dementia. He was adamant he didn't want it all raking up again. He's a difficult character.'

'Difficult?'

Mae paused and I knew she was taking the time to choose her words. 'Obviously it's hard for the siblings left behind. It's classic prodigal child – the one who disappears is the one the family's attention is focused on. Remaining siblings can experience feelings of jealousy, isolation.'

I didn't want to think too much about sibling rivalry. I pushed the thoughts from my head, made myself focus on the investigation. If Vicky's necklace was proof she had had a sister, we could cross Marcia off the list. Which left two possibles. 'Danielle had a sister who died when she was just a few days old – Louise Goodwin told me that last night.'

'You spoke to her? Good. Yes, I know. Mrs Goodwin keeps in regular contact. Poor woman, she's been through so much. She's on her own: her husband died. There's just her and her grandson, Danielle's son.'

'She said.'

Jo leaned across me. 'What about the last one, Jenny something?'

'Jenny Crawley. I'm pretty sure she only had a mother, in Poland. That's why the social worker contacted us, when she retired. She was worried that no one else knew of Jenny's existence – not in this country anyway.'

No one knew of her existence. I thought about that for a moment. We believe we're part of society when really we're so alone it's possible to die without anyone knowing your name. No matter how shit I am at relationships, I don't want to die like that. I knew there was a risk, though. I mean, I only really have Jo and Aunt Edie and let's face it, Aunt Edie isn't going to be around forever. 'Have you managed to get hold of the social worker?'

'I left a message. I'll try her again.'

I ended the call to Mae and turned to Jo. 'Marcia didn't have a sister. And you'd think if Jenny had a sister she'd have been in touch with Missing Persons. It's got to be Danielle.'

I was determined to bring Mrs Goodwin closure, even if it wasn't the kind she was hoping for.

Jo turned the key in the ignition and the van growled into life. 'You said the mother sounded pretty certain that Danielle would never commit suicide.'

'No one wants to believe their loved ones would commit suicide. Maybe Danielle was more upset about her sister's death than she'd let on. I'll get Martin to look at the residents of the flats again. If there's a married teacher living there, we might be able to prove he's the father of Danielle's child. That would explain why she did it there.'

'Didn't Mae say there are hundreds of missing women who have never been reported? Chances are it's someone we've never heard of.'

I lit a fag. 'Great.'

'That's what happened when they caught Fred West – they were digging up bodies from his back garden – the bodies of all these young women and no one had the slightest clue who they were.'

'Great,' I said, again. 'Fucking great.'

'Where now?' asked Jo.

It was the middle of the afternoon and my stomach hurt. 'Let's go back to Roundhay Park. We can get a coffee and see if there's anyone around at the flats. It's time to go door to door. Somewhere, someone knows something.'

The sun had come out and the trees were just getting their leaves. The world teetered on the brink of spring and we drove up through the city centre, the world getting greener as we headed north out of the city towards Roundhay Park. We parked the van and bought takeout coffees from the Lakeside café.

The park looked even more inviting, basking in the sunshine, as we climbed the steep hill to the flats. We walked through the gates into the complex and saw an older couple threading their way through the car park. 'Morning,' Jo called out. 'Beautiful day.'

'Isn't it just,' said the man. 'Are you visiting someone?'

He looked at us both, waiting for an answer. He seemed to stare more at Jo's Afro than at me and the expression on his face said he didn't think we belonged, which of course was true. We didn't.

I decided to go for broke. 'We're private investigators,' I said, flashing him my badge. 'How long have you lived here?'

'Private investigators?' He frowned at us and his whole manner suggested he didn't believe us. He glanced at his wife and then back to me. 'Investigating what?'

'Just answer the question,' I said. I don't often drink coffee and the caffeine had hit my bloodstream like speed.

He scowled at me but he was too polite not to respond, even though it was obvious he didn't want to. 'We bought the flat twelve years ago.'

'Ah, then you'll know all about it,' said Jo.

'What's that?'

'The body that was found round the front, the one tied to the statue.'

'Oh that dreadful business,' his wife said. She shuddered and pulled her gloves a little tighter around her wrists. 'I don't know why you'd want to be bringing all that up again.'

'We're trying to find out who she was, why she did what she did.' I fixed her with my hardest stare. 'Aren't you curious?'

'No. Not at all. I'm just glad we weren't here when it happened.'

'I thought you said you'd lived here twelve years?'

'We were at our summer house in Portugal when they found the body.' She smiled at her good fortune. 'We're never here in August. We only heard about it afterwards.'

'Are there any teachers that you know of, living here?'

'I rather think a teacher's salary wouldn't stretch to a flat here. Not unless they had family money. It's mainly successful entrepreneurs, lawyers, we've even had celebrities.'

'Have there been any developments?' her husband asked. 'In the case of the body? I assume there must have been if you're interested after all this time. At the time, nobody knew who she was or where she'd come from; the police never managed to find out anything, far as we knew. Has that changed?'

'We're working some new leads, yes,' said Jo. 'Obviously I can't give you the details.'

'Well, I'm afraid we can't help,' the wife said, linking her arm through her husband's. 'And please don't go making a song and dance about it: it's not the kind of thing that happens round here.'

I could see what she meant, as the sun beamed down on the white stucco and bounced off the windows. 'Don't worry, property prices won't be affected,' Jo mumbled as the couple walked off, the woman pulling her jacket around herself, because even though the sun was shining there was still a cool breeze.

'They weren't exactly what you'd call forthcoming,' I said to Jo. 'Let's hope there's someone more helpful inside.'

'I wouldn't hold your breath,' said Jo. 'They're all the same round here. Tory voters, every last one of them.'

'You can't make sweeping generalizations,' I said. 'Not from where a person lives.'

'Want to bet?'

'Makes sense to start at the front,' I said. 'They're the flats most likely to have seen something.'

*

We made our way down the path that led round the side of the building and out to the front of the property – the side that overlooked the park. Fixed to the wall by the door was a keypad with twenty buttons on it, arranged in four rows of five. I pressed the first five buzzers, starting at the bottom of the keypad, and waited. No one answered. We waited another minute more and then Jo pressed the next five.

Again nothing and I was just about to start on the third

row, when a disembodied voice crackled through the intercom. 'Yes?'

'Hi. We'd like to ask some questions about ...'

The intercom clicked and fell silent.

'Hello?' said Jo.

No one replied.

'See,' she said.

'Just because he's hung up on you doesn't mean he votes Tory.'

Jo pressed the five buzzers on the third row. Again, no one answered. 'They're not exactly socially minded, though,' I conceded. 'Or maybe they just go out a lot.'

Jo pressed the next five. 'They're the kind of people that don't get people popping by. You'd make an arrangement to see these people. Book in advance.'

'Come in,' said a voice, and we both jumped. It was hard to tell whether it was male or female. Or even human. It had a dalek quality to it. The door beeped and a green light flashed on the keypad. 'I've been waiting for you.'

Chapter 15

The door clicked. Jo glanced at me before putting her hand on the door and pushing it open. It swung back to reveal the lobby. Jo leaned into the intercom again. 'Just remind me of the flat number,' she said, but there was no reply.

We stepped into the lobby. Postboxes lined one wall. I saw a staircase off to the left and a lift directly in front of us. 'Let's take the stairs,' said Jo, which seemed like a good plan, seeing as we had no idea which floor we were heading for. We climbed the steps slowly, as I wondered who we were going to meet.

At the top of each flight of stairs was a door. We opened each one as we reached it and looked down identical corridors, all carpeted with a rich russet brown carpet. There was no sign of life in the first five. Jo's breathing got louder the higher we climbed.

I pushed open the sixth door we encountered and looked inside the sixth identical corridor, only this time there was someone standing towards the end of it. It was difficult to make out their features as behind them, at the far end of the corridor, was a floor-to-ceiling window, with light streaming through it, which threw the figure into silhouette, but it was clear the person was female. Or at least, someone wearing a skirt. I shouldn't make assumptions.

'Come on,' they said. 'I haven't got long.'

I turned to Jo who nodded at me to go down the corridor, towards where the figure stood. When I turned back though, the figure had disappeared. Jo gave me a nudge and I made my way down the corridor towards where she'd been stood, Jo a step or two behind me. We passed the closed doors of two other flats and as I got closer to the window I saw an open door to a flat on the right-hand side.

We drew level and paused outside for a moment, peering into the flat through the open door. There was no sign of the person, and the place was so creepy I wondered whether she was a ghost. All I could see was a small hallway where a large chest of drawers dominated one wall. On top of it were twenty or more photographs all in frames, all jostling for position. All portrait pictures, one face, sometimes two. Children and adults. Jo nudged me again and I stepped across the threshold.

'Come through, I'm in the lounge,' a voice called out.

I frowned at Jo. I counted four closed doors off the hallway – how were we supposed to know which one was the lounge? I moved towards the most likely suspect, and pushed the door ajar. My stomach clenched, unsure of what to expect. The first thing I noticed was the windows, big windows that came almost to floor level, and beyond them the gardens. We were at the front of the building – the side that overlooked the park. The next thing I noticed was the statue, down in the garden, the place where Vicky Doe's body had been found.

I knew then that this was the flat, this was the woman who'd been watching us when we'd visited two days before, on Thursday morning: the ghostly face I'd seen, pressed against the glass. The face I wasn't sure whether I'd imagined.

'I saw you, the other day. You were watching us,' I said to the lady sitting in the armchair.

The next thing I noticed were the stuffed animals. Not real ones. I mean not dead ones. Stuffed toys – teddy bears, but not just teddy bears. There were stuffed bunny rabbits, monkeys, giraffes, polar bears, a lemur hung from the ceiling. She could have opened an entire zoo from the looks of things. Some of the teddy bears wore clothes. She had a fluffy cat, all curled up on her lap. At first glance I thought it was real, but it was too still.

'I always knew someone would come looking for her,' she said. 'Stands to reason. Eventually someone would have to come.'

She was small, frail, but not so old as I'd thought when I'd been stood outside, when I'd caught a glimpse of her. Probably in her fifties, her hair still dark, perhaps a little too dark.

'We're sorry to bother you. I'm Lee, Lee Winters,' I said. 'What's your name?'

'Linda Pamela Jenkinson. Flat 44, Park View Court, Roundhay, Leeds.'

'Hi, Linda. I'm Jo,' Jo said. 'What a lovely flat.'

'I chose the colours,' she said, and I nodded as I took in the lilac and pale green colour scheme.

'We run a missing persons' bureau,' I said.

'She's not missing.'

I didn't understand at first, and then I remembered I'd made the same point, the night that Martin had first told us about this case. I turned to Jo and let her explain.

'Are you talking about the woman they found tied to the statue out there?' Jo crossed to the window and pointed out. 'Seven years ago?'

'The dead girl.' The woman put the stuffed cat to one side and joined Jo at the window. 'Down there.'

'No one knows who she was,' said Jo. 'Somewhere out there is a family that misses her. They don't know that she's dead.'

Tears welled in the woman's eyes. 'They didn't want her to die.'

I thought that was an odd thing to say but I let it pass. It was obvious Linda Jenkinson was odd, but it takes all sorts to make a world. And I've never trusted anyone who claims to be normal.

'Let's all sit down,' Jo said.

I guided the woman back to her chair, and Jo and I glanced around for a place we could both sit, which wasn't obvious. I noticed a tray on the coffee table with a china tea set – matching teapot, jug, cup and saucer, the teaspoon placed on a folded piece of kitchen roll. In the end I sat on a large pouffe I think they're called – not quite a chair but too big to be called a footstool. Jo perched on the arm of the settee. There wasn't any room on the settee itself on account of all the stuffed toys. I noticed Paddington Bear in amongst the creatures, wearing his trademark duffle coat and red wellington boots. He sat next to a teddy bear dressed as a nurse.

'You were here when she was found,' Jo said. It wasn't really a question, more a statement of fact.

'I have a job.'

I glanced at Jo again. 'That's great,' she said.

'I work nights.'

'Are you a nurse?' I couldn't really picture her as one but it was the first thing that came into my head.

'I work at Tesco. It's open twenty-four hours a day. Except on Sundays. On Sundays it closes at four o'clock in the afternoon.'

'What do you do there?' asked Jo. 'At Tesco?'

'I stack the tins onto the shelves. In the night-time because there aren't as many customers because most people are in bed.'

I felt the blood in my veins pulse a little quicker under my skin. 'What time do you finish?'

'Sometimes I'll work until four o'clock in the morning and sometimes I work until six o'clock. I like working until six o'clock the best.'

'Why's that?'

'It's better because it's daylight when I leave work at six o'clock. I don't like the dark.'

'I can imagine,' said Jo. 'I don't like it either.'

'In the summertime it's light when I leave work at four o'clock in the morning. In the winter it's still dark, but it won't be long until it gets light.'

'Can you remember what time you finished work on that night – the night of 29th of August – seven years ago? When they found the dead girl in the garden?'

Linda reached for the stuffed cat, put it on her knee again and stroked between its ears, all the way along the length of its back. 'That night was different.'

'Different because?'

'Because I was supposed to finish at four o'clock but Daniel asked me to sort out the frozen cabinets. I don't usually do the frozen cabinets because they are very cold.' She performed a mock shiver, and I couldn't help it, I almost laughed.

'So you worked a bit later?' said Jo. 'On the night of the 29th of August?'

'I worked until quarter to five in the morning. Three quarters of an hour extra. Then you get paid overtime, which is twelve point five per cent more than ordinary time.'

'How do you get home at that time?' asked Jo. 'Do you walk?'

'Daniel rings a taxi for me. I get the same taxi driver every night, unless it's Saturday morning because Tariq doesn't work Saturday mornings. He has to take his boys to football practice in Dewsbury. They are growing up fast. Then I get Samir but he doesn't like talking so much.'

'And the taxi drops you at the back of the building? By the car park?'

'Yes.'

'And you walk round to the front door?'

'I get my bird feed from Tesco. Daniel lets me.'

I remembered the array of different tubes and containers hanging near the statue. My skin goose-bumped. 'You went to fill your bird feeders?'

No one said anything for a moment as we all allowed the

implications of this seemingly simple decision to sink in. It was August, probably around five o'clock in the morning – just beginning to get light. Poor Linda, making her way in the half-gloom to put out seeds for the birds and instead she sees a naked woman, tied to the statue. Must have frightened the living daylights out of her. I kept my voice low. 'Can you tell us what you saw?'

'The dead girl. Her skin, shiny, like it was wet. I didn't touch her.'

'Was it you that called the police?' asked Jo.

She shook her head and looked at her hands, folded around the cat on her lap. I glanced over at Jo and told her with my eyes not to push it.

'Did you see anyone else?' I asked.

'No. Just her. All alone.'

'Did you check whether she was dead?'

'I didn't touch her.'

'What did you do?'

'I put the bird feed back in my bag. They eat berries too. And worms although in dry weather the worms can burrow too far underground.'

'Did you notice anything strange?' As soon as the words were out of my mouth, I cursed their stupidity. 'I mean, apart from the woman.'

'She didn't have her clothes on. It wasn't cold, but it must have been horrible for her, that everyone would see her without her clothes on.'

'Did you see her clothes?'

'They were folded up. I didn't touch them.'

'You went up close to her?'

'Did she have a handbag?' asked Jo.

'I didn't touch it.'

'I knew it,' said Jo. She turned to me. 'So where's her bag?'

'Are you sure?' I asked Linda. 'Are you sure she had a handbag?'

'It was on top of the pile of clothes. A white handbag, with a silver clasp. It had a scratch on the front, where the leather was peeling off.'

'You've got a very good memory,' I said.

'Yes,' she said, and her eyes darted to the photographs on top of the bureau. 'I remember everything.'

'How can you be so sure she had a handbag? It was a long time ago.'

'The letter was on top of it,' she said.

'The letter?' My throat went dry and I heard a ticking. I traced the sound, saw the clock on the mantelpiece, one of those ones with gold balls underneath it that are in some kind of perpetual motion. 'What letter?'

'She wrote me a letter,' Linda said, and I saw the tears well in her eyes again.

'She wrote you a letter?' Why would the dead woman write Linda a letter? We were in the presence of madness. I pulled a face at Jo. She had picked up the large stuffed panda sitting next to her and was holding him on her knee.

'How do you afford the rent on a place like this working at Tesco?' I asked.

'It's not rented,' she said. 'I bought it with my inheritance, nine years ago.'

'Your inheritance?'

'When Mother died.'

'Did your parents live in these flats? When they were alive?' Jo added, rather needlessly in my opinion.

'No.' Linda's eyes widened. 'They lived in Harrogate because the air in cities isn't clean. Father would never live in the city. Cities are full of sin.'

I swallowed. Linda's father didn't sound like a barrel of laughs, although he may have had a point. That's probably what I like about cities. That they're full of sin. Takes the focus off my own shortcomings. 'Did you know the woman in the garden?'

'No.'

'So, why would she write you a letter?'

Jo pulled a face at me, put down the panda and moved closer to Linda. 'What did the letter say?'

Linda placed the cat down on the floor by the fire. It remained in its curled-up position, quite lifelike for a stuffed toy. Linda stood up and crossed to a bureau in the corner of the room. It was an elegant piece of furniture, its surface covered in framed photographs like the chest of drawers in the hall. Most of the photographs were old pictures, black-and-white and sepia. Posed, formal portraits in photographers' studios. Linda pulled at the top of the bureau and the leaf dropped down and formed a desk. Inside were lots of little cubbyholes, all stuffed full of papers. Without rummaging at all, she plucked out a small white envelope.

'You kept the letter?' I said, unable to keep the excitement from my voice.

A thin envelope. Nothing written on the outside. Linda handed it to me and I had this moment where I felt proud that she trusted me. 'This is the letter you found by the body?'

'Linda, did anyone ever come here and ask to see this letter?' Jo asked as she moved to sit next to me on the pouffe. 'Did the police ask you about this letter?'

'I don't like men,' she said. 'Men do bad things.'

My hands trembled as I opened the flap. A piece of paper inside, with a fancy kind of silver edging. I tugged it out and unfolded the sheet of paper. It was handwritten, the sentences sloping to the right across the page. The handwriting was easy to read, the letters more printed than joined up. I read the words aloud. '"I know. You know. And somewhere, out there, someone else knows. I want you to live the rest of your days knowing that. That out there, somewhere, someone else knows."'

Chapter 16

I read the note another two times in my head before I handed it to Jo. What did it mean? My brain tried to make sense of the words. Who knew what? I turned to our rather weird hostess. 'You didn't know this woman. The woman by the statue?'

Linda shook her head.

'You'd never seen her before?'

'No.'

'How did you know this letter was for you?'

'It says that I know.'

'You know what?'

'And she knows.'

I pleaded with Jo to make sense of things for me, but she raised her eyebrows in a way that gave me the impression I was on my own. 'What do you both know?' I asked Linda.

'I cannot talk to you about that. That is a secret. I promised. Please do not ask me again.'

Linda picked up the tray with the tea set and left the room.

I turned to Jo. 'What the fuck?'

Jo shrugged. 'Amazing that she's kept it all this time. Seven years she's had that. I bet she's never spoken to the police. She can't have, or they'd have taken this.'

I stood up and followed Linda through to the kitchen. There was a teddy bear wearing a plastic bib sitting in a high chair at the kitchen table. 'Did you tell the police about the letter?'

She picked up a folded tea towel and refolded it before placing it back down in the exact same spot. 'I think you should leave now. It's time for my boiled egg, with two slices of toast but no butter and then my sleep.'

'Do you know if there are any teachers living in the flats? School teachers?'

'I don't speak to my neighbours. It's best not to get involved.'

'Come on, Lee,' said Jo, behind me. She turned to Linda. 'Thank you so much for all your help, Linda. You did exactly the right thing and now you don't need to worry about this anymore. It's our job now. OK? We'll take the letter. You're not responsible for it anymore.'

'What about the other person?'

'We'll sort that out too. It will all be OK, I promise.'

I stared at Jo. She sounded so certain I didn't even mind that I had absolutely no idea what she was on about. I let her steer me back into the hallway and out of the main door. 'Bye, Linda,' Jo said at the threshold. 'Enjoy your lunch and well done. You've been really brave and you've helped the girl in the garden. You did absolutely the right thing.'

Linda closed the door without saying goodbye. Jo and I

turned and made our way down the corridor towards the staircase.

'What the fuck are you on about?' I said as soon as we were out of earshot.

'Ssh.' Jo pulled my arm and made me walk faster. 'She's doing her best.'

'Why would Vicky Doe, whoever she is, write a letter to Linda?'

'Well it obviously wasn't to her, was it? Linda just happened to find it and assumed it was for her. You can't legislate for that.'

We headed through the door at the end of the corridor and back down the stairs. 'So who was the note to?'

'That's what we need to find out. Whoever the note was to, is the reason Vicky killed herself.'

'And she did kill herself. The note proves that at least.'

Jo continued like she hadn't heard me. 'They're the reason she came here in the first place and the reason she did what she did. She came here to unsettle someone – and that same person took her handbag so the police didn't find it. Whoever that person was, they didn't want her identified.'

I mulled this over as we descended the last flight of stairs. 'And the train ticket fell out of her bag?'

'Must have done. Martin's notes said the ticket was found in bushes near the body.'

We hit the lobby, me still trying to process what we'd just witnessed. 'If Vicky is Danielle, the note could be aimed at the teacher, the father of her child.'

'It's an act of defiance, as well as surrender. Vicky killed herself in the worst way possible because it was better than what she was living with. But whoever she wrote the note to – she's telling them that the truth will out eventually.'

I pictured the note again. "Out there, someone else knows.' Which is sort of true. Danielle's mother knows. Maybe Danielle told her DJ boyfriend too.'

'Vicky tied herself to the statue so that she couldn't be moved. Couldn't be swept aside, hidden.'

'Naked?'

'She's accepted her own powerlessness – she can't bring the perpetrator to justice, but this other person will.'

'Why did Linda think the note was for her?'

'Well, number one, she's bonkers. Number two, it hit home. Linda knows about secrets. About keeping other people's secrets. That's why she thought the letter was for her.'

How the fuck Jo works all this stuff out is beyond me.

'Come on, Lee. It's not rocket science. Fifty quid says Linda's been abused. Probably by her dad, and she's never told anyone.'

'We don't know that.'

'She doesn't sleep at night and she surrounds herself with teddy bears,' Jo said, like that was incontrovertible proof. I opened my mouth to argue but Jo didn't let me get a word in. 'She said men do bad things. She lives in the city because her father would never live in the city. She sees Vicky's dead body, sees the envelope, not addressed to anyone and she opens it.'

'She's got balls,' I said. 'If I found a dead body at that time in the morning, I'd run a mile.'

'Probably not the worst thing that's happened to her.'

'So she reads the note and thinks it's for her?'

'A suicide note from someone who has a secret. Linda's obviously going to think they've got some kind of connection. And the truth is, she's right.'

This was stretching the bounds of credibility too far. 'You think her dad abused Vicky?'

'No.' Jo hit me on the arm. I hate it when she does that because she really doesn't know her own strength. 'Although I did wonder. But her dad lived in Harrogate. And it's too much of a coincidence. No. What I mean is, Linda can identify with Vicky's situation – with her suicide, with her letter, with her desire to get revenge. I bet you next month's wages that Vicky Doe was abused by someone who lives in these flats. She killed herself outside his flat to ...'

'To what?'

'I don't know. To teach him a lesson, to show him what damage he'd caused? To make him sleep less easy?'

'Why didn't she go to the police? Why didn't she name him in the suicide note? Why didn't she put his name on the envelope, for fuck's sake?'

'Because she's a victim. And victims aren't heard or believed most of the time, no matter how many times they tell the truth. And the reasons for that are complex, before you ask.'

I was about to ask but Jo was already pressing the keypad on her phone. I followed her out of the foyer and back into the garden, glad to feel the sun on my skin again, to be reminded that the rest of the world was still there, still going about its business.

*

We walked back down the hill. Jo rang Martin and told him about the note. I could hear the pride in her voice – that we'd found something the original investigation had missed. She asked him to check again whether anyone living in the flats had a criminal record. 'Something might have come out since. You never know.'

We got an overpriced sandwich in the Lakeside café. The place was crammed with buggies and high chairs and crying babies and toddlers having meltdowns. I flinched, couldn't help myself. Why anybody had children was completely beyond me – like tying yourself to an anchor and trying to go for a swim. I tried not to notice that some of the women didn't look much older than me.

We would have sat outside but all the tables were taken so we found ourselves squashed in a corner on a turquoise settee with bright orange cushions and half-eaten jacket potatoes not cleared from the table. Jo stacked everything on a tray and left it on the windowsill.

We'd almost finished when a mobile phone rang. It took me a moment to realize it was mine.

'OK. So you've brought your phone.' Jo gave me the thumbs up. 'Next step is to answer it.'

'It's Nikki,' I said, once I'd checked the screen. 'What am I going to tell her?'

'You can tell her we're taking her case so seriously we're willing to go to an all-night party. Surely that ought to earn us some brownie points.'

I pressed the decline call button. 'We'd have to deliver Matt back to her, with a plausible explanation of where he's been for the past six days, before we're going to get any brownie points with Nikki.'

Chapter 17

When we got home, I wrote up my notes of the day's events and ran a bath. I put my Bluetooth speaker on the shelf and shuffled my favourite chilled-out playlist. I needed to calm down, couldn't understand why I felt so hyper, but something was unsettling me.

I jumped when Jo banged on the door. 'Aunt Edie just rang,' she shouted through. 'She's making us dinner. Figured we should get properly fed up if we're going to an all-night party. Lancashire hotpot. I told her we'd be there for five.'

Jo was right – food was a good idea. I hadn't eaten anything except for that overpriced, half-sandwich in the Lakeside café. Maybe that was why I felt weird. I turned the hot tap on with my toe. I can lie in a bath till I look like a prune.

'I'm going to see Mack,' Jo continued. 'Just in case.'

I knew what that meant. And again, Jo was right. We couldn't go to an all-nighter without something to keep us awake. But apart from a small lapse on our last case, it had been almost a year and a half since I'd had a drink, let alone anything else. I wasn't sure my head was ready for recreational drugs. My mind raced and I tried to slow my breath. Calm.

Undercover was part of the job, but it was taking me back to face my demons.

Aunt Edie had only been in her flat a couple of weeks but it looked like she'd lived there forever. We'd hired a van and brought over all her furniture for her – furniture that'd been in Aunt Edie's house since I used to visit as a child. Her new flat was half the size of her old house, which had itself been tiny, so it was fairly cramped. We sat at her dining table, its wood bleached by the sun and years of vigorous polishing. I tried to eat as much as possible – to line my stomach for the onslaught ahead. My throat didn't seem to want to open though.

'What's the thinking behind this party business?' Aunt Edie asked as she ladled another spoonful of hotpot onto Jo's plate. 'What are you hoping to get?'

'Ideally, Matt,' I said, although as I said the words I realized I had two goals – to find our missing person and to come back with my head still in one piece.

'And if not Matt, someone who knows where he is,' Jo added. 'According to Sara it's the same crowd following the sound system each week. Someone's got to know where he went.'

'I used to love going dancing,' Aunt Edie mused. 'Friday nights at The Empire. Never thought about doing it in a field though. Is there a dance floor?'

'Doubt it,' I said. 'They're usually in woodland.'

'Sara went to one in a cave once. An underground cave.'

My stomach lurched. I couldn't think of anything worse

than being trapped underground with a bunch of off-their-heads ravers. This night was shaping up into a fairly decent attempt at my worst nightmare.

*

We played a game of Scrabble – Aunt Edie kicking our asses like always – and then Jo used Aunt Edie's WIFI to get onto the Facebook Group and get directions. She tried three times. On the first two, there was no mention of a party and I allowed myself to hope that perhaps there wasn't one this week and we could stay at Aunt Edie's, eating her fresh-baked parkin with spoonfuls of cold tinned custard. But at half past eight a cryptic message appeared, with a set of directions. Jo wrote them down, which seemed to take an age.

When she finally closed down Facebook and put down her phone her eyes shone and I knew this kind of thing was right up her street. 'A place called New York. Serious. It's in Lincolnshire. Miles away. We'll need to fill the van.'

'Wish I was coming,' said Aunt Edie. 'I could do with a boogie.'

'I'm glad you're not,' I said, without thinking. I caught sight of her crestfallen face and tried to make amends. 'We don't know what it's going to be like. Could be awful.' I realized Aunt Edie was more up for a party than I was, which didn't make me feel that good about myself, given that she's at least half a century older than I am.

We set off at ten o'clock, stopping at the garage to buy the essentials – cigarettes, chewing gum, bottles of water and petrol. I'd put the photos of Matt that Nikki had given us in an envelope in my jacket pocket. Butterflies danced inside my belly. I hadn't been out for months, not since before we set up the business, not since, well I don't want to think about that, but not for a long time. If I'd known what was in store for us, of course, the butterflies would have fled, and I would have followed them. But I didn't and so we headed off, dance music blaring.

Chapter 18

It was past midnight by the time we arrived but we didn't take a single wrong turning, thanks in part to my superior navigational skills, but also, credit where it's due, to the accuracy of the directions. The roads got darker, thinner, we passed through villages then hamlets until finally we came to a track marked only by a wooden board that someone had propped by the gateway with an arrow hand-painted on it in luminous orange paint that reflected our headlights.

'This is it,' said Jo. I could see the white of her teeth as she took the turn. We drove down the track and as we did another car appeared behind us, the first I'd seen in ages, and followed us down. At the end of the track we found a field full of parked cars. Headlights provided odd beams of illumination.

'Are we ready for this?' I said.

'You bet your ass,' said Jo.

We climbed out of the van and followed a group of people making their way down a muddy track towards a wood. After a minute or two, I heard the bass line pushing its way out through the trees. We moved towards the music like moths to the firelight. Impossible to see much, people dancing, a lorry, some fairy lights, a fire. The music pulsed inside my body, taking over from my regular heartbeat.

As we got closer, I relaxed. A woman with a shaved head smiled at me. I couldn't get over how easily we blended in and how I felt like I belonged, despite the fact I didn't know anyone. But everyone looked like someone I could have known. Hippies with dreadlocks, a woman in a silver lamé dress and green wellies, bare-chested lads with skinheads and goatee beards, sweating in the night air. The music reached into me and my strings yanked like a puppet. It was so long since I'd been out.

'We're not going to get any sense out of any of this lot for hours,' said Jo.

'Good job we've got hours then,' I said.

'Shall we?'

I knew what she was asking and I inhaled. I felt, like really felt, that nothing bad could happen here. It reminded me of the demonstrations I'd been on – where you knew everyone was on the same side. And it was obvious just from glancing around that every partygoer was on something. I shrugged my shoulders. 'Everyone else is. If we don't, we'll stick out like a sore thumb.'

'We're going undercover?' Jo clapped her hands.

If I'd have thought about it, I might have remembered that our last experience with undercover work didn't turn out so well. But I didn't think about it. I couldn't because Jo had thrown her arms around me, and we were hugging and swaying to the music, Jo's laughter in my ears. I laughed too and said to her, 'I just hope we make it back.'

We made our way back up the path to the van and sat inside it while Jo sorted us out. We smoked a few cigarettes, drank some water and waited for the rushes of excitement as the van throbbed to the bass and my scalp shiver-prickled. My knees itched to dance. When we could hear it no longer we stumbled back down the path to the clearing and found ourselves space.

*

The next few hours are a bit of a blur. I know that we danced and that I probably had my eyes closed, because I can't remember seeing anyone else. I love those moments when you can truly switch off. This was the most space I'd had for ages. We live on top of each other, in the city, like caged rabbits. It sounds weird to talk about space at an event where we were crowded together in front of the sound system, the speakers housed on the back of a small lorry, cranking out the beats, but it's about headspace. I had acres of it. The air was fresh, my legs never tired. Occasionally I'd open my eyes and catch the loved-up gaze of someone else. A guy hugged me and I didn't even mind; I recognized him as a fellow traveller, doing his best to get through this thing we call life. Gender boundaries blurred; we are all human, doing what we can to survive.

The music was amazing; I got lost in the melodies, the bass keeping my feet moving but the rifts taking me all over the place. My mind emptied of all the mundane, day-to-day thoughts, the negative soundtrack I run in my head. I got rid of it all and I was just there. It's hard to describe, impossible to describe, but presence. Emptiness.

I know.

I sound like a right old hippy.

*

The next thing I remember is seeing a thin streak of light across the base of the sky. I've never been so disappointed to see dawn. I tried to focus, couldn't see Jo anywhere. A bald-headed, bare-chested man handed me a bottle of water and I smiled at him as I drank some. 'Thanks.'

We danced together, and I made a promise to myself that I'd be more socially minded when I returned to Leeds. I'd been reminded of humanity, our tribalism, our need to belong.

'First time?' asked my new dance partner.

'Amazing.'

'Tea?'

Tea. Now there was a thought. I considered it carefully and nodded. 'Tea might be good.' I could feel my mouth gurning and talking wasn't easy so we smiled some more instead. He took my hand and led me away from the clearing where everyone was dancing, the music slower paced now. We stumbled through the woods, tripping over tree roots, the ground uneven and my legs unable to judge distance, to where a group of people had built a small fire.

'Josh.'

'Lee,' I said.

'Lee? That's a boy's name.'

'No.'

'If you could have one wish right now, Lee, what would it be for?'

I thought about this for a few minutes, weighing up the options. What would I really, really like? 'Watermelon,' I said.

He moved across to the other side of the fire, rummaged in a bag and, I swear to God, pulled out a watermelon. The synchronicity of this single event blew my mind. He took a penknife from his pocket and hacked me a slice. I bit into it, the juice running down my chin. I laughed. Better than I'd imagined. 'You've done this before.'

'Come most weeks. I love it, me.'

'Space.'

'Right. Dodging the rat race.'

We sat together for ages, watching the fire. I couldn't decide whether to go dance some more. My body wanted to but my legs resisted. The sky grew lighter. A grey dawn. Gradually the number of people dancing thinned and the number of people making small camps around the clearing grew. 'Are these parties always here?' I said.

'No, all over. Got to keep on the move so no one can break it up. Police turned up at one a few weeks back.'

'Shit. What did they do?'

'Told us to turn the music off and waited till everyone left. Way to bring everyone down.'

I glanced around, half-expecting to see vanloads of coppers. The scenery had changed. Colour had returned; the trees with their new leaves looked fluorescent as the light got brighter. I noticed more people – probably a couple of hundred in total

– maybe more. I saw Jo with a group of girls sitting around their own fire. Jo was on her back, blowing smoke rings in the air. I don't think I'd ever felt such peace, not for a long time, not since before, well before everything. Not to think of things like that, not here, not in this state. I closed down that part of my mind.

'How'd you find out about the party, Lee?'

'A friend.' The thought of Matt reminded me of why we were here and I flushed. I couldn't have looked for him less in the time I'd been here – I'd spent most of it with my eyes literally closed. 'He came to one somewhere round here last week. Did you?'

'Nah – couldn't get a lift – Johnny, that's who I usually come with – he had a gig to go to. In Sheffield. That's where I'm from.'

'I'm looking for him.'

'Who?'

'My friend who came last week.'

'He's here?'

'Said he might be.'

'Boyfriend?' He said it without any trace of jealousy, or curiosity, just an open question.

'No. Definitely not.'

'You gay?'

'No.' The question seemed bizarre. I realized if pushed I'd describe myself as asexual these days, it had been that long since, well, since anything. Sex seemed like another world, a planet I didn't inhabit.

'Want me to help you find him?'

'That would be great.' I couldn't do it alone. Talking wasn't as easy as it used to be.

'What's his name?'

'Matt. Matty.'

'Where's he from?'

'Leeds.'

'Distinguishing features?'

I tried to remember. 'He's pretty. Long hair, skinny.'

'A pretty boy from Leeds. Can't be that many of them.'

I grinned. 'He's a student, doing an MSc.' Details filtered into my brain as I brought myself back to the reason why we'd come here. 'He's got to hand it in soon.'

'Better not mention that. Don't want to bring him down.'

'Good thinking.'

'I'm single and ready to mingle.' He passed me a joint. 'Don't go anywhere.'

After dancing for five hours without a break, I didn't think my knees would let me. I watched him wind his way back to the dance floor, his knee-length shorts and canvas boots giving him the appearance of a boy scout, albeit a topless one.

I leant back and closed my eyes. My brain emptied again. I was reminded of my place in the universe, of the fact that really all my problems were insignificant. How wrong I was.

Chapter 19

A spliff helped bring me back to earth. I drank the tea, and ate the rest of the watermelon. I couldn't see any sign of my bald-headed, bare-chested new dance floor friend. I got to my feet and stumbled around the clearing and found Jo dancing on her own down a little path that led into the woods. She was still wearing her parka.

'Lee.' She grinned. I grinned. Like we hadn't seen each other in months. She put her arms around my shoulders and pulled me into a full body hug and I wondered why on earth I think I don't like hugs. Jo stepped back. 'I'm having the best time. I love this.'

'You're the best friend in the whole world.'

'You too, fuckface.' She hugged me again. Even though my knees were knackered, I couldn't resist a bit of a dance as we held each other, although dance was a bit strong. More of a sway, with perhaps a bit of a jiggle.

I opened my eyes. 'This is the best place for a party.'

Jo let me go and we took a moment to appreciate the surroundings. The sun had broken through now and shafts of light dappled the trees. 'I saw you dancing your pants off,' said Jo. She shook her head. 'With your eyes closed.'

'I met a boy.'

Jo raised her eyebrows. 'About fucking time.'

'Not like that.' I pushed her and she nearly tripped.

She laughed. 'Thought it was too good to be true.'

'I'm delegating. He's looking for Matt for us. I'm on it like a car bonnet.'

'Matt.' She laughed again, this time so hard she bent at the waist. 'I'd forgotten about him.'

I shook my head. 'Some business partner you turned out to be.'

'Just biding my time. Waiting for the right moment. There's a travellers' camp down there.' Jo pointed into the trees. 'I went for a wee, and there's all these caravans. Right bunch of hippies. Think we should ask around?'

'Dunno. I'm still a bit twatted. Fancy a brew first?'

I led Jo back to the group I'd been sat with earlier. We cadged a cup of milky tea, served in a tin mug, the kind I imagine they use in prisons, and shared it between the two of us. I tried to roll a cigarette but I didn't have the spit to stick the Rizla paper down and the tobacco just fell on the ground. I gave up after the second attempt. My limbs ached but sitting still felt too sedentary, so we decided to wind our way through the trees and see if we could find the travellers' camp Jo had seen. Sure enough, a few hundred yards into the woods were about half a dozen caravans, including a VW camper van, and two white tents – the circus tent kind – pitched with rope and wooden pegs. A bloke with dreads was building a fire while a greyhound with a bad leg hobbled along next to him.

He smiled when he saw us. 'You lost?'

'Exploring.'

'Having fun?'

'Fuck, yes,' said Jo. 'Can't believe I've never been to one before. Music's awesome.'

'Thanks,' he said.

'You're a DJ?'

'My set was two till four.'

'Awesome,' I said.

He grinned. 'You danced?'

'Didn't stop,' I said truthfully.

'Take a seat,' he said. There were bales of hay arranged around the fire and I sat down on one of them.

'You DJ every week?' asked Jo.

'Every week there's a party.'

What a weird life. Travelling round the country throwing parties in woods. I wondered what they did during the rest of the week. Not much, if the way I felt now was anything to go by. I lay on my back on the hay bale, gazed up at the clouds.

'Do you live here, then?' asked Jo.

'Some of the time. Mostly we move around. Spend the winters in Spain. More sun, fewer coppers – better than here.'

'Do you know a guy called Matt?'

'Don't think so.'

'A student from Leeds?'

He shook his head again. 'Why you asking?'

Jo took a seat on the hay bale next to mine and picked up a stick to poke the fire with. 'He came to one of these last week, and no one's seen him since.'

'What's he look like?'

I remembered the photos I'd put in my pocket. I hadn't thought to give them to Josh. My brain was waking up, a cell at a time. I was returning to the world and the experience hadn't scarred me. In fact it had been good. It had been so long since I'd been out of my head. Like a holiday – times out of your brain are necessary, but for addicts like me there's an obvious danger. That's what makes an addict. They're the people whose heads aren't good places to reside – they're the ones who become addicts. Because going back is too hard. It's easier to keep going, to take the next set of pills, the next drink. The drugs are passports – a passport to leave behind the rain and head for sunshine. Who doesn't want to live where everything's lovely? I sat up and tugged the photo out of my back pocket and handed it over to the bloke in front of me. 'Like this.'

He frowned for a moment, scratched at his dreads as he examined the picture. He turned to me. 'What's it to you?'

'He's my friend's boyfriend. She's worried about him – no one knows where he is.'

'Dunno.' He handed me the photograph back and put a blackened kettle on a flat stone in the firepit. 'Nothing to do with me.'

The events of the night and the morning are a bit hazy, but I do remember thinking it was warm enough to sunbathe as we made our way back through the clearing. Which means it must have been getting on for about nine o'clock when I tripped. My foot caught against a dead weight and I fell forward.

Jo grabbed me, or at least tried to grab me, but she missed. My reactions weren't quick enough, my body didn't have time to put my arms out and I was on the ground before I knew what had happened. I lay on the floor and got hit in the stomach by a wave of tiredness and it occurred to me that sleep might be a possibility at some point in the future. I mean, not right there and then, but sleep became a thing again, after a night of feeling more awake than I had in a long time. It made me laugh, which might also have had something to do with the cigarette we'd shared with the DJ.

'Dickhead,' Jo said as she held out an arm to pull me up.

I put my left hand down on the ground to steady myself and that's when I noticed. I hadn't tripped over a log.

I'd tripped over a leg.

A man's leg.

And as I followed it along I saw the rest of him, the Converse boots, the long shorts and the bare, hairless chest. My dance floor friend, the man I'd last seen as I sent him off looking for Matt.

'Oh my God. Josh.'

Chapter 20

Jo must have seen the look on my face change, because she squatted down next to me.

'Josh?'

He lay still in a foetal position, his arms up around his head. I brushed the mud from his shoulders. 'Christ, what's happened to him?'

Jo tugged at his right arm, pulling it away from his face. A trickle of blood ran from above his eye down past his ear and round the back of his head. 'Shit,' she said.

The adrenalin hit the other stimulants in my bloodstream and for a moment I thought I might explode. 'Is he dead?'

Jo leaned the side of her head onto Josh's chest. 'He's breathing. Who is he?'

'The guy I told you about. The one who said he'd look for Matt.'

'Let's sit him up.' Jo took his right arm and I took his left and we hauled the top half of his body up off the floor. He flopped forward, his head almost hitting his knees. The blood flow from the cut above his eye increased.

'Better idea,' said Jo. 'Recovery position.'

We laid him back down and turned him over onto his side. 'Maybe he's taken a bad pill?'

'Don't be stupid,' said Jo. 'Look at his face. We'd better ring an ambulance.'

'Maybe he fell.' I'm ashamed to say it, but I really didn't fancy interacting with any kind of emergency services. 'Maybe banged his head on a rock.'

I searched in vain for the offending article.

'Make sure he's not swallowing his tongue.'

I parted Josh's lips with my fingers and made myself grab his tongue and pull it to the front of his mouth. He gagged. An involuntary reflex. Jo worked to bring his knees closer to his waist, and as his body moved, he vomited. I tried to get out of the way but wasn't quick enough. Bits of sick flicked down my leggings.

'Thank fuck he doesn't need mouth to mouth,' said Jo.

'Give us some water.'

Jo pulled the bottle out of the pocket of her parka. I poured a splash into the bottle cap and tipped it over his bottom lip. It dribbled down his chin. 'Put your coat over him,' I said to Jo.

'Think we should tell someone?' Jo asked as she took her arms out of the sleeves of her coat.

'He's bruised here too, look,' I said, tracing the purplish outline on his ribs. 'Shit, this is my fault.'

'You don't know that.'

'He was looking for Matt.' I poured some of Jo's water onto my fingers and rubbed gently at his face. As well as the cut over his left eye there was the beginnings of another bruise on his cheek. One side of his face was covered in mud. I dabbed at it some more with my damp fingers. He groaned. 'He's waking up.'

He opened his eyes and stared at me like he was trying to place me. 'Shit, man, are you OK?'

'I'm fine,' I said. 'What happened to you?'

'My head hurts.'

'Who did this?'

He put his hands to his rib and winced. 'I was talking to someone. About your friend. He told me to get lost. I said that wasn't the spirit. And then I can't remember.'

He tried to sit up. 'Shit. That hurts.'

Jo wrapped her coat round Josh's shoulders as he shivered despite the sunshine. I pulled the photos of Matt from my back pocket. 'Was it him?'

'Fuck. Yes. That's your friend?'

'I'm so sorry. I had no idea he'd do something like that.'

Jo avoided my gaze.

'He's the boyfriend of a friend. I never actually met him. Last thing she heard he'd come to one of these – no one's seen him since.'

'Tell her she's well rid of him. I've never seen any trouble at one of these. That's not what they're about.'

'Someone must have seen something,' Jo said.

Josh shook his head and grimaced again. 'I was coming back up this path. He said, "What are you looking for?" Thought he was trying to sell me drugs. I told him I was looking for someone called Matt from Leeds. He asked me why and I said because this cute girl asked me to.'

It took me a moment to work out that I was the cute girl and the surprise made me grin. I've never been called cute in all my life.

'Go on,' said Jo, shooting me a glance.

'He asked me what cute girl, and I said his girlfriend. That's the last thing I remember.'

Josh rubbed his ribs again. 'Feel like I've been kicked by a horse.'

'I'm so sorry, Josh. I had no idea.'

'It's not your fault.' He sat up a bit straighter, and crossed his legs in front of him. A bit of colour returned to his cheeks. 'Got any smokes?'

Jo rolled him a cigarette while I poured more water onto the tissue and cleaned up his face as best I could. We shuffled along a bit, away from the vomit and on to a log.

'How long was I out for?'

'Hard to say.'

Jo sparked up the cigarette and handed it straight to Josh. 'Who are you here with?'

He described the people he'd come to the party with and I sat next to him on the log while Jo went to find them. His friends arrived with a blanket and expressions of concern, said they'd drive him straight back to Sheffield. We watched them walk back through the trees together, arms around Josh. He seemed OK, but I knew from experience that he'd never be able to relax in this environment again. Your body stores the imprint of traumatic events so it can keep you safe even when your rational mind knows there's no threat. It's why I avoid nightclubs.

'What should we do?' asked Jo as Josh and his friends disappeared from sight. 'Matt's here somewhere.'

'Which means,' – my brain struggled to grasp hold of the possibilities – 'it means he's been here all week. You wouldn't go to a party, rape someone, disappear and then come back to the same party the next week, would you? That makes no sense.'

'He must be hanging out with the travellers – the caravans.'

'I thought it was odd,' I said, as thoughts fought their way to my consciousness. 'The DJ, at the fire – he said, "Nothing to do with me" when I showed him Matt's photo. That was a weird thing to say, wasn't it?'

*

The shock of finding Josh had straightened us both up a bit. We linked arms and made our way deeper into the woods to the site of the caravans. There was no sign of the hippy we'd spoken to earlier, but a woman lay in a hammock strung between a tree and one of the caravans. She'd tied a rope to a second tree and was using it to swing herself gently back and forth. 'Where's Matt?' I asked.

'Don't know,' she said. 'Who are you?'

'He's here, isn't he?'

'Do I know you?'

'A friend of his. Lee,' I said. 'Nice to meet you. Where is he?'

'Don't know,' she said.

'You're covering for him.'

'Are you the police?' She sat up in her hammock and looked at us like we might possibly be that far undercover.

I pulled a face. 'No, but we need to find him.'

'You're very agitated,' she said, like she was some kind of psychotherapist. She was older than the party crowd, looked like she'd been off-grid for a long time.

'We need to find him,' Jo said. 'He's been accused of a serious crime.'

She sang a line from a song I vaguely recognized, her voice high and perfect pitch.

'D*Note,' said Jo. 'That's going back a bit.'

'Why would you want to hide someone who's been accused of rape?' I asked.

She frowned and swung her legs over the side of her hammock. 'Who's been accused of rape?'

'Matt.'

'No way.' She picked a bottle of water up from the floor and took a mouthful. 'Matt's sound as.'

'Trust me, he isn't,' Jo said.

She squinted into the sun to stare at us. 'Thought you said he was a friend of yours?'

'Sorry,' said Jo. 'We should have said he raped a friend of ours.'

'No way.'

'Yes way. If you want you can meet her. Ask her yourself.'

'Fuck.' She paused and I knew she was examining her memories, like we all do when we're presented with a fact that doesn't fit the picture we have in our heads. 'He said the police were after him.'

'And you think he's sound?'

She frowned at me, like she didn't get the connection.

'He told you he was on the run,' I said. 'Didn't you think that might mean he'd done something wrong?'

'He said it was for organizing raves in Newcastle.'

'Likely,' said Jo. 'The police aren't going to hunt you down for organizing a party.'

'You'd be surprised. Last year they arrested a couple of—'

'He raped a woman, here, at one of these parties, last week.'

She shook her head. 'He gave me a foot massage.'

'Are you saying you don't believe his victim? Why would she make something like that up? Why would any woman make something like that up?'

'Shit,' said the woman, rocking back into her hammock. 'He's gone.'

'Gone where?'

'Dunno.'

'Fuck off,' said Jo. 'We know he's here.'

'He was here,' she agreed. 'But he left.'

'When?'

'Dunno. Half an hour ago? He took the VW.'

I looked around and realized she was right. The VW, the orange hippy van with painted flowers, had gone. I cursed myself for my lack of observational powers. Had I been more aware, I would have noticed. OK, it had been necessary to go undercover, but being undercover so deep you can't actually see doesn't help anyone. 'Did he say where he was going?'

'No. I did ask, but I don't think he heard me. He was in a rush. Shit.' She took her sunglasses off and I saw the wrinkles around her eyes, deep grooves in her skin. 'I can't believe it.'

'You're sure he's not said anything about where he's going?'

'He's been asking Dan about Spain. God, you'd never think—'

'Spain?' I said. She wasn't the first person to mention Spain to me today. It took me a moment to remember that the DJ we'd spoken to by the fire, the one with dreads, had said they spent the winters in Spain.

'There's a camp over there – Beneficio, in the south. Beautiful place, totally offgrid.'

'You think Matt's going there?' I asked.

'Dan'll go apeshit about the van. If he's not planning on bringing it back, I mean.'

'Which way did he go?'

She gestured behind us. 'There's a track – leads up to the village.'

I grabbed Jo's arm. Her pupils were almost as big as her eyes, made her eyes look black rather than the bright blue I'm used to. 'Come on,' I said but even as I said it, I knew it was useless. We stumbled back along the path, past the party, back towards the field where we'd parked the van. The van was still there surrounded by thirty or forty other cars, all parked at different angles. It felt like another lifetime that we'd left it there.

Jo got in the driver's seat and exhaled. 'Where are the keys?'

'You've got them,' I said.

We got out of the van and wasted a few minutes patting down every pocket. It took a few moments more to realize Jo wasn't wearing her coat. 'Shit,' she said. 'I gave it to Josh.'

I remembered Josh slipping out of it as his friend wrapped a blanket around his shoulders. 'It's back in the woods,' I said.

*

There were still a few people dancing as we made our way back across camp. Jo's coat wasn't in the clearing. 'Did Josh take it?'

'How we going to get home?'

'That guy's wearing it,' she said.

I followed her gaze to a guy with a shaved head who was indeed wearing Jo's coat. I marched over to him. 'Excuse me, that's my friend's coat.'

'Sick.'

'Can I have it back?'

'Yeah, course.' He slipped it off and handed it to me and smiled. I thought I could probably ask him for the shirt off his back and the same thing would happen.

I checked the pockets and found the van keys. By the time we'd made it back to the makeshift car park, I estimated we'd wasted quarter of an hour, but as time had lost all meaning, I couldn't be sure. 'Don't know if I can remember how to drive,' Jo said.

She turned the key and the van coughed into life. It took twenty minutes to negotiate our way out of the field. People had randomly parked their cars wherever they'd left them and there were so many ditches and bumps in the field I had to get out and push twice. The second time three people helped me.

'This is crazy,' I said, when I climbed back into the van. 'We aren't ever going to find him.'

'Still time to go though.'

I looked where Jo was pointing and saw a police car and two vans on the road at the bottom of the track. 'What we going to do now?'

'Got anything incriminating on you?'

'No.'

'Should we have a chat? We are here on official business.'

We stared at each other as we mulled the idea over. It was hard to see the police as anything other than the enemy, especially the state we were in. 'Do you think we should warn everyone?'

'We've not got time. They'll be here in two minutes. What do you want to do?'

We'd arrived at the entrance to the field. Left would take us past the oncoming police procession, right would swing us around the woods, the direction Matt had gone. 'Let's go right,' I said. 'He's in a VW camper van – he can't be going that quick. It's worth a shot.'

I wasn't in a fit state to handle the police. Besides, our job was to find the missing and Matt was the one we'd been paid to hunt.

As we bumped along the dirt track, I wondered whether we had a chance of catching up to him. Volkswagen camper vans aren't known for their speed, but Jo wasn't up to her usual driving. 'I can't remember when to turn the wheel,' she said as we mis-negotiated a bend and narrowly avoided the ditch.

'Come on, we need to look a bit more lively than this.'

She pushed the accelerator further to the floor and the van picked up the pace. 'Where do you think he's going?'

'He's off to Spain,' I said. 'He's made up a cover story, which means he knows what he's done. He knows, or he thinks, the police are after him. He can't stay partying forever. He can't go back to Leeds. He's got no choice but to leave the country.'

We reached the end of the dirt track and turned left onto a small country lane. We drove on in silence for a few minutes until the road bent to the left. Jo turned the wheel but didn't quite get the ratios right and we mounted the kerb. 'I can't do this,' she said.

'OK, let's stop at the first place we come to. Get a cup of tea.'

*

I don't know who was more relieved, me or Jo, when we saw a village hall, with a sandwich board outside that offered cream teas. It was half past ten on Sunday morning. We probably looked a bit of a state but the pint-sized lady behind the counter was too well-bred to mention it. We ordered two cups of tea, a bowl of soup and I placed a banana from the basket by the till on the tray. There were only a few other people in the café, mostly mothers and babies. We kept our heads down as we made our way to the table in the far corner, furthest away from anyone else.

'Don't know if I can eat,' Jo said.

'He'll need a passport,' I said.

Jo didn't reply.

'We have to ring his parents,' I said. 'We tell them he's missing. They've a right to know.'

I wasn't sure about our legal obligations. Did we have a responsibility to tell the police? Trouble was there was so much we couldn't tell them. Sara didn't want the rape reported, and I was fairly sure Josh wouldn't be in a rush to press charges either. It made me think about how unprotected those that live on the outskirts of society are. If you live a life you don't want examining, it's difficult to access the criminal justice system.

Jo stirred a couple of packets of sugar into her tea. 'None of this answers the real question.'

'What real question?'

'What are we going to do when we find him?'

'Tell Nikki.'

'And then what? I'm serious, Lee. We know he's a rapist; he's attacked your mate, Josh. I mean, do we even want to find this prick? Nikki doesn't need him in her life.'

I sat on my hands. 'I'm not letting him swan off into the sunset. He has to pay for what he's done.'

'If Nikki decides to keep the baby, what kind of dad is he going to be?'

I didn't want to think about that. I tried to quieten my mind by focussing on our client. What did Nikki want from this?

I sighed and reached for my mobile. Only one way to find out.

Nikki answered the phone on about the second ring. 'Yes?'

'Nikki, it's me, Lee.'

'Any news?'

The desperation in her voice broke my heart. I glanced at Jo but she was focused on her tea, her hands wrapped around the body of the mug. I exhaled and felt the after-effects of too much stimulant in my bloodstream. My scalp shivered. 'We think he's hanging out in Lincolnshire, with the organizers of the parties. We came down last night.'

'He's there?'

'Once he got wind we were looking for him he ran.'

'He ran? Did you tell him I need—'

'Listen, Nikki, has Matt got a passport?'

'A passport? You think he's leaving the country?' Her voice screeched down the phone and I had to move it a few centimetres from my ear.

'It's a possibility. We're looking at the possibilities.'

I ended the call knowing I'd only made things worse. Nikki told me Matt had been to Thailand the summer before she met him. So he had a passport, but she didn't know where he kept it.

'If it was in Leeds,' I said to Jo, 'he could have gone back and got it. He's had a whole week to make plans. Odds are he has his passport.'

'So what do we do?'

'We have to tell the police. Before Matt leaves the country.'

'We can only do that if Sara agrees,' said Jo. 'And she won't. I know she won't.'

I folded my arms. 'We can't let him run to Spain. Where's the justice in that?'

'There are thousands of men walking around who've done the same thing, or similar. That's how the world works, Lee. Don't know why you're acting so fucking surprised.'

'It's not how my world works.' I knew I must have raised my voice because a couple of the people in the café looked across in our direction. I took a breath and leant in closer to Jo. 'There's no way I'm letting him sail off into the sunset while Nikki's left to decide on her own whether to bring up a rapist's baby. That's not going to happen. No fucking way.'

Chapter 21

We stayed in the café ordering random items from the menu at half-hourly intervals until Jo felt ready to drive and so it was late afternoon by the time we got back to Leeds. I fetched the duvets and we put the sofa cushions on the floor and watched shit films on Netflix. 'I could murder a glass of wine,' said Jo. She must have noticed the look on my face. 'Soz.'

'No, you can if you want,' I felt obliged to say. Although I'd probably kill her if she did. My hands had got the shakes and I had a thirst that I couldn't quench no matter how many mugs of tea I drank. Jo opened her mouth to say something, but my phone rang. The screen said number not recognized, but I answered it anyway. 'Hello?'

'Could I speak to Lee Winters, please?'

'This is she, I mean her. I mean, I'm Lee.' I took a breath, swallowed. 'Who's this?'

'My name is Frances Wilson. Mae Greenwood from the Missing Persons Helpline left a message on my answer-machine, regarding a former—'

'You're the social worker?'

'Retired social worker, yes.'

'Oh wow.' I sat up and my heart rate jumped by about thirty beats a minute. 'I mean, thanks for ringing. Mae said you had a missing person, a ...' My throat was too dry to get the words out.

'She told me you're working on a case that might have something to do with Jenny Crawley?' Frances Wilson might be retired but the professionalism in her voice was impossible to miss.

'Yes. There's a body. I mean, might be. I'm sorry. I mean, we don't know at this stage ...'

'I've been convinced for some years that Jenny isn't with us anymore. I know that sounds strange.'

I guessed that Frances Wilson was around sixty years old; I imagined her as small, a gentle but firm presence. 'No, it doesn't. I know. I mean ...' My sentences refused to form. Jo put a hand on my knee. 'Doesn't matter,' I said.

'What makes you think your body might be Jenny?' the voice on the telephone asked.

'There was a train ticket, near the body, from Nottingham to Leeds, so we've been looking at anyone with a connection to both cities. That's how Jenny's name came up.' I glanced at Jo, trying to decide how much information to give to this soft-spoken woman I'd never met. It couldn't hurt I thought. I took a deep breath to steady myself. 'Yesterday we got given a necklace that the victim was wearing. Did Jenny Crawley have a sister?'

A pause. I waited it out. 'Yes, she had a sister,' said Frances. 'Do you know how we might be able to get hold of her?'

'I'm afraid, no, that's not possible.' I heard her sigh 'Jenny's sister, Maureen Kozlowska, was murdered.'

'Murdered?' I stared at Jo as dread seeped under my skin. 'When?'

Jo took my phone from my hands and pressed the speakerphone button so that suddenly Frances Wilson's voice projected into our front room.

'A couple of years before I met Jenny. Could you tell me a little about the body? Where was it found? How did she die?'

Jo gave me the nod. We had nothing to lose.

'Suicide,' I said. 'She left a note. Her body was found in the garden of a block of flats, close to Roundhay Park.'

'Roundhay Park?' she said, like I'd hit a nerve.

'Yes. You know it?'

'I'm sorry. It's been such a long time.'

I heard the catch in her voice and knew she was having difficulty speaking. I tried to think of a question that might help ground her in the present, rather than take her back to the past. 'How come Jenny had a different surname to her sister?'

'Kozlowska was their mother's maiden name. I suspect Jenny changed hers back to Crawley, perhaps after what happened to Maureen.'

'Can you tell us more about Maureen? What happened to her?'

'I only know what Jenny told me, plus the bits I've pieced together from the news reports.'

'News reports?' I mouthed to Jo. She frowned at me.

'Jenny and Maureen's mother was Polish,' Frances continued.

'She came to England as a young woman and married an Englishman – I assume that's where the name Crawley came from. Jenny had no memory of her father; I gathered he left before she was born and the girls were raised by their mother. She did the best she could, but there were problems.'

'Problems?'

'With regards to the mother's mental health. In fact she was sectioned on several occasions. The girls were in and out of institutionalized care for much of their childhood.'

Jo reached across to me and we held hands as we listened to Frances sketching out the background to Jenny Crawley. Perhaps it was the consequences of what we'd taken last night, but I felt Frances Wilson's words like they were wounds.

'When the girls were teenagers, their mother returned to Poland, but Jenny and Maureen wanted to stay in England. It was their home, the only country they'd ever known. Jenny wanted to complete her GCSEs. She was a bright kid. Oh my goodness.'

The social worker paused for a moment, and I let her regroup.

'Maureen was a few years older than Jenny, and had a job, working in a cardboard box factory. She convinced the authorities she could look after her younger sister. But, somewhere along the line, to make ends meet no doubt, Maureen turned to prostitution. She was murdered by one of her clients.'

'Fuck.' I cleared my throat. 'Sorry.'

'Of course, I didn't know Jenny at that time. Everything I know about Maureen's murder is from what Jenny told me afterwards.'

'Maureen was killed in Leeds,' I said it as a fact, had the feeling the pieces of the jigsaw were slipping into place. I raised my eyebrows at Jo. Jenny's suicide made sense to me now. 'In a flat on the edge of Roundhay Park?'

'No,' said Frances Wilson. 'It wasn't far away though. The girls had a flat in Harehills.'

There went my theory. 'Maureen was killed in their flat in Harehills?'

'Jenny only ever spoke about it once, but I never forgot the conversation. She told me she was supposed to keep out of the way while Maureen attended to her clients, but I think Jenny often hung around, kept an eye out for her sister.'

'Can you think of any connection Jenny might have had to the block of flats overlooking Roundhay Park?' asked Jo, leaning over.

'Who's that?' asked Frances.

'Sorry, I should have introduced you earlier. That's Jo, my business partner.'

'We wondered whether she was trying to get back at someone who lived there,' Jo added.

'Maybe she just wanted to be near where her sister died,' I said when Frances Wilson didn't respond to Jo's question. Roundhay Park was only a stone's throw from Harehills, geographically, even if culturally it was a million miles away.

'When was Maureen murdered?' asked Jo.

'Let me see now, I think Jenny was around fifteen years old at the time. I'm afraid I don't have my notes anymore.'

I glanced across at Jo. I knew we were both thinking the same thing.

'I didn't meet Jenny until she was pregnant with Sasha.'

'Sasha?'

'Jenny's son.'

I thought of Martin's notes on the autopsy. The victim had given birth. I didn't know if I wanted to hear too much about the child who must be out there, somewhere, motherless.

Frances Wilson seemed intent on filling in the gaps for me though. 'Jenny was referred to social care by her midwife, while she was pregnant. The midwife was concerned because of Jenny's age – she was only seventeen when Sasha was born – and because she knew Jenny had no family support network to turn to.'

I wrote the figures down. Fifteen years old when her sister was murdered. Gave birth at seventeen. I could barely look after myself at seventeen, let alone a child.

'I worked with Jenny for a year, a year and a half and it must be nearly ten years since I last saw her, which would make her around twenty-seven or twenty-eight years old now, if she's still alive.' I could hear the hope in her voice but I think we both knew she was clutching at straws.

'What happened to Sasha?' asked Jo.

'This is what troubles me most. I don't know. We monitored the pair of them during that first year and it wasn't plain sailing. I don't doubt for a moment that Jenny loved her child.' She paused again and I knew not to rush her. 'The baby's father was still around, and considered a positive influence. But when their relationship broke down, Jenny fell in with a bad crowd and we suspected a drugs issue. Ultimately the decision was made to take Sasha into care. I think Jenny got wind of what was happening and she ran I never saw her again.'

'Did you try and trace him, the father of her baby?'

'When they broke up she told me he'd gone to Nottingham. He had relatives there and Jenny said he'd wanted to buy some kind of smallholding. He used to sell fruit and vegetables on the market. I think the plan was to try and cut out the middleman by growing his own produce.'

'What did you do when she disappeared?'

'In truth, not a lot.'

I couldn't stop the judgement in my voice. 'What?'

'A week or two after she failed to attend a meeting, I forget the exact timescale, I received a card through the post, from Jenny. In it, she said she'd gone back to Poland to live with an aunt. She didn't give an address but the card was post-marked from a small town. I looked it up and it was very near to where her family was from originally. The card said she'd decided to return home and not to worry about her. We didn't have the budget to track people overseas. I wrote to the Polish equivalent of social services but I never heard anything. I think I chased it once. We had such high caseloads.'

My skin chilled. 'And you never heard about Sasha?'

'No. He'll be eleven years old now. And his mother, if this is Jenny, has been dead seven years.'

'You didn't report her missing until four years ago. Why?'

'I retired. And I knew that when I left, I'd be the only person who ever thought about her. If I'm honest, I didn't believe she'd gone back to Poland, not even at the time. She had a very difficult relationship with her mother and she'd lived her whole life in England. I also didn't think she had the money for the plane ticket.'

'Did you have any thoughts as to where else she might have gone?'

'I hoped she'd gone to Nottingham, maybe patched things up with her ex. I only met him a couple of times but he always struck me as one of the good guys. I thought maybe if she'd left Leeds, got away from some of the people she was hanging out with, maybe she'd have a chance.' She sighed. 'You want to believe in happy endings. Perhaps you start to need to believe in them. No news is good news in social care.'

I knew Frances Wilson had spent her whole life doing a job where she probably got little thanks and plenty of blame, but I couldn't stop myself feeling disgusted at the scant protection the state affords the vulnerable. I stood up because my stomach had cramped and I worried I might be sick.

'Did they catch Maureen's killer?' asked Jo.

'Yes, they caught him. Well, Jenny thought they did.'

'Come again?'

'Jenny believed Maureen was the victim of a serial killer. He was arrested and charged with the murder of four women in Leeds, although, I should point out, he wasn't charged with Maureen's murder. But the case never came to trial – the alleged perpetrator committed suicide soon after he was arrested.'

The coincidence was too much, even for my addled brain. 'You mean, Jenny's sister, Maureen, was murdered by the Park Killer?'

'Yes. Or at least, that was what Jenny believed.'

I could hardly speak. 'I thought the Park Killer only killed people in parks?' As I said the words, I realized how ridiculous they sounded.

'Jenny never stood a chance,' said Frances Wilson. 'The odds were stacked against her.'

'No one gave her a chance,' said Jo.

'There are hundreds more like her,' said Frances. 'It's an impossible situation. If people knew what life was really like for those on the fringes then maybe ...'

She didn't finish her sentence, I suspect because she'd long since stopped believing that any kind of meaningful change was possible. 'We were applying sticking plasters to people whose legs were hanging off.'

'At least you were doing something,' said Jo. 'I mean, at least you tried.'

'Wasn't enough for Jenny. It wasn't enough for an awful lot of others, either.'

'If it is Jenny,' I said. I didn't want us to get carried away. We still hadn't found anything that linked Jenny to the flats at the top of Roundhay Park.

'She wouldn't kill herself without taking care of Sasha. For all her troubles, she loved that little boy.'

'Have you got the name of Sasha's dad? We could really do with speaking to him.' From what I could gather, the only person who might have the slightest idea what had happened to Jenny Crawley's son was the man who'd fathered him.

'I'm not sure I should be giving you this information, but then I've been down all the official channels and they didn't want to know. As far as I could see it was just one less case to worry about. I remember his name because it was like the poet. Blake. His name was Winston Blake.'

I scribbled that on the piece of paper in front of me.

'Young, black, nice guy, from what I saw.'

'Did Jenny ever mention anyone she knew who lived near Roundhay Park?'

'Not that I remember.' Frances Wilson took a breath and I sensed what she was about to tell me was important. She wanted to get the words right. 'I tell you something about Jenny Crawley though. She was scared. Not scared, petrified. Couldn't sit still. If someone opened a door she'd flinch. I knew her for the best part of two years and of course it was a professional relationship, not a friendship – but if I had to describe her in one word that's what I'd say. Petrified.'

I don't know why, maybe it was needing to do something with my hands, but I wrote that word down on the piece of paper next to where I'd written Winston Blake's name.

Silence filled the flat as Jo and I sat cross-legged on the floor staring at the screen of my mobile. It lay like a small unexploded bomb between us, neither of us wanting to end the call, but at the same time not knowing what else to say. Jo leant across me again. 'I'll send you photographs of the necklace,' she said to Frances, 'and the suicide note. You never know, might jog your memory.'

'She was such a bright girl,' Frances said. 'Didn't deserve the life she got.'

'If we have anymore questions we'll be in touch.' I finished the call as Jo made a note of Frances Wilson's mobile number and pinged her over photographs of the note and the necklace.

'What a life,' I said as I read through the notes I'd taken while Frances had been speaking. 'Dad fucks off, mum's mental. Grows up in and out of care. Sister's murdered when she's fifteen. Pregnant at seventeen, missing since she was nineteen, and most probably dead by twenty-one. And the only person who seems to know, or care, is a retired social worker.'

'She's our best bet for Vicky,' said Jo. 'There's the Nottingham connection. She had a child. She had a sister. The Park Killer gives her a connection to Roundhay Park.'

'We don't know for certain that Maureen was killed by the Park Killer. Just that Jenny thinks she was. The police can't have found any evidence to link him to Maureen's death, otherwise why not charge him with it?'

'In the seventies the police said the Yorkshire Ripper only killed sex workers in Yorkshire. You know why?'

I shook my head.

'Because they wanted everyone to believe that so long as you weren't a dirty prostitute living in the grim north, you were safe. They disregarded loads of evidence that didn't fit the profile. Sutcliffe killed dozens more women, all over the country, and abroad. But even now, forty years later, they don't want to admit to it.'

'But—'

'Same with the Park Killer. If you're not out at night on your own in a park, you'll be fine, girls. Stay in and stay safe. That's what the police want you to believe.'

'But Jenny didn't kill herself in the park, or at their flat in Harehills.' I stood up and stretched my back. 'Time-wise,

Danielle's a better fit – Jenny disappeared two years before Vicky's body turned up. Where was she for those two years? And if Jenny believed the Park Killer murdered her sister, he was already dead by the time she committed suicide, so who's the note to? And what's the point of tying herself to the statue?'

'Maybe it's not about her sister. Maybe she was abused while she was in care, or something. Maybe one of her care workers lived in the flats.'

'Vicky took everything off except the necklace. It's got to be about her sister, whoever she is.' I thought back to my conversation with Danielle's mother, and that reminded me I'd left a message for her the day before. 'Mrs Goodwin hasn't rung back. I'll phone her in the morning. I need a bath.'

*

I stayed in the lukewarm water for hours, depression wrapping itself around me like a second skin. I thought about Vicky, about Jenny, about Danielle. I almost hated Vicky, whoever she was, for committing suicide, for taking her own life and leaving behind so many unanswered questions, but I sensed her desperation – the determination in her note, the brutal way she chose to die. What had Martin said – he couldn't think of a worse way to die. Why not stick her head in the gas oven? She'd had the whole journey from Nottingham to Leeds to change her mind. To think of her child. I'd memorized the note and the final sentence burned into my consciousness.

Out there, somewhere, someone else knows.

Chapter 22

I'd never been so grateful to fall into my bed than I was by the end of Sunday. I couldn't remember the last time I'd pulled an all-nighter, but it was clear I didn't have them in me anymore. And now I didn't have the option of a glass of something strong enough to switch off the voices, turn out the lights. I fought to empty my mind but when I finally got to sleep, it was worth it.

I woke the next morning with the thought that Matt, for one, could go fuck himself. No way was I letting him waltz off to live in the sunshine with a bunch of hippies. Perhaps I couldn't do anything about the past, but I sure as hell could do something about the here and now. Men have been getting away with this kind of shit for too long. Not anymore. This time was going to be different. The culture is changing and the sooner men like Matt get used to that fact, the better for us all.

I couldn't stop my mind returning to the past though. To a woman who'd got used to being invisible, who had died trying to leave a mark on the world and failing. Petrified. The word Frances Wilson had used to describe Jenny Crawley played in my mind. Jenny hadn't got justice or closure. Fear comes from the not knowing, from the images and thoughts our brain conjures up as it tries to fill in the gaps. Men, getting away with murder.

Which made me think about Danielle and her ex-boyfriend, DJ Ink. If Vicky Doe was actually Jenny Crawley, then Mrs Goodwin's suspicions about her daughter's boyfriend were probably correct. The chances were he'd killed Danielle and disposed of her body somewhere. He was out playing records while his ex-girlfriend's mother raised her own grandchild and spent every day wondering whether her daughter was dead or alive.

When I feel this way, on a downward spiral, I know there's one way to make myself feel better. You have to become active. The trouble with women is we're taught to be passive, to internalize, to turn things in on ourselves. It's the flight or fight instinct. Women are taught to run, to hide. Historically, that attitude hasn't helped us much. Women need to learn to turn their emotions outwards. Don't bottle it up, suck it up, take it on. Instead, make it work for you. Anger is fuel. Rocket fuel.

I went downstairs, made a cup of tea, and took it through to the front room. My phone was on the coffee table. There was a missed call from the office, so I called Aunt Edie first. She said Mrs Goodwin had left a message on the answer-machine over the weekend, returning my call.

I told Aunt Edie we'd be in later and fired up my laptop. It didn't take me long to find the hippy community in Spain that the woman in the hammock had told us about. Wiki didn't have a right lot to say about it, beyond the fact that it was situated in a valley in the South, with most of its inhabitants living in tents, benders and tipis. I made a note of the coordinates and brought it up on Google Maps. It looked pretty damned near idyllic from the photographs, a lush green paradise, basking in sunshine. The thought of Matt being there while Nikki and Sara both dealt with the consequences of his actions burned me. I was going to bring him back, whatever it took.

Once I'd decided on that plan of action I read up on the Park Killer. There wasn't much I could do about him: he'd been dead for nearly nine years. He'd never said a word in police interview and had hung himself three days after his arrest. Why was Jenny still so afraid of him? And how had he managed to hang himself in police custody? I thought belts and shoelaces were removed as a matter of course. I found a small newspaper article about Maureen's death, thirteen years ago. It had warranted barely a line or two of print.

I decided to concentrate on the living. The predators I could do something about. I googled DJ Ink and got the details of the gig he was playing that night in Bristol. Plans formed, broke up and re-formed in my brain.

The internet is amazing. A few minutes on the Skyscanner website, considering our options and I rummaged through the drawers in the dresser in the lounge and found both my and Jo's passports and stuffed them in my duffle bag. If Matt's parents didn't come through, I was damned well going to go to Spain myself and drag his sorry arse back to Leeds. Even if Sara didn't want to tell the police about what he'd done, Nikki deserved a face-to-face meeting.

I was just about to go upstairs to wake Jo when she pushed

through the front room door, her hair an explosion on the top of her head. I hadn't heard her come down the stairs. 'It's half past ten,' she said. 'We're late for work.'

'You're dressed,' I said. And she had her shoes on.

'Oh, I went to see Sara.'

'This morning?' Jo never got up before me. Never ever. Jo is not what you'd call a morning person.

'No, last night.' She didn't meet my eyes. 'She rang. She was upset. You were asleep.'

'Right.' I crushed my roll-up in the ashtray. I stood up too quick and the blood ran from my head. 'Time to get moving.'

'You OK?' asked Jo.

'I'm going to get dressed. Then I want a word with Tuff. I've a bone to pick with him.'

'We've promised Sara we won't tell anyone,' Jo reminded me.

'Tuff already knows,' I said as I stalked past Jo and headed upstairs for my bedroom.

The van was still parked outside the flat, so we drove up to Headingley, and I jumped out at the kerb outside Matt's house. 'Two minutes,' I said to Jo.

I hammered on the front door and Jan opened it a moment later. I marched past her without saying anything. Tuff was in the kitchen, wearing a pair of sweatpants and eating a bowl of cereal.

'He's gone to Spain,' I said.

'How do you know?' he asked and I knew it was news to him.

'You know what he did,' I said. 'You can't cover for him.'

'Don't know what you mean,' he said, but the spoon he'd been holding dropped to the table.

'I want his parents' number.'

He stood up, left his cereal bowl on the table, still half-full of Crunchy Nut Cornflakes. He scratched his arm. 'What you going to do?'

'I'm going to tell them what a worthless piece of shit their son is.'

'And that's useful because?'

'They're going to bring him back to this country and get him to face up to his actions.'

'You've not met his dad,' said Tuff.

'Matt's done a runner, Tuff,' I said. 'You know what he's done. Give me their details or I'll go to the police and I'll use every contact I have there to get them to charge you too.'

'Me? What've I done?'

I put my hands on the table and leaned in towards him, so that our faces were only inches apart. 'Failure to report a crime. That's an offence.'

'I—'

'You knew what had happened and you did fuck all.'

'That's not—'

'You asked no questions.'

'I thought—'

'You're a scientist, you know that that kind of evidence degrades over time.'

I sensed Jan standing behind me in the doorway.

'So you can throw in perverting the course of justice. That's an imprisonable offence.'

'But—'

'You made her feel like it was her problem, not his. You're as bad as him. Worse, because you're a cowardly piece of shit.'

His eyes brightened. 'I didn't know what to say.'

'Not my problem.'

'I haven't got their number.'

'Bullshit.'

'I haven't, honest. They live in Orchard Portman.'

Sounded like a name from a Disney movie. 'Where?'

'It's a village in Somerset.'

'You've been?'

He nodded. 'A couple of times.'

'Give me the address.'

'I don't know the address. But it's a big house on the left just past the post office. You can't miss it. The village is tiny. I didn't tell you this, though.'

Jan hovered at the kitchen door, her hand over her mouth. I took a last look at Tuff. 'You make me sick.'

*

I got back into the van and slammed the door shut. 'Fucking spineless coward.'

Jo started the engine. 'Office?'

'No,' I said. I needed to keep moving. 'Ever been to Somerset?'

'Somerset?' said Jo. 'That's miles away.'

'What else have we got?'

'Why would we want to go to Somerset?'

'Matt's parents are there. I want to talk to them.'

'What are you going to say?'

'Someone has to get Matt to face up to what he's done. If Sara's not going to go to the police, and his best mate isn't going to do anything, then it's up to his parents.'

'So ring them.'

'I don't want to ring them. I want to speak to them. Face-to-face.'

'They might be on holiday.'

'If they are, we move to Plan B.'

'Plan B?'

'We go to Spain.'

'Spain?'

I nodded. 'We can get a flight from Heathrow for about fifty quid. I'm serious. We've been paid to find Matt and that's what I'm going to do.'

'What about Vicky? Did Frances Wilson get back to you about the suicide note?'

'Vicky's not going anywhere. It's been seven years, another day or two isn't going to make any difference. We can sort that out when we get back.'

'It'll take all day, driving to Somerset.'

'Great.' I needed momentum, movement. 'And, while we're down south, we can check out Danielle's ex-boyfriend. Even if we just let him know we're investigating – might be enough to unnerve him. He's got a gig tonight, Bristol – that's down south too. If we get a shift on we might make it in time.'

'South is a fairly large geographical area,' Jo said.

'Get the satnav on it,' I said. I watched the clouds move across the sky. 'Come on. Perfect day for a road trip.'

The satnav lady confirmed that there was only an hour's drive between Orchard Portman and Bristol, where Danielle's ex-boyfriend was DJing that evening. With a bit of luck we could make it down to Matt's parents', have a chat with them, work out what to do and then call in to see the gig on the way home. Jo didn't seem overly impressed but she agreed to go along with it. I rang Aunt Edie and told her the plan.

'You do what you've got to do. I can hold the fort here.' She sounded in her element. 'What do you want me to say to Martin? He'll be mithering me every five minutes.'

'He can wait. Tell him to get on to everything he can find about the Park Killer, and about Jenny's sister, Maureen Kozlowska. I want to know everything about her murder, every single detail. And he needs to see if there's anything that connects the Park Killer to the flats in Roundhay Park. That should keep him busy. We'll be back in a day or two. Nikki's got a deadline, Martin hasn't.'

It took us the best part of six hours to drive to Orchard Portman, but I felt much better being on the move. I used the time to make some calls. First I rang Louise Goodwin but there was no answer. Then I rang Mae. She'd checked the files and Edward, Marcia's brother, was her only sibling, so it seemed unlikely that Marcia would be wearing a necklace that said 'Sisters Forever'.

Next, I got a number for Mr Williams in Orchard Portman from directory enquiries. I called and an answer-machine picked up. I didn't leave a message because I didn't know what to say.

We only stopped off once, at a service station, and I bought lunch from the Marks & Spencer's and we ate it in the van. We played music all the way down, and I felt like I might be in with a chance of outrunning the come down.

I rang Matt's parents two more times on the way down and on the second time a very well-to-do woman's voice answered. I switched off the call. 'Not on holiday,' I said to Jo.

Jo pressed down on the accelerator and we headed on down the M5. The world got warmer and greener the further south we travelled.

*

Orchard Portman is a tiny village and it didn't take us long to find the post office. 'So, it must be that one, there,' I said, pointing to a large house set back from the road.

'What are we going to say?' Jo asked.

I'd been thinking about this all the journey down and, truth was, I hadn't come up with much. 'Let's play it by ear,' I said.

'Plan,' said Jo, although I detected a faint hint of sarcasm.

'Got any better ideas?'

'No. But remember we promised Sara—'

'Nikki is our client. We're doing what we've been paid to do. Find Matt.'

'But Sara wants—'

'We have a duty to our client. If that means telling Matt's parents he's been accused of rape, because that's the truth—'

'If it's honesty you want, why don't you tell them about Nikki being pregnant?'

I paused and considered this for about a fraction of a second. 'I don't think we should mention that.'

'So only some truth is important?'

'Oh, shut up,' I said.

Chapter 23

We parked the van near a duck pond at the far end of the village, and then walked back towards the post office. It was early evening, just after six o'clock, warmer than it had been when we left Leeds, and the air felt different. Fresher, bigger. We circled Matt's parents' house and noticed the two cars parked on the drive. The gravel crunched as we made our way to the front door, where a beautiful tree with what looked like bunches of purple grapes curled round the porch. I glanced at Jo before I pressed the doorbell, but she stared straight ahead. I like that about Jo. She's never fazed by other people's wealth.

A woman in her fifties came to the door, wearing an apron over her skirt. She wore a soft pink jumper with three-quarter length sleeves. A gold bracelet dangled from her wrist. 'Mrs Williams?' I asked.

She had the good manners not to frown at us but it was clear she was perplexed by our appearance. 'Yes?'

'I'm Lee Winters and this is my partner, Jo. We run a missing persons' bureau, in Leeds. May we come in?'

'My husband's here.'

'We'd like to speak to him too. It's about Matt.'

'Matthew.'

'Matthew,' I said.

'You'd better come through,' she said. 'Alex is in his study.'

She led us through to the rear of the house, through a thickly carpeted corridor. The house felt bigger towards the rear, like the ceilings had been raised. I tried to work out why I was feeling weird, and realized it was because Mrs Williams hadn't asked any questions. She hadn't even asked why we were there.

'Take a seat,' she said. 'I'll let Alex know that you're here.'

Jo pulled back one of the kitchen chairs and sat down. I did the same at the other side of the table. Patio doors opened out onto the garden and I noticed a glass of white wine, half drunk, on the table outside. I wondered why she hadn't sat us out there. She returned a moment later with a tall man, also in his fifties. His forehead creased when he saw us. 'What's this about?' he said.

'I'm Lee Winters,' I said, standing up. 'And this is—'

'My wife said. What's it about?'

'We run a missing persons' bureau in Leeds.' I held out a business card but he didn't take it. 'We've been hired to find your son, Matthew.'

'Ridiculous,' he said. 'Who on earth has hired you?'

'His girlfriend.' I put the card back in my jeans pocket. Jo remained seated at the table.

'Matthew doesn't have a girlfriend. He's completing an MSc.'

'He's about to fail his MSc; he's supposed to hand it in this week, but he missed his last tutorial. He hasn't been seen in Leeds for over a week.'

'I think you'll find he has requested an extension in order to broaden his research.' Mr Williams folded his arms across his chest.

'What?'

'When?' asked Jo.

'When what?' Alex Williams fixed his gaze on Jo, and I have to say I felt relieved to have the attention off me.

'When did he request the extension?'

'I can't see what on earth it's got to do with you.'

'We've been hired to find Matt,' I said, trying to keep my voice even. 'We spoke to his tutor. She hadn't heard from him.'

'When was that?'

'Wednesday.'

'Well, that explains it. The request was only approved this morning. I spoke to Matthew's tutor myself.'

'You've seen Matt?'

'As I've made clear, I don't think it's any of your business.'

'It is our business. It's precisely our business,' said Jo. 'We've been hired to find him. By his girlfriend.'

'And I told you he doesn't have a girlfriend.'

'Mr Williams,' said Jo, in a voice that implied it was time to stop the nonsense. 'We would like to speak to Matt. Is he here?'

'I am not explaining the whereabouts of my son to a couple of strangers who've had the temerity to come to my house at dinnertime, to interrupt my evening without—'

There was a scraping noise as Jo pushed back her chair

and stood up. 'If we can't find Matt, we'll have to contact the police, report him as a missing person.'

'For the love of God, I've told you he's not missing.'

'So, where is he?'

'Would you like a cup of tea?' Mrs Williams asked, like we were all having some lovely friendly conversation about the weather rather than Jo standing there hands on hips in front of Mr Williams who looked like he was about to punch her.

'Have you seen Matthew, Mrs Williams?' I asked. She glanced at her husband, like she was looking for the answer to the question.

It struck me that we all had our secrets, every single one of us, standing there in the room. We were keeping some of the secrets on behalf of other people. Sara didn't want us to tell about the rape; Nikki didn't want us to tell about the pregnancy. Mr and Mrs Williams didn't want to tell where Matt was. The room was bursting with secrets. Secrets and lies.

'We've driven all the way from Leeds because your son has been reported missing and we're trying to make sure he's OK.' I realized as the words came out of my mouth that they were in fact also a lie.

'I'm his next of kin,' Mr Williams said, crossing the room and standing next to his wife. 'If I say he's not missing that's all you need to know. I suggest you head back to Leeds and tell this so-called girlfriend that Matthew has postponed his studies for a year.'

'He's not coming back?'

'He's broadening the scope of his thesis.'

'In Leeds?'

'Not at the moment, no.'

'What about his house? His flatmates are worried about him. All his stuff's there.'

'Eileen and I will see to that.' He crossed the room to stand next to his wife. He put an arm around her shoulders and pulled her into him. She didn't respond, stood there like an ironing board.

'What about his share of the rent?' Jo asked.

'You can tell his cohabitants they have no need to worry. I'll sort it out.'

'I see.' I glanced across at Jo. 'Matthew's done a runner, supported by you, his parents.'

'He's taking some time out—'

'He's gone to Spain,' I said. I watched Mr Williams's face as he registered the fact I knew this. 'He's done a runner and you're colluding with him.'

'Colluding is a strong word.'

'You must know that no one runs to Spain, without telling any of their friends, leaving behind all their possessions, giving up on an MSc the week before it's due, unless they've done something that they need to run from.'

Mrs Williams stepped out of her husband's embrace and took a step towards the sink. She busied herself rinsing a cup.

'What did he tell you?' asked Jo.

'I think it's time you ladies left.'

'Because I can only think of a few reasons why someone would run to another country.' I stared at Jo and she nodded. She moved across to me so that we were standing opposite the Williams, the kitchen table separating us. We'd clearly all taken sides.

'I don't have time for—'

'Nervous breakdown?' said Jo. She paused. 'Only a family like yours, you'd step in and pay for some kind of therapy.'

'Drugs?' I said. 'But then ditto rehab.'

'You have no authority and no business here.'

'Money troubles?' Jo said.

I glanced around the kitchen, with its designer units and oven that could cater for thirty and shook my head. 'I don't think that's an issue here.'

'Relationship breakdown?' said Jo. 'But then, his girlfriend still loves him.'

'So what does that leave us?' I said. 'The only other thing I can think of, is crime. Matt's done something wrong, something he doesn't want to face up to.'

There was a clatter at the sink and Mrs Williams turned towards us. 'He needs a holiday,' she said.

'Something very wrong.' I didn't take my eyes off Mr Williams's face.

'And if he's done something very wrong,' said Jo, 'we all know running away isn't the answer.'

'If you try to make trouble for my family, you'll regret it,' Alex Williams said, his voice narrow.

'Is that a threat, Mr Williams?' Jo put her hands on her hips.

Mr Williams cleared his throat. 'It's a statement of fact. Eileen can see you to the door.'

What would Matt have told his father? He'd obviously been

in touch with his parents, which made me think he was desperate. Parents like these weren't easy to talk to, that much was immediately obvious. It crossed my mind that maybe he'd told them that Nikki was pregnant, but there's no way Matt could have known that if we were to believe Nikki. She'd only found out about the pregnancy after Matt had disappeared. I bit the bullet. 'Your son has been accused of a very serious crime, Mr Williams. I suspect you know that.'

His eyes narrowed. 'I have no idea what you're talking about. If he's been accused of a crime, why aren't the police here?'

I glanced across at Mrs Williams. She had her hand to her throat.

'The police aren't here because there was no crime, anyone with half a brain can see that.' Alex grinned at me. A grin that made me curl my hands into fists at the side of my body.

Tosser. 'Your son has been accused of rape, Mr Williams.'

Out of the corner of my eye, I saw Mrs Williams step backwards, so that her back was against the kitchen worktop. Matthew's dad, on the other hand, didn't move. 'Rubbish. My son has no need to force his attentions on anyone, believe me. He has girls queuing up—'

'You're making a mistake, Mr Williams,' Jo said. 'A big mistake.'

'She's right,' I said. 'We're here to help. We're the nice guys. The police won't be half as reasonable.'

'I tell you something,' he said, his lips thin and mean, 'the problem with your generation is you think you can go out, get drunk, and whatever else, without any consequences.'

'Consequences?' said Jo.

'I've seen girls, half-naked, in the city centres on a night out, paralytic – can't stand up straight, let alone make sensible choices.'

'Are you saying they're asking for it?' said Jo, 'Because that's an outdated, misogynistic, shit-for—'

'They do something they regret and think they don't have to take responsibility—'

'Matt told you what happened?' I said. I tried to imagine how that conversation played out.

'I've said everything I'm going to say. Eileen, show them out.' Mr Williams turned and left the room. I heard the door of his study bang closed.

Eileen had a red rash that had spread down her throat to her chest. 'I'm sorry,' she said. 'You'd better leave, I don't want him getting upset.'

She headed off through the corridor we'd come in through. I followed her. 'You need to talk to us, Eileen. You need to talk to us for Matt's sake.'

'I've got four sons,' she said.

'Mrs Williams,' Jo said. 'Matt's in trouble and he needs you to step up and help him do the right thing. He can't run from this. You know that. I know you know that.'

Her cheeks coloured as she opened the front door. 'I don't know what you're talking about.'

'Do the research,' said Jo. 'It's not rocket science. If sex offenders aren't caught, their behaviour escalates.'

'Eileen!'

We all jumped at Alex's voice, shouting from his study.

'Give me a ring,' I said to Eileen, handing her a business card. 'We can help. If you try and hide this, it'll explode somewhere down the line. Trust me, I know.'

She held my gaze for a moment before slipping our business card into her apron pocket.

'Eileen!' Alex's voice sounded like it was getting nearer. I touched Eileen on the arm and stepped out through the front door. As Jo and I walked back down the drive, I felt Mrs Williams watching us.

'Well, that was a fucking wasted trip,' said Jo as we turned onto the street. 'All that way for that twat.'

'He didn't flinch when I said Matt's been accused of rape.' I remembered the steel in his eyes. 'What kind of man would cover for his son, if he'd been accused of rape?'

'Most men.'

'Rubbish.' I don't know why, but for some reason I hold out more hope than Jo for mankind. I think it's to do with personality rather than any considered examination of the facts. I'm an optimist – I have to be, or I'd go under. I have to believe in human decency, in man's humanity, otherwise I don't know that I'd see a reason to go on. Jo seems able to live with the idea that we're all fucked.

Chapter 24

We looped back round the duck pond and climbed into the van. 'I almost feel sorry for Matt growing up with that wanker,' said Jo. 'And Christ, can you imagine, living in that house with all that testosterone? Poor Eileen.'

'Think she'll do the right thing?'

'Doubt it. Her job is to keep it all looking good, to stand by her man. Shame she's got five of them. That's a lot of standing by.'

'Fuck it,' I said. I knew I had to keep moving. 'Let's go to Spain.' I checked my phone. One missed call from an unrecognized number. I flicked to the internet. 'We can fly from Bristol.' I called up Skyscanner and checked out the flights I'd bookmarked earlier. 'There's one at 5 a.m.'

'And what do we do when we get there?'

'We can tell Matt what a complete cunt he is, for starters.'

'You think that's going to make you feel better?'

'Not massively, no. But we've got to think of Nikki. She's our client. We've been paid to find Matt. If we can tell her where he is, that we've spoken to him, got his side of the story – then at least she'll know what she's dealing with.'

'OK.' Jo strapped her seatbelt in. 'Airport here we come. What about passports?'

I love that about Jo. As I said, she's always up for the party.

'Packed,' I said. 'And, if we get the flight from Bristol, we can pay DJ Ink a visit on the way. See what he's got to say about his missing girlfriend.'

Men.

I despaired until I thought about Martin Blink. He was a good one. Possibly the only good man I'd met. I pushed away thoughts of another, much younger man, but not before a flash of dark curls came into my mind. I lit a cigarette and felt the burn in my lungs.

We didn't speak again until we got to Bristol. We parked the van in a city centre car park and ate at Nando's. We had time to fill. According to the Facebook page, DJ Ink's set didn't start till 9.

We found the club and paid the entrance fee. Music pounded above us, making the ceiling vibrate. Whatever lay dormant in my bloodstream from Saturday night woke up and I felt hyper almost as soon as we climbed the stairs. I don't like clubs. They make me claustrophobic. I like space, which was why the outdoor party had been so good for me. After dancing in the open air, this felt dirty, confined, the oxygen recycled too many times.

Still, we swayed around a bit, and Jo went to the bar and bought two bottles of water. I must have raised my eyebrows because she shrugged. 'Don't want to fall asleep on the way to the airport,' she said.

The music was actually good. A mix between dance and funk. Jo nodded over to the far side of the room, where there was a raised section, with waist-high wooden railings all around it. A tall thin man was bent over the decks with headphones on.

'DJ Ink, I presume. Shall we say hi?'

'How we going to handle this?' Even though it had been my idea to come, I hadn't really thought about what we would do when we got here. It wasn't like it was our case. We had no authority to act when it came to Danielle Goodwin.

'All we can do is put the willies up him.' Jo grinned which looked weird in the fluorescent light. 'Just for the laugh.'

'Let's dance a bit first,' I said.

So we danced and I tried to shake the down feeling that was threatening to engulf me. As my mind emptied of everything except the music, I tried to concentrate on the good things in my life. I had my own business with my best mate. We didn't have anyone to answer to. I wasn't living in fear of my lover, or my father, or my brother. I hadn't been attacked by a man I thought was my friend, I wasn't pregnant to a rapist. I wasn't so desperate that I saw strychnine as the better option.

It took me a moment to realize that my phone was ringing in my pocket. I pulled it out and glanced at the screen. Unrecognized number. I swiped to accept the call. 'Hello?'

She had to say her name three times before I realized it was Danielle Goodwin's mother. 'Hang on, I can't hear you. I'll take you outside.' I pushed my way through the crowd on the dance floor, holding my phone down by my side, and made my way back the way I'd come, down the stairs and back outside. 'Sorry about that.'

'Sounds like quite a party. Sorry to ring so late, it's been one of those days. I've tried a few times.'

'I know, we keep missing each other.'

There was a pause as I tried to think what to say.

'I'm returning your call,' she said. 'Did you have something to tell me?'

'I wanted to ask you a question. I hope you don't mind, but you said you had another baby.' I found getting the words out difficult.

'Sophie,' she said.

'Yes. Sophie. I know this might sound odd, but did Danielle know about Sophie?'

'Of course she did. We visited her grave together. I take Kyle. It's important for them to know about her. I can't pretend like she never existed.'

There was a silence you could have cut with a blunt pair of scissors.

'Why are you asking about Sophie?'

'We've found a necklace. A necklace the victim was wearing—'

'The suicide girl? I told you, that's not Danielle.'

'We want to make absolutely sure.'

'Danielle had too much to live for. If she's not alive anymore it's not because she chose to die.'

'I'm sorry, I didn't mean to upset—'

'It's because of him,' she said, and I had to hold the phone away from my ear. 'If she's dead, it's down to him.'

I wondered whether she'd had a drink, thought I could hear a slight slurring of her words, but it might just have been the bad line. Drinking alone, I knew from experience, was never a good thing. Poor woman. 'Well,' I glanced up at the windows of the club. Shafts of lights hit the pavement, changing colour every few seconds, blue, green, purple. 'We're looking at him too.'

'What?'

'If we can help at all in Danielle's case, I mean, even if she's not our ...' I didn't want to use the word body, 'victim.' I hesitated. I wanted to tell Mrs Goodwin I knew how it felt, to live with the kind of uncertainty she lived with every day, but of course I didn't. I lost a parent, not a child. I can't imagine what it must feel like to take on the responsibility for another life, and then to lose that life.

But I did know how it felt to live with the hope that one day that missing person might turn up. I spent my entire childhood hoping my father would one day walk through the door, that he'd take one look at the situation I was growing up in and resolve it. Of course, he never did. I swallowed. 'I'll do what I can, is what I'm saying.'

'I didn't ask you to get involved.'

'Oh no, I don't mean ...' I was embarrassed, thought she'd got hold of the wrong end of the stick. 'I mean, I'm not going to charge you. It's just, if he's done something to Danielle, he should pay for that.'

'No,' she said and it sounded like she was shouting at me. My cheeks burned and I glanced around to see if there was anyone nearby. 'Don't go stirring it all up,' Mrs Goodwin said.

'It's not good for Kyle if I go getting all upset. Leave it to the police, it's their job.'

'But the police aren't—'

'I don't want you getting mixed up in this, I'd never forgive myself. He's a dangerous man, stay away from him. Do you hear me?'

'Yes,' I said. I did hear her. I glanced up at the windows again, the lights had changed colour, the windows now bathed in a red orange glow that made it look like the building was on fire. 'I'd better go. I've left Jo.'

'Where are you?'

I could hear the suspicion in her voice but I pretended not to. 'Yes, see you soon,' I said, like we'd just finished discussing the price of teabags. I switched off my phone and tried not to feel disgruntled. A bit of gratitude from someone wouldn't go amiss. My legs were heavy as I climbed the stairs. If I was honest, there was more than one reason why jumping on a plane to Spain was exactly what I felt like doing. When I got back into the club I tracked Jo to the edges of the room and saw her threading her way through the crowd towards the DJ booth in the far corner. My fingers itched from the change in temperature as I caught up with her.

'Great set,' I heard Jo say.

'Thanks, man. Been before?'

'No, first time.'

'Well, check it out. Every Monday 9 till 11.'

'We're from Leeds,' I said, joining the pair of them on the raised platform.

'OK, maybe a bit far. This is a great track,' he said. 'If this don't get you dancing, nothing will.' He looked at us, like it was odd we hadn't turned and gone back down the steps. Realization dawned that the moment to leave after a moment or two pleasant chit-chat had gone and none of us had moved.

The silence was broken by two women who marched up the stairs carrying a box of records between them. 'Played, Ink.'

'Cheers.'

The two women set down their box of records, as Ink put one of his records back in its sleeve.

'Can we buy you a drink?' Jo asked Ink.

'I'm meeting my girlfriend.'

'Ace. We'll buy her one too.'

He looked a bit bemused but he followed us over to a corner near the bar. I went to get the drinks. When I got back he and Jo were engrossed in a conversation about music, which I couldn't really follow.

'So, what you doing down in Bristol?'

'We're on our way to the airport,' said Jo. 'Just thought we'd drop in.'

'We're investigating a case,' I said.

He laughed. 'You don't look like coppers to me.'

'We're not, we're private investigators.' He stopped laughing as I spoke. 'We run a missing persons' bureau.'

Someone on the dancefloor cheered as 'Who's That Chick?' started up. DJ Ink shifted his gaze from me to Jo. 'Fucking hell,' he said.

'Yes,' said Jo. 'Fucking hell indeed.'

He put his drink down on the table and turned away from us. 'I'm going for a fag,' he said.

'Good idea,' said Jo. 'Could do with one myself.'

He started running almost as soon as we got through the main door. Jo stood to one side to let me past and I chased after him. Running away from someone on a staircase is never a good idea, particularly not one that's heading downwards. I launched myself on him, landed on his back and we fell down the last few stairs together. A bouncer at the bottom helped us both up.

'You all right, Ink?' he asked.

Luckily Jo was only a few steps behind. 'He's not feeling very well, wants some air. Don't worry, we'll look after him.'

I don't know whether Ink was dazed, or whether he was embarrassed to ask a man for help dealing with two women, but he didn't say anything and Jo linked arms with him as we dragged him to his feet and out of the main door.

I didn't say anything until we got round the corner, down a back alley that led behind a restaurant with the smell of fried chicken. 'If there's one thing I've learned in this business,' I said, 'it's only people with guilty consciences run.'

He sat down on the steps outside the kitchen doors, surrounded by large wheelie bins.

'We know about Danielle,' I said.

'Someone's hired you to find her? After all this time?'

'It might seem like a long time to you, but for her mother, bringing up Danielle's child, wondering every single day what happened to her, it probably doesn't feel like all that long ago.'

'Her mother hired you?' The incredulity in his voice was obvious.

Jo passed me a cigarette. I lit it. 'I didn't say that.'

'Has something happened to Kyle?'

'No.' Jo offered him a cigarette but he shook his head. 'Kyle's fine.'

'So why?' he said. 'She's got no right.'

'No right? She's bringing up her own grandson and she's got no right to try and find where her daughter is? She believes you killed Danielle.' I couldn't keep the words inside me anymore. Perhaps he was getting what I hadn't dared give to Matt Williams's dad.

'No, she doesn't.'

I fixed him with my hardest stare. 'She does. She told me.'

'She's not starting to believe her own bullshit?'

'Come again?'

'Truth is she doesn't deserve a daughter. That's the truth.'

'Go on,' said Jo.

'Nah, I've said enough.'

'You killed Danielle to get back at her mother?'

'I didn't kill Danielle. She wants to believe that, let her. She knows the truth.'

'The police interviewed you.'

'The police interviewed me for eleven hours. They didn't charge me. The night Danielle disappeared, I played my set and I went home. My mate Ned came with me – crashed on my sofa. We were together all night. There's no way I could have killed Danielle. She's the best thing that ever happened to me.'

'She is?'

'What?'

'You said she is the best thing that ever happened to you. Present tense.'

He shrugged. 'Never met anyone else that comes close.'

'Do you know where Danielle is?'

He ran both his hands through his hair. 'How is Kyle?'

'You left Nottingham soon after Danielle disappeared,' Jo said, exhaling a cloud of smoke. 'Why did you do that?'

'I needed a change.'

'What if she'd come back? I mean, if she was the best thing that ever happened to you, and you didn't kill her, why didn't you wait around to see if she turned up?'

'If she wanted to contact me, she could. I'm easy enough to find. Ned's still there – still sees Lou Goodwin marching around the place. He'd tell me if Danielle ever showed up.'

'What about your girlfriend?' I remembered he'd told us at the bar that he was meeting his girlfriend. 'She can't like knowing that Danielle was the best thing that ever happened to you. What would she think if Danielle turned up?'

'She's not really a girlfriend.' He checked his phone and stood up. 'I'd better go – she'll be wondering what's happened to me.'

Jo flicked the butt of her cigarette towards a drain. It hit the metal grid and sparks flew up in the night air. Ink pushed past her and Jo made like she was going to grab his arm, but I shook my head. 'Let him go,' I said. Ink ran off into the alleyway, like a scalded cat. 'He knows something.'

'Isn't that reason to not let him go?'

'Give him a minute.' I watched him make his way back

towards the club entrance. When he got there, he glanced around and I ducked back into the side street. When I next peered round the corner, he was further down the street. 'Not going to meet his girlfriend. Funny that.'

Jo leaned against me. 'We're letting him get away.'

'No, we're not. Do that find your phone thingy.'

'What?'

'I put my phone in his pocket, when I was riding him down the stairs.'

Jo grinned. 'Knew there was a reason I chose to go into this business with you.'

'He'll give it ten minutes to make sure we're not following him, then he'll text his girlfriend and get her to meet him somewhere else. In the meantime,' I said, linking arms with Jo, 'there's a chance we might spot her in the club.'

'Unlikely seeing as we don't know what she looks like.'

'She'll look like a young woman, trying to find someone she knows in the club. She'll look puzzled until she gets a text message. Then she'll look worried. Can't be that hard to find.'

*

But Jo was right. We didn't spot her. We wandered round the club for a while, Jo got a pint and I got a sparkling mineral water. I asked the barman to add a splash of lime because why the fuck not. Twenty minutes later I nudged Jo. 'See where he is now.'

*

We left the club and followed the signal on Jo's phone. It led to a residential street, a small row of terraced houses fifteen minutes out of the town centre. I sloped off round the back of the houses, and Jo knocked on the front door three minutes later. In the still of the night air I heard the banging – she has a knock like a policeman's battering ram, does Jo.

Nothing happened.

Thirty seconds later I heard Jo pound the door again. As she did, the back door of the house opened and a young woman stepped out, pulling on a coat. I waited until she stepped into the back street, and the glow of the streetlight made her dark hair shine.

I took a gamble.

'Hi, Danielle,' I said.

Chapter 25

Danielle Goodwin looked me up and down like she was assessing her chances of running, or perhaps overpowering me. Flight or fight. She had no chance on either count. I don't mean to blow my own trumpet, but I'm built like a whippet, born for the chase – she was slightly overweight and wearing heels. And boxing has taught me to stand on the balls of my feet, keep my arms loose, my fists lightly curled. She thought about her options for all of about two and a half seconds. 'I'm not called Danielle,' she said.

'Right.'

'No, I mean, I was. I've changed my name. No one's called me Danielle for seven years. It's Laura now.'

'Can we go inside?'

'Please don't tell my mum.'

'I need to make sure you're OK. If you are, I promise you, I won't tell your mum.'

'Honest?'

'Cross my heart.'

'Si says you're working for her.'

'Not true. We're working for a retired journalist.' I watched panic cross her face. I moved to reassure her. 'He wants us to identify a dead body that was found seven years ago. You were one of the possibles. Obviously, it's not you, being as how you're not dead, so you're not involved in the case we're working on. But, I still need to know you're OK and making good choices. That's all.'

'You'd better come inside,' she said.

The house was small, a little galley kitchen at the back that we stepped through into a small room that was full of records. It had speakers set up on stands and I noticed fairy lights, switched off but hung over the walls. I heard Ink talking to Jo out the front.

'It's all right, Si, let her in,' Laura called. 'The other one was waiting for me out the back.'

'How did you find us?' asked Ink, coming into the back room.

I crossed the room to where his jacket lay on the small settee. I picked it up and pulled my phone out from the pocket. 'We're private investigators. It's our job.'

'Nightmare,' he said.

'You need to give us a chance,' said Jo, as she followed him to the room. 'We're actually really nice people.'

'They're not working for my mum,' Laura said.

'Don't suppose you've got a beer handy?' asked Jo, taking her jacket off. She took a seat on the settee, made it clear we weren't going anywhere anytime soon.

Ink moved to stand by Laura. He put his arm around her shoulders, but she shrugged it off. 'They're trying to identify a dead body. They got my name from missing persons.' Laura turned to me. 'Thought she'd have given up by now.'

'You've not asked anything about Kyle,' I said.

'No,' she said. She paused. 'I guess I've had to put him out of my mind.'

'Right,' I said. I tried not to let my resentment show, but I know what it's like to grow up with a parent with that attitude. Ink stepped out of the room, into the kitchenette.

'Have you met my mum?' Laura asked.

'No, just spoken to her, on the telephone.' I didn't want to sit down next to Jo, preferred my height advantage. 'Lucky for Kyle that she's there. She thinks you're dead. She thinks Simon killed you. Can you imagine what it's been like for her – not knowing where you are, what's happened to you?'

Ink came in from the kitchenette with a couple of bottles of beer. He handed one to me but I shook my head. Jo took one and Ink opened the other.

'What did she say about Kyle?'

'That you had him when you were very young.'

Laura took a seat in the large chair and Ink sat down next to her, balancing himself on its arm. He put his arm around her shoulders again, and this time she didn't remove it. He offered her the bottle of beer, and she drank a mouthful before speaking. 'Did she say anything about his father?'

'She doesn't know anything about him. Beyond the fact that he was married and he's had nothing to do with Kyle, not even since you disappeared. She's raising your child single-handedly.' I tried to keep the judgement out of my voice but I admit I wasn't finding it easy.

'He's not my child.'

'What?' asked Jo, digging her keys out of her jacket pocket.

She opened her bottle of beer with the opener she has on her keyring.

'Do you want to explain that?' I asked. 'Everyone thinks he's yours.'

'You really want to know?'

'We've driven all the way from Leeds,' I said. And I did want to know. I wanted to know what made a parent abandon their child, even a parent as young as Laura.

'My mum had seven miscarriages. And a baby who died.'

'She told me. Must have been awful for her.'

'The doctors told her to give up, said the odds were stacked against her, but she wouldn't give up.'

I saw the look on Jo's face, but I didn't understand it.

'Because she wanted another child more than anything.'

'Losing a baby must be terrible,' I said. 'I mean—'

'My dad couldn't take anymore. Her grief, the obsession. He drove his car into a wall when I was twelve years old.'

'Christ,' said Jo.

'Must have been awful for you both,' I said. I noticed Simon tighten his hold on Laura.

'It didn't make her stop,' Laura said.

'Didn't make her stop wanting a child?' Jo asked. 'But how ... I mean, if your dad was dead?'

I closed my eyes. I didn't want to hear anymore. I didn't need to hear anymore. The weight of me fell onto my knees and I dropped to the floor.

'Jesus,' said Jo. 'Are you saying ...?'

'When I was fourteen, she bought us a bottle of champagne to share. I came home from school and she was making my favourite dinner. I was so relieved to see her relaxed, almost happy, I didn't even ask what we were celebrating. It was the first time I'd ever had a drink. It was the first time I can remember her being kind to me, and I actually thought maybe she'd turned a corner. That maybe she might be starting to focus on what she had instead of what she'd lost.'

Laura laughed. Well, laugh is probably the wrong verb. 'As if.'

I wasn't sure I wanted to hear anymore. In fact, I knew I didn't, but I also knew that I'd asked for this. I owed it to Laura to listen.

'It was three weeks after I'd got my first period. She'd been online. Found a sperm donation clinic that asked few questions.'

'You poor thing,' said Jo.

'She had it all planned. She said we could tell everyone I'd had a one-night stand with a married man. She said no one could force me to reveal his identity. All I had to do was go along with her plan.'

Ink tightened his grip on Laura's fingers. 'She's fucking insane.'

'When I said I didn't want to, she slapped my face so hard, my lip split.' She held up her face and pointed to a small white scar that ran from her top lip to under her nose. 'She went on about it for days. Begged, cried. I woke up one night to her hitting me with her shoe. She didn't feed me for three days. In the end, I agreed. I thought it might make her like me. I thought maybe if she got what she wanted we could be happy.'

Tears stung my eyes. I couldn't help it. 'She made you get pregnant?'

Laura nodded. 'She took me out of school – told the authorities I was being home educated. It took six tries. I'd just turned fifteen when the pregnancy test turned blue. As soon as I saw the line, I cried. She was over the moon. She said I wouldn't have to do anything, that it was like me giving her the best Christmas present I could get for her.'

I know we have higher expectations of women than we do of men, and that isn't really fair. I know men do all kinds of sick, hurtful things to their own children, to their own daughters and we've become almost immune to the idea of it. But what I was hearing about Mrs Goodwin made my skin crawl. I thought of her voice on the telephone. How could a mother do that to her own child?

'But nothing changed,' Laura continued. 'Even after she'd got what she wanted. It didn't make her happy. If anything it made her worse. She barely let me get out of bed the first three months – she was so scared I'd have a miscarriage. And then, towards the end of the pregnancy I think she hated me more than ever – because my body could do what hers couldn't. The birth was the worst moment of my life.'

No one spoke for what seemed like about five minutes. I felt hot, light-headed. What could I say to that?

'What a fucking cow,' said Jo.

'She didn't let me near him, after he was born. She was terrified of me telling anyone the truth, said she'd kill me if I ever breathed a word to anyone. I was hardly allowed out of the house. She wouldn't let me get a job. And then, when Kyle was about six months, she started talking about having another. And that's when I realized,' – Laura swallowed – 'I knew, there was no way out. She'd never let me go.'

'You planned to disappear?'

'It was my idea,' Ink said.

'How did you two meet?' asked Jo. I don't know whether she was thinking the same as me – thank God they had each other.

'We used to go to the same school, though Si was two years above me.'

'She used to come to the Spar – I was working there, trying to earn enough money to go travelling.'

'We got talking.'

'You mean, I eventually got up the courage to ask you out. I'd fancied her since about Year Nine.'

Laura grinned. 'My mum hated him.'

'Your mum hates everyone,' Ink said. He saw the look on Laura's face and added, 'Apart from Kyle.'

'She always wanted a boy. Never liked girls. I thought so long as I didn't tell anyone anything, she'd let me go. I thought she'd tell everyone I'd had a breakdown, or something.'

'I made sure I had an alibi for the night Danielle went missing,' Ink added. 'I knew Louise would say anything just to keep the focus off her.'

'How come the police never found you?'

'I'm surprised my mum reported me missing. I really didn't think she'd care. But she did cos they went to Si, asking questions.'

'I said she'd been talking about going travelling after Leeds Fest. Danielle took her passport with her.'

'We wanted them to think I'd just run away from the responsibility of having a child.'

'A couple of my mates came to uni down here,' Ink said. 'So I asked if Laura could crash for a couple of weeks.'

'I went to the library and researched for babies that had died in the same year I was born – got the birth certificate of a girl called Laura James. I started using her name – on the tenancy agreement of my first flat, on electric bills. It wasn't that hard; in fact I still can't believe how easy it was.'

'What did you do for money?'

'I got a job working in a café, cash in hand. For the first year I lived here that's all I did. I went to work in the morning and came home at night. I volunteered for every extra shift going.'

'Don't you worry about Kyle?'

'Laura didn't choose any of this,' said Ink, his dark eyes boring into mine. 'She was fourteen ...'

Laura put a hand on his thigh. 'Course I do,' she said to me. 'My mum's a time bomb of suppressed rage. But she got what she always wanted. A boy.'

'Ink's right,' said Jo. 'It's not your fault. None of this is your fault.'

'I still find some things hard. Like I can go to the fridge and eat something without asking and I don't have to feel like I'm stealing because I bought the food. I can make a cup of tea. I still can't look at Nice biscuits.'

'Nice biscuits?'

'We had to eat one at four o'clock every single day. A Nice biscuit with a glass of orange squash. My mother spent her whole life trying to control everything. She's sick.'

'Do you think you'll ever contact her?'

She shook her head. 'It's taken me the best part of seven years to stop living always looking over my shoulder, always wondering whether she's watching. I can't let any of it back in. I know you think I'm a terrible mother, but I had no choice.'

'I don't think you're a terrible mother,' I said.

'She took over as soon as he was born. I just incubated him for her. I was still a child. It's taken me years to realize that. I wasn't ready to be a mother. Don't think I ever will be.'

I watched Simon's hand tighten around her. 'Doesn't matter. We've got each other,' he said in a low voice. He raised his head and spoke to me. 'We did the best we could for Kyle. I rang social services not long after and made an anonymous complaint – so that they'd keep an eye on him. We did the best we could with a shit set of circumstances. None of it is Laura's fault.'

*

We left them not long after that. I'll never forget sitting in that small, cold but kind of homely back room, Simon with his arm around Laura. They still looked like children even though Laura was just a couple of years older than me. It's not often I meet people I think had worse upbringings than I did. My mother wore depression like a shield. It kept her away from people, from interaction. I never saw her laugh; she never put her arm around me. But she also never hurt me. We shared a house, just the two of us, for eighteen years and I know nothing about her. I couldn't tell you what she believed in, who she voted for, what her favourite song was. She squatted on the settee watching *Coronation Street* as the life seeped out of her one day at a time.

But what Laura's mother had done to her child was something else. Neglect I can forgive, because neglect is passive, it's without energy. Abuse is active. Abuse requires action and the actions Louise Goodwin had taken went beyond forgiveness.

Chapter 26

On our walk back into Bristol town centre, Jo and I decided to forget about the 5 a.m. flight to Spain. Hearing Laura's story had wiped us both out. There was another flight at eleven the next morning. A few hours' delay wouldn't do any harm and we could book into the Premier Inn we'd seen on the way into town and get a few hours' sleep. It was almost midnight when we checked in through the automated screen on the twenty-four-hour reception. We got a twin room and Jo bought a bottle of beer from the twenty-four-hour Tesco Express round the corner. I took my jeans off and got into bed in my knickers and T-shirt. I was looking up flights on my phone when it rang. I frowned at Jo. My phone didn't recognize the number.

'Hello?' I said.

There was a silence.

'Hello?' I said again. I was on the verge of hanging up, assuming it was someone messing around, when Eileen Williams's voice trembled down the line.

'I'm sorry to ring so late. I had to wait until Alex was in bed. I don't know what to do.'

'You've done the right thing,' I said. 'Ringing is the right thing.'

'What do you want from me?'

I swallowed to give myself a moment to think. 'I want you to come to Spain with me. I think Matt, Matthew's gone to Spain.'

'He has. Alex told me.'

'Matthew came home?'

'Yesterday. I came back from church and caught him breaking in to the house. Kept saying over and over again he'd done something wrong but it wasn't his fault. I thought he'd taken something. I was about to ring for an ambulance when Alex arrived back from golf. He took Matthew into his study and told me to get on with lunch. The next thing I knew, Matthew had gone.'

'What did Alex say?'

'That Matthew was worn out from studying too hard and needed a break, so he was going to go away for a few weeks, to stay with some friends who were working in Spain for the summer.'

'Do you know whereabouts in Spain?'

'I saw the receipt for the flight on his desk. Matthew flew to Granada.'

Granada was the nearest airport to Beneficio.

'He said Matthew would be fine after a few weeks off in the sunshine.'

'Right.'

'I don't know what to do for the best.'

'Yes you do. You know he has to face up to what he's done.

He needs help. He has to explain what's happened to his girlfriend. He has to take—'

'I didn't know he had a girlfriend. He doesn't tell us anything about that side of life.'

'Well, he has. She's called Nikki and she seems to adore him.'

'Nikki? This isn't the woman who says ...'

I paused, waiting to see if she could complete the sentence but she didn't. 'No,' I said eventually. 'I can't tell you the name of the person he raped at the moment. She's traumatized, needs time to recover. But when she does, she will report him to the police, and once they find out Matt's run to Spain ... Well it doesn't look good.'

'Where is she? This Nikki?'

'She lives in Leeds. She's worried about Matthew. All she knows is he's disappeared off the face of the earth.'

'Is she nice?'

I thought about that for a moment. Nice probably wasn't the first word that would jump into my mind to describe Nikki, but in the absence of anything else, it would do. 'Yes, she seems very—'

'I've made so many mistakes.'

I thought of her husband. 'We all make mistakes,' I said. 'It's not about not making mistakes, it's about making amends when we do.'

Me. The voice of experience.

'Alex will be terribly upset if I get involved.'

'Eileen, you're Matt's mother. And, Alex is your husband, not your father. I'm telling you right now the best thing for you to do is to help your son face up to his mistakes. Come with me to Spain.'

'Alex didn't give me a chance to speak to Matthew, before he left.'

'Well, take the chance I'm giving you. I can book us two plane tickets right now. All I need is your passport number.'

'You'd have to come and get me. If Alex knew what I was doing he wouldn't let me leave.'

'Wouldn't let her leave?' I mouthed to Jo. Thank Christ I've never been in a relationship where I've reached the point where I could say that about my partner and not even seem to recognize its absurdity. 'You want us to come and get you now? We're in Bristol.'

'How long will it take you to get here?'

'An hour?'

'OK. I'll meet you by the post office in an hour. I'll bring my passport.'

She hung the phone up on me, and I stared at Jo. 'We've got to go and get her right now.'

Bless Jo, she was already pulling on her trousers. 'Good job you don't drink,' she said. 'You'll have to drive.'

Less than twelve hours later I found myself sitting on an aeroplane, next to Eileen Williams. The urge to say yes to the air stewardess's offer of a glass of wine or gin and tonic had never been stronger. There had only been two available seats on the flight, so Jo had elected to stay in Leeds and keep Aunt Edie in line. I'm not good with strangers, and eleven hours in the company of Eileen had not made her seem like she wasn't a stranger. Half of those hours I'd been asleep – although not in the Premier Inn in Bristol – after picking up Eileen, we'd headed straight for Heathrow, as it gave us more options, and we'd booked the first flight out to Spain. Malaga. Not the nearest airport, but we decided we needed to get out of the country as fast as possible, before Alex realized his wife was missing.

Eileen probably had fewer social skills than I do, and there's not many people I can say that about. Obviously she had a thing or two on her mind, what with her son being a rapist, her husband being a bully and her being on the run. Well not on the run exactly but when I asked her if she'd left a note, she'd shaken her head and said, 'It's best I deal with all that when I get back.'

It's weird, isn't it? I mean, presumably no girl says, 'When I grow up I want to marry a man who treats me like a servant and doesn't let me decide when to take a trip.' So, how do women end up in that situation? I have a theory it's all about parenting. If you were well-parented, if you had parents that were looking out for you, who wanted the best for you, and steered you away from bad decisions (for that read bad men) then you were in with a chance of a happy life.

If not, if you grew up with bad parents, ones that had too many issues of their own to ever get around to some active hands-on nurturing, then you're fucked. You're already in a cycle of abuse – your parents abused, neglected or disappeared and so you end up recreating the relationship because that's your normal. You end up with friends that abuse, neglect or disappear, because that's your pattern. Breaking the pattern of childhood is a lifetime's work, so if you are born into a pattern that needs breaking the main focus of your life will be spent on breaking the pattern, or succumbing to it.

If you were one of those lucky kids that got born into a great pattern, a healthy pattern – well then you get to choose how to spend your life; you can set your own goals, and they can be creative goals rather than reactive goals. Sometimes, I tell myself I feel sorry for those kids though, because really the only way is down.

I dozed a bit on the plane and so it didn't seem to take long to get to Malaga. I switched my phone on in the airport and waited till its European package kicked in. There was a message already from Jo, telling me where to pick up the car she'd hired for us. The heat enveloped us as we jumped into a taxi and got dropped off in the centre of Malaga, near the car hire place. Jo must have got back to Leeds because she'd emailed them a copy of my driving licence – or maybe she'd got Aunt Edie to do it. All I had to do was sign a few forms and we were away. We checked the car over on the lot and the assistant handed me the keys. My hands were sweaty from both fear and the heat. It was getting on for noon and so much warmer than Heathrow at 7 a.m. I hadn't even got a change of knickers with me, and it was way too hot for the jeans I was wearing. 'We might need to go shopping,' I said to Eileen.

*

I can think of a hundred things I'd rather do than trail around town buying stuff. It's not something I ever really do. Clothes seem to arrive in my life, other people's cast-offs, charity shops. I don't like new clothes. They're too shiny and unyielding. I prefer the lived-in feel.

We left the car on the lot and walked the short distance into the centre of Malaga. I'd never been shopping with an older woman. The experience was weird but Eileen was an expert. She seemed to know exactly where to go and what part of the shop to target. It didn't take long before I had new shorts, a couple of T-shirts and a pair of light canvas shoes.

'My treat,' said Eileen and for the first time I saw something that wasn't sadness in her eyes. 'I absolutely insist.'

After we'd got kitted out, we found ourselves an agreeable pavement café that had lots of shade and sat down.

'I don't speak Spanish,' I said.

'You don't need to,' she said.

We ordered lemonades that tasted more like Bitter Lemon, and I ordered a burger, and Eileen had something she said was called calamari and looked like onion rings although I'm sure she said it was fish.

I've only been abroad twice. The first trip, to Paris, was the worst experience of my life. The second time, Thailand, was the best – the place where I was reborn. I didn't really want to think about what this third trip might mean. I try not to believe in signs or destiny or things coming in threes. 'Have you rung Alex?' I asked Eileen.

'No.'

'Right.'

'He'll be furious. He's not used to ... He's used to giving orders.'

'I got that.'

'It's the only way he knows. He's a doctor,' she said. She took a sip of her lemonade. 'And when Matthew was seven and at boarding school in Surrey, his appendix burst. Alex and I were living on base in Singapore.'

I lit a cigarette, just so I had something to do with my hands. I wasn't sure I wanted any of the background to Matthew's life.

'Luckily there were doctors in the UK too. But it probably wasn't a doctor Matthew needed most then.'

'Lots of people grow up without having their mothers around all the time. They don't turn into rapists.'

She flinched. 'Please don't use that word.'

'You have to use that word. I can't make it sound better for you.'

'He always seemed so angry.'

'Alex?'

'No. Well, yes. But I meant Matthew. He always seemed so angry with me, not just with me. With women. I found a hidden store of pornographic magazines once, in his bedroom. I had the gardener light a bonfire and I burned them. They were distressing.'

'Maybe talking to him would have been a better idea.'

'Do you think I've not spent the last twenty-four hours thinking of the things I could have done differently?'

'I'm sorry, I didn't mean—'

'It's my fault. How Matthew treats women, how he feels about them, it's my fault.'

'You can't take the blame for him, you know.' I thought as the words came out of my mouth that I was lying through my teeth. I'd blamed my parents for quite a lot of things that I've done wrong in the past. I blame my mum for my lack of social skills and I blame my dad for the rest. His absence left a hole in me and most of my addictions are an attempt to fill that hole.

If my dad was here, I knew I wouldn't be saying, 'You can't take the blame for your offspring.' I'd be saying the opposite. That every wrong thing I'd ever done in my life was because of him. I wanted him cursed with guilt for all eternity. I didn't want him ever to be free of the feeling that he was responsible for everything.

'Cheeseburger?' the waiter asked.

I didn't feel as hungry as I had when I ordered.

Chapter 27

It was almost four o'clock by the time we'd eaten and we were both knackered, having hardly slept at all the previous night, so we decided to book a hotel in Malaga and head out to Beneficio early in the morning. The early bird catches the worm. Google Maps had told me it was about a two-hour drive – I wanted to get there before anyone got moving.

'We should aim to set off about 5.' To be honest, I had another reason for such an early start – I was hoping to drive when there wasn't any other traffic around. Driving's not my strong point at the best of times, and I'd never driven on the wrong side of the road before.

We found a hotel, and a mini market where we bought a few provisions, including a toothbrush for me and some snacks for the evening. I said goodnight to Eileen in the lift – she was on the third floor, I was on the fourth.

I rang Jo from the hotel room. 'Hola.'

'Hey, you.' She sounds more Liverpudlian on the phone than in real life. 'How's it going?'

'Good. Hot. I'm knackered. We're hunkering down for the

night – going to get there early doors tomorrow. Thanks for sorting the car.'

'No worries. Remember they drive on the right.'

'Thanks. I'll try to keep that in mind.'

'How's Eileen?'

'Quiet. Guilt-ridden. Posh. What time did you get back to Leeds?'

'In time for breakfast.'

'Bloody hell. You must have floored it.'

'Do you know what's interesting?'

'What?'

'One of the Park Killer's victims was attacked right outside those flats. I mean, literally, right outside.'

'By the statue?'

'No, in the park. But honestly, you couldn't get closer to the flats. Which is weird when you think about those huge windows. If someone had been looking out, you'd be certain they'd see.'

'So, Jenny was making a protest about the Park Killer? Maybe she wanted the police to acknowledge he should have been charged with Maureen's murder?'

'Well, if she was, you'd think she'd have killed herself in the same spot he attacked his victims, in the park, outside the gardens of the flats. I think the flats are the key. It's interesting she tied herself to that statue. She didn't want her body to be moved. Why didn't she want her body to be moved?'

'I don't know. It's a bit—'

'Or, more importantly, why was she worried her body might have been moved?'

'Why make a protest about the Park Killer when he's already dead?' I undid the laces on my trainers.

'That's my point. I don't think she was making a protest about the Park Killer. I think she was making a protest about, or to, someone who lived in the flats. But I think it involves the Park Killer in some way.'

'Run that by me again?'

'What if the Park Killer wasn't acting alone? What if someone knew what he was doing? What if someone was protecting him?'

'Why would anyone do that?'

'What if he had an accomplice?'

'A serial killer with an accomplice? Fuck off.'

'Oh come on, Lee. What about the Moors murderers? What about Fred and Rosemary West?'

'You think the Park Killer had a wife?'

'He did. I checked. Well, a girlfriend who lived with him. But she didn't live in the flats. And there was never anything found that suggested she knew what he was doing. She distanced herself from him as soon as he was arrested. Didn't go to his funeral.'

'A girlfriend.' I tried to think of the kind of woman that might go out with a serial killer. I remembered reading that the Yorkshire Ripper's wife was supposed to be on the spectrum somewhere. I thought back to our visit to the flats, to the odd woman with her stuffed animals up on the fourth floor. 'You don't think, Linda?'

I could hear the exasperation in Jo's voice. 'No, I don't think Linda. I don't think Linda does relationships. But I think someone in those flats is connected to the Park Killer and I think Jenny knew about the connection. Frances said Jenny was scared. Not just scared. Petrified. So it's someone who doesn't want anyone to know about the connection and it's someone who's threatening.'

'Great.' I glanced around my hotel room, wondering whether I'd locked the door.

'I'm meeting Martin tomorrow morning, first thing. We're going to go through all the residents that were living in the flats at the time Jenny killed herself. The answer's staring us in the face, I'm sure of it.'

'OK. Well, good luck. Say hi to Martin for me.' I sat back against my pillow and yawned. 'Sorry, I'm knackered. Haven't recovered from Saturday yet. You must be too. Early night?'

I heard the hesitation in Jo's voice. 'Er, well, no. Said I'd call and see Sara. See how she's doing.'

'Oh.' As soon as I said the word I knew I sounded like someone's mother. Lemony.

'We might go to the pictures.'

'Right.' I tried to make my voice lighter. 'Good idea.'

'Something to take her mind off it all.'

'Did you tell her Matt's in Spain? Did you tell her I'm in Spain?'

'No. Thought I'd break that to her tonight. That was another reason for seeing her, actually.'

I wasn't convinced. 'Right. Do you think she'll be pleased?'

'I don't think she knows what she wants. She doesn't want to tell the police, but she doesn't want to let him off the hook either. She needs some kind of closure.'

'And to make sure it doesn't happen again, to some other woman.'

'She's got to recover first, Lee.'

Jo sighed and I knew she was pissed off with me. 'You seem more keen on making it her responsibility than you do on making it Matt's.'

'Get lost,' I said as my cheeks grew warm. 'How can you say that? I've just flown to Spain.' I stretched out the last word.

'You're doing that for you, not for Sara.'

'I'm doing it for Nikki, who is our actual client in case you'd forgotten.'

'All I'm saying is give her time. She's an amazing woman.'

'Right.' I picked up my bottle of water and held it against my cheeks. 'So amazing she can't face reporting a rapist to the police.'

'Oh, fuck off, Lee. This is your problem, not Sara's.'

'Why's it my problem?'

'God, you drive me mad.'

'Me?'

'You're so fucked up, you don't even know.'

'Know what?'

It took me a moment to realize Jo had ended the call. I hurled the phone across the room. It hit the wall and bounced onto the floor. I kicked off the sheet, knowing I wasn't going to be able to sleep now. The minibar called out to me. I told it to shut up and put on my new pair of shorts and refastened my trainers. Times like these all I can do is run.

Chapter 28

It took me ages to work out where I was when I woke up the next morning. I switched off the alarm on my phone and realized it was low on charge. While I had thought to bring a charger, I'd forgotten to pick up one of those two-pin plug adapters you need to plug it into the socket. Jo would kill me. I didn't care.

I was in the shower when I heard another phone ring. I ran through to the bedroom and picked up the landline next to my bed. It was Eileen checking I was up. We met in the lobby. She looked like she hadn't slept at all.

'Shall we get some breakfast?' I said.

'You can,' she said. 'I'm not hungry.'

In the end I went back to the mini mart just round the corner and grabbed us a couple of croissants and a half-dozen small bottles of water. My stomach felt tight, I think because of the thought of the drive ahead – not what we might find when we got there. I'd use the car journey to try and come up with a plan of action once we found Matt.

*

We barely spoke all the way there. The good thing about getting a hire car was that the steering wheel was on the wrong side, which kind of reminded me to drive on the right. There were a couple of instances where I saw Eileen's knuckles tighten on the door handle, but once we were out of Malaga and onto the open road, heading east along the coast, we were fine. The car had its own satnav system which seemed to be saying we'd arrive at three minutes past seven. The perfect time.

We drove into the sunrise, and being away from Leeds made my world feel bigger, made me realize that my little bubble, which is all-consuming when I'm in it, is only that – a little bubble on the face of the world. I wanted to switch on the radio but I sensed Eileen preferred the silence.

We stopped in a town called Órgiva, the last town before we reached Beneficio. I bought some potatoes and bananas from the local market, which was just setting up, because I'd read it was always better to arrive with a gift. And then we headed for the mountains that we could see rising beyond the town.

We passed the entrance to the site twice before I spotted it, despite the satnav. I parked the car at the bottom of the steep hill and we walked up a stony track for about ten minutes. The sun was breaking through the early morning haze and the air smelled fresh. A river tumbled down the hill next to us. At the top was a car park of sorts, where dozens of clapped-out trucks and motorhomes were gathered. Some had been painted with hippy symbols, flowers and the peace sign, some had curtains up at the windows. It was still early – not quite 8 a.m. By the time we reached the entrance to the site Eileen's face had taken on a pinched look, like she'd swallowed a wasp.

The Runaway

At the entrance to the camp there was a sign welcoming us and stating the rules. No alcohol, no hard drugs. We followed the track up the hill through beautiful scenery – pine and eucalyptus trees – until we came to a massive tepee. We hadn't seen a single living person since we arrived, but as we approached the tepee a man with the longest dreadlocks I've ever seen walked past us.

'Excuse me,' I said. 'We're looking for someone called Matt.'

He frowned at us and I wasn't sure whether he understood English.

'He came here, probably two days ago.'

'The new guys sleep there,' he said, pointing to another tepee I hadn't noticed that was nestled between the trees to our right. 'The visitors' tent.'

'Cheers.'

'I doubt anyone will be up yet. Grab a cup of tea from the kitchens.' He stared at Eileen. I knew already that she didn't look like the typical visitor to Beneficio. 'This is your first time?'

'Yeah,' I answered for her.

'Well, you're welcome. Everyone is welcome here.' He wandered off along the path through the trees.

'Do you want a cup of tea or should we get straight to it?'

'Straight to it.' Eileen said in a voice that made me think she wouldn't be persuaded to drink or eat anything while we were here.

There were four people asleep in the visitors' quarters. Four people and one dog. The dog opened an eye, and I paused a moment, but after a moment's thought, it shut its eye again and everyone else stayed sleeping. I only had the photos Nikki had given me to go off, but I knew I didn't have to recognize Matt. I heard Mrs Williams inhale and I followed her gaze to where her son lay sleeping inside a sleeping bag, his face soft.

I made my way over to him and put a hand on his shoulder. His eyes opened and then narrowed. I pointed towards his mother. 'We need to talk to you, Matt,' I whispered. 'Can you come outside?'

He rubbed his face and I guess he was trying to figure out whether he was dreaming. Or having a nightmare. His face went through several expressions, and I waited until he slid out of his sleeping bag. He was wearing a pair of loose-fitting shorts and not much else. His shorts bulged in a way I didn't want to think about. I don't think his mother did either because she turned away and made for outside. I let Matt go before me and he followed his mother outside.

'What are you doing here?' he said to his mother as he wrapped a blanket around his shoulders. He had stubble on his chin, like he hadn't shaved for a couple of days.

'Your father told me.'

The colour drained from Matt's face, despite the suntan.

'Let's find somewhere to sit down,' I said.

'Who's she?' he asked his mother.

'I'm a private investigator. I run a missing persons' bureau in Leeds. I was hired by your girlfriend.'

'Nikki?'

'You can't run, Matt. You'll never stop.'

'Nikki.' He stumbled along the path until we came to a

wooden hut building that was fairly open plan – it had a roof but no walls. There was a table and benches. 'The school,' he said.

'Have you met Nikki?' he asked his mother.

'No.'

Matt exhaled like that was a weight off his mind. For some reason this really annoyed me. 'Why haven't you introduced your girlfriend to your mother? You've been going out with her nearly a year.'

Matt didn't reply. He just stared at Eileen. She seemed to wither under his gaze. 'I'd like to meet her,' she said in a voice that didn't sound like hers.

She might like to meet her but she wouldn't approve, even I knew that. Especially when she found out Nikki was pregnant. I still hadn't decided whether to use that information, thought I'd store it like a weapon – only bring it out if absolutely necessary.

'You wouldn't get on, trust me,' said Matt.

'Lee told me about the other woman,' Eileen said. 'The one that's accused you of …'

'Shut up.' He stood up. 'Don't know what you're talking about.'

'Matthew, you need to explain to everyone what happened. I'm sure if you—'

I cut through the bullshit before we all sank in the stuff. 'Sara's going to go to the police,' I said. 'She's not the kind of woman that will let you get away with this. I found you in less than a week. The police will get here much quicker. The very fact you've run makes you look guilty.'

I glanced at Eileen. 'Even your mother knows it's true. There's no point trying to deny it, or rewrite it.'

His chin dropped. 'I don't remember. I don't know what happened.'

'If that's true, Matt, why are you here? Why didn't you go home? Why didn't you call your girlfriend and tell her what's going on?'

'It's Tuff's fault. It was his idea to go—'

'If the only thing standing between you and rape is your mate deciding to go to a party, you've got serious problems. A serious problem that you need to get help for.'

'We can get you help, Matthew.' Eileen glanced at her fingernails. They were painted a soft-shell pink colour.

'What you going to pay for now? Therapy? Rehab? Where can you send me next?'

'I'm not sure your father—'

'When are you going to get it into your stupid head that you can't just fix things by throwing money at them?' The anger in his voice took me by surprise. Eileen's cheeks flushed.

She hesitated and there was a silence that I wanted to fill but didn't have the words. Eventually Eileen said in a quiet voice, 'I know I haven't been the best mother.'

'You were no kind of mother. You sent us away at four.'

'I didn't have a choice, Matthew. Your father went to the same school.'

Four years old? It's possible to send kids to boarding school at four? God, we're a fucked-up country.

'I wouldn't mind if you had a job. Or a reason to not have

us at home. Your life has been the most meaningless existence I can think of. What's the point of you?'

I flinched. But then, sometimes it's best to put the truth out there.

'Your father didn't want me to work.'

'Don't blame this on Dad.'

'I would have loved to have been more involved. I was, with Ollie, but when he went, I thought what's the point of getting attached when you're all going to be sent away?'

'We were four years old.'

'None of your brothers has been accused of rape,' I said. 'Presumably they had the same upbringing?'

'You're right.' I thought Mrs Williams was talking to me but she was addressing her son. She tried to put a hand on his arm but she didn't have the courage to land it. 'I shouldn't have let you go. I knew how much you hated it.'

'I'm sure Singapore had its compensations.'

'It wasn't exactly a bowl of cherries, Matthew. Living with your father on army bases around the world. Half the time I didn't know anyone. I didn't have any friends.'

'I bet you it was a fuck of a lot better than military boarding school,' Matt spat back, and I got the feeling he was probably right.

'I can't change it, Matthew. I wish I could. I've made so many mistakes.'

'You never once stood up to anyone in your whole life.'

'Why do you blame me and not Dad? It was his decision.' Her voice sounded like a child's and I knew she wasn't far from tears.

'You're pathetic.'

'I don't think this is getting us anywhere,' I said.

'No, it's all right,' Eileen said. She dabbed at her eyes with a tissue she'd brought out of her bag. 'It's the truth.'

'Don't try and make her feel sorry for you,' Matt said to his mother. 'It's always all about you.'

'You're being unfair. I might have—'

'You don't actually exist. You're just a reflection of other people.'

'Matthew, please.'

'All you care about is what other people think, how we're perceived, whether we present to the world as a successful family – you and your boys.'

The noise sounded like a pistol had been fired. A crack. I looked up and realized from the bright red mark on the side of Matt's face that his mother had slapped his cheek. I don't know who was the more surprised, me, him or Eileen.

'Don't you speak to me like that.' Her mouth was a long thin line. 'You have no idea who I am or what I think. You don't know what I go through; you don't know the half of it.' Flecks of spit flew onto the table. 'Your problem is you've never had to compromise. You don't contribute anything. None of you ever did.'

'We were never there.'

'You think you're entitled to whatever you want, always did. If someone had something and you wanted it, you thought you should get it.'

'This is getting us nowhere,' I said. 'Eileen, why don't you go back to the community kitchen bit, see if you can find us a cup of tea. I need to talk to Matt.'

Eileen nodded. She brushed imaginary dirt off her tunic-like top. 'I won't be long,' she said.

When she'd gone I turned to Matt. 'You've got a choice: you can come back with us to England right now and go and see Nikki and explain it to her.'

He winced at the thought. I handed him a cigarette.

'Or you can stay here and I'll make it my business to tell every single person what you've been accused of.'

'Is Nikki OK?'

That was a hard question. I settled for, 'She's really worried about you.'

'Does she know ... about ...?'

'Yes.'

'She'll kill me.'

'Might be doing you a favour.'

'I've never done anything like that before,' he said.

'That doesn't make me like you.'

'I don't know what happened, what I was thinking.'

'You want my advice? Stop thinking about you, start thinking about Sara. What she might want. What she might need. And when you're done thinking about her, think about Nikki.'

'I miss Nik,' he said, in a quiet voice.

'You're actually – yet again, by the sound of your life story – in a very privileged position,' I said. 'Your mum seems to be suggesting she'll sort out some kind of treatment programme for you, which I recommend you book into, and when charges are pressed, at least it will look like you're doing something about it rather than running away.'

'I didn't mean to hurt anyone.'

'No? Well, let me tell you, Matt. There's no way on earth fucking someone while they're unconscious isn't going to hurt.'

'I didn't know she was unconscious. I thought she was tripping.'

I folded my arms across my chest. 'You thought you could get away with it. You didn't think she was a person. That's the attitude that needs fixing. It doesn't take a fucking therapist to work out you're angry with your mother and you're taking it out on womankind. Grow the fuck up.'

'Piss off.'

I stubbed out my fag. 'Not an option. I'm not leaving until you do. Think of me as the ghost of Sara. I'm going to haunt you until you face up to what you've done.'

He rubbed his chest and I realized I was totally unmoved by his obvious physical attributes.

'What you going to do, Matt? Are you coming back or are you going to wait it out here, wondering every day if the police are going to arrive?'

He wiped his eyes and I realized he was crying. 'I'm going to come back,' he said.

Chapter 29

We drove to Granada, the nearest town with an airport, and Eileen booked us into a hotel, just so that Matt could have a shower. That's what life is like when you have money. While Eileen went with Matt, the helpful man on the desk rang the airport for me. I booked three tickets on the next available flight, which was the next morning at 7 a.m., on the company credit card. The hotel rooms were going to come in useful. I rang Jo to tell her the news, but she didn't answer. I thought about leaving a message but I knew I'd find it too hard to keep the sarcasm from my voice. I can't tell you how many times she's had a go at me for not answering my phone. I hung up and rang Aunt Edie instead.

'Pet. I was just thinking of you.'

'Where's Jo?'

'Oh. She left straight after her meeting with Martin. Said she was having lunch with ... a friend. She's taking a half day, said you'd been working all weekend.'

'Right.' I tried not to sound like a jilted bride but even I could hear the stuffiness in my voice.

'All things do pass,' said Aunt Edie.

I ignored her. 'What did Martin have to say?'

'Oh you know Martin. Thinks he's MI-flipping-5. Won't breathe a word of anything to the mere office dogsbody. No wonder he's single.'

I didn't point out to Aunt Edie that she had been single for as long as I'd known her. She had been married once upon a time, but all I knew about Uncle Arthur was that he'd been a butcher and had dropped dead while cutting up a pig carcass. They hadn't any children. I often wondered whether Aunt Edie got lonely, but she'd never tell you even if she did. 'Well, if you want you can tell Martin I've demanded an update. I won't be back in Leeds until lunchtime tomorrow. I need to be kept informed. All information needs to be shared with you. Tell him I said so.'

She sniffed. 'I'll try.'

'Didn't Jo tell you what they'd discussed?'

'She was in a rush. She'll tell me in the morning.'

*

I wandered back upstairs and knocked on the door of Eileen and Matt's twin room. Matt was in the shower so I told Eileen we'd be here for another day. 'Have you still not rung Alex?'

'It's probably best to wait until I see him face-to-face.'

In other words, avoid the conflict. A mode of operating I suspected she'd spent a lifetime perfecting.

The afternoon stretched in front of us, and as Matt and Eileen were barely speaking to each other, I felt apprehensive about it. It wasn't what you'd call a convivial atmosphere, so when Eileen suggested we visit the Alhambra, I thought what the hell. I'd never had the experience of being dragged round interesting monuments while on holiday, although I suspected Matt had.

*

The Alhambra is a palace dedicated to beauty and the pursuit of leisure. There's an outdoor swimming pool with a balcony above it where blind musicians used to play while the women swam. Blind so they couldn't feast their eyes on the women's nudity. A different take on the interpretation of the idea that men shouldn't look on women lustfully, which is also where the hijab come from.

'We need a plan for when we get back to England,' I said to Matt while Eileen cooed over the plants with some English woman she'd met.

'I thought we had one. The shit hits the fan.'

'Still feeling sorry for yourself?'

'Wouldn't you?'

'No. I feel sorry for your mum, who's risking her marriage and the world as she knows it to stand by your side. I feel sorry for Nikki who's spent the last week worrying about what the fuck's happened to you. But most of all I feel sorry for Sara, who came round from a bad experience with drugs to find you sticking your dick inside her.'

'I was off my head too you know.'

'I'm going to ring Nikki and tell her I've found you. She's going to choose whether she wants to meet you, or whether she wants me to kill you. If she chooses the former, you will sit and listen to what she has to say. After that, I swear I'll be doing everything I can to persuade Sara to report you. So your best bet, if you want my advice, is to own up to what you did and sort your shit out.'

I stalked off.

*

When we got back to the hotel we ordered burgers from the bar, which Eileen paid for. I called Jo again, but got the same electronic message. I had less than five per cent of battery remaining. 'The person you are calling is unable to take your call.' Not unable. Unwilling. I took a deep breath and waited for my chance to leave a message. 'All right. I'm behaving like a dickhead. I'm sorry. Hope you had a good time at the cinema. Let me know how you got on with Martin. Love you.'

I hung up and scrolled through my contacts. I kept telling myself this was a successful resolution of the case and I should be feeling proud of myself. I'd found the missing person and I was about to bring him back, to make him unmissing, restored. But my stomach felt heavy as I pressed to call Nikki. She answered on the first ring as usual.

'Lee?'

'Hey, Nikki. Listen, my battery's about to go. Are you OK?'

'Kind of.'

'You told your parents?'

'I think it's better to write them a letter. I think it's—'

'I've found Matt.' I surprised myself by grinning.

'Oh my God. Really? Where?'

'Spain. I'm bringing him back tomorrow.'

'Spain? What the fuck is he doing in Spain?'

'We'll be flying into Manchester. Tomorrow morning. With his mother.'

'His mother?'

'Long story. Do you want to see him?'

I could hear her breath down the phone. 'I don't know,' she said.

'It's your choice. I've told him he has to explain everything to you.'

'Have you told him about ...?'

'I thought that should be up to you. I'll tell him if you want me to.'

'No. I want to tell him. What time do you land?'

'Just after nine.'

'I'll be there,' she said, as my battery died.

Chapter 30

I hate flying. There's just something about it that makes no sense to me. I picture the passengers and the contents of the aeroplane suspended in the sky without the shell of the plane surrounding them and it looks absurd. Landing is the best bit of the whole experience. I sensed I was the only one of the three of us happy to be back. My sunburned cheeks smarted. I'm born for the north of England.

Nikki was waiting for us at the arrivals gate, looking like she hadn't slept since I spoke to her on the phone. Possibly none of us had. We left Matt and Nikki to talk and Eileen and I headed for the airport Starbucks. I ordered a chai tea latte; she had an Americano, no frills.

'Are you OK?' I said. She'd barely spoken for the last forty-eight hours.

'Not really. No.'

'I'm sorry,' I said. And I was. I knew I'd blown down her house of cards.

'I've made an utter mess of life.'

I took a slurp of my latte and wiped the froth from my mouth. 'Been there.'

'How do you deal with the guilt?'

'Focus on the here and the now,' I said, recalling Yuki's words to me, words that promised an escape from the negative energy I carried round with me every day. I met Yuki in Thailand. He taught me how to box and he taught me so much more than that. His way of seeing the world changed my life. Every time I feel overwhelmed, I try to focus on his voice, his words to me. 'There is only this place and this moment. Nothing else exists. Everything else is only a memory or a projection.'

'We all can change how we react to things,' I said to Eileen. 'If there's something you haven't done right, don't do it again and it's gone. The here and the now is all our life is.'

'I don't want to be married to Alex.'

That didn't come as a surprise. 'Don't be,' I said.

'I wish I'd been a better mother.'

'Be a better mother. Here and now.'

'You make it sound easy.'

It isn't. I know it sounds simple but it's the hardest lesson ever to learn. It's still not automatic, although Yuki promised me that if I practised enough, one day it would be. 'You have to keep at it.'

Nikki appeared at the table. 'Your son is a dickhead,' she said to Eileen. She turned to me. 'Are you coming?' Without waiting for me to reply, she hitched her bag onto her shoulder and marched off in the direction of the sign to the railway station.

I gulped my chai tea latte as I scanned the crowds and picked out Matt wandering across the concourse. He didn't look happy, but then he didn't deserve to. I pointed him out to Eileen. 'Let me know how it goes.'

'I'm scared,' she said. 'I'm scared of my own son.'

I put a hand on her arm. 'You can do it.'

'What if—?'

'Good luck.'

*

Nikki and I made our way to the station and I bought a ticket from the machine. We were in luck – the train to Leeds was sitting on the platform. 'Did you tell him?' I asked her once we were sitting together.

'No. I nearly did and then he told me about the party and what happened and I thought he couldn't cope with knowing about the baby right now and then it hit me. If he can't cope with knowing I'm pregnant, he's never going to be able to cope with being a dad. He said he might go to prison. Is that true?'

'It's a possibility,' I said.

'If I'm going to do this, I'm doing it completely alone. He didn't even apologize. Like he thinks I should feel sorry for him. Dick. Head.'

I wasn't expecting thanks, and I didn't get any. I sat back in my seat and closed my eyes. If I looked at the situation through Nikki's eyes, this probably wasn't anywhere near the outcome she'd been hoping for. But at least she had the facts to make her decision now. Once you know the cards you've been dealt, you stand the best chance of playing your hand to its full potential. Truth levels the playing field.

I'd solved our second case. We were now two for two, which was a pretty good feeling.

'Don't know why you're smiling,' Nikki grumbled.

Once we arrived in Leeds, we caught a taxi to Hyde Park – Nikki got out at Hyde Park Corner and I rode all the way back to the office. It was almost eleven.

When I walked through the office door, Aunt Edie jumped up from her desk like she'd been scalded. 'Where have you been?'

'I said I wouldn't be back till lunchtime.'

'Why haven't you answered your phone?'

I pulled it out of my pocket. 'I forgot to get one of those plugs to charge it abroad.' Dread seeped into my veins as I took in the look on Aunt Edie's face. 'What's happened?'

'Oh, Lee.'

'What?'

'There's been an accident.'

'What?'

'Jo.'

I put my arm out and held on to the filing cabinet. I don't know how my arm knew to do that. 'What?'

'An accident,' she repeated.

'Where?'

'She's in intensive care.'

'Intensive care? What do you mean?'

'Oh, Lee. Pet, I'm so, so sorry.'

My knees buckled as my brain refused to accept what Aunt Edie's shaking hands were trying to prepare me for.

'No,' I said.

Chapter 31

I can't remember much about the next few hours. There's a blank space in my brain and no matter how much I try to pull the pieces together there are bits missing.

I didn't go to the hospital.

I know I should have and I was going to, really I was, but Aunt Edie wouldn't let me. She locked the outer office door and barricaded us both into the back room, refusing to let me out, no matter how much I screamed. She said there was nothing I could do – that the nurses wouldn't even let me in to see Jo. Intensive care is next of kin only, apparently. I remember Aunt Edie saying that because it confused me – Jo's the only family I've got and if something were to happen to me, Jo would be the only person I had to stand by my bed.

Aunt Edie held my arms and said it was different for Jo. She said Jo's mum was there – and her dad, which made me realize how serious it was because he would have probably had to fly back from somewhere like Japan or South Korea or somewhere. I thought, Christ, Jo would kick off when she woke up and saw him by the end of her bed. She's not close to her dad – I've never even met him. He's always away on business trips and when he is back in the UK he's too busy with his twenty-something-year-old wife to have much to do with Jo. I wanted to go down to the hospital to tell him to do one, but Aunt Edie said that Steve, Jo's brother, was already there and I knew he'd do what was best for Jo. He's not a massive fan of their dad either.

In truth, although I put up a fight, I probably could have fought harder. I'm not good in hospitals and I don't like illness. It unnerves me, reminds me that at the end of the day the veil between life and death is too fine. In the pictures in my mind, Jo is always moving, always reaching out and I didn't know that I could bear to see her any other way. It kind of freaks me out when I see her asleep because she looks much more vulnerable than she does when she's awake. I knew it made sense to wait and see her when she was better – when she was at least sitting up in her hospital bed, arguing with the doctors, taking the piss out of her fellow patients.

That's what I told myself.

OK.

I hate my obsession with truth.

I wish I was one of those people that could just believe the bullshit, especially about myself. But there's this voice inside me that nags at me, whispering that that's not how it was, refuses to let me lie.

I knew Jo was mad at me, although I didn't understand why. And I thought that maybe if I went to see her it would make her worse. She needed all her strength to get better; she couldn't afford to waste energy on being angry with me. And until she told me what I'd done wrong, I didn't know what to say to make it right.

The idea of seeing Jo's mum wasn't appealing either. After our last case she made me swear on my life I wouldn't put her daughter in any kind of danger, ever again. She said she'd have my guts for tennis rackets if I did. She'd been kind of joking at the time, but the way she'd been holding onto Jo's hand made me know she was serious too.

Why didn't I take Jo with me to Spain?

We should have stayed together. I should never have let her come back to Leeds alone.

Aunt Edie tells me the police came to the office and interviewed me and that must be right because I have a signed copy of my statement, dated that day, although I don't remember speaking to them at all. It's here now, in front of me and I can read the words but it's like I'm reading about someone else's life. It's clear that they'd been focused on that last phone call I'd had with Jo. What had she said? What mood had she been in? Had she said where she was going, what she was working on, what her plans were?

My answers, according to the typed sheets of paper in front of me, were monosyllabic, which doesn't surprise me because, even now, I still can't bear to think about that last conversation. It's like my brain presses the pause button any time I try to replay it in my mind. Aunt Edie told them to leave in the end, said I was in shock. They said they'd be back to see me later. I knew before they were out the door that I wouldn't be there when they returned. What good was talking to the police going to do Jo?

Aunt Edie didn't let me out of her sight until Martin

turned up. I don't know if that was before or after the police had gone. Someone told me Jo needed surgery – that her pelvis was broken – and I pictured her in the woods at the all-night party from the weekend and prayed that people with broken pelvises mend well enough to dance again.

I still feel the heat of Aunt Edie's arm around my shoulders, no matter how hard I tried to push her away. It's like the imprint of her has somehow got under my skin.

When Martin arrived, his skin was white, like he'd been in a flour storm. 'I'm going to get him, if it takes my last breath,' he said as he limped through the door.

He might as well have been speaking Russian. I couldn't connect words – couldn't make them into sentences, not ones that made sense. A cup of tea would be on the table and then it wouldn't be, but nothing joined together. I couldn't spot the relationship between things.

'I'll not stop until I do,' he said.

'What?'

'My last breath.' He said this like he was swearing an allegiance to his country or the king or something.

'It was an accident.' Aunt Edie said with a fierce look on her face.

'My arse.'

Aunt Edie stepped behind me and I sensed her shaking her head. I turned round. 'What?'

She had her hands in this funny position. Like a concert pianist about to start. Her fingers bounced up and down. 'They don't know,' she said. 'No one knows. They're still trying to work out what happened.'

'It was an accident. In the van?' I hadn't even questioned how the accident had happened, not when Aunt Edie had first told me. The police had mentioned a crash. I guess I'd assumed it was Jo's fucking awful driving. Christ knows I've been in enough near misses with her.

Martin levered himself down into Jo's office chair and spoke slowly to me. 'She was hit, by a car, in the middle of the night, in the middle of a case, the driver didn't stop and you think it's an accident?'

'She was walking?'

That couldn't be right. Jo never walked anywhere if she could help it. Unless she was drunk.

Aunt Edie folded her arms under her bust. 'It's not worth getting upset until we know the facts.'

I stared at Martin. He hadn't shaved. His bristles were a mix of white and grey, with the odd dark brown one thrown in. 'You think it's to do with the investigation?'

Martin looked at me like he couldn't believe I was stupid enough to ask the question.

My veins burned. Flayed. 'You think someone deliberately ran her over?'

Martin tried to cover my hand with his own.

I shook it off. 'What time?'

His eyes never left my face. 'Quarter to one this morning.'

'What the fuck was she doing out at that time?'

Aunt Edie sat at the desk and for the first time in my life I thought she looked like an old woman. 'We don't know,' she said, her voice more trembly than I'm used to. 'She'd told Sara she'd be back about 10 p.m. She never showed up.'

'Sara?' I couldn't place the name. 'Who's Sara?'

'You know. Sara. Jo's friend. I had to tell her,' Aunt Edie said. 'She was terribly upset.'

I turned to Martin. 'I was with Matt when Jo, when it ...'

I couldn't put it into words, the possibility that someone had deliberately aimed their car at Jo, it was beyond the reach of my brain. Aimed and pressed down on the accelerator pedal. If someone had done that, they were a dead man walking. Sweat pooled in my palms. 'She said you'd had a meeting.' A flashback to our last phone call. 'The suicide. Jenny Crawley. You think it's to do with that?'

'I think so, I think—'

'What the fuck did you talk about?'

'Jo brought me up to speed. Said you'd identified the vic. as Jenny Crawley. She showed me the suicide note.'

'And?'

'We went through the list of everyone who lived at the flat at the time of Jenny's suicide.' Martin reached down and pulled his briefcase onto the desk. 'I've got it here.'

Martin opened his briefcase and pulled out a notebook.

I'm not proud to admit this, but there was something freeing about thinking about Jenny, about the case, about work. It presented me with a window, a window I could climb out of, away from the blackness of my own thoughts. Away from my fear of what might be. 'What did you think?'

'Same as you. The note must have been written to someone in the flats. Someone that had done something bad, either to Jenny or to her sister.'

'Her sister was killed by the Park Killer. Jenny told her

social worker. And he was already dead by the time Jenny killed herself.'

He flicked through the pages of his notebook. 'I know and I can't find any connection between the Park Killer and the flats, aside from the fact that he attacked two of his victims right outside of them.'

'Then, there's something else.' I tapped my fingers on the desk. 'Jo said she thought the Park Killer must have had an accomplice.' The content of our last phone call came back to me in waves. 'Like Brady and Hindley, she said.'

'A serial killer with an accomplice?' Aunt Edie grimaced and crossed herself. 'I thank the good Lord my days on this earth are numbered.'

I crossed the room to retrieve the case file from the filing cabinet. In it was Jenny's last note, tucked between the few pieces of paper the folder contained. I plucked it out and a thought hit me for the first time. 'There's no name,' I said. 'Jenny didn't put a name on the envelope. She must have thought that the person she wrote it to was going to be the person who found her.'

'Which means someone who gets up early,' said Aunt Edie. 'Someone who gets up before everyone else. Or someone who gets home late.'

'Unless she told whoever it was what she was about to do,' Martin said, and I wasn't sure if he was playing devil's advocate just to wind up Aunt Edie. 'She could have rung someone once she'd tied herself to the statue.'

'She didn't have a phone,' I said.

'Maybe they took her phone.'

I shook my head. 'I think Linda was the first person to find the body, because the note was still there at that point. And the handbag. And Linda didn't mention a phone.'

Martin thought about this for a moment. 'Maybe it was in Jenny's handbag. We don't know that Linda looked inside the bag.'

Aunt Edie ignored him. 'So, someone that lives on that side of the building: the side that overlooks the park.'

I closed my eyes and called up the note. I didn't need to take it from the envelope. I could see the loopy handwriting in the front of my mind. '"I know. You know. And somewhere, out there, someone else knows. I want you to live the rest of your days knowing that. That out there, somewhere, someone else knows." Someone else knows what?'

Martin scratched at the bristle on his chin. 'Might not be anything to do with her sister's murder. Might be something else entirely. Something we know nothing about.'

'She took off everything except her necklace,' said Aunt Edie.

'You're right,' I said, as I caught her train of thought. 'Nothing else mattered but the necklace. This has to be about Maureen, someone implicated in her death. Maybe it was someone involved in the investigation. Was there anyone connected to law enforcement on the list?'

Martin shook his head. 'Not that I saw. Here.'

I took the notebook out of his hands and scanned it. There were over a hundred names, grouped by gender, age and the date they left the property, if they had. 'Wonder if Rob Hamilton would speak to us?'

Martin peered over my shoulder. 'He moved out a year or so after the suicide. He'd be easy enough to track down. And that one,' – he pointed to the name Jimmy McFly – 'he runs that posh restaurant in Ilkley; he was on TV too, back in the nineties. Used to present a cookery programme, but then he got done for drink driving, went to prison for six months.'

'Any connection to the Park Killer?'

'Not that I can find. Seems to have kept his nose clean since. Restaurant is doing really well. Just got its third Michelin star.'

'What about Blake Jeffries? Didn't you say something about him?'

'He used to run a club. Can't be him though, he's dead. Nearly four years.'

'It's seven years since Jenny took her life,' Aunt Edie said. 'Four years doesn't rule him out.'

'It was last night that Jo got run down,' Martin said. 'That makes our suspect very much alive.'

'Could have been someone trying to protect his memory.' Aunt Edie pulled the tissue out of the sleeve of her cardigan and blew her nose.

'How did he die?' I asked.

'Heart attack linked to excessive drug use.'

I crossed a line through his name. I didn't think anyone would go to those kind of lengths to protect the memory of someone who had been dead four years. One down.

'And Steve Thompson is a crime writer. His first novel was published two years after Jenny's suicide.'

The names swam before my eyes. 'So, who were you talking about? What did Jo think? Who did you suspect?'

'I've been over and over it,' Martin said and I recognized his frustration. 'We tried to narrow the list down by looking at single men, under sixty years old. That's Group A. Thirteen of them, including a retired judge but he was magistrates, not Crown. And he retired before Maureen was murdered. I've looked whether anyone worked with children, in the care system, anyone who might have had contact with Jenny or Maureen that way. I asked a contact within the prison service to see whether the Park Killer had any visitors, whether any names matched. Nothing.'

'It's got to be a person on this list. And whoever it was, Jo went and challenged him.'

Martin's fists clenched.

'Aunt Edie, did you get the plan of the flats from the management company?'

'Damned straight, I did. They didn't want to give it to me, but I played merry hell with the upstart on the phone.' She pulled open the filing cabinet and took out a rolled-up piece of paper. 'Here it is.'

'We need to know which flats overlook the statue. It's got to be someone living at the front of the building. Someone using the front entrance, so they'd see her body before anyone else did.'

Aunt Edie unrolled the paper and spread it across her desk. 'Well, that's easy enough. Chuck me one of those highlighter things.'

I lobbed a fluorescent pink felt tip across to her and she

caught it in her left hand, while still holding the plans on the desk with her right. 'Martin, can you have another look at occupations. Who gets up early?'

'The postman,' Aunt Edie said.

'Or comes home in the morning – night shift workers, taxi drivers.' I thought about the kind of people I see on my morning runs. The people who don't keep normal hours.

'Radio presenters, milkmen, dog walkers.' Martin took his jacket off and rolled up his shirtsleeves.

'OK, once you've got a list ... cross-reference with Aunt Edie. See where that gets us.'

What else? I closed my eyes and tried to conjure up the image of Jenny tied to the statue. What was she trying to tell us? 'The strychnine – where did that come from?'

'I looked into that at the time,' said Martin. 'It was banned by the EU in 2006 although the government appealed.'

'Why did they appeal?'

'Because before that it was used by pest controllers.'

'What kind of pests?'

'Mainly moles. Farmers used it.'

'So where did Jenny get it from?'

Martin shrugged his shoulders. 'It's not that hard to get hold of on the internet – it's still used in other countries.' He flicked open his notebook and licked the tip of his pencil.

I envied them both their ability to sit and focus. I couldn't stop pacing. What had Jo seen that I hadn't? I thought about Jenny's suicide note again. I took it out of the envelope and read it to myself. *Someone else knows. Out there, somewhere, someone else knows.* 'She told someone,' I said out loud. 'Jenny told someone. Who? Who would she have told?'

Martin took off his glasses and rubbed his eyes. 'Her mother?'

'Her mother's in Poland. Too far away. And a nutcase. She wouldn't turn to her mother.' In that we were kindred spirits.

'Best friend?' said Aunt Edie, as she poured over the plans.

'Did she have any friends?' Martin asked. 'No one ever reported her missing.'

I jumped up off the desk and paced the floor. 'Jenny's social worker said if she could use one word to describe Jenny it would be "scared". "Petrified", she said. And by the time Frances met Jenny, the Park Killer was already dead. But she was still scared.' Thoughts rushed out of me, faster than I could put them into words. 'But if the Park Killer did have an accomplice … then his accomplice is still out there. That's who Jenny was scared of. She's expecting him to come for her. Which means he's dangerous. She takes out an insurance policy – she tells someone.' I tried to put myself in her shoes. 'She'd tell a man, not a woman. She wouldn't put another woman in danger; not the kind of danger she was in.'

Pacing helped me think. Aunt Edie scribbled numbers on a notepad and I noticed a smudge of ink across her top lip that made her look like she had a moustache.

'The father of her child.' The thought hit me like a six-foot-high wave. 'She'd tell him. The social worker said they had a good relationship for a while, that he was considered a positive influence. She'd have told him about her sister. She told him about what happened to Maureen. What was his name? Like the poet, she said. Begins with B.'

Martin shrugged his shoulders. 'Byron?'

'No.'

'Blake?' said Aunt Edie. '"He who bends to himself a joy, Doth the winged life destroy."'

'How do you know that?' I asked.

'William Blake,' she said.

'Not William,' I said. 'Winston. Winston Blake. That's it. We have to find him. He's the one who knows.'

Chapter 32

Winston Blake. What had Frances Wilson, Jenny Crawley's social worker, told me about him? He was black, Afro-Caribbean, I think she'd said, and he was the father of Jenny's son, Sasha. He'd lived in Leeds and then moved to Nottingham, because that was where the Nottingham connection had come from. I knew he'd once had a relationship with a woman named Jenny Crawley. That was quite a lot of information, I thought. It would have to be enough.

It had been nine years since Jenny disappeared from social services' attention and seven years since her naked body had been discovered in the grounds of the luxury flats next to Roundhay Park. What had she done during the two years she'd disappeared off social services' radar before her death? Frances had admitted that at the time Jenny had taken off they hadn't looked too hard. One less case to worry about. The assumption had been she'd gone back to her mother in Poland, but subsequent events proved she hadn't. What if Frances's hunch had been right – what if she'd gone to Winston? Jenny Crawley had travelled from Nottingham to Leeds on the day she decided to end her own life. According to Frances, the last known address for Winston Blake was Nottingham.

I left Aunt Edie and Martin Blink working on the list of residents and went through to the back office. I fired up the laptop and googled 'Winston Blake Nottingham'. Nothing. I remembered Frances had told me Winston used to sell fruit and vegetables from a barrow on Roundhay Road, so I googled 'Winston' plus the words 'fruit and veg stall', but that didn't bring up anything either. Frances had said that Winston Blake had gone to Nottingham to grow his own produce and at that moment two separate thoughts joined up. Farmers and pest control. Winston growing fruit and vegetables. Maybe Winston had a problem with pests. Did moles eat vegetable crops? Was that where the strychnine Jenny had ingested came from? As the question formed in my brain, the hairs on my arms stood up.

Three companies came up when I searched for 'mole-catchers Nottingham'. I rang the first one and asked if they'd ever had a customer called Winston Blake. The prim woman on the phone told me that she couldn't give out any information about their customers. I took a deep breath and spent a bit of time explaining who I was. She hummed and ahhed and I said I could ask the police to ring if that was easier for her. In the end she agreed to have a search through their database and said she'd call me back. I wasn't holding my breath.

The next company I rang were more helpful, possibly because their receptionist sounded about fifteen. It took him all of two minutes to say there was no one of that name on file.

The Runaway

The third number I rang was a mobile number and I got to speak to the mole-catcher himself. In contrast to the receptionist at the previous company, this man sounded about seventy-five. 'I know it's a long shot,' I said. 'But I'm trying to find a man called Winston Blake, and I believe he may have had a problem with pests, moles or rats, at one time – possibly a long time ago.'

'Black guy?' he said.

'Yes.' I stood up so quickly my head swam and I had to hold onto the back of the chair. 'You know him?'

'Can't forget a guy like that. Hands like shovels. Blighted by 'em, he was. They'd got into his tunnel.'

My mind boggled. 'I'm sorry?'

'He had one of them polytunnels. Growing his own, he was, but the buggers had played merry hell.'

'You've got an address for him?'

'I don't know whether you'd call it an address, but I know where his moles were.'

Aunt Edie wasn't happy about me going out. Martin offered to come with me, but we both knew he'd slow me down. I promised I'd keep in touch. Aunt Edie unplugged my mobile from the charger and handed it to me. I stuffed it into my pocket.

Less than an hour later I was on the train to Nottingham, my heart thumping. Truth was, I couldn't get out of Leeds fast enough. The city didn't hold anything for me without Jo. And I may have told the police I couldn't remember what we'd talked about in that last phone call, but that was a lie. There's a sentence or two she said, that I know I'll never be able to forget. Because she was right.

I am fucked up.

The doors closed on the train and I left part of me behind on the platform. My memories. My thoughts. The times spent with Jo. I dug my nails into my forearms in an attempt to stop my eyes welling.

My phone rang on the train, which I hate, because I always think that anyone talking on a phone on a train is a wanker.

'Hello?' I tried to keep my voice as low as possible.

'Lee? Is that you?'

'Yes,' I whispered.

'Oh. It doesn't sound like you. Sorry. It's Frances Wilson, Jenny Crawley's social worker. I've managed to get into work and have a look through the archived files.'

'OK.'

'I'm sorry it's taken so long. Most of them are in the basement, covered in dust.'

'Right.' I couldn't bring myself to say the words, *I'm on a train*.

'Can you hear me OK? It's not a very good line.'

I switched ears and pressed my head up against the wall of the train. 'Yes. Go on.'

'I found a card that Jenny sent to me, supposedly from Poland. I checked the handwriting against the photo your partner sent of the suicide note. I'm almost a hundred per cent. The body, it's Jenny.'

She wasn't telling me anything I didn't know, but it still felt good to get the confirmation. Small steps towards a destination at which I had to arrive, however much I knew it wasn't going to be a nice place. 'Right,' I said.

'I can't stop thinking about Sasha,' Frances said. 'It seems clear that Jenny never actually went back to Poland, so where is he? I had a look through the current system; this is strictly between you and me. He's not in any of the live files. Not in Leeds, anyway.'

'Did you ever hear anything from Jenny's ex-boyfriend – Sasha's father?' I asked, trying to give the impression I hadn't given him much thought.

'Winston Blake? No, nothing.'

'You said he was a good influence.'

'Well, that was my impression, but based only on two short meetings.' She sighed into the phone. 'I don't know what to do. I mean, she disappeared nine years ago. Chances are ...' She let the sentence hang in mid-air.

'I've got to go,' I said.

'If anything's happened to that child, it's my responsibility.'

'If it wasn't for you, no one would ever have known what happened to Jenny Crawley. At least we know the truth.' Although as I said the words I realized they meant nothing. What good did knowing the truth about what had happened to Jenny do if we didn't know why?

'If you hear anything ...'

'Yes.'

I hung up and spent the rest of the journey with my eyes fixed on the window, my mind trained on Jenny. Twenty-one, three years younger than me, when she'd made this journey in reverse. A young woman brought up in and out of care, a girl without parents, whose sister had had to resort to selling sex in order for them to get by. She was fifteen years old when Maureen was killed, she'd had a child at seventeen and by nineteen she'd disappeared off the face of the earth. Two years later she'd killed herself. What had happened to her in those intervening two years? We knew she'd come from Nottingham on the day of her suicide. As the train pulled into the station I felt like she was with me and I knew deep down that this was where she'd been. Winston Blake sounded like the only good thing in a life that had capsized in a sea full of sharks. She'd come here to find the man she hoped might save her. Now I was doing the same.

*

I withdrew a hundred quid from the cashpoint at the station and made my way to the taxi rank out front. I gave the driver the directions the mole-catcher had given me and sat back in my seat. Fifteen minutes later, when the taxi driver stopped the engine I half-thought he'd brought me to the middle of nowhere so he could rape me and mutilate my corpse. 'You sure this is it?'

He nodded and made no threat towards my life, so I gave him twenty quid, told him to keep the change and climbed out of the car. I wandered down the road towards a wooden gate that had a rope tied around it, keeping it closed. The gate was only waist height and behind it was an overgrown plot of land, with a couple of half-hearted wooden buildings and chickens scratching around.

I let myself through the gate and hung the rope back over the fencepost so that the chickens didn't escape. I noticed a few raised beds, on the right, some of which might have contained potatoes, although I'm no gardener. Behind the wooden shacks was another gate, and through that another patch of land which looked better tended. The plants here were in lines, like they'd been planted with purpose. Further on I noticed a spiral of smoke rising into the air. I walked down the crazy paving path, past a greenhouse that had a couple of smashed panes of glass. A collection of plant pots surrounded a water butt, and a watering can lay on its side. I followed the smoke and found another patch of land, with a huge compost heap at one end. The further away from the road I got the more tended the land became. A dog barked from a plot to my left. I instinctively veered to the right, still heading for the smoke.

When I found the bonfire, I found a person. A woman, mid-sixties I'd guess although hard to tell. Her cheeks made me understand the word ruddy. She wore a skirt that reached the floor and an apron and she reminded me of Mrs Tiggy-Winkle.

'Hi,' I said. 'Sorry to bother you.'

She grinned at me. 'That's all right. Is it logs you're wanting?'

'Er, no, actually. I'm—'

'Manure?' She gestured towards a dung heap and for the first time I noticed two horses in a field to the right. In the field was a barn with a corrugated roof.

'No. Thanks. I'm looking for someone. Winston. Do you know him?'

She frowned. 'Bought the place from him. Couple of years back. He'd had enough.' She snapped the branch she was holding and added it to the fire.

'Do you know where I could find him?'

'Is he in trouble?'

'No, not at all.'

'Someone died?'

'No,' I lied.

'Won the lottery?' She gave a bark that I think was supposed to be a laugh.

'Do you know where he is?'

'He was looking to buy a bigger place. He's a man full of big ideas. Nice guy though. Decent.'

'If you could help me find him, there's a reward.'

'A reward? How much?'

I thought how much cash I had on me. 'Fifty quid.'

She held out a hand. 'He used to supply all the fruit and veg for the Marcus Garvey Centre. Someone there will know where he is. They stick together, that lot. Safety in numbers.'

I took the remaining money from my pocket, peeled off thirty and held out twenty. 'The Marcus Garvey Centre? Where's that?'

She took the notes from my hand. 'Directions are extra,' she said.

'That's all I've got,' I said, which was kind of true. I needed the rest for the taxi back. 'And fifty quid for the name of a building? Don't you think that's a bit steep?'

'He who pays the piper calls the tune,' she said. She picked up an axe and moved towards the large pile of logs. 'That's all I've time for.'

I thought about arguing but she was fairly handy with the axe, so in the end I decided against it. I made my way back through the different plots to the road, and called up an Uber on my app. It took the driver twenty-five minutes to find me.

*

While I was waiting for the cab, I googled the name of the centre the old woman had given me. Marcus Garvey. Who was he? Didn't take long to find out. A black politician, active in Jamaica and the US, died in 1940. The centre that took his name ran as a club venue and a meeting point for members of the black community. I had a feeling I'd heard the name before. I took a note of the postcode and gave it to the driver when he finally showed up. It was a long shot, but I had to start somewhere.

The Uber dropped me right outside the centre. We have something a bit like this in Leeds – The West Indian Centre, in Chapeltown – so I knew the type of place, where the old guys hung out and shot the breeze. They know everything about everyone, these guys, which is surprising because they give the impression they are men of few words.

Inside was a huge hall, with a bar across one end of the room. Committed drinkers sitting around, only one white guy, who nodded at me as he scratched at his beard. I thought about what to do. I needed to fit in. I hadn't eaten all day. I was thirsty. Difficult to believe I'd woken up in Spain this morning. Felt like a lifetime ago. A wave of panic hit me, like it does when I lose track of my place in space and time. My clothes smelled of woodsmoke. I thought of the fire at the all-night party we'd been to. Got a glimpse of Jo dancing.

The bar was open.

A warm light calling to me.

Fuck it.

I needed to fit in. I didn't want to alienate anyone. I wanted to show I belonged.

I made for the bar and ordered a pint of Red Stripe. The AA meetings could go to hell for the time being. I was only going to have one. Not that big a deal. I paid for it on the company bank card.

An old man sitting at one of the tables to my left raised his pint in my direction, like he was saying cheers, so I moved across to his table and nodded at the wooden box perched on the table in front of him. 'Fancy a game?'

He stared me up and down for a moment or two, like he was assessing my chances, then slid the lid off the dominoes. The thing about being an outsider – you instinctively get recognized by other outsiders. It's like being part of a gang – a gang of misfits, of people that don't belong. An oxymoron, if you think about it.

He racked up the tiles and beat me three times straight, and I'd bought him a drink before I asked him if he knew a guy called Winston who sold fruit and vegetables. He shook his head.

Half an hour later, I was thinking what my next step should

be when a guy with dreads walked in. 'He's your man,' the old fella said. 'Knows everyone.'

So I picked up my glass, sidled over and asked the guy with dreads if he knew Winston Blake. He asked me why I was asking and I told him I was a friend of Winston's ex-girlfriend, which felt close enough to the truth. He took my phone number and said he'd let me know.

'Let me know what?' I asked, but he didn't answer, just turned and wandered towards the toilets. I figured what the hell and ordered another pint. I was enjoying the feeling of blurred edges; the slight distance from reality that I crave. Bad thoughts drain from my mind. It's like the person inside me, the one that's obsessed with truth, gets sent on holiday when I drink. And I love taking a break from her.

On the other side of the entrance hall was a café I noticed, so I wandered over and ordered a portion of rice and cheesy peas. I asked the woman serving whether she knew Winston Blake but she just shrugged her shoulders and smiled at me. 'You need more meat on your bones,' she said. 'Too thin.'

The food was delicious and mopped up some of the surplus liquid in my stomach. I ate slowly, chewing the food and my thoughts at the same time. What next? I knew Winston Blake was here in Nottingham and I knew he held the answers I needed. That's the other side – the good side – of alcohol. The rational part of my brain might pack up and go home, but my gut instinct focuses, grows stronger. It sounds stupid but I trust myself more when I'm drunk.

I didn't want to go back to Leeds, not till Jo was better. I had this sense that the longer I stayed away, the quicker she would recover. A superstition almost. I used to do it as a kid — if I could hold my breath till I walked to the end of our street, my dad would be home when I got there. Course it never worked, but that doesn't stop you trying.

I checked my phone. Aunt Edie had rung but I wasn't in the mood for talking to her.

I sat in the corner with my pint and sensed that the regulars were talking about me. That's what I wanted so I didn't react. I don't know how long I'd been there when the younger guy with the dreads returned. He asked me if I fancied a smoke and we went outside to an area near the car park which had obviously been designated the smoking corner. There was a picnic table with benches attached, a rubbish bin, and the railings were painted yellow but the paint had chipped over the years. He handed me a ready rolled one-skin cigarette but I knew by the size of it that it didn't contain just tobacco. I knew it was a test, but one I've aced on plenty of occasions. Some people are good at science. My speciality is my tolerance levels, all the more remarkable when you take my BMI into account. My shoulders relaxed by a fraction of a centimetre.

'What you want with Winston?' he asked.

'Just need to talk to him about something. Something that happened in Leeds a few years ago.'

'What that?'

'It's complicated. I mean, well, it's actually about an ex-girlfriend of his. I'm hoping he can help me fill in some blanks.' I was aware I was speaking louder than normal.

'Jenny?'

My ears pricked up. Or at least it felt like they did. 'You knew Jenny?'

He shook his head. 'Only what he told me.'

'Where is he?'

'On his way. Told me to keep an eye on you till he got here.'

'Well, that was easy.' I couldn't help a feeling of pride that might have had something to do with my third pint. But fuck, I was good at this shit. This finding people thing.

'How's Jenny doing?' he asked.

'I should probably wait until Winston gets here.'

He shrugged his shoulders like it was no skin off his nose. 'Does he have a kid, do you know?'

He grinned at me. 'I should probably wait until Winston gets here.'

'Jinx.' I passed him the spliff. The combination of the beer and weed made me unsteady. Bollocks to my AA meeting this week. What they didn't know they couldn't guilt trip me with. I was sick of listening to the same old story, told a dozen different ways. Besides, it wasn't like Jo was going to be on my case for a while. I bit my tongue.

'Where you from?' the guy asked.

'Leeds,' I said. 'What about you?'

He didn't answer. Instead he gestured towards the car park. 'Winston.'

I watched a tall black man jump out of a dark-coloured car. He was way tall and lanky, his hips swayed as he made his way over. His shoulders bobbed as he walked. He wore a beanie hat, which might have been a bit warm – it was a sunny day. Not boiling but warm enough. I tried to guess his age as he approached, but it was difficult. Could be anything between twenty-five and fifty, I thought.

'You looking for me,' he said, without introducing himself. It was a statement not a question.

'Winston?' I held out a hand.

He ignored it. 'This 'bout Jenny?'

I nodded and knew the third pint had been a mistake.

He stared at me for a moment that seemed to last too long. 'You come to tell me she's dead?'

I swallowed, felt the blackness tug at me. ''Fraid so. I'm sorry, man.'

'When?'

'Seven years ago. August.'

He nodded like that information didn't surprise him at all.

'You want me to leave you to it, bled?'

I'd forgotten about the other guy. Winston was one of those people that commanded your attention, took over the space. He didn't look at his friend but the friend stubbed out his smoke and stepped away. I watched him amble across the car park, back towards the centre.

'She killed herself.' Each time Winston spoke his voice was soft, like he was asking a question, but a question he knew the answer to.

'Yes.'

'And they only just found her?'

'No. They found her straightaway. But, back then, the police never identified her. No one knew who she was.' I didn't know quite where to start. I tried to put myself in his shoes. What would he want to know first? What was best left unsaid?

He cut through my thoughts, cut to the chase. 'Why you here?'

'I run a missing persons' bureau.'

He frowned at me, waited for me to explain. The sun warm on the back of my neck.

'A journalist hired me. An ex-journalist. He reported on the case at the time, the time when Jenny's body was found.'

'What it got to do with him?'

'Can we sit?' I said. I led the way to the picnic bench, grateful for the support. The sun was low in the sky, the clouds had thinned to almost nothing and the light was hurting my eyes. 'It bugged him, that they never found out who she was. He said no one ever pushed for it to be solved, so it slipped between the cracks. He thought maybe a new pair of eyes on it – so we had a go, found a necklace, found some other things. A social worker had reported Jenny Crawley missing in the meantime. We got lucky – found the match.'

Winston didn't sit; he towered over me and I had to squint not to get sun in my eyes. He stood up a bit straighter and nodded. Seemed to brush himself off, mentally speaking. 'So you came to tell me she's dead? We split up a long time ago, man.'

'It's like she was trying to tell someone something. Like she had a message.'

'Like I said, we split up. Ain't my problem anymore.'

I didn't believe his I-don't-care attitude. 'The journalist says he feels like she's out there, trying to tell him something.'

'Let sleeping dogs lie.' He made to walk away, but I grabbed his arm without thinking.

'They aren't sleeping all that well.'

He stared at my hand on his arm. 'Come again?'

I let go. It wasn't like me to initiate physical contact. 'I'm not the lead investigator on this case. My partner was.'

He screwed up his eyes and rubbed his nose.

'Jo,' I said, because I wanted him to know her name. 'She's in intensive care.' I took a moment, let the words settle. For me as much as for him. I drove my fingernails into the palm of my hand. 'Someone ran her over, in a car, last night.'

He looked up at the sky. 'Man, I'm sorry for you.'

I swallowed and willed him to shut up. I didn't want his sympathy. 'It wasn't an accident.'

'Oh boy.'

'She got too close to something. Something to do with Jenny.'

'Seven years is a long time. Too long.'

'What did Jenny know? What did she want everyone to know?'

'I can't help you.' Winston turned his back to me.

'She killed herself in the garden of a block of flats. She tied herself to a statue and poisoned herself with strychnine. You know what that does to your system?'

He took a couple of steps away from me, his arms swinging at his sides.

I raised my voice. 'It's not a nice way to die.'

He paused for a moment, looked over his shoulder at me. 'There is no nice way to die.'

He headed towards the centre, following the path his mate had taken.

I took a breath, raised my voice more. 'I spoke to someone who said you had a pest control problem on your land a while back. Strychnine is still considered the best way to get rid of moles and rats. Only it's been illegal in this country since 2007.'

He carried on walking.

I waited a beat and shouted after him. 'You gave it to her.'

He turned to face me. 'Why would I do that? I didn't want her to die.'

I saw the look on his face and felt bad. 'I know. I'm sorry.' But I knew I was onto something and I couldn't stop now. I lowered my voice. 'She got it from you though, didn't she?'

He raised his gaze up at the sky for a moment and then back at me. 'She took it from me. I didn't know, I swear.'

I saw the guilt in his deep brown eyes. I recognized it because it's what I see whenever I look in a mirror. 'It's not your fault,' I said.

'I didn't notice, not till weeks after she'd gone. We weren't together no more, but she used to show up occasionally. Once or twice a week. But I didn't see her for a while. I used to keep it down at the allotment. Only used it once.'

'If it hadn't been that, she'd have found another way.'

He took a step towards me. 'When I realized, I hoped she'd taken it to ...'

'To what?'

He shook his head. 'Nothing.'

'She left a note, Winston.'

He closed his eyes.

'It said she had a secret and only one other person knew.

339

It was like it was the only thing she had left. Her one last possession. She said that, out there, there was one person who knew the truth. That was the thought she clung to as she died. That there was a witness, that someone believed her.'

He sat down on the bench opposite me, the picnic table between us.

'Why didn't you help her, Winston?'

'Man, what the fuck could I do?'

'She was trying to get back at someone, wasn't she? Something to do with Maureen?'

'She'd never hurt another person. Not even him. Not even after what he did.'

'Tell me who.'

'You don't want to know.'

'You see, that's where you're wrong. I do want to know.' I'd never wanted to know anything more than I wanted to know this.

'If you know, you'll be like Jenny. She didn't sleep.'

'I don't care about sleep.'

'You'd care if—'

I leaned towards him. 'If someone drove their car into my best friend deliberately on purpose, I don't care about anything except they need to pay for what they've done.'

There was a pause and we stared at each other. He hesitated, softened. 'Men like that never pay,' he said in a quiet voice.

'She told you.' I slapped the table. 'I knew it.'

'If I tell you, you just become another woman that suffers because of him.'

'You don't know me. I'm not the suffering kind.'

'I know the way this world works.'

'Jenny's sister was murdered. Jenny knew who killed Maureen.'

'They're both dead, what does it matter?'

'The Park Killer killed Maureen.'

'He's dead too. Died in prison.'

'There was someone else.' I knew Winston knew. I'd have bet everything I owned on it. 'If you don't tell me I'll keep going. Jo found out, I will too. All you're doing is helping me get there faster, cleaner.'

He pulled out a tobacco pouch. When he spoke his voice was softer, older. 'I knew she was dead. Knew there was no way she'd have fought this long. But it's still a shock, you know?'

I didn't want to talk about death. I wanted to talk about justice. 'Jenny's social worker said she disappeared nine years ago. They assumed she'd gone to Poland, back to her mother.'

'That's what she wanted them to think. She knew they were thinking she wasn't capable of ...' His voice trailed off and he buried his head in his arms.

'Of looking after Sasha?'

He didn't answer, didn't move.

'Don't you owe it to Jenny to tell me? She must have told you what she knew because she trusted you to do the right thing, Winston. Now, you're the only person who knows what happened. If you don't tell, it stays a secret forever. This is Sasha's mum and Sasha's aunt we're talking about. Are you going to let it get covered up? Forgotten?'

After what seemed like a long, long time, he lifted his head and stared at me, like he was trying to decide something. Eventually he said, 'She sent a couple of letters back to a mate in Poland, got her to post them back here, back to the social workers.'

'But she was with you? In Nottingham?'

'I convinced her to give it another go, but she was right, it was never going to work. She was too fucked up.'

Jo's voice, our last telephone call.

'She knew it. I knew it. You don't want to hear 'bout the things that happened to her. All her life. Her mum, in care, Maureen's murder. She put up with more shit than anyone. It broke her. They broke her.'

'I'm sorry.'

He shrugged my sympathy off. 'I could never blame her, after what she'd been through, but it didn't make her ideal relationship material.' He tried to smile, but it didn't work. 'But I wanted Sasha.'

'Sasha. Where's he now?'

His eyes fixed on me. 'I'll tell you what happened to Jen, but on one condition. Forget you ever heard about Sasha. He's doing fine.'

I trusted him, there was something about him that told me he was a good man, a good dad. I didn't hesitate. 'Deal.'

'Maureen was the only good thing in Jenny's life, far as I could see. I mean, before she met me and Sasha came along. Once Maureen was murdered, Jen didn't stand a chance.'

'Jenny was fifteen when that happened?'

'Something like that.'

'And Maureen was selling sex.' I wanted to hurry him along.

I was starting to feel thirsty again and I knew another pint wasn't the answer.

'You know, there are men that target girls like them, girls in care – cos they know no one gives a shit what happens to them. There's a whole system set up to get those girls.'

'I know,' I said. I thought back to what Jo had said in The Brudenell. 'They're the invisible. You can do what the fuck you like to them because no one's watching.' We stared at each other for the moment and the intensity of his dark brown eyes unnerved me. 'You think the Park Killer targeted Maureen?'

'Right.'

'And he had an accomplice?'

'No.' He paused for a moment and I knew we were on the precipice. The brink. 'Not an accomplice. He had a boss.'

I swallowed the beer that regurgitated itself into my mouth. 'The Park Killer had a boss?'

Winston shrugged. 'Men like him, they take whatever they like.'

'The Park Killer was killing to order?' My mind struggled to accept the idea. How did men like that find each other? How did the conversation start? 'Someone was telling him to kill?'

'That's what Jenny reckoned.'

'Why?'

'You sure you want to know?'

'Dead sure.' I'd never been more sure.

'The Park Killer killed Maureen so his boss could have sex with her dead body.'

'Fuck off.'

He shrugged. 'Told you.'

'Jenny told you that?'

'She saw it happen.'

'What?'

'Jenny and Maureen had a system, for when Maureen was working. Jenny used to keep watch – they lived in a flat in Harehills, in Leeds. Jen would hang around, keeping an eye out. Outside. Maureen didn't want any of her clients to know she had a sister. So, Jen took car registration numbers, sometimes photos, when she had a phone.'

'She took photos?' The ramifications of that bent my head.

'The Park Killer had been before, a few times, Jenny said. Obviously she didn't know then that he was the Park Killer. That night, Jenny saw him go into the flat – all as normal. But he didn't come out. Instead, another man turns up and gets let into their flat. Jenny don't know what to do. She waits. I don't know how long. Twenty minutes, maybe. Half an hour. She creeps up, lets herself into the flat with her key. And that's when she saw him.'

'She saw him?'

Winston nodded, and his eyes reddened.

'She saw him with Maureen?'

He nodded.

'And the boss?'

He nodded again, and I saw the Adam's apple in his throat bob.

I couldn't imagine; I didn't want to imagine.

'Jen ran, but they'd seen her.'

'She didn't tell the police?'

He looked at me like I'd gone down in his estimation. 'What's she going to get from the police? Man. They'd send her back into care – back to the people she's been running away from. She never went home again, lived on the streets for nearly a year. She was messed up, in shock.'

Neither of us spoke for a minute. I rolled my own cigarette and saw my hands shake. I tried to think of questions to ask, but I couldn't think of anything except of a fifteen-year old girl seeing that happen to her sister. I didn't want to believe what he'd told me but I knew I couldn't afford not to.

Because that's what the abused are up against. Deep down, we don't want to know. We don't want to believe what human-kind, mankind, is capable of. How many broken people are out there, guarding truths we don't want to know.

I needed to change the subject, even if just for a moment, to let the ground settle. 'How did you two meet?'

'I was working on Leeds' market. Fruit and veg. Noticed her hanging around – we used to give what we couldn't sell to the hungry at the end of the day. We got talking. This is like a year later, after Maureen. She'd got herself a place – a bed and breakfast – and she was trying to turn it around.'

'She sounds tough.'

'Yeah.' He smiled. 'She was tough. Funny too. Only sixteen, when I met her. She didn't tell me that till we'd been together a while.'

'You sound like the best thing that happened to her.'

'It was a low bar,' he said.

'When did she tell you, about Maureen?'

'The Park Killer had been arrested. It was all over the

papers. Jen was acting weird. A couple of days later, he killed himself, in the cells. We was walking through the market and it was written on one of those boards. Suicide – the Park Killer. She sat down on the floor and cried. She told me a day or two after that.'

Goosebumps had formed all down my arms. I rubbed my skin.

'She was pissed off he'd killed himself. She thought the truth would come out, if there had been the trial.'

A line from a song I couldn't remember popped into my head. *There ain't no justice. Just us.*

'She moved in with me, and got pregnant not long after and things got worse. Wouldn't sleep without the light on. I'd wake up and she'd be soaking wet, shivering, crouched in the corner of the room, her back against the wall. She'd put a knife under her pillow. She convinced herself the boss was coming for her, freaking out he'd try to hurt the baby. She wasn't making sense.'

'This other guy, the boss. You know where he lives?'

He shook his head.

'His name?'

He stared at me and I knew he was deciding. I met his gaze, willed him to take me on, to trust me. I knew I could handle it. I knew this was the right thing to do.

'You know his name,' Winston said eventually. 'Everyone does. He's ...' Winston's voice trailed off, like he didn't quite dare release the knowledge.

I closed my eyes and saw Martin's list in front of them. I finished the sentence for him. 'A chef.'

'A chef?'

I opened my eyes and saw Winston frowning at me. At that moment another name from the list jumped into my head. A name that everyone knows. 'No,' I said.

I couldn't believe it, didn't want to believe it, even though at the same time somewhere inside me I already sensed it was true. 'Rob Hamilton? The Rob Hamilton?'

'You knew?'

'Rob fucking Hamilton?' I swear I felt my brain bulge. 'Christ.'

Rob Hamilton. A name everyone knows. A household name. A name associated with celebrity, with wealth, with success. A predator hiding in plain sight.

'He wasn't famous at the time, not when Maureen ...' He couldn't finish the sentence, instead started a new one. 'Jenny didn't know who he was, not even when the Park Killer was caught. It wasn't until later – Sasha was a baby. Jen struggled at first, after the birth, but I thought, maybe she was starting to settle. Sasha gave her what she'd never had. Roots, stability. Family. My old man passed; I thought we needed a new start, out of Leeds where the memories were. We weren't loaded, but we were doing OK. My old man had a bit of land, here in Nottingham. For the first time I could see a future.'

He smiled, but it didn't reach up to his eyes. 'And then one night, we were watching TV and he came on and Jenny, man, it was like she'd seen her own death. She recognized him straightaway.'

'We need to tell the police.'

'You going to go to the police and say a dead woman said

she saw a famous celebrity raping her sister's corpse thirteen, fourteen years ago?'

I flinched at his words. Anger made my stomach hurt.

'It's the past,' Winston said. 'You have to let it go.'

No fucking way.

'Jo was knocked down last night. That's not the past.'

The here and the now.

'If I can prove he had something to do with that, the police can start investigating. He's going to pay for what he did.'

Chapter 33

I left Winston at the Marcus Garvey Centre. He hugged me, and it didn't feel weird, which was odd because I'm not a touchy-feely person. Maybe we were both saying goodbye to Jenny. He smelled of cinnamon and woodsmoke, or perhaps the smoke was me. I gave him my number and said to ring me if he wanted an update. He took the number but I didn't think I'd ever hear from him again.

I rang the office on my way to the station and spoke to Aunt Edie. The first thing she told me was Jo had rallied, and was considered strong enough for surgery. I had to stop walking for a moment, but the news didn't surprise me. Jo's the strongest woman, the strongest person I know. It would take more than a car to get rid of her. I opened my eyes and offered up a small smile of thanks. It's not like I believe in God, but it's good for the soul to feel grateful.

'You can visit her tonight, her mum said to tell you. She's going to ring when Jo's out of theatre.'

A car blared its horn at me as I stepped across a side street. I waved at the driver. He mouthed something at me in return.

'I'm going to go and pick up a few things, so you've got

something to take with you. I thought grapes and maybe some magazines.'

'Great. That's absolutely great.' I laughed out loud, laughed up at the sky. 'How are you getting on with the list?'

'The list. Right, yes.' I heard her rustling sheets of paper in the background. 'OK, we've cross-referenced group A – that is single men, under sixty years old at the time of Jenny's death – with those that live in park-facing flats and have or had jobs that might involve early mornings. We're down to four.' I could hear the pride in Aunt Edie's voice. God love her. 'Hang on,' she said. 'I've got the names here.'

Aunt Edie read the list out to me. Rob Hamilton was third. 'Can you give me their flat numbers?' I said. 'I want to check something.'

'What about you?' she asked, once she'd given me the flat numbers of the four. 'Are you staying out of trouble?' There was a tone to her voice that I recognized but didn't acknowledge.

'Course. Think I might have a lead on Winston.'

I said I'd ring Aunt Edie back when I knew more and ended the call. I ducked into a Starbucks near the train station, ordered a chai tea latte and hooked my phone up to their internet. It wasn't difficult to find out where Rob Hamilton lived now. He'd sold his flat by the park less than a year after Jenny's body had been found outside, according to the *Our Property* website. I needed the police to investigate him, but I also knew he had to be fairly good at covering his tracks. I had to assume he'd made sure there was nothing that linked him to the car that had hit Jo. He might even have set himself up an alibi. I was about to accuse someone famous, someone really famous, of something almost unbelievable. I struggled to believe it myself, and I'm fairly cynical about the world. I'm also unimpressed by celebrity, but I know that puts me in the minority.

I don't know whether the #metoo movement has changed the world, but I knew the odds were against me, against Jenny. A dead woman with no relatives to care about her – just a mad mother, a dead sister, and a son whose father wanted to protect him from the knowledge of this.

I was up against a man with a reputation to protect, a man who had already shown he was willing to do anything to protect that reputation. I was up against a man who embodied privilege, celebrity, success. The world wants to, needs to, believe in those ideals.

I sat there for an hour or more, letting the alcohol drip from my system, hyping myself up with caffeine, thinking about my next step. The longer I sat there, the clearer it became. There was only one thing I could do. An hour later I walked out of Starbucks with considerably more information than I'd had since this case started. And even in these celebrity-obsessed times we live in, knowledge is still where real power lies.

I caught the train back to Leeds, picked up the van from the station car park and drove to Thorner, a small village on the outskirts of Leeds where Rob Hamilton now lived.

You'd be amazed how easy breaking and entering is, once you put your mind to it. We like to think we're safe within our own four walls, but the truth is we're all a single pane of glass away from the outside world. And anyone who's ever been to the bottle bank knows how fragile glass can be.

Rob Hamilton had come up in the world, even by the standard of the luxury flats on the edge of Roundhay Park. The house had gates that had a remote-control locking system, but there was a wall at the side, probably six foot high but easy enough to climb. It was made out of old Yorkshire stone and the gaps between each slab were big enough to get my toes into and I climbed myself up and over. I had a mosey around the outside of his house, which was a new build, redbrick and square. I broke into his double garage, but there wasn't a car parked in there, nor on the drive. There were oil spots on the garage floor though, and a space big enough to park at least two vehicles.

I sat on the step inside the garage and tried to put myself in Rob Hamilton's shoes. A private investigator, Jo, turns up, almost seven years after Jenny killed herself, just when he's starting to relax. One thing I know about Jo is that she doesn't pussyfoot around. She'd have been straight on to him, once she knew.

I didn't know the law well enough. Was there a statute of limitations on the kind of crimes he'd committed? Was Maureen a one-off or part of a pattern? What the #metoo movement has emphasized more than anything is that predators never fill up on their prey. There's always a next time. How many Maureens had there been for Rob Hamilton?

How had he come to know the Park Killer? How long had they known each other? I'd checked out Rob Hamilton's career online. At the time of Maureen's murder, fourteen years ago, he'd been working as a doctor at Leeds General Infirmary, with a part-time gig on local radio – a weekly, twenty-minute slot on healthy living.

No one would have known him outside of Leeds. Let's be honest, not many people in Leeds would have known him – who listens to local radio, even fourteen years ago? But not long after that, he'd got his break – his own chat show on late-night, local TV, discussing the health issues of various minor celebrities. When he'd interviewed a pop star on her battle with breast cancer, a battle she'd never shared before, his gentle yet fearless interview style had caught the public's attention and his career had skyrocketed. He was moved to a prime-time slot on the BBC and there he proved himself as someone who could get anyone to open up – from politicians to actors to the prisoners he'd worked with in the early days of him being a doctor. Rob Hamilton could hold the hands of people from every walk of life as he cajoled them into sharing the secrets of their lives with an audience of millions. By the time Jenny had tied herself to the statue outside his flat, seven years ago, he was a household name, hosting one of the biggest celebrity interview shows on TV – the UK's answer to Oprah.

I'd found an article about him going into rehab, which was dated less than six months after Jenny's body had been discovered in the grounds of his old apartment block. Had he recognized her dead body? Did he know that she was connected to Maureen Kozlowska? Did he realize his terrible secrets were at risk of being exposed?

On the night that Jenny took her own life, someone had stolen her handbag. I knew that had to be him, so he had to be anxious. But he'd never seen the suicide note, thanks to Linda, so maybe, once he'd succeeded in ensuring the police hadn't been able to identify the body, he'd thought he was safe. Less than a year later, Rob Hamilton had quietly moved house and moved on.

Until, another seven years later, Jo turns up. There's a Buddhist belief that we shed our skins every seven years. Rob Hamilton must be beginning to realize he wasn't going to be allowed to shed his. Jenny had turned up almost seven years after Maureen's murder, and Jo seven years after Jenny's suicide. Each time he allows himself to think he's got away with it, along comes another woman with the power to unmask him. And what a mask it was he wore. I couldn't imagine a bigger fall.

But how did Jo make the connection? How did she know it was Rob Hamilton and not one of the occupiers of the other flats? She hadn't found Winston. What had led her here, or to Rob Hamilton? And how?

I stood up and made my way back onto the drive. The house was uPVC double glazed which made breaking in a little more tricky. Tricky but not impossible. I went round the back. The great thing about rich people's houses is they aren't often overlooked. Rich people, in my experience, value privacy. That's one of the main differences between the classes, from what I've seen. The working class live their lives under other people's gaze. Rich people have more opportunity to hide, to create a false impression.

The Runaway

Sure enough there were lots of established trees and bushes in the back garden to ensure that anyone in either of the two detached houses in the vicinity couldn't see me. I dug up a stone from the rockery near the patio with my fingers and smashed it against the pane of glass in the back door. It took several attempts but double glazing is still glass, when all is said and done.

I snaked my hand through the broken shards but misjudged the gap, saw the thin line of red appear on the back of my hand. On the other side of the door, I felt the key sticking out of the lock and turned it. I heard the clunk and the door popped open.

I glanced behind me. Nothing had changed, nothing had moved, life went on around me, without me. My pulse quickened and I stifled the urge to laugh as I stepped inside and paused for a moment on the threshold, allowing myself to grow accustomed to the noises of the house. New houses tend to be quieter than old houses. I waited a few seconds more, possibly a minute all in all, straining to hear any sounds of habitation – movement, the TV or music playing. I heard nothing. I was in what I think estate agents call a utility room. By the back door was a row of jackets, with a pair of wellies underneath, and two state-of-the-art washing machines, sitting one on top of the other. I couldn't imagine why anyone would need two washing machines. I took a couple of steps forward and crossed the room and into the kitchen.

You can tell a lot about a person by their kitchen. This one was cold and you'd be forgiven for thinking it had never been used. The worktops were the hard, granite kind, shiny and black. Each one was empty, no baskets of fruit, or tins of biscuits, no washing up by the sink.

I jumped a mile in the air as my phone rang. I scrambled to pull it out of my pocket, my heart pounding against my chest so loud I could see my ribcage moving. The office number flashed up on screen. I swiped the screen to ignore the call and switched the phone to silent, cursing my own stupidity. Good job no one was home. I checked the time before stuffing it back in my pocket and making my way through the kitchen and out into the entrance hall, a square room in the centre of the house. A large wooden staircase squatted in the middle, and a kind of balcony arrangement ran around the first floor. I counted half a dozen doorways on the ground floor before I put my foot on the first step. Start at the top. Work down.

All of the four upstairs rooms looked like hotel bedrooms, waiting for the next set of guests to check in. The duvets neatly folded back in a triangle, so that whoever was going to climb into bed wouldn't have the inconvenience of having to lift the sheets out of the way before getting in. It made me think of climbing into an envelope. I searched each room, but the furniture contained very little – a couple of towels and an extra blanket. A dog's bed in the bottom of a wardrobe and a box of CDs. In the smallest bedroom I found a stash of hard-core pornographic magazines and some DVDs hidden in a built-in cupboard that ran into the eaves of the house, alongside a plastic box containing some fairly heavy-duty bondage gear, including a rubber ball on a piece of metal that, minus the ball, looked like something you'd put on a horse. I put the rubber ball up against my lips. It seemed almost too big for a person's mouth.

I closed the cupboard door and sat down on the floor for a moment. I didn't know what I was looking for. He'd have got rid of anything connecting him to Jenny, or Maureen, I imagined. He'd moved here a year after Jenny's suicide, which would have been seven years after Maureen's murder. It's not like he would have carried around anything implicating himself to that, as he moved house. So what was I looking for? Something that gave insight into his sexual deviancies, that I could use to prove what kind of man he was. What kind of something would that be?

I needed more than porn. More than sadomasochistic sex toys. I needed to prove a link to the Park Killer. I needed to show the kind of company Rob Hamilton kept.

His computer.

I ran down the stairs and found an office at the front of the house, just off the square hallway. It contained a desk, several tall, dark wood bookcases and the walls were painted a deep crimson, almost blood red. A large TV dominated the room and an armchair was in the corner, big enough for two. A standard lamp hung over the armchair, and a small table next to the armchair. An odd place to watch TV when the house was this big. For starters this was the smallest room I'd been into so far and it was decorated in a way that made me think of a womb. A den. On the desk was a small laptop – so lightweight I could pick it up in one hand. I flicked up the screen and pressed the on button. It came to life immediately, the screensaver a picture of Rob Hamilton, a still from a TV studio, him sat knee to knee with another face I recognized, the frontman of a band that had been around all my life. I'd loved them as a teenager – even my mum had thought the lead singer was something special. The pair of them were shaking hands and smiling at the camera, like they'd just done something they were proud of. I wondered whether the singer knew what kind of person Rob Hamilton really was.

My skin prickled. I could sense Rob Hamilton in this room, sitting in the armchair, watching fuck knows what on the enormous TV screen late into the night. I shivered and forced myself not to think along those lines, not while I was in a house where he might turn up any moment. I needed a clear mind. I needed to be alert. If there was nothing to tie Rob Hamilton to Maureen, what about something that tied him to what had happened to Jo last night?

I went back into the hallway, where I'd seen a landline. I dialled 1571 – and the automated voice told me I had no messages. I rang 1471 and listened to the last number that had rung the house. As the computerized tones talked out the number my blood chilled. The call had come at 5.07 p.m. the previous day. A number I know off by heart.

The number of Jo's mobile.

I needed to piss. A sudden urgent need. I went through to the downstairs toilet, making a mental note to get Martin and Aunt Edie to find out what had happened to Jo's phone. I could show a link between Jo and Rob Hamilton: now maybe the police would be willing to reopen the file on Jenny's death.

I fastened my belt on my way back to his den. My knees

felt less sure of their ability to move me around, to support me. I bumped my hip bone on the doorframe. Jo had been here. Or if she hadn't been actually here, she'd been in contact with the owner of this house. I peered out of the window. His car wasn't on the drive, or in the garage. I thought of Jo, in the dark, walking along the street and Rob Hamilton, sat behind the wheel, aiming and pressing his foot down hard on the accelerator. A feeling I couldn't contain raged through my body and I picked up the laptop, the picture of him coming back to life right in front of my face, and I hurled it across the room. It bounced off the wall, leaving a scrape on the blood-red wallpaper.

I crossed to the desk and yanked open the middle drawer. It contained a hundred signed photographs of the man himself, smiling at the camera, his teeth white, too white to be true. I threw them on the floor behind me. As I went through drawer after drawer, no longer bothering to put things back as I'd found them, my mind was in hyper-gear. I went over everything I knew about Jo's movements the day before. She'd met Martin, gone through the list, and then taken the afternoon off. I remembered Aunt Edie had told me Jo had gone to meet a friend for lunch. Sara, I'd presumed at the time. Whatever Jo had done between lunchtime and 5.07 p.m. had led her here, into the path of Rob Hamilton.

I found an old address book in the third drawer down and wished I'd brought a bag. I retraced my steps back to the utility room and helped myself to a small rucksack hanging with the coats by the door. I scurried back to the den and picked up the laptop. Its screen was still intact, although there was a chunk missing from the wall. I put it in the bag, along with the address book and picked up a bunch of keys from his desk. Perhaps there was a safe somewhere? A lock-up? I pulled the two framed prints he had off the wall to see if there was anything behind them. Nothing. I examined the keys. Five in all. Two that looked like house keys – one mortice lock and one Yale. A car key and two keys that looked like filing cabinet keys – small, silver. I hadn't seen a filing cabinet anywhere. I slipped the keys into the bag.

Where was Rob Hamilton now? Disposing of his car? Covering his tracks? Leaving the country?

I didn't have long to wait to find out.

Chapter 34

I was on my hands and knees in the den, trying to lift up the edges of the carpet to see whether there might be a loose floorboard underneath when I heard the front door bang. I got up off my knees, and noticed for the first time the extent of the mess I'd created. I closed the drawers to the desk as quietly as I could, and glanced out of the window just in time to see an Uber pulling out of the front gates.

I don't watch anything on TV. And it's not just because I think it's all crap. I mean, I do think it's all crap, but that's not the truth, not the whole truth. The truth is I can't sit still and watch TV because it gives space for the negative thoughts to come in.

Truth is I have to keep my brain creatively engaged or the darkness gets me. Watching is, for me, too passive a pastime – before I know it, I'm in a state of anxiety, worrying about this or that, whether my shallow breathing and my high heart rate means I'm about to die, whether that niggling pain I hadn't noticed in my spleen is some kind of cancer, whether my sister would still be alive if I hadn't done the things I've done. I'd rather read a book, because then my brain is engaged with the imagining. TV leaves my brain with too much time on its hands. And as Aunt Edie keeps telling me, the devil makes work for idle hands.

My mum used to watch *Coronation Street* every day of the week, her equivalent to catching up with her mates. She once got me to post a letter to one of the cast – she'd written to her to tell her her husband was cheating on her. It was addressed to Deirdre Rachid, 1 Coronation Street, Weatherfield. She couldn't post it herself, on account of the fact her agoraphobia prevented her from walking to the end of the street. I didn't post it, of course. I ripped it into small pieces and threw it into the bin outside the chippy.

I don't watch TV and when people have those conversations about how great *The Wire* is, or *The Bodyguard*, I have no idea what they're talking about. I'm resigned to the fact that I live in a different universe.

But there are some things you can't escape, because they're so ingrained into our culture that they transcend the screen. Like Ross Kemp, and *The X Factor*. I know about them, even if I've never seen them in action. So, when I stepped into the hallway, and faced Rob Hamilton for the first time, it was like having Ken Barlow standing in front of me. Someone you think you know but actually you've never met. It's a weird feeling. Familiarity and its opposite both in the same moment. I recognized Rob's white-grey hair and dark eyebrows that made him look both old and young at the same time.

'I'd expect someone as famous as you to have a chauffeur, not an Uber,' I said, because that was the first thing that came into my head as I wandered into the hallway.

'Who the fuck are you?' he said. He didn't sound angry, more confused. His voice was more familiar to me than my own father's. Not that that's saying much.

'I wanted to see where you lived,' I said.

'I'm calling the police,' he said. 'You have no right.'

'I'm such a fan.' I blinked on purpose a few times. 'Can I have your autograph?'

'Are you out of your mind?' he said. It sounded like a genuine question. He stared at me and I knew he was trying to work it out. Crazed fan or something to do with Jo? He wanted to believe the former, but we both knew coincidence was on the side of the latter, and I probably didn't look like your average fan. I wasn't sure who Rob Hamilton's average fan was, just that it wasn't me. I watched him struggle with his own rationality.

'Go ahead, call them,' I said, trying to keep my voice as steady and level as possible. I put my hand into my back pocket and pulled out my phone. I tapped in the code and held it out to him. 'My mum's not going to believe this.'

He put the bag he'd been carrying down on the floor by his feet. 'What do you want?' he asked.

'I said. Your autograph. And maybe a photo?' I raised my eyebrows as if to say I knew I was pushing it, but I was willing to take the chance.

'And then you'll leave?'

'Yes. Course. You've got a beautiful house.'

'How did you get in?'

I hesitated and that hesitation cost me. 'You left the back door open,' I said.

'I don't think I did,' he replied.

We circled each other, switching positions so that I was now in the corridor nearest to the front door, and he was nearer the rear of the house. He waited for me to say something.

He didn't take the phone that I still brandished so I slipped it back into my jacket pocket. I saw his Adam's apple bob. 'Where's your car?' I asked. 'You do have a car, I take it. I mean, I'd imagine someone as famous as you to have a really nice car.'

'I do. Or rather I did.' He tried to smile. 'I reported it stolen this morning.'

'Stolen?' I nodded, like I might be seriously considering the prospect.

'It wasn't you, was it? I mean, you've broken into my house. You can't blame me for thinking you might be responsible for stealing my car?'

As his hard, grey eyes met mine, I heard my voice saying, 'Where were you at quarter to one this morning?'

He didn't stop to think. 'I was out, last night,' he said. 'With a friend. We had dinner. Spent the night together.'

'A friend who can vouch for you?'

He removed his jacket, turned and hung it over the stair bannister. When he spoke his voice had authority, confidence. 'There's been a spate of burglaries round here lately. If you ask me it's a bloody crime wave. Too many poor people. That's not their fault, of course, but there's always someone who thinks they can take without asking, someone who wants the high life without being prepared to put the spadework in.'

364

'Have the police found it?'

He removed his gloves and laid them on the hall table, next to the telephone. 'That's where I've been. The police station. My car was set alight, somewhere down in Scott Hall something or other they said. Sounds like joyriders. Lucky for me I've a robust insurance policy.'

'Does it cover hit-and-run?'

'I beg your pardon.'

'Last night, at quarter to one, my best friend was involved in a hit-and-run. The driver didn't stop.'

'That's dreadful. You surely don't think my car was involved?'

'I think she was run down on purpose. I think the driver wanted to kill her.'

'I'm very sorry for your loss but it was nothing to do with me.'

'She's not dead,' I spat.

I saw his eyes bulge and for the first time in our conversation I knew I'd told him something he didn't already know. A surge of something stronger than whisky hit my bloodstream.

'And when she comes round, she'll have no trouble telling the police all about the phone call she made to you, yesterday, at 5.07 p.m., and the arrangement she made to meet you to discuss what happened to Jenny Crawley's sister, Maureen Kozlowska. You see, we're not only best friends, we're business partners, which means everything that Jo knows, I know.'

I let that information settle for a moment. Rob Hamilton cleared his throat like he was about to say something, but nothing came out.

'Things like why, seven years ago, Jenny Crawley decided to kill herself right outside your flat on the outskirts of Roundhay Park. Beautiful location. You can't imagine bad things happening there.'

'That person was never identified. The police couldn't find out who she was.'

'You used to work as a prison doctor, I hear. You must have met all kinds of people in there. I understand the Park Killer spent some time in prison, for domestic violence, before he started attacking women in parks. Ever come across him?'

Rob Hamilton stepped towards me, his hands curled into fists. I wasn't worried. If there's one thing boxing has taught me, it's that most people don't know how to fight. I lifted myself up onto the balls of my feet, ready. 'Time's up,' I said. 'Bet you thought you were in the clear, but that's the thing about Karma. You never know when she's going to sneak up and bite your balls off.'

'I don't know what you're talking about.'

'She left a note.'

'Who did?'

'Jenny Crawley.'

'I don't know anyone by that name.'

'No. You knew her sister. Maureen Kozlowska. Only you might not have troubled to learn her name either. Maureen was a sex worker. She was killed by the Park Killer.'

'This has nothing to do with me.'

'Jenny, Maureen's little sister, used to keep watch when Maureen was working. They were very close. Jenny used to take photographs, car registration numbers, that kind of thing.

It was Jenny that discovered her sister's body, in their flat, in Harehills. You see, Maureen's latest appointment was taking too long. Jenny was worried. She went back to the flat. She saw what you did to Maureen.'

His face had gone white, the blood drained from it.

'And yes,' I said. 'Jenny left a note. She left that note for you. Only someone else took it.'

'Please.'

'The person who took it kept it all these years.'

'I can give you anything you want.'

I spat at his feet, needed to clear the bile from my mouth. 'You don't have anything that I want.'

'Anything at all.'

'Don't you want to hear what the note says?'

'Name your price. Just name it. I'll give you everything.'

'Did you offer that same deal to Jo?'

'Please. Please, don't. You don't know what it's like to live with what I've done.'

'That's because I'm not a disgusting pervert.'

'I've changed. I'm not that person anymore. I swear on my life I'd never do anything—'

'Shut up,' I said. 'I don't want to listen to a word that comes out of your dirty, lying, disgusting mouth. You ran my best friend over to stop her from telling what she knows about you. If you think for one minute I'm going to be bought off by you, you're fucking insane.'

He stepped backwards until his back was against the hall wall. 'You can't do this to me. I've got friends. You'll never be able to step out of your house.'

'Don't threaten me.'

'I'm a sick man.' He sank his head into his hands and his shoulders sagged. 'Please, don't. I'll do anything. I'll kill myself. Please. I'm serious, I'd rather die than—'

'Like your mate? The Park Killer?' I shook my head. 'There's been too many people who can't live with the thought, the sight, of what you've done. But if you think I'm going to let you take the easy way out ...' I had a hard a time keeping my hands by my sides. I wanted to rip his throat from his body. I reminded myself to breathe. 'I want you alive, so that you can suffer every single day for the rest of your pitiful life. You see, every night I go to bed, I want to think about how you're suffering. You know what happens to men like you in prison?'

He was crying openly now, snot running down his face. He didn't look anything like the handsome man of the TV screen. Up close the minor cosmetic procedures were taking their toll. His pores were too big, his skin not quite the right colour, his eyebrows too straight, his teeth didn't match the rest of him. He looked fake. A plasticine image of what handsome should look like.

'Jenny Crawley spent the last seven years of her life sleeping with the lights on,' I said, as my fingers twitched at my side, the adrenalin in my system yearning to be put to use. 'Scared every day of her life, because she knew that men like you exist.'

'I didn't mean—'

'She knew no one would take her word against yours.'

'It wasn't like that. I didn't—'

'Men like you rely on women being too scared, too ashamed

to speak up. But you must have known it was coming. The world is changing – there's no hiding place anymore.'

I reached inside my jacket pocket for my phone and switched off the recording function before calling up the keypad. I pressed the 9 button twice. I didn't get to press it for a third time, because Rob Hamilton charged at me. I dropped the phone and grabbed him by the waist. He reached for a fistful of my hair but I put my knee up and hit him as hard as I could in the stomach. He doubled over and I clasped my hands together and used them like an axe on the back of his neck. He dropped to his knees and I kicked him in the face. Twice. Blood splattered onto my boots and across the cream of the hall walls, and I felt a feeling I don't get very often. It's a feeling I don't like to examine too much, but it's about as close to happiness as it's possible for me to get. It's a feeling of power, and of excitement and it's probably not how we're supposed to feel, especially not as women. But when you win something, even a fight, it's hard not to feel, well, to feel like a winner. I haven't won much in my life so the feeling is unusual, and that makes it even better.

I never had myself down as a fighter. Once when I was at school a girl hit me and I was so shocked, so embarrassed, I just stood there, open-mouthed, while she hurled abuse at me. Later it turned out it was a case of mistaken identity – she thought I'd sent a text message to her boyfriend, only it wasn't me. She never apologized and I never asked her to. As a child I avoided conflict, sloped around life's edges, tried to stay out of trouble, off radar, out of the way. The world had other plans.

369

Women aren't taught to fight; they aren't taught to stand their ground. Women are taught that at the first sign of trouble they should run. Which is stupid advice, if you think about it, because your average man will always run faster than your average woman. It's something to do with the thigh muscle. Men have narrower hips, so their quads get to work in a straight line, which also happens to be the same direction in which their legs are moving. Women's hips tend to be wider, so their muscles have to work at an angle. Means their muscles are never going to be as efficient, no matter how many hours a woman might train. Added to that a man's leg is about eighty per cent muscle, whereas a woman's is about sixty per cent. Bigger leg muscles working more efficiently. You've only got to look at the world records for sprinting. Running is never going to be the answer.

Added to that we teach women to run and then dress them in clothes that are actively designed to ensure running is not an option. Ever tried to run in stilettos and a skirt? You might as well just lie down and get it over with. All running does in those circumstances is add to the thrill of the chase. A chase that the man is always going to win.

But fighting ... fighting is different because fighting requires another skill set altogether. And not many people – men or women – bother to learn those skills. A woman who has learned to fight has a massive advantage over a man who hasn't. Fighting requires intelligence, patience, precision and discipline, skills women have by the bucketful.

Brute strength plays its part of course, but only if you come up against a man who's taken the time to learn the basics. As a general rule, men don't take the time to learn the basics, because their testosterone tells them they don't need to. They think being big and heavy is enough. It isn't.

Rob Hamilton clambered to his feet. He'd got a rush of adrenalin – his fight or flight response. And men aren't taught to run. I lifted myself up on to the balls of my feet again. Thai boxing teaches you to use the natural weapons of your body. You have eight in total. Two elbows, two knees, two fists, two feet.

As he came towards me, I drove at him with my fist to his face first, my elbow to his throat second. I raised my right knee and aimed for his groin but my calculations were out of date – he'd collapsed, shrunk down so by the time my knee had completed its trajectory it got him in the chest. The final kick, the kick with my foot, connected with his skull and I heard the crack of bone. Something rose up in me, something that I like to keep buried most of the time, but I thought of Jo and what he'd done to her. I don't know how many times I kicked him while he lay on the floor, but I know I'm not going to waste my time feeling bad about it. I doubted he'd spent much of his life giving thought to Maureen or to Jenny or to Jo. Or to any of the other women he'd abused. It's better to let anger out.

*

I went back upstairs into the smallest bedroom and retrieved the plastic box filled with sex toys. I used the handcuffs to fasten his wrists behind his back, and I forced the rubber ball into his mouth, the job made slightly easier by the fact he was now missing a front tooth. I fastened the clasp at the back of his skull. There was a blindfold so I put that on him too. Then I retrieved my mobile phone from its resting place across the hall floor and called the police.

Rob Hamilton was groaning by the time the first police car arrived. The police officer looked younger than me and I'm willing to bet he'd never seen a scene like the one in front of him before. Blood streaked the front of Rob Hamilton's white shirt and as the policeman struggled to take the blindfold off, I got a taste of what I was going to be up against. 'God, is that Rob Hamilton? *The* Rob Hamilton?'

I nodded at the young copper. 'Don't untie him,' I said. 'Wait till the big boys get here.' I'd asked specifically for Detective Inspector Fowler when I'd called 999. I'd dealt with him on my last case and I knew that he'd at least be willing to hear my side of the story, hopefully cut me a bit of slack.

A bit of slack.

I looked at Rob Hamilton's slumped form again. I'd tied him up with what looked like a dog lead that had also been in the plastic box. I'd looped it around his ankles and then connected it to the handcuffs behind his back, which had made his back arch. I think they call it the bow position in yoga. I'd had to fight temptation when I'd noticed his exposed throat, as his head bent back, but I'd managed to restrain myself. Discipline, you see.

I felt sorry for the young copper as we waited for the rest of the squad to arrive. Nothing in his training had prepared him for this. He radioed through to chcck where the rest of the squad were, the panic in his voice obvious. I took a photo of Hamilton with the camera on my phone so I could show it to Jo. If that didn't cheer her up, I didn't know what would. I couldn't help grinning. I couldn't wait to go and see her. Our friendship had moved on; we could let go of whatever that stupid argument had been about. Of course it didn't matter about her and Sara. Our friendship goes beyond that. Way beyond.

Detective Fowler arrived about ten minutes after the first cop car. The young constable had gone to stand by the front door, at a complete loss as to what to do or say.

'What the hell?' asked DI Fowler as he stepped into the bloodstained hall.

'It was him. He tried to kill Jo. He claims his car was stolen but it was him.'

'Rob Hamilton?'

'Listen to this.' I played him the recording on my phone three times while his officers removed the sadomasochistic restraints from Rob Hamilton and allowed him to be examined by the paramedics. They didn't remove the handcuffs though.

'It's not exactly a confession,' DI Fowler said.

'"You don't know what it's like to live with what I've done?" Come on. He had sex with Jenny Crawley's sister, after the Park Killer had murdered her. Jenny killed herself outside his flat.'

'You have proof? A witness? Anyone who's willing to testify to any of this?'

I thought of Winston. I thought he'd come through, if not for me, then for Jenny. 'Yes.'

Detective Fowler rang a few people, barked orders down the phone. 'We'll need to get the house sealed; I want that car looking at under a bloody microscope. We're going to need something that puts Rob Hamilton at the scene of the crash. And take a look see what we've got on the original murder. Maureen Kozlowska. Fourteen bloody years ago. Have a word with the pathologist. I hope to Christ he keeps better records than we do.'

He switched off his phone and turned to me. 'This is going to be a difficult one. Tying him to a murder that happened that long ago.'

'You'll be able to get him for attempted murder at least. That happened last night. Jo will tell you, soon as she comes out of surgery. She'll tell you.'

'You don't know,' he said.

I realized that my right knee, the one I'd used to kick Hamilton in the stomach, was really hurting and wasn't capable of holding me up anymore. 'I think I might have broken my kneecap,' I said. 'Are the paramedics still here?' I thought maybe they could take a look at it. Give me an injection of something. I hadn't noticed the pain at first but now it was excruciating.

'I'm sorry, Lee,' Detective Fowler said, and his voice was softer than normal. 'I was informed an hour ago. The surgeons did everything they could but Jo's injuries were too extensive.'

He had something stuck between his front teeth. A dot of

black. Like a seed or something. I frowned at him as he put his hand under my elbow and took the weight of me. 'What?'

'Jo hasn't regained consciousness.'

I didn't want to know what that meant. But Detective Inspector Fowler seemed hell-bent on informing me.

'She's in a coma.' Each word spelled out with precision, like he wanted me to grasp the meaning of every separate word. 'She's not responding to treatment. The doctors aren't hopeful.' He motioned to another policeman who I hadn't noticed stood by the door. 'I'm sorry, Lee. I know how close you were.'

Chapter 35

I know how close you were. Those words haunted me for days afterwards. Like they'd got into a loop in my brain. Close.

I've never thought about it before, but how can the same word mean being close to someone and something coming to an end? As in close the book, or this road is closed. Close like a dead end.

I met Jo during my first week at university. I'd been so glad to leave home – a poxy Lancashire town that was dying on its feet, although no one ever talked about it. Everyone went about their business as shop after shop got boarded up around them. We were being picked off, one by one, and I never really noticed it until I left, but no one ever mentioned the future. A business went bankrupt, a store closed, a drug user died, a young mother got sectioned. Small town Russian roulette – you stopped wondering who or what would go under next.

I'd never really had a friend. In my home town, the only newspapers our corner shop stocked were *The Sun* and the *Daily Star* and it's hard to find like-minded spirits when the whole town is fed on a diet of tits and hate. I never invited anyone home, because I was too ashamed of my house and more specifically my mother, a whale beached on our reinforced settee, guzzling herself to death.

Jo was my first proper friend. In truth, the only friend I've ever had. She swooped down on me, in Freshers' Week, like she knew I needed feeding. She filled me with insight, ideas, concepts. She made me realize that it wasn't me, it was them, and that realization is the most liberating feeling in the world.

She made me laugh, that first day as we were walking through the Students' Union. A group of lads, messing about, and one of them had said something to her – I can't even remember what – and she told him he should go and wank off to *Top Gear*. He was so surprised, the expression on his face made me laugh till I cried. I'd never done that before. Never laughed until I was worried I might die because I couldn't breathe.

Friends change you. They alter your genetic make-up, so that the pathways in your brain function differently. Their DNA interacts with yours – a chemical reaction – and you are changed by the process. I'm not the same person I was before I met Jo and I'll always be different from now on. I don't like to think about the person I'd be if I hadn't met Jo.

For the first few weeks, after, I didn't want to get out of bed, but I made myself. I made myself walk through the park, past the university and down to the hospital. I'd sit by her bed, alongside her mother and Ste, her brother. Sometimes I'd be there on my own and I'd play music to her. At night when I couldn't sleep I wrote her letters and read them to her the next day. I took Aunt Edie with me on a few occasions, and we read out loud, bits from *The Guardian* about the Tories and austerity and Brexit in the hope that something would make her angry enough to spark her back to life.

Over the weeks Jo's face grew thinner.

Twice when I got there, I saw Sara at Jo's bedside. Luckily, both times she didn't see me. I wasn't ready, wasn't sure what the words I wanted to say were, even though I knew I wanted to say them, so I left her to it and went for a walk around the hospital and when I came back she'd gone.

I talked to Jo about Rob Hamilton and what I'd done to him. I told her how the police had reopened the investigation into Maureen Kozlowska's death, and Jenny Crawley's suicide. She never once moved. Not a single flicker.

The longer a person stays in a coma the less chance there is of them waking up. That's the trouble with Google. You can find out the answers to all the questions you never wanted to ask. As the days slipped into weeks I sat by her bed and prayed to swap places with her. It got harder to visit and harder to stay away. I wondered whether she might recover quicker if I didn't visit. Maybe I was making her worse not better. I was her best friend, the person supposed to drag her through but I couldn't find a way, and every day just highlighted my failure more.

I hoped to die. Didn't want to wake up, didn't want to eat, didn't want to see anyone. Aunt Edie moved in. I didn't even realize. It was only when I dried my hands on her pop stockings that were hanging over the towel rail in the bathroom that the penny dropped.

'You can't live here,' I said.

'I can't leave you on your own.'

'I'm doing OK.'

'Crapsticks, you are.'

'Get out,' I said.

Two days later the pop socks were gone. I celebrated by staying in bed and not getting dressed. The doorbell rang, three, maybe four times but I ignored it. I was in my bedroom in the attic when I heard footsteps on the stairs, and a man's voice. I don't know any men.

Maybe I was hallucinating. I hadn't eaten much in the last few days. I crawled out of bed, peered round the doorframe.

And there he was.

On the staircase outside my bedroom, halfway up.

'Edie made me come,' he said.

As if life couldn't get any worse.

My dad. Thinner than I remembered. Not just his body, his hair. He'd diminished. Maybe it was my elevated viewpoint.

It was so bad, I nearly laughed. I held onto the railing. 'Is she trying to finish me off?'

He hovered on the stairs, one foot on the next step, but not moving. 'She said I'm all you have.'

'I never had you,' I said. 'I never had you before and I don't want you now.'

'She said we both have to learn to live with losing the person we love the most. She said—'

'You didn't lose Fiona. You fucking killed her.'

He nodded, like he knew I was going to say that. Like the

conversation was going just as he'd been told it would. 'She said you think you've killed Jo.'

'Rob Hamilton ran her over. Not me.'

He half-smiled. 'Edie said when you realize that, that's the first step.'

God, that woman drives me mad. I wanted to scream but I knew I didn't have the energy. I felt light-headed standing at the top of the stairs looking down on him. It's weird looking at my dad – kind of the opposite experience that I had when I stood in Rob Hamilton's hallway. Rob Hamilton was a stranger I'd seen a lot. My dad is someone I've hardly ever seen, a face I don't know, and yet in his features, there's parts I recognize. I didn't meet him till I was nineteen, never even saw a photograph. But there's something about his eyes that reminds me of something, something deeper than I can put into words. It's about familiarity – some people might call it family, even though we never wer]e one. He must have sensed my lack of fight, because he took a step up, a step towards me. 'Let's go for a walk,' he said.

*

I'm not going to say what we talked about, and I'm not going to say that talking to my dad made everything better. But it did serve one useful purpose. It reminded me that there's always someone worse off. And that's nearly as bad as Aunt Edie's, 'Whatever doesn't kill you makes you stronger' tripe, but maybe there's some wisdom in her. Buried. Deeply buried.

But thinking that at least I didn't physically cause Jo's

condition, like my dad caused my sister's, was liberating. Because then I remembered Jenny and what she went through that made her poison herself and die the way that she did.

Women are taught to turn their anger in. They take responsibility, take the blame, punish themselves and in doing so they embrace the role of victim. And if I stay home, blaming myself for Jo, I'm doing the same thing.

That doesn't help the world.

Staying small does not help the world.

A friend is someone who encourages you to be your best self. Jo always did that for me and now it's my turn to do it for her. The only way I can carry on, make sense of what's happened, is to try to be my best self, until the day Jo comes back.

I'm not sure I knew that while she was still moving, but that's how I'm going to try and deal with her now, because on some level I believe I can bring her back to life that way. Until she wakes up, I'm going to live for the both of us – I'm going to take the best bits of me and the best bits of her and blend them to create a best self.

That thought keeps me going, keeps me getting out of bed each morning and walking down the hill into work, into the office. I'm doing it for the two of us.

Aunt Edie flutters round me, never quite getting close, but hovering all the time like she's about to put a bucket in front of me in case I vomit. I don't talk to her yet because I don't know the right words. But I know she's there.

I can't talk to Martin either. Can't bear to see the guilt I feel mirrored in his eyes. So the two of them totter around, bickering in the background, but keeping the place ticking over. Rob Hamilton has been charged with Jo's attempted murder, and that will be a whole other mountain to climb. The court case, the trial, the raking over the past. That day, he asked me to let him die and I thought it was too easy an end for him. Now I wish I'd killed him, because it would have been an easier end for us – for Aunt Edie, Martin, for Jo's family, Sara, me.

At the moment, the only way I can get through the days is to spend them alone. Writing this report gave me the chance to do that. Sitting in the back office, day after day. To be honest, I'm scared of what will happen now it's coming to the end.

Nikki came in last week to tell me she'd had her first scan and the baby she's carrying is a boy. We stared at each other for a moment, and I know we both had the same worries because she said to me, 'It's my chance to make a difference.' I asked her what she meant and she said it was no good women going on about what absolute twats men were if we weren't prepared to stand up and have a go at shaping the men of the future. She said she'd been thinking about it and masculinity didn't have to be toxic.

'What about your parents?' I'd asked her.

'Totally flipped out.' She shook her head and the bells in her hair tinkled again. 'They'll come round, eventually, maybe. And uni have said I can take a year out which is ace. Give me time to get my head around it.' She put her hand on her belly and I thought the extra weight suited her. 'It's only a baby. How hard can it be?'

'What about Matt?'

'I got a letter from his counsellor. He's in this rehab centre, in Bristol. They ask all the family to come, like an intervention kind of thing. And they asked me.'

She sounded pleased to be asked.

'And are you going?'

'My first thought was no. He's a dickhead and I don't want anything to do with him. But it feels like too big a decision to take on my own. I mean,' – she cradled her bump – 'he's not just my dickhead ex, he's this little thing's dad. I can't change that. So I rang the counsellor and said that in order to make my decision I needed to speak to Matt's mum, and he said he'd give her my number. She rang me the same day. And she's actually all right.'

'Really?'

'She came up to Leeds. And I told her she was about to be a grandma, and she cried. I mean, I was expecting, well, I don't know what I was expecting. But she's the first person I've told about the baby who was actually happy for me. She's happy she's going to be a grandma. She's happy about the baby. She's split from Matt's dad, did you know?'

I wasn't surprised by that news.

'Yeah. Matt never said much about his parents, but she's nice. She's got a flat in Bristol and she's said, if I want, I can go down there. She'll help me with the baby. I went down, last week for a few days. It's by the sea. That would be good for a baby, wouldn't it?'

I didn't really know much about babies, but seeing the happiness in Nikki's eyes made me feel better. 'So did you see Matt, while you were there – did you go to the intervention?'

'We went together, me and Eileen. I don't know. He did say sorry and that he was never going to take drugs again. But I still think he feels most sorry for himself. Eileen was awesome. She told him he had to stop blaming other people for his own shit. She actually said those words to him.'

'Did his dad go?'

She shook her head again. 'He's taking the divorce badly. When she told him she was leaving, his exact words were, "I forbid you to do that". She said it was well awkward because there was a taxi with its engine running in the drive, her suitcase in the boot. He told her he'll never agree to a divorce and he's cut off all her access to their bank accounts.'

'What's she going to do for money?'

'She says she'll get a job. But also she's not stupid. I think she helped herself to a large chunk of cash before she told him she was leaving. And she's flogging all her designer clothes and jewellery. She even sold her engagement ring.'

'So you're going to move down there?'

'I might. At least for the year till I come back to uni. What have I got to lose?'

I admired her for her courage and I told her that and we both cried. And after she'd gone I felt like I'd taken a step somewhere. Another small step. I don't know where but I guess that's not the important thing. The important thing is that something moved.

*

On the day they transferred Jo to Liverpool, where her mum lives, I rang Sara and asked if we could go and say goodbye together. Part of that was cowardice. I couldn't bear the idea of saying goodbye to Jo on my own; the thought of walking back afterwards knowing that she no longer lived in Leeds terrified me. But it wasn't just cowardice. I wanted Jo to know that I'd look after Sara, until Jo's back in Leeds.

She came to the office and, even though we hadn't seen each other since what happened happened, we hugged and I felt her whole body tremble, like a dog that's been left outside a shop.

We walked down through the park together. I asked her about the last day she'd spent with Jo.

'I don't know. She never talked to me about work, but we had this conversation, where I said I'd been changed by what had happened to me – you know, with Matt. I said I felt I'd joined this kind of club, and I could spot both abusers and the abused. I still feel like that – like I've got some kind of weird X-ray vision. You know?'

I didn't know but I believed her.

'Jo got up and I knew something I'd said had meant something to her. She rushed out – said she had to go to see a woman about a dog. She said she'd be back later that evening. And that was it. I had a missed call from her on my mobile later that day, but I didn't answer it because I was in the bath. And when I rang back, the call went to voicemail.'

She rubbed her eyes with the heels of her hands, and I knew she'd always punish herself for taking a bath. I wondered whether Rob Hamilton was beating himself up as much.

I didn't push it any further because it was too hard for either of us to talk about – Jo as she was before, busy, bolshy, bossy – but one day I'll get round to going to see Linda because I'm guessing that's what Jo thought when Sara said what she did. Prey has a nose for the predator, because it needs to know when to become invisible, when to keep out of the way. I guess Linda sensed what Rob Hamilton was, and that Jo somehow persuaded her to part with her secrets.

*

Jo's mum was there when we got to the hospital. I could hardly bear to look at her – but she pulled me into a hug and said she'd come and get me anytime I wanted to visit Jo. She said not to forget how much Jo needs me.

Jo's mum went to get a coffee before she had to get in the ambulance with Jo. Jo looked thinner, paler. Attached to so many machines, eerily still.

'Hey you,' I said and my eyes hurt.

Sara stood on the other side of the bed and we took a hand each. I lined Jo's fingers up in the palm of my left hand.

'Sara's here too,' I said. 'We've come to say goodbye.' I bit my lip. 'Not goodbye, cos we'll come and see you in Liverpool, long as you promise not to talk Scouse to us.'

Tears fell onto my hand, the one holding onto Jo's fingers. I rubbed them away with my thumb.

'I reported Matt to the police yesterday,' Sara said. 'They took a statement and said they'll talk to him, but without any witnesses, they told me not to get my hopes up. I had to agree to accept a caution for the drugs.'

I wrinkled my nose. 'Fuck, really?'

'To be honest,' Sara said, looking at me, 'I'm hoping they don't charge him. I know I'd never win, and Jo's right – the whole experience would be like being raped all over again. But it's on record, and Matt will know it's on record, and so if any other woman reports him in the future, at least it's there, and the police will know that I'm here, ready to testify, to stand up next to someone else and say me too.'

'What made you change your mind?'

'I read this article, written by another survivor. She was talking about how a lighthouse doesn't chase around looking for people to save, it just stands there shining, like a beacon, to those that need it.'

*

On good days, that's what I want to be for Jo. I'm here to say that she is still here, that her life matters, even though, at the moment, she can't contribute to it. She isn't one of the invisible – women like Jenny who move amongst us but no one sees. Not like Marcia, the third possible identity for the body in the flats. Maybe no one will ever know what happened to her. The women that leave no trace.

That's not going to happen to Jo. I am testimony to her. I stand to say that she exists, that she's strong and honest and that she sees things the way that they are. Until she wakes up, I'm going to live my life for her, doing the things she would be doing if she could – making a difference, encouraging change, helping women to be free, to stick up for ourselves and for each other.

'Until you're back,' I whispered to her. And I don't know whether I imagined it – the brain does all kinds of things to get us to see what we want to see – but I swear I felt her fingertips press down in my palm.

Acknowledgements

All the events in this book are fictional but the idea for it came not long after I saw a photograph of Jimmy Savile and Peter Sutcliffe together at Broadmoor. I am grateful to The Arts Council who provided me with the opportunity to develop the idea into a complete work of fiction.

I know I wouldn't have made it to the end without the support of The Society of Authors, through their Authors' Foundation grant. It wasn't just the money (although that did really help!) but knowing that someone believes in you – that's priceless. I can't thank everyone enough.

I've visited some dark places while writing this one and I wouldn't have been able to do that without my family and friends. You know who you are – Bekki, Lydia, Cathy, Orla, Mark and Kate.

There's also all my writing friends and in particular The Northern Women Writers' Network – specially Anna, June, Emma and SJ. And Jason, Sarah, Charlotte, Cary and Katja – thanks for the chats and the hot chocolates. Thanks too to Fiona Gell, from The Leeds Big Bookend, and all those who work so hard to promote books and reading.

Thanks to Jamie, for always being there and telling me what he really thinks, and to Kathryn and the team at HarperCollins. Thanks to Janette for making me not look like an idiot …

And finally thanks to everyone who read my first book, *The Disappeared*, and shared it, reviewed it, invited me to their book group, sent me a nice message and generally lifted my spirits. Knowing there are people out there reading my books is one of the best feelings ever. I hope you like this one.

If you enjoyed *The Runaway,* make sure you've
read *The Disappeared*, Ali Harper's first novel
featuring Lee and Jo ...

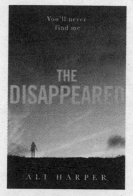

A distraught mother ...

When Susan Wilkins walks into No Stone Unturned,
Leeds's newest private detective agency, owners Lee
and Jo are thrilled. Their first client is the kind of
person they always hoped to help—a kind woman
desperately worried about her son, Jack.

A missing son ...

The case seems simple—kid starts college, takes up
with the wrong crowd, forgets to ring his mother. But
very quickly, Lee and Jo suspect they're not being told
the whole truth.

A case which could prove deadly ...

Their office is ransacked, everyone who knows Jack
refuses to talk to them and they feel like they're being
followed ... it's clear Lee and Jo have stumbled into
something bigger, and far more dangerous, than they
ever expected. Will they find Jack, or will their first
case silence them both for good?